D0499305

RLH
4706

CRAFT
* 10-00

It Is Just That Your
House Is So Far Away

It Is Just That Your House Is So Far Away

STEVE NOYES

Signature
EDITIONS

© 2010, Steve Noyes

All rights reserved. No part of this book may be reproduced, for any reason, by any means, without the permission of the publisher.

Cover design by Doowah Design.
Photo of Steve Noyes by numberbox.ca.

Acknowledgements
Thanks to the editors of *Quarry*, who published a long excerpt from this novel in 2001, in somewhat different form. The Canada Council made free time in China possible in 2007. Many people contributed greatly to Jeff Mott's Chinese: Zhang Xuan, Zhang Kai, Cheng Wei Feng, Liang Qi Wen, Meng Shao Lu, Qu Fang Li, Wang Jian and Richard King were especially helpful. Jay Ruzesky commented on early drafts and helped sharpen the text considerably. Finally, a lifelong shout of thanks to Catherine Greenwood. *Zhong ai yi sheng.*

The lyrics on page 47 are from The Guess Who's "Share the Land" and on page 175-176 from "King of the Road" by Roger Miller. The excerpt on page 162 is from "The Man with the Blue Guitar" by Wallace Stevens; on page 128, the poem is by Emily Dickinson. The quotations from Chinese poetry throughout are from *Golden Treasury of Tang and Song Poetry,* translated by Xu Yuan Zhong, 1995, Peking University Press.

This book was printed on Ancient Forest Friendly paper.
Printed and bound in Canada by Marquis Book Printing Inc.
We acknowledge the support of the Canada Council for the Arts and the Manitoba Arts Council for our publishing program.

Library and Archives Canada Cataloguing in Publication

Noyes, Steve
    It is just that your house is so far away / Steve Noyes.

ISBN 978-1-897109-42-7

    I. Title.

PS8577.O9618 2010   C813'.54   C2010-902183-5

Signature Editions
P.O. Box 206, RPO Corydon, Winnipeg, Manitoba, R3M 3S7
www.signature-editions.com

for Miranda

You must have heard of the young man who went to Handan to learn to walk in the graceful Handan manner; he was not successful in learning how to walk like them and in the process forgot his own way of walking and had to crawl all the way home.

—Chuang-tzu

If you could read my mind, love,
What a tale my thoughts would tell.

—Gordon Lightfoot

Part One

Hanzi

汉字

The Characters

Chapter One

Virtually the first thing Jeff Mott saw upon landing in Beijing was a fight between two taxi drivers over him and his friend Mark. The drivers blocked the end of the taxi queue-rails and went at it, pointing, shaking fists, flailing arms, spitting out Mandarin at vehement speed. A matter of honour, no less. The two foreigners stood there, jet-lagged, hefting their bags.

Jeff had never been in China before. When Mark, back in Canada for a visit, had learned Jeff was at loose ends, jobless again, he offered to put Jeff up in his Beijing apartment — a base — since his wife Sandy was in Victoria having her pregnancy monitored. "By Western doctors," Mark said. "The best."

Jeff gawked at the young women and their long, black hair, wheeling their suitcases across the parking lot. Mark stomped around his bags, looking for options, as the taxi drivers went at it. He had papers to grade.

Soon a policeman strolled over and started yelling too, but not before another driver sidled up to Jeff and Mark. "Taxi?"

"Come on, let's go," said Mark. When they were in the back seat, he said, "You see that? That's typical. The problem with the Chinese is half of them don't know what the other half are saying. But does that stop them? Hell no, they keep yelling at each other."

Jeff said nothing. He was watching the green exit signs advance and pass, trying to recognize characters. It didn't seem possible for there to be so many neighbourhoods in one city. Jeff was thrilled — the mystery of signification. That night he stood on Mark's balcony, tasting the spring sand from the desert in the air, and watching the progress of four successively neon-lit characters across a billboard. 北。。海。。餐。。厅.

"Take your shoes off, eh? Outside's just a bunch of gob and germs all over the place," Mark said.

Mark had lived in China for four years and spoke no Chinese. This perplexed and amazed Jeff, especially since Mark was fond of beginning his sentences with the phrase, "The Chinese," as in, "The Chinese never show their emotions." This was not the most risible of his insights: that honour fell to his pronouncement, "To speak Chinese you have to really know what's being talked about."

His apartment was in San Li Tun, the embassy district of East Beijing, and it was well-insulated from China. Chinese citizens had to sign in and out. For their safety, of course, Mark sneered. The apartment was gloomy and cool, and it was wired for expatriates: the phone was hooked up to Canada Direct and CNN was coming in twenty-four hours a day on the satellite. But what struck Jeff were the photographs and relics. There were shots of Mark and Sandy camping at the Great Wall, in a tuk-tuk in Bangkok, with backpacks on some mountain trail. Replicas of the terracotta soldiers sat sternly in the far corners of the apartment. Calligraphy hung on the walls. Bronze bells, Burmese lacquer tiffin-stackers, Xi Shi market silk carpets, rattan furniture and heavier end tables made of exotic hardwoods. They would furnish a whole house back in Canada with the finest Oriental tourist artifacts.

"You have a lot of pictures," Jeff said.

"Marriage is a shared memory," he said. "We are building a set of memories together. That's how we know we love each other. I would never do anything to damage those memories."

Jeff thought about that.

He looked at the photographs again. Mark and his wife were together in all of them. But something bothered him. Four years and there were no Chinese in any of the pictures. All of these excursions must have been with other expatriates. There seemed beneath all this comfortable nostalgia a loneliness; and yet Jeff was grateful to Mark for giving him a jumping-off point in China, and he envied his financial security. They were both approaching forty.

"We really had to change our focus here after three years or so, from being in China, having the Chinese experience, to teaching in

China. That's why we moved to the International School. Each year I think, this is the year I'm going to take Mandarin lessons, but I'm just too busy."

The smiling figure of the Dalai Lama was in evidence around the apartment. Jeff read on a dust jacket of his benign refusal of the Chinese — "They have taken everything from me; should I let them take my mind as well?" — and Jeff thought this set a sort of moral tone for the *lao wai*, the foreigners in China. On the other hand, Jeff was unaffected by Buddhism, because he still had his Muslim indifference to other faiths. Jeff picked up and put down several other books that preached *mindfulness*, and perhaps it was this discipline Mark relied on as he set to mastering a software program that would archive his family photos on CD-ROM, while, night after night, the spring wind howled and the sand from the Gobi infiltrated the plastic-sheeted balconies. In Canada, before he flew here, Jeff had read Mark's emailed, widely circulated updates — they were full of rent-to-own calculations for Beijing condos and bitter laments as to the cost of Chinese hotels.

"Deepak Chopra's latest book was good, but he seemed to be saying that spirituality is all about making more money," Mark said.

"Perhaps that is what sells."

"What are you doing here?"

"I don't know. I'm just here to see what's here."

"Don't get carried away, eh? Keep on doing what you're doing. Be mindful."

China is like stepping onto another planet, Jeff thought, as he balanced among hundreds of bikes waiting for the traffic cop to wave them on. But it is our planet, the one we have forgotten about. We forget that people earn a living carrying loads on poles through the streets, that there are places where the crush of people is the norm. We forget just how big an impact humans can make on the earth.

He lost balance, had to push off. A little girl eyed him ruefully, sitting sidesaddle on a rear-wheel rat trap, sucking on a Popsicle.

From the top of the Fragrant Hills, whose heights afforded no relief from the coal smoke and monoxide, factory upon factory appeared farther and farther back in the yellow haze. Sitting in a traffic jam near Wu Dao Kou, a hellishly busy corner in northwest Beijing, smoking a pleasingly cheap Camel, he watched the people keep coming and coming, bicycle upon bicycle out of the side streets, cheery and multitudinous, a market of some sort, barbecue smoke and blankets hung with pin-up calendars, the merchants jabbing hands, lusty with argument and deliberation, and stiffened rabbits piled high on the tables.

And the Chinese characters, barbed, complex, everywhere. When Jeff was a little boy, in Winnipeg, he would wander around the Chinatown behind City Hall and stare at the characters on the restaurant signs. Even then he thought, Why don't we know any of these people whose words are so fantastic, full of swoops and hooks and boxes and hats and tails, such intricate surrounded figures?

One day, years ago, when he was on welfare and had only ten dollars left in his account, Jeff withdrew it and headed for an all-you-can-eat Chinese buffet. There he could sit and eat for hours, digest for a week. Beautiful young Chinese women flitted about the chandeliered room escorting customers to tables, but it was not them he was interested in. He was interested in soggy bean curd, and fried rice, and egg foo yung with scallions. In greasy egg rolls, in crisp, thin batter. In chili sauce. In gummy, curried noodles with yellow onions and yellower shrimp. There was a plainer woman, a little older, who trundled out of the kitchen to stir around the food in the steam trays and replenish the knives and forks. She seemed sad and lonely.

"Ni hao," he said to her. *Hello.*

She looked up, startled.

"Ni hao," she said.

"I don't know any more Chinese than that," he said. "Where are you from?"

"Beijing."

"Your English is very good. Have you been in Canada long?" He had to repeat this.

"Ah, long." She looked around; probably she wasn't supposed to talk to customers. Then she said, "My husband in Beijing. I wait for him."

"How long?"

"Years, maybe."

"Are you okay?"

"Yes. Okay."

She went and filled up the fork dispenser. He never saw her again. He tried to connect with what she might have felt like. He had no idea.

And now, here he was, pedalling his borrowed bicycle past Gu Gong.

After a couple of weeks in Beijing, restless, he bought a ticket to Kunming in Yunnan province and took off. He was the only foreigner on the plane. Just before they landed, the stewardesses tossed dolls dressed in tiny ethnic Bai-people costumes at the passengers; one stewardess smiled and placed this tasselled doll in Mark's hand.

"Xie xie," he said. *Thank you.*

Before long, he was on a sleeper bus headed for Dali. Whole families were stuffed in the narrow bunks and the bus was rank with Yunnan tobacco and sweat. The peasants did not exhaust their enthusiasm for him but did exhaust his interest in rudimentary English conversation. The bus inched through the night on a precarious highway of clay washouts and long-term construction projects. The birds were faintly singing in the false dawn when the driver stopped in the middle of nowhere for a piss break, and Jeff followed a couple of men into a small roadhouse. When Jeff drew back the bead curtain, the men had already disappeared. A girl of no more than fifteen or sixteen sat on a rucked-up bed, painting her toenails beside a red oil-lantern; as she turned to acknowledge him, her housecoat fell open.

"Ni hao," he said.

"Lao wai," she said. *Foreigner.*

He backed away from her gentle laughter.

A few minutes later, the men emerged from the other rooms and ran back to the bus fastening their pants.

In Dali he hung around. The main drag was full of other foreigners in flip-flops and tie-dyed T-shirts drinking milkshakes and eating fries. Jeff scrupulously avoided them, and, aware of the urge's strangeness, instead sought out the mosques. In fervent surges, he would still practise Islam, then fall away. Spending time with Chinese Muslims was an entirely colonial experience; for Jeff it was a daguerreotype of lattice-sunlit mosque interiors among bearded and turbaned men kneeling in a circle and reciting by turns the *Qur'an*. As fragrant incense burned, the men circularly murmured the *suras*, and then the prayers, their foreheads in strict rows all touching the carpets facing Mecca. Back in the street again in the delirious Yunnan sunlight, Jeff's washed feet felt light in new shoes, and he was eager for the bowls and bowls of noodles and chili and beef and mint that awaited him.

One evening he went to the post office and phoned home to talk to his daughter Melissa. His ex-wife told him she'd been trying to reach him at Mark's. His father had died. Alzheimer's. Jeff had not spoken to his father for years. Nonetheless.

He stood outside the post office and chain-smoked. The smell of summer skin and motorcycle exhaust was heavy in the air. His stomach churned. His father was from England, and consequently Jeff had retained both a frozen distaste for and smug belonging to that heritage. His father had had a stiffness of mien matching even the celebrated Chinese reserve.

Jeff's body knew what to do.

He washed himself, his feet, hands, face, rinsed his mouth out, breathed water into his nostrils, wet his hair and walked to the mosque again, through the courtyard and the carved, red, wooden doors, the dark inside instantly enfolding and flooding him. He faced Mecca alone and prayed.

His father, an unsuccessfully transplanted Englishman. Whose sense of his own superiority, the son reflected, deteriorated to the point where he grew isolated, abusive. The lashings he had given Jeff for wanting his boyish freedoms. The slide past even that into his occult beliefs — channelling, UFOS, a new age when misfits like him would be proven right. That was what it was all about. Being right. Then the disease had come. Jeff had seen his mother feeding his father ice cream with a spoon, like a baby, and the old man, wasting, had smiled and drooled and had not recognized Jeff in the slightest. And now it was over.

Fragments of lived actions shot by in sunlit jaggedness there in the gloom of the mosque. Striding to keep up with his father's long steps. Five years old? Flying a kite. Learning to swim. His father impatiently urging him to let go, the coiled, frightened boy grasping the edge of the pool. And the fights — the taut, long arms pinning him on his bed against the wall, the hand yanked back to strike.

Another man entered the mosque and began to make his prayers.

His father had never talked about his life in England. Jeff remembered his mother, years ago, on his last trip to Winnipeg, telling him what little she knew. His father had already retreated, deep into his mind, and could no longer be reached. Who would have guessed that he was the equerry for the Royal family before the war? Whereas Jeff had thought his father's ominous reticence — ("What did you do in the war, Dad?" "My duty.") — had to do with important espionage, it was in fact a girlish modesty about the cunning drop-shots he deployed while teaching the Princesses tennis.

He left the mosque, feeling porous, as if the other worshipper could read his private thoughts, and he went to see Abu Bakr, an elderly Chinese Muslim whose daughter, Ma Li, ran a café on the main drag. Abu Bakr was not doing so well himself; he had come into town for the festival and it had cost him: his hands shook and he walked in a slow, painful stoop. His face was gaunt. Ma Li had told him that the lao wai's father had died, so Abu dragged himself downstairs. He clutched at his heart a pocket-sized edition of *Ya Sin*, the Qur'anic sura usually read at funerals. Jeff's Chinese was minimal. Abu spoke no English. Their real common tongue was the memorized Arabic.

BismillahirraHmanarraHiim,
Ya sin,
Wa al-qur'an hakiim,
Innaka min al-mursaliin,
:alaa aS-SiiraTa al-mustaqeem...

Abu recited until Jeff's eyes filled with tears and he had to leave, walk, think.

A week earlier in Kunming he had happened upon the funeral of a Muslim, the swiftly stepping white-robed figures bearing the dead in the white-draped wooden box glided shoulder-high in utter silence, twenty people and a coffin turning as one into a side street, and in their sudden absence the noise in the street increasing, ringing from every bicycle bell in Kunming.

He walked through the Dali market seeing only the innumerable shapes of marble, each souvenir a surrogate headstone, ashtrays, Buddhas, fossil-patterned table tops, marble-framed mirrors, ink trays and penholders and marble balls and rolling pins.

He was bewildered. He was thirty-seven, a prime number, alone on the planet. His father was dead.

\#

A couple of weeks later in Dali, at another café, Jeff met Nu Ling. He was killing time. So was she. The instant he smiled at her, she whisked herself from behind the bar she tended and introduced herself — "Tell me about your hometown." — and before long they were scribbling Chinese characters and English words on napkins. She pouted when she didn't know something. She had full lips and her nose was delightfully wide. They weren't communicating much, but it was a sort of fun; Jeff warmed to it. Then she asked him if he wanted to see where she taught. "Have you ever been to Xiaguan?" And so it was arranged.

The next morning, when Jeff told Ma Li about this expedition, she spat out dire warnings and shook her table-rag — the last white guy who had been to Xiaguan had ended up being taken for sixty thousand kuai and the divorce was still pending. Warned, but curious,

Jeff showed up at the gate of Nu Ling's middle school, and repeated all the possible tonal variations of her name to a bored security guard who, finally, screwed his tea-jar lid on tight and led him across the dirt playground and to the second floor.

There was no glass in the windows. Nu Ling was chatting with another teacher among stacks and stacks of English composition books with *Wish you friendly* on the covers. The friend was an English teacher; predictably, she was terrified to speak English with a native speaker. "Hello," she managed. The school was not noticeably formal; Nu Ling's buddy wore grubby sweatpants and a U2 T-shirt.

"Hello Jeff, we have class now," said Nu Ling, and strapped on an accordion which weighed her down; it was far too big for her. It had rows and rows of buttons and a spangled finish.

"She teach music," said the English teacher.

Jeff's entry caused a huge stir and babble in the classroom, which was open to the delicious Yunnan summer air, the tall palms and lichee trees and rhododendrons, the distant blue-white mountains; Nu Ling lifted her sweet young voice above the accordion's wheeze and led the students in a mindless song about a *pengyou*. There was a lot of giggling and pointing at Jeff.

Things were to go downhill. At lunch industrial-sized woks of pork and vegetables offended him in the cafeteria. Jeff was in strict Muslim mode after his father's death, in a way he could not explain even to himself. "I can't eat pork," he said.

"Oh," she said. "Come with me."

They ended up in an unlit shack on the other side of the playground, where the few Muslim students were doled out their beef and noodles. Jeff and Nu Li ate at a stone picnic table, shunned by the other students, and still hammering away at discovering the basic facts about each other. She wasn't beautiful, Jeff decided. And she wasn't much fun; there was a brooding, hurt quality about her, an anxiety, as though she were pushing herself forward against all odds. After lunch, she collected her monthly salary, which a sneering man slipped her from his wallet near the main gates. It was ninety kuai.

Ninety kuai, thought Jeff, that's *fifteen dollars*.

They were about to leave when the English teacher hailed her and she excused herself, ran to her friend across the dusty yard. The friend talked seriously, and, Jeff noted with horror, clasped Nu Ling's shoulder in full fealty as though Nu Ling were *embarking on something that would change her life forever.*

They said little on the bus that rattled and shook through Xiaguan. His Chinese brain had shut off. Her father's apartment was small and gloomy, the light blocked by tall house plants growing in plastic tubs on the balcony. Her father, who had one leg in a cast, lay on the sofa watching a war movie, in which Chinese soldiers barked imperious commands. Nu Ling plunked an English-Chinese dictionary down between them as though to say, *Communicate!*, and retired to the bedroom to prink — through the open door Jeff stole glimpses of her before a mirror touching her face with puff then pencil.

Well, well, off work, eh? Where do you work?
Electric company. You?
Not working, travelling. Your daughter is very nice.
No comment.
When are you going back to work?
Next week.

They returned in the early evening to Dali, to her café. Her mother laid out a candlelight dinner — *a candlelight dinner*; she beamed and flitted from one attention to another. I just *met* this girl, Jeff thought. He had to get out of there.

"Look, I'm tired, I have to go. I'll maybe see you around."

Nu Ling said nothing. She stood in the café doorway, her face still.

He walked home under the hanging spray of grey dissolving fireworks and the faint roar of the festival outside town, the huge market where he had seen ten-year-olds exhibited in Penman's underwear. How was that evening supposed to end? Would a bed have been procured, another candle? Ma Li had been right. Jeff heard Nu Ling's voice lifting in song in the morning classroom. She was an ordinary girl, perhaps dreaming of escape from the heavy accordion and the ninety kuai.

And her father worked for an electric company.

And her parents were obviously separated.

And her nose was delightfully wide.

And I have been to Xiaguan, thought Jeff. *Weile jiandao yi ge shagua wo dao Xiaguan qu le, hai you wo xiguan chi fan xigua*; in order to visit a foolish woman I have been to Xiaguan, and I am accustomed to eating watermelon. This is the sort of Chinese sentence I can fabricate with intense study of my grammar book, and I am none the better for it. He shook his head.

Chapter Two

When Jeff returned from Yunnan province, he had a renewed desire to speak Chinese. But how? Nervous, he offered his few phrases to random strangers. He talked to the cab drivers, he talked to the mink-pelt, rhino-horn and bear-claw-powder salesman, to the Beijing police, the cigarette hawker, he talked to students and they staunchly replied in English, he scanned the signs on windows and recognized one character out of fifty, he copied characters onto the impossibly thin Chinese notepaper and taped these to the wall.

In Mark's apartment, he watched TV, his lips occasionally moving. His head bobbed, up, down, left, right, as he tried to mouth the tones. Mark would take a break from his archiving and make comments like, "Really into the lingo, eh?"

That's how he thought he started to learn, the rote digestion of the signs, but he was aware that the truth was more mysterious. Every morning a faint cry from the distant pavement would reach him, *You rou bao, rou de rou de, ni mai le ma, yi kuai wu, ni mai le ma, yi kuai wu le*. Selling something. Want to buy. A kuai and a half. Not much of an epiphany, but it made him happy.

It would be months and months before he would start to see the radicals in the characters, the heart, the hand, the sun, the earth, the small pictures of ideas that composed the whole. He studied storefront after storefront looking in vain for the characters he had mechanically copied and memorized.

Before very long, he accepted a position teaching English in San Tiao, a small town north of Beijing. Mark's doing — a teacher at the International School knew a Party official who knew someone in the Bureau of Foreign Experts who needed a native speaker.

He was escorted to San Tiao by a cross woman who spoke not at all to him but plenty to her chauffeur. There was a framed photo of Deng Xiao Ping on the dashboard. They set out from San Li Tun, and proceeded to skirt the airport and race past long dewy fields of cabbage lined with scholar trees, then found their progress stalled outside Beijing by a huge market near the river: sat in stock-still traffic for better than an hour. The country people, mostly men in shiny suit jackets short in the arms, were selling vegetables off the back of street-blocking trucks, and Jeff quickly annoyed his escort by asking the Chinese names of every fruit and root vegetable he could make out from the window.

"What am I, your personal Chinese teacher?" she said.

When they arrived at San Tiao College, he was bundled out of the van and led into a private room off the cafeteria, where a small group of Chinese faculty solemnly shook his hand before they sat down to a meagre lunch served on metal trays. Jeff talked incessantly; they said nothing, seemed nervous. No one's name was offered. When they were finished eating, they shook his hand and filed out.

"What are their names?"

"You wouldn't remember their names anyway. Foreigners never do. Come."

She led him to an apartment big enough for a family and the driver dumped his luggage in the living room, which had three chairs, a small table and a full-length mirror leaning against one wall, and she said, "You put chili oil in your cream corn soup."

"Yes?"

"This they thought very strange. They would have put sugar in it. I will show you your classroom."

Soon he was on his own, walking through San Tiao, whose scale was welcome after the seas of pavement and monumental buildings of Beijing. It was a hick town. For him at first take, it epitomized struggling, but apathetic China, created solely so students could walk across its dusty crossroads wearing flip-flops and spitting sunflower seeds, their first and last crack at peasantry. There were condos for sale in San Tiao, he noticed from the roadside signs with the photographed interiors.

There always would be. Nobody in their right mind would want to live there, unless they were from true deep village land, straw-roof territory. He stopped outside a building clearly announcing KARAOKE, and heard The Carpenters playing at the top of a dank stairwell. The local market was a solid half mile of dried, cracked mud. Many of the peasants sat on their produce in wheelbarrows. On the main drag, the shops made no attempt to attractively or even visibly display their products. They just heaped boxes into vague aisles in the middle, slashed the cardboard sides for access, until they had to start a new heap, and hoped the boxes would empty before the baby got out of diapers.

Jeff heard shouting on the street and turned.

A gang of boys caught up with another boy, whose desperate escape had ended in a lurch and a ditch: they pushed him to the ground and surrounded him and the leader slapped him hard across the face and began to yell. The victim gave up, rolled over and protected his head, prone in the comforting dust. The ring of boys all wore identical track suits, red and white, and the boy on the ground was in yellow. They all had crewcuts. The leader was chubby, taller by a head than his band.

It was not so much a fight as it was a denunciation. The adults in the vicinity lined the roadside and watched. No one said anything. Perhaps this was normal. Jeff decided to say nothing either, but stayed to watch in case they started to seriously hurt the boy. Even if he managed to break it up, he reasoned, they would always catch up with their prey later. They didn't seriously hurt him. They humiliated him. That was enough. The boys chanted in their ring around their victim and the leader of the gang yelled into his face, and made him say apologetic, pleading things through his tears. It was too terrible to watch, perhaps because it was solemnly approved by the others in the street, watching, silent. He was out of his depth.

At that moment, Jeff felt like a substantial coward, roaming the earth in search of atrocities to witness. Eventually he walked on to the vegetable market, to have his typical, hackneyed conversations with the vendors, a sort of relief.

Where are you from?

Canada.

My uncle has been to Canada.

Really?

Yes, Texas, Canada.

He met his students the next morning: a score of pampered and tanned electric company workers. A couple of them, he learned from their oral résumés, lived in the executive compound, a city unto itself with iron gates and flower gardens and ponds and sports fields and apartment blocks, and a couple of guards out front, not far down the main drag. Most of the students insisted on using their English names. Dutifully, he tried to match Tom and Mary, Bill and Rosie, Daisy and Sue with the Asian faces. They were raucous among themselves, distant with Jeff.

That first class, he split them into groups and gave them a subject to discuss and wasted his time walking between the tables listening to them converse — in Chinese.

"We need the book to learn," said David, the class monitor.

"The book it is," said Jeff. "Turn to page sixty-eight, where 'Bobby' and 'Cindy' are discussing the plans for their beach-blanket barbecue near their home in sunny Burbank, California."

In one of the first classes, Jeff joked, "I'd like to meet a nice girl from San Tiao, settle down, buy a nice house in San Tiao."

Silence.

One evening, Mary and David, the two class monitors, led him away from the main road and down a lane into an orchard. As dusk was beckoning stars and bats into the apple-scented air, David turned and told him, "We in China have rules, you know. You cannot see any of the young women."

Jeff's jaw dropped, but, instantly realizing he was in a place where reactions were unseemly, froze his face.

Mary explained, "Their supervisors will watch them if they spend time with you alone. They will be punished. Maybe they would not graduate."

The rules did not stop Tian Kang. Jeff met her in his first week. To his surprise, she teetered up to him in her high heels: "Excuse me, are you the foreign teacher?"

"No, I am a very important oil company executive with key ties to the Chinese Communist Party. I am here to recruit new hockey players for the Vancouver Canucks. Of course I'm the foreign teacher. My name's Jeff."

"My name is Sophie."

"What's your Chinese name?"

"Tee hee. Tian Kang. I wanted to ask you a question. I have made up a résumé in English. I want to look for work in joint venture companies. Where should I put the date on it?"

Tian Kang actually said "tee-hee," the only person Jeff had ever met who did so. "You don't have to put a date on your résumé."

"No? That's good, because I did not, tee-hee."

Jeff liked Tian Kang — there was something about her that he couldn't place, an odd mix of boldness and childishness. She was not in the class of workers he taught, and she seemed older than the other students at the college. During evening walks around San Tiao, and trips to the Summer Palace and Xidan Street in Beijing, she opened up to him. She told Jeff that she'd had a long affair with an English teacher; she would go and live with him in Beijing on weekends; his Chinese level was quite high, but he encouraged her to speak English. "I think he is a good man, a kind man, but he would not marry me. Tee-hee."

"Why not?"

"He finally say to me, Tian Kang, you have to think more about what you want to do, not what your parents want you to do...but I know he is a kind man...a kind man...yes, a good man, I think."

"That's very sad."

"Sad, yes."

Tian Kang sat in worried silence for a spell. Then, "There is a story, a song-story about a young woman in ancient China. She is being thrown into the lake to meet the dragon king who live at the bottom. Before they throw her in, they ask her if she has anything she want to say to the dragon king, and she say, I tell him next life I want to be a man."

"That is a very sad story," Jeff said.

"What a terrible fate, to be born a woman," Tian Kang said.

She brooded. "I like very much to have children, especially a baby boy. But I know I will die in childbirth."

"Tian Kang! That's ridiculous! How many women in China had babies this year? Like three hundred million. Did they die in childbirth?" But his voice trailed off because her face was not moving in the slightest.

"I'm sorry. Okay, it isn't ridiculous. It is a fear. Fear isn't logical. I'm sorry."

"Mei guanxi." *It doesn't matter,* she said. But he kept it in mind. He had no idea where she and her fears had come from; he had no right to dismiss them.

That night Jeff woke up in San Tiao's masking silence, surprised to be yearning for the smell of his daughter's hair. She lived with his ex-wife; he saw her on weekends. They played in the park together. He missed the smell of her hair, and how her arms turned a light cinnamon in summer. Melissa. She, his old life, felt very far away.

June came to San Tiao. In the humid heat girls flip-flopped to the public showers dandling hair brushes, their long black hair shining on the way back. The roads teemed, when he looked hard, with tiny hopping frogs, green-brown; many were squashed and their bodies became indistinct stains on the concrete in the June rains.

He learned a type of ivy was called Pa Shan Hu, the tiger climbs the mountain.

The roadside peasants sold whole watermelons and carved them with huge cleavers, slashing the sides first, and Jeff sat by the roadside and spat seeds with his students. And there were *cao mei,* strawberries sprinkled with clingy sugar and served on toothpicks, devoured with students in dormitory rooms.

He began to meditate in the mornings, before he taught, in the garden behind the college; he sat in a cramped lotus under a willow, and kept returning to the thought that there must be some reason he was in China. He would likely leave before he realized it; in retrospect it would come flooding in.

The power failed often in the evenings and students would mill in the darkness outside their dormitory, holding lit candles, and the mosquitoes would descend out of the dusty darkness; candles held up by their spent wax burned on the edges of pool tables on the main drag; boxes were turned over on the sidewalks and card games started.

There was a pelting rainstorm that filled the overhanging awnings on his favourite noodle shop, snapping the supporting poles and drenching the patrons. Jeff stood on the street wringing out his shirtsleeves and laughing with the others.

The sun returned and he had to change his shirt thrice a day.

He played pick-up basketball on the outdoor courts with short, scrappy students slick with sweat.

He went on evening walks with students to the Chao Bai River, over fields and down stream banks, and when the women could not leap the streams, the men tore out clumps of bulrushes to make small bridges. One night beneath the spilling stars, the students told him the story of the Weaver-Girl and the Herd-Boy, their hopeless, separated love, and the bridge the birds formed in the sky so they could cross the Milky Way and be together.

A huge red sun set every evening behind his apartment building in a desolate dirt field, which was slowly patrolled for no evident reason by a pair of bent-backed peasants.

There were competitive videos on TV because Hong Kong was returning to China at the end of June, and a chanteuse of beguiling beauty strolled by the sea in Hong Kong's harbour, she sat musingly on streetcars, she sang that Hong Kong was the most beautiful city in China; and behold, the shrimp and crab she serenaded were the most sensuous pink imaginable. With fireworks and tumbling acrobats and long pans of the red roofs of Gu Gong, Beijing responded — *it* was the most beautiful city in China, and the Northern Capital, there could be little doubt.

He noticed during his day trips to Beijing that more and more policemen appeared at the intersections; Chang An Avenue, which fronted the Forbidden City and Tian An Men Square, was to be restricted at the end of June to taxis, official vehicles and buses. There was coverage in the *Ren Min Ri Bao* of previous bombings by Uighurs from the Xinjiang autonomous region, and a photograph of a public gathering in Hong Kong with all signs and placards cropped out of the frame, which made Jeff snort with derision. He knew from talking with Mark in Beijing that the gathering was a commemorative protest of Tian An Men Square.

When he visited Beijing, he loved wandering in the *hutongs*, the thousands of narrow lanes in which two bicycles could barely pass. They twisted and turned, becoming no more than footpaths between high brick walls and iron gates, until he could not see the sun. Parked bicycles, sudden openings on small courtyards and drying laundry, two ancient faces distracted from their chess. The people hidden, folded in the pockets of these crooked lanes. The unmistakable sound of a mother scolding a child became a pop song slicing into another pop song. Strong smells of fried meat, garlic, rotting garbage.

Once he had phoned his daughter from the post office and wandered into the wrong *hutong* coming back, got lost. He couldn't hear the main road. He tried one *hutong*, then another; it divagated, he chose, again, the wrong one, and passed a skinny man in shorts squatting, slicing mutton on a wood block, turned the corner and ran straight into five or six armoured personnel carriers blocking a larger lane. There were perhaps twenty soldiers, tall, eyes purposefully blank, leaning against the vehicles, not in crisp uniforms but in fatigues, the sleeves rolled to mid-bicep. Even Jeff could tell they were not from Beijing; their language was strange, devoid of the Beijing hard R, whining. They were sharing cigarettes as they cleaned their weapons with rags. One kept flipping open and twirling a foot-long knife.

He asked them for directions.

No one spoke.

"Okay, thanks, *xie xie*," said Jeff.

He looked back. A soldier leaned the automatic weapons one by one on their stocks against a wheel, and they gleamed hard in the sun. He turned the corner and two boys were playing badminton across a couple of parked bikes.

"Ni hao," he said.

"Lao wai," they said.   .

He emerged from the maze of alleys somewhere near Chang An Avenue, and had to walk a mile to get to the next underpass. The huge hotels, far, far from the street, were hazy, ethereal, hardly part of the city and yet dominating it. His sense of scale was completely gone. Throw away the maps, he thought, for we have found the city, larger and more substantial than the realm of our senses. Nowhere was this more apparent than at Da Ping Kou, where he caught the San Tiao bus. He waited in the exhausted bliss of the crowd, its freezers full of Popsicles and Cokes, its peddling and shouts and constant harangue, its tendency to wipe its forehead, to slump and stare, its chewing on folded pancakes with hoisin sauce, while ranged all around it, impervious to the blast of horns, the backfiring motors, the new and monstrous buildings floated far above in their draping of fine, green netting, and from within the netting came the solid drill, drill, drill, the distant chunk, chunk, chunk, and cranes swung above even this, as though conducting this music of the heavens. As he sweated on the street, Jeff knew all of a sudden that *Beijing ate humans...* It was as near as he could articulate his fear of being engulfed by Beijing's raw immensity.

The bus was jammed. On the way back, he had to stand and sway. It stopped once at a roundabout of more flustering confusion, of *shao kao rou* vendors choking over their barbecues, of endless stacks of empty pop bottles, of identical tile-fronted shops, and the brown-armed peasants and their bulging loads, toothpicks in their mouths, kneeing baled purchases out the back doors of the bus where others were pushing in, a constant urgent clamour.

Then a slim young woman in a halter top and yellow miniskirt ran into the throng from nowhere, a blonde doll bouncing from her backpack like a tail, and she had confidently swung her leg high to gain the bus-step when a peasant lugging a sack of rice zoomed in from the left and a young man in army fatigues vaulted in from the right and they absolutely crunched her on the step. When their bodies divided, and she stepped up and on, she was shaking her head, distaste darkening her face.

Jeff watched her compose herself. She sharply tugged her skirt down and, twisting, drew a slim book from the backpack, *College English Exercises,* which she brought close to her nose and began to read. Her hair was swept up in a bun held by a glittering silver clasp in the shape of a fish. A faint smile flickered across her profile.

Jeff pushed his way over. "Oh, you read English books, *ni hao,*" he said.

"*Ai, ni hao.*"

"What is your name?"

"My name is Wang Bian Fu. English name is Lucy."

They started chatting at Jeff's pidgin Chinese level. A student appeared at Jeff's elbow and started to translate.

"I don't need you to translate," Jeff said. "I'm talking to her, not you."

The student indifferently drifted back to his place.

Then the woman beside them asked Jeff, Who are you? Where do you work? What town? Are you a student? Jeff looked at Wang Bian Fu for explanation. "Ah, yes, maybe we should say nothing right now. This is a habit of Chinese people; they are very curious about you."

Before she got off, Jeff gave her his phone number, suggested they could get together to practise Chinese and English. Or play tennis. He didn't expect to hear from her again.

The following day she phoned.

He met her at the gates of his apartment compound, where she was lightly hopping from one foot to another, as though she needed to pee, her hands on the straps of her backpack, not exactly hiding behind the tree, but not in plain view either. She stepped out and greeted him.

"You want to walk? Let's walk to the river," she said.

They went for a walk to the river. "Oh, ho, we can communicate," she said. "We are like the North Chinese and the South Chinese."

They passed factory after factory on the main road. They asked each other simple questions about their families. She said she lived with her father; "He try to control me," she told him.

They left the road and crossed rain-drenched fields of low green wheat, having to wait for a long line of white ducks at a bare patch: they were headed home for feeding in an elegant chortling queue.

Jeff paid a kuai and a half to a grinning farmer so they could cross a makeshift bridge over a stream, and took Bian Fu's hand and helped her in her high heels. As she stepped onto the far bank, he had a good look at her face, her downcast eyes and her interestingly shaped nose.

He said, "My students took me here. To the Chao Bai He."

"Yes, it is very *liang kuai*. Very cool."

They sat on the bank: from sparkling skeins of sunlight on the waters, small fish were leaping, skimming the surface, then dropping in the water, gone.

"What about your mother?" he said.

"My mother live in Beijing."

"Oh. Why's that?"

She did not answer for a while. Then she said, "My parents do not live together."

Jeff banged on with another question. "Where do you like living better? With your mother or your father?"

Her smile became tenser.

Presently she said, "You are very rude I think, ask these questions. I am the child. I love them both. I want them to live together."

"Sorry."

"*Mei guanxi*. It is all right."

A fish jumped again in midstream.

"*Xiao yu tiao tiao*," she said.

"What's that mean?"

"Little fish jumping?" she said.

"You are a fish," he said.

"Yes, I am a beautiful fish."

He turned his face this way and that. "What am I?"

"Your nose, it is big like a bird. You are a bird."

He flapped his arms.

She seemed embarrassed by their joking, and again they fell silent. Then he reached out and brushed his fingers against the oval pocking on her upper arm. "What is this?" he said, knowing full well it was a vaccination mark.

#

That week it got hotter and hotter.

Among the students, there was a rumour that entry to Beijing would be allowed only to those with Beijing *hukou*, or identification cards, another preparation for the return of Hong Kong. The room was abuzz one morning with their plans to get around this restriction. He had to question them to get at it. "The government is doing it for our own safety," one said. There were a few snickers. Some students, he gathered, believed and repeated everything they read in the *Ren Min Ri Bao*. That was their duty.

His duty was to drill students in English conversation. "And what, 'Bill,' do you do in the morning when you go to work?"

"Yes. I am asking my secretary make me cup of coffee."

Howls of laughter.

"Then what?"

"Please?"

"What do you do after you drink the coffee?"

"Lunch."

Only two more hours of this knee-slapping stuff.

There was a knock on the classroom door. A stern plump woman with her grey hair in a bun came in and spoke to the monitors. David indicated that Jeff was to join them in the hall.

"What is it?"

"This is Sister Ma, our leader."

The woman addressed herself to her subject in short, trenchant sentences. David nodded and spoke to Jeff. "She says that leaving your shirt untucked is not respectable. Teachers should also not put their feet up on tables."

"Yes, I see," said Jeff.

"She says that there are standards for foreigners and regrettably you are not meeting them. And your hair is too long."

Sister Ma nodded curtly and left.

"Thank you," said Jeff.

He learned there was to be a speech contest, on the theme of Hong Kong's return to China. Inside the auditorium it was sweltering; outside, towering black clouds. A teacher handed him a glass of water when he entered, and he sat down beside her, realizing after a few minutes that he was sitting in a judge's seat and she was too polite to tell him to move. He retreated into the middle rows. The auditorium filled. The student-orators sat in their best clothes and held last-minute coaching sessions with relatives and teachers. Jeff sat sweating, trying to visualize Bian Fu's father, how he tried to control her. He didn't get far. A short man in a silk housecoat, barking out orders? He wanted to see her again.

The speeches started.

David sat down next to him; he had Alice with him. Alice was always snotty towards Jeff, telling him, in fact, once, that she didn't like it when he looked at her. "You are a friend," he said. "Why shouldn't I smile at you?"

"I do not like it."

Now she asked him what he had thought of Tiantan Park in Beijing.

"It was very beautiful."

It had also been very hot, and indescribably boring. The concentric altars for sacrifices, if viewed from an airplane, he imagined, were a marvel of concinnity; at ground level, they were endless backdrops for provincial families parading with cameras.

"Beautiful? Is that all?"

"Shh," said David.

A women wearing a red *qi pao*, a snug, long dress with a high collar, was waving her arms on stage. The man on the other side of Jeff wiped his brow. "She is saying that Chinese people suffered greatly during the Aggressive Invasion of the Foreign Countries," went Jim.

"You see the buttons on her *qi pao*, they are very special. Those are handmade buttons. I made some myself for my *qi pao*," said Alice.

In his mind's eye, Jeff saw Bian Fu taking a long cool drink of coconut juice, tugging her sarong, and opening her journal to write about him.

"She is saying that now the children can return to their mother, China, who has suffered greatly since they have gone," said Alice.

A young man mounted the stage and struggled with his Adam's apple and tie for the next obligatory ten minutes, managing to say that China had suffered. *Tong ku*, Jeff got that much. He looked around. People were indeed suffering; they slumped, catatonic, in their rigid little seats; newspapers became fans. David left and returned with bottles of mineral water.

"He is saying the shame can be erased now that Xiang Gang returns to the Motherland," David said, and drank half his bottle.

"If you could understand what he is saying," Alice made a point of saying, "then you would agree with it completely."

The judges conferred after each speaker, awarding high 8s and 9s to all, except for the first, who received 9.5s. Was the fix in? Jeff wondered. Had Sister Ma, the school headmistress, already picked the winner, straining tea leaves through her stained teeth?

One of the last speakers, an indomitable young woman called Han Xiu Ling, committed the ignominious sin, near the end of her paean, of inviting a dozen schoolchildren on the stage with her, and having them unfurl a banner with badly drawn harbour skyscrapers. The winner, as it turned out, was the first woman in her red *qi pao*. People made for the doors as though there were a fire.

The drumming rain in the middle of the night woke him, and he lay wondering if Bian Fu was awake too.

The next morning, returning from his morning meditation — ("There is no reason, there is some reason, be in the zone of no reason I am here.") — he ran into his neighbour, one of the judges, lugging three thermoses of *kai shui*, boiling water.

"I saw you at the speeches last night. Pretty good, eh?" Jeff said.

The neighbour's eyes became cross and incredulous. "*Bu hao*," he said.

"Okay, *bu hao*, not so good?" Jeff said.

"*Zhen bu hao!*" the man said, glad to have corrected him, and walked away.

That afternoon, his students were to deliver a short speech on a new English word they had learned.

Charlie swaggered up to the head of the class and said, "My new English word is *dictionary.*"

Uproarious laughter. Students bent in their chairs, howled.

Jeff felt irritation mounting within him and then something fierce took over, darkening his countenance: Sister Ma would have been proud, for it was a sternness intense and paternal; he imagined it, even as he reacted, as practically Confucian in its injured sense of betrayed propriety. "Did you know that word before you got the assignment?" Jeff said.

Charlie seemed puzzled. "Yes," he began.

"Then what did you learn?"

He returned to his seat, chastened, and the rest of the students smiled stiffly at Jeff, who was worried. After that outburst, he had two hours to fill.

He was relieved when the silent and uncooperative afternoon was over. At the top of the stairs, at his door, Bian Fu stood, scribbling a note. She wore the short yellow skirt and her hair was in a bun.

"Come in."

Jeff made her tea.

She made a big show of getting up and washing out the wok when he suggested dinner.

Jeff found himself checking out her legs.

"What is in the refrigerator?" she asked, aware where his eyes were.

"*Qiezi.* Eggplant."

They stir-fried the eggplant together, and she dumped in about a half cup of salt; during their meal she kept asking for more glasses of water.

"Gee, I wonder why?" he said.

A half hour later, she let down her hair, and tossed her head so he could see it fall around the flimsy straps on her shoulders. Her eyes shone. They both wriggled in their chairs. They laughed. She began to stroke the fine hairs on his arm, fascinated.

"You have these hairs," she said.

He leaned in towards her. "You don't," he said.

They kissed, once, lightly, achingly. The nearby whine of a mosquito broke it off.

"I must go," she said.

The next evening a few of the students showed up to take Jeff for a stroll. They had just purchased a watermelon near the gates of the Electric Company compound, when, cruising at an unusually fast clip, anguish on her face, Bian Fu blew by in a patterned blue sarong.

"Bian Fu!" Jeff said.

She turned, surprised, and then came shyly over, her eyes down. Jeff introduced her to his students; a ranking ceremony took place, in which each asked each where they were from and what their parents did. Jeff had noticed that it seemed necessary for Chinese students to do this before any kind of interaction. The outcome was the students decided Bian Fu was not worth speaking Chinese to. They seemed markedly suspicious of her, in fact, downright hostile.

Alice said, "Pleased to meet!" to her but would not shake her hand.

David asked her what she was studying. She replied she was a student of English at Er Wai Language Institute. "Ho, I suppose you want to learn English from Jeff, ah?" David said. She smiled.

They passed the student dormitories and headed down a dusky, dusty road on the fringe of San Tiao. There were many long red brick walls with *hanzi* chalked and painted on them. "Ho, that sign, it says making love within your family is bad for your health," said David.

"That one is saying, Inside here we are all prisoners," said Alice.

Jeff strongly suspected that some of these institutions had been re-education centres during the Cultural Revolution.

Bian Fu began an awkward conversation with Han Xiu Ling.

David sidled up to him. "Ho, Jeff, very beautiful young student from Er Wai."

"I didn't notice," he replied.

Then Bian Fu did a curious thing: they were waiting for a horse and cart to pass, the light was fading, and Bian Fu sidled over to a tree and bent as if to supplicate before it, then stretched to pluck a pair of pale green leaves, which she offered to Jeff.

He accepted the leaves, not knowing what to say.

Shortly thereafter the students cleared out. They cast worried glances backwards at the pair of them, standing all alone in the middle of the road. A couple of men pedalled past; one shouted "Guoji, guoji," *international,* and the other laughed and spat.

"Why don't you invite me your place? For a chat?" Bian Fu said.

He did, but only a few minutes later she hopped up, and said, "I have to go."

"Why?"

"I have to go to disco. To see my boyfriend."

"Your *what*?"

"You want to come? Let's go."

He stood in the doorway, then shrugged and sat down again. Bian Fu's leaves were on the coffee table, a pair. He picked them up, twirled them. What did they mean?

Next afternoon, he sat at his desk attempting to study Chinese. A word formed deep in his head: Boyfriend.

He had noticed that his usual restaurant had a sign in English: DON'T'T SPIT.

He looked out the window. The peasants who lived in the row of brick shacks behind his block continued to trudge around, unperturbed, with pickaxes, shovels, saws, anything that would rust. These tools they banged away at patiently, often crouching for hours trying to bend a tool back into shape. Sometimes they held them up to the sky, as if sharpening the sun. There was no particular urgency to their movements. Jeff suspected they were happy. He suspected they were retained by the college for their proletarian aspect.

His classes were winding down. In about a week, he would return to Beijing. In another two weeks, exactly when Xiang Gang returned to the Motherland, its citizens patriotically holding their handmade *qi pao* buttons aloft, he would return to Canada.

Bian Fu showed up the next evening, frowning.

"What's the matter, get tired of your boyfriend?"

She shot him a look of manufactured misery. Again she wriggled in torment on the couch. "Your hair, your hair," she managed to say, and then began stroking the hair on his arms. Jeff drew her up from her seat. He couldn't breathe. His arms were around her. He saw them come together in the mirror, his fantasy of pleasure with her suddenly confirmed. His reddish hair and the full length of her black hair, crowning her beauty, a vivid picture — they came together. He saw himself gather her hair in his hands, and his hand caress her neck. And their lips touched. Her eyes opened wide, watching him. He kissed her again and his hand touched the small of her back, bringing her closer. In the midst of the next kiss, long, enveloping and satisfying, there came a knock on the door.

Bian Fu gave a startled gasp and, looking at the door, the window, fled into the bedroom.

Jeff answered the door.

It was one of the basketball players. With a curious formality, this tall young man, whom Jeff had played one-on-one with twice, proceeded to thank Jeff fulsomely for his friendship and wondered if he could come out for a few beers, or would Jeff be gracious enough to invite him in, because he had to leave for Xinjiang tomorrow?

"Have a nice trip," Jeff said. "Sorry, I'm busy."

He closed the door on an unhappy face. As he hurried to the bedroom, certain that Bian Fu had already jumped out the window, the first pang of fear entered him, the possibility of retribution, and it clouded his eyes for an instant with revolving shadows of the dead tree frogs.

Bian Fu shuddered against the balcony wall. He kissed her. "It was just a friend. I sent him away," Jeff said.

"I have to go."

He went to follow her and she turned in the stairwell, put out her hand and said, "No."

He stood there, weak with the taste of her lips.

Chapter Three

It didn't take long. David came up to Jeff after class, and, in a strongly insinuating tone, said, "I think Jeff must be very happy."

Jeff erased the blackboard with short strokes and did not turn to reply. Out in the hallway, a group of female students stopped talking when he passed. Sister Ma came out of her office and coolly regarded him as she sipped green tea from a jam jar.

That weekend they went to Beijing on the bus — at 7:30 in the morning. "Why don't we take the electric company bus, the one that leaves at 9:00?" said Jeff.

"Oh, no."

"Why not?"

She wouldn't answer. He figured it was her father again. Father, boyfriend.

She is just a friend, he thought. A casual attachment. Some attraction thrown in.

She did not speak all the way into Beijing. Nor did she speak as they walked through the Museum of the Chinese Revolution off Tian An Men Square. Jeff fumbled through the transactions with ticket sellers, water vendors, minibus drivers with his elementary Chinese all morning, paying for her as a matter of course. It did not escape him that they were universally sneered at.

"Are you rich?" said a man selling crackers. "How rich are you?"

By mid-afternoon, they ran out of sight-seeing steam and went to Ritan Park, where, by a red wall on a bench, they played paddy-cake with Jeff's Chinese vocabulary. "A red wall."

"The tree's leaves are green."

"The green roof and the red wall."

"The blue sky."

Switching to English, Bian Fu said, "You know, I have become quite attached to you. I have only seen you these recent days. I almost lose myself," looking into his eyes and then away.

"I have become close to you too."

But they sat on the bench in an unbearable gloom, unable to say more.

They wandered out of Ritan Park and Bian Fu said she had to buy a hat — could they stop in that shopping centre over there, across a six-lane street? They took the underpass. At the bottom of the steps, Bian Fu stopped, stiffened; it was dark; mounds of garbage were underfoot. He took her hand and they went on. On the third floor of the *zhongxin* she found a hat, a straw monstrosity with a brown band and a big yellow flower. "*Haokan bu haokan?*" she asked him. *Pretty or not?* It made her look rural in a Western way, almost.

"*Hen haokan,*" Jeff said, and he bought it for her.

On the way back to San Tiao Jeff noticed that the secondary roads were two-tone, pale yellow, deep black. Bian Fu explained that the peasants had laid their wheat crop out on the roads, one lane only, to dry. In the fields near the Chao Bai River other peasants burned their stubble, the birds frustrated in their attempts to hunt and feed, wheeling away and upwards from the flames, the smoke.

She stayed on the bus when he got off.

The next night as he sat by the roadside munching and spitting watermelon with students, one of them suddenly said, "There is a river nearby, Jeff *Lao shi*, do you know it? Some of the students go there to swim."

"Oh yeah, do they wear any clothes?" he joked.

Alice looked disgusted and said, "Jeff, do you know the meaning of the Chinese word *rang*?"

Someone said something he didn't understand. He did know *rang*, though. It meant to allow or permit. He lowered his eyes and excused himself. He walked away quickly. Not so much longer to go, he thought. And then: but I want to stay.

In San Tiao's only decent store, he bought a tortoiseshell *jiazi*, a hair-clasp, shaped like a fish. Then put it away, scared to give it to her just yet.

When Bian Fu showed up that evening, unannounced as usual, she was evidently upset. She tugged his arm downwards, indicating he must sit and she must speak and he must listen. She was having trouble breathing as she spoke, so difficult were her thoughts, so difficult in English.

"I live with my boyfriend and his parents in an apartment at the electric company. They always try to control me. When I got down the tennis rackets because we wanted to play tennis — remember? — his father started to question me. Who are you going to play with? A friend, I said. He said he would organize a tennis game with people he knew, and told me to put the tennis rackets away. He is very traditional."

"I thought you said you lived with your father."

"He live in Bing He, in the neighbour province."

"You're not married, are you?" Jeff asked.

"Ah, no."

"That's good. If you were married I would never go anywhere near you."

"Ah, yes. My boyfriend say to me, You are seeing the foreigner? Yes. You have fallen in love with him?" She looked shyly away. "I do not know what to say. I will kill you, he say. I'm not afraid of you, I say. Later he say, look, if you want to leave me, Bian Fu, you can leave me, just pick any Chinese man, but please, please, do not go with the foreigner."

"And so he knows you are out with me, now."

"Ah, yes."

"Does your boyfriend hit you?" Jeff's voice had become quiet.

"If he hit me I would hit him right back. No, he does not."

"I don't know what to say," said Jeff. "I like you very much. You have a problem with your boyfriend. Perhaps you should work it out."

"The problem is I like you," she said.

"I need to think about this," he said.

They sat in an imponderable silence for a few minutes, and Jeff tried to look at her eyes, to see them without admitting their magic, so he could say something simple like, "I don't want to see you anymore," but he couldn't do it. Then she got up to leave. Jeff tried to kiss her, and she pushed his chin away. She let herself come close to him, in one hesitant step, and they embraced, and kissed. He started to say something and she said, "No," and walked out.

He thought about her ceaselessly without exactly wanting to. He had the feeling of slipping — into something he didn't understand — of being on the verge. He remembered a conversation with his friend Terry in Victoria when Jeff had broken up with his last girlfriend: Never again, he'd sworn, would he get involved with a woman who was breaking up with a husband, boyfriend, whatever. Terry had listened and said, At this age, buddy, you don't have much of a choice. Everyone is either involved or getting uninvolved. There aren't too many people walking around without any relationship baggage. And Jeff had acknowledged this wisdom — Terry was worldly, in a crude way — but said, I don't want to bother. Terry had shrugged. So don't bother, he said, and laughed.

Nonetheless, Jeff now had waves of paranoia, or an uneasiness that gave way to broadly comic fantasies of paranoia. Sister Ma would bang on the door any second, accompanied by policemen, and sternly supervise the packing of his bags, the removing of his clothes and the donning of prison garb. She would be unruffled; long years of experiences with similar miscreants would give her the authority to say, "Teachers whose shirts become untucked, and who consort with Chinese women, this we do not appreciate."

He told himself to get a grip. But the bad movie kept playing in his head.

They permit him to smoke a last cigarette, but it is a Chinese cigarette and the tobacco falls out before he can light it. To his greater horror, once they are in the police cruiser, one of the cops pulls out a TOEFL primer and says, "I wonder if you have time to answer a few questions about your language? What is the difference between *incarcerate* and *incinerate*?"

Laughing it off in a little room.

He had never noticed before how many people *smiled* at him.

David grinned at him from behind a textbook outside the teaching building, and wagged his finger. "*Pa shan rong yi, xia shan nan.* It is easy to climb the mountain, and not so easy to descend." Jeff ignored him.

The next day Bian Fu phoned to say she was moving to her mother's place in Beijing.

"Oh," he said, his caution instantly evaporating, as though being with Bian Fu were suddenly much less tense, weightless, than thinking about being with her. "So do you want to get together? I can meet you in Beijing."

"Ah, yes!"

They met in Da Ping Kou, the cleared corner of the city. Again he was made minuscule by the huge office-building projects cocooned in green canvas and netting. People swerved around him, got on buses, got off buses. A stench of tar. Minibus tycoons hung out the side doors and crooned their short snatches into the monoxide streets: *Tiananmen, Tiananmen, liang kuai, Xidan, san kuai!* He was munching on a *bing-qie,* one of those Beijing crepes with egg and coriander and plenty of hoisin and chili smeared on it, when Bian Fu showed up with a worried smile. It was nine in the morning. Jeff's shirt was soaking.

"I am late, so sorry. My mother's place is — I had to take three buses!"

"Oh, yeah?" His mouth was full. "What's your mother's place like?"

"Oh, it is very modern."

In her speech this morning there were noticeable pauses. She was clearly bothered by some fallout — family, boyfriend — caused by her defiant actions, and she had to keep busy. She dragged him by the hand. There was no use prying; today she would just deflect it. She was not going to let on that she was in trouble.

"Bian Fu, what does your mother say when you tell her you are with a foreigner?"

"She say *Mei guanxi.*" And her head tilted.

Jeff heard what he wanted to hear: there would be no problem with her mother.

She had to find a phone. Jeff waited a little way from the magazine stand. She came back and asked him for three kuai. Jeff tried to listen as she bent her head over the receiver, as someone told her something worrisome, but he couldn't make out anything. Russian couples, the men in leather jackets and the women in heavy jewellery, walked past with their latest purchases — jeans, carry-on luggage, rolled carpets from Xi Shi market. The men seemed drunk, the women annoyed.

Bian Fu was beside him again. "Okay, let's go."

"Everything okay?"

"Ah, yes."

They had planned to visit Wang Fu Jing Avenue, which was probably the most Western of Beijing's shopping districts, and to see *Ya Pin Zhan Zheng, The Opium War*, the latest big-budget Chinese movie, which carried the imprimatur of the Chinese government — part of the Welcome Home Hong Kong package. It promised to be a shining example of revisionist history. Jeff had watched an English interview with the actor who played Lin Zexu, the Qing dynasty official who had impounded and then destroyed the British stocks of opium, and had declared the use and the sale of the drug illegal, which actions had eventually led to the British capture of Hong Kong. The actor's remarks had set a new standard for entertainment industry clichés: "I wanted, you know, to add some life to the historical character, to portray Lin as a *real person*."

Make no mistake, this would not be a comic book, he thought.

Wang Fu Jing Street was teeming with streamers, balloons and shoppers. There was an outdoor karaoke bar going outside the Foreign Language Bookstore. It was nearly forty above. Nothing amused Bian Fu. Everything they did and looked at held her attention for a minute, then she fretfully, tugging at his hand, licking her lips, looking about for distraction, had to move, had to fill the time. They sat on the steps of some Overseas Chinese hotel. Bian Fu was chewing her lower lip.

"Maybe we should stop," she said.

"You want to stop?" His voice was high. "Okay," he said.

"Ah."

A huge energy drained from him in the heat. He found his voice, but it took awhile. "I don't want to stop," he managed.

"Maybe we should just forget it. I am a woman and you are a man. Okay?"

She took his hand and started rubbing it with her thumb.

"Maybe if you told me what is bothering you so much I could help you."

"How are you going to help? You can't speak Chinese and they wouldn't talk to you anyway. His parents phoned my parents. His mother is really mad. She talked with my mother for two hours. They want me to come home immediately and work it out with him. No, I said. I am finished with him."

She looked at her fingernails. Gaggles passed, in that Beijing male uniform of light short-sleeved shirt, dark pants, laceless loafers, gold watch, in that attitude of patient suffering the summer streets required, with that special condescension reserved for those who try to solve their problems by crouching on hotel steps with their bums resting on flimsy Chinese stationery.

Bian Fu moaned softly.

"Let's go see the movie," said Jeff.

In the theatre they sat dead centre and the hall soon filled up with the entire population of a Chinese high school come to be edified with their chaperones. Jeff felt highly conspicuous, the only foreigner in a shrieking crowd anticipating the definitive statement on the treachery of foreigners.

The foreigners in the movie were rugged nineteenth-century types, with big sideburns, who wore heavy coats entirely unsuitable for the Southern Chinese heat they were subjected to. They ate bloody cuts of roast meat. They drank immoderately, especially when placed under house arrest. They were blasé about addling the entire Chinese population with their stores of Indian opium. The Chinese didn't get off easy either. The Emperor himself was portrayed as an outrageous fop, more concerned with the state of his finery and fingernails than with the Celestial Empire. While drugged Mandarins tottered around, falling ever deeper into the foreigners' trap, the Emperor received manicures in his Gu Gong chambers.

Bian Fu rubbed his palm again with her thumb.

The schoolkids chattered at a volume more appropriate to a denunciation meeting than a movie theatre.

Particles of meaning penetrated his brain via the Mandarin subtitles. *Ru guo...ya pin...ying guo ren...*

An English boat was boarded by Lin Zexu, who had a conversation with a British captain with the help of a very cute translator. Lin Zexu said something, to which the translator responded in English. The entire audience roared with nasty laughter at the subtitles.

That's so Chinese, They never say yes and they never say no.

He looked over at Bian Fu, but couldn't make out how she took that.

The scene that shook Jeff was about halfway through. At the end of a party the court courtesan made a pretty speech. "My sisters may entertain you with their laughter and smiles, but I can stay to attend to your every need." The British captain found himself in agreement with this proposition.

"See," said Bian Fu, "he likes *her* hair too."

Not more than a couple of minutes later, however, the captain dragged the courtesan out of his bedroom by her hair, as he waved a pair of scissors she had concealed.

Now, the scene. The river disburdened itself of early morning mist, as the courtesan was shackled and dragged to the riverbank, as Lin Zexu stood waiting. She was bound to a huge boulder. The soldiers gathered together behind the boulder, with their hands on the rock, ready to push, their legs bent and their quadriceps bulging, Lin Zexu began to count and the camera went closeup on the courtesan's face, which opened wide in fear and desire and she screamed YE YE!: her cry flew across the bank to a bent old man gathering firewood, who straightened at his name YE YE!; Lin Zexu shouted Ah! and the boulder plunged under the water in a last blast of storming bubbles. Ye Ye, crippled, picked up another stick.

Bian Fu's neck pulsed.

Steve Noyes

After the movie, she had to find a phone. She listened for a long time to her mother. Then she called her sister. Again, a long listen. Then she phoned the boyfriend and started yelling. Jeff backed away, and stood with his arms crossed, dully watching the street. Passers-by looked and looked away. She screamed immoderately for a couple of minutes, then hung up.

"I have to go back to San Tiao," she said simply. "I have to face them."

"I'll walk you to the minibus."

It came all too quickly. Bian Fu was in shock. Jeff explained to her that he was moving from San Tiao to Beijing in a couple of days, after the graduation party.

"Here, this is my sister's number," she said, scribbling on a scrap of paper from her purse. "Call and leave your number with her. She will get it to me."

"I will be thinking of you," he said. "Good luck. I know you know how to handle yourself."

She said nothing. She put one foot up on the minibus step.

"I love you and will be thinking of you," he repeated. "Call when you can."

She nodded.

"Zai jian."

"Zai jian."

Then the minibus started to move. She found a seat and looked out the back window, waving as the bus moved off in the evening traffic toward San Tiao. Jeff realized he was eating from the bag of popcorn in his hand. It tasted like shit. What he really needed now, he thought, was some opium.

The graduation party was held on the second floor of the teaching building in San Tiao. The young men sat on one side of the room, young ladies on the other. Han Xiu Ling was there, imperious as one in a short skirt can be; Tian Kang was there, looking like the Chinese version of Doris Day in a white dress and pumps. The emcees were the best looking of the bunch, tall slender people destined to become anchors on provincial television stations. The main event was karaoke, hours upon hours of karaoke, students singing in nervous groups, soloists, teachers rising to tell funny stories; funny, that is, to everyone but Jeff. The room was sweltering, and Jeff and the teachers sat at the front, drinking endless bottles of Evian water and eating candy, chips. It was like being back in high school.

They asked Jeff to sing. But I can't read the characters on the karaoke machine, he tried to beg off. Sing, sing, they insisted.

And so he rose to his feet, took a deep breath, gripped the microphone and, with a last look at the graduating class of San Tiao College, threw back his hair and began a chant from his homeland, a lament of the wheatfields and north-end streets of Winnipeg, the hum in the spurlines: he had no idea how he was sounding, but he put some soul into it, sustaining the notes, polishing it with a remembered singer's sarcastic tremor, yes, this tune was home grown, it didn't come from Hong Kong —

> *Ah — maybe I'll be there to shake your hand*
> *Maybe I'll be there to share the land*
> *That they'll be giving away*
> *When we all live together*
> *I'm talking about together now...*

The emcee took the microphone back in awe. Or disbelief.

"*Fei chang hao,*" he told his classmates, spurring them to applause.

They had soon run through all the possible permutations of karaoke and the machine was programmed to play a whole dance tape; the mirror ball sent small roving discs spinning around the hall as the lights dimmed and a modest program of dancing started. Jeff was searching for a means of escape — he had already been through a couple of hours of silent obligatory banquet with the teachers. Alice condescended to dance with him. It was about as much fun as getting a needle. She loudly complained about his foxtrot inadequacy and stepped all over his feet, her body held stiff lest it actually touch his. Then he went to dance with Tian Kang. She was delightful, at her merry best. She told him she was going home to Xi'an to get married.

"What! So you're not taking any of those jobs you got in Beijing?" Earlier in the summer, he had spent many hours coaching her in English interview skills.

"I am a daughter." She smiled sweetly. "I listen and obey."

"Yes, but what about what you want?"

She squeezed his arm, and said, "I'm afraid you don't understand China very well, Jeff. You have many things to learn."

He supposed this was true.

Tian Kang dropped in to see him before he quit San Tiao for a hotel in Beijing. She listened patiently to him rant about the reaction of Chinese when he and Bian Fu were out together. "They are so prejudiced! They don't even know me and they hate me! I even see the students here have this sort of reaction. Why do they hate foreigners so much?"

Finally she said, "You don't understand. It is not you that they hate. It is the girl they hate — they do not like that sort of girl do anything to get out of China."

"No," he said. "She's not like that. Do *anything*? Am I that repulsive?"

"Listen; there was another foreigner here about two years ago. A Chinese woman married him. I tried to warn him. When they got back to Germany the woman lasted maybe one week; then she took off. You should get to know this girl very well and try to figure out her intention."

He kept quiet. Tian Kang slipped into considering herself; perhaps it was her impending marriage, or the freedom that talking with a foreigner allowed her. "I do not know about my marriage, what it will be like. I do not think I will try very hard, tee hee."

"Who are you marrying?" Jeff asked.

"One of my father's business colleagues. I know him a little," she said, as if the question were completely unimportant.

"I have memories," she said. "Once there was a boy in one of my classes; we were very friendly with each other. I could not help myself. I would go and look for him in the cafeteria. He came and visited me in my dormitory. After he was gone, one day I picked up my jacket and he had left a note in my pocket saying, I am thinking about you all the time. I still think of him. What was the matter with me? He left this school two years ago. I still think of him. He would stand near the basketball courts and watch me walk into the teaching building. I think he is married now."

"There's nothing the matter with you. The heart extends in many directions. There are many kinds of love. Some of them are obsessive."

"Obsessive?"

"Like you say, you cannot forget about them. They are like fevers. They are not choices you make."

She drew herself up in her chair, to become a little larger, a little more veracious. "I am a Chinese woman," she said. "This is my fate. I take it seriously."

This is the official version, thought Jeff. "Oh, I know, I know," he said. "I'm not saying you won't." (Though he had his doubts, just as he knew she did.) "But these things happen. People have feelings for each other. Sometimes people do strange things. Let it go, Tian Kang, let it go. You don't have to feel bad about it."

She wrote "obsessive" in the notebook she carried around. "What was the other kind of love you mentioned?"

"Romantic love — it too starts as a kind of obsession. It is not balanced. It consumes. It is irrational."

She copied out these words too, but was unsatisfied. "We will not see each other for a long time, I think. Maybe never."

"I will think of you," he said.

"I have to go to class."

So this was it. Another finite friendship.

"'Obsessive' love," she repeated. "Not like real love."

"No. *Very much* like real love," he said. "Hard to tell the difference. Sometimes."

Bian Fu and Jeff were in an air-conditioned hotel room, drinking coconut milk. She lay at the end of the bed, with her knees up, a book in her lap. Her hair fanned over the counterpane. He watched every tribulation of her lips as she read, every deepening of her eyes:

> *Chuang qian ming yue guang*
> *Yi shi di shang shuang*

Ju tou wang ming yue
Di tou si gu xiang

She handed the book to him.

"'Before my bed a pool of light —/ Can it be hoarfrost on the ground?/ Raising my head, I see the moon bright,/ Lowering my head, in homesickness I'm drowned,'" he read.

"Yes," she said softly, "it is a very beautiful scene."

They were taking the afternoon *xiuxi* on the eighth floor of the Tiantan Hotel. There were only three or four days to go before he returned to Canada. Bian Fu had said little about her family and boyfriend, other than they were extremely annoyed with her; she and Jeff were touring Beijing with the energy to see and feel normally only granted to those risen from the dead. Gu Gong, Tiantan Park, Lu Xun's old house, where they spent hours holding hands poring over his notebooks and manuscripts. A blur. They drank each other. At the Meishuguan, the National Art Gallery, there had been an exhibit of calligraphy specifically curated for the return of Hong Kong to the mainland.

"This is one of Deng Xiao Ping's sayings," she said, beside a very long scroll of tiny characters. "He said it to Margaret Thatcher." She rattled it off; the words *Zhong Guo ren*, Chinese person, figured prominently.

"What's it mean?"

She paused in mock-difficulty with a possible translation. "Maybe later I will explain."

One piece of calligraphy was only four characters, huge. Jeff had difficulty imagining the brush-size it was done with, possibly the kind of brush you paint houses with. The effect was stark, bold. The *hanzi* writhed and bulged at their junctures, and where the strokes ended there were fiery black wisps as if the brush had been torn from the paper in a storm of emotion; the scroll pulsed with an inner malevolence. Cursive as the scrape of branches against a window, the characters defied identification; there were no easy radical shapes, no *kou*s or *shou*s or *xin*s to pick out; it was the shape of someone's guts as they shrieked from the crowd.

Bian Fu noticed Jeff staring at it and whispered, "That one says — ah — something like — 'now the shame can be killed.'"

She drew a tiny package of Kleenex from her purse and wiped her neck. "I saw my sister other day."

"And what does your sister think of us?"

"*Zhong li*. She stand in the middle. She does not say yes, she does not say no. It is our business."

Jeff dropped it.

At the hotel, once they got past the anxiety of negotiating the lobby and entered the privacy of their room, Bian Fu lost her circumspect public manner — sometimes she liked holding hands but more often she preferred not — and became erotically playful. As they lay kissing, Jeff rubbed her breasts and the backs of her legs with increasing ardour. She undid his top button and fondled his chest hair, wound her legs around his. Jeff had a hard-on constantly. But they did not make love: she was in control. She suddenly snorted and said, "Buh! I feel desire!" and tugging down her skirt, bounced over to the other bed, where she turned her big eyes toward him and said, "I have to run away now!"

"Do you want to make love?" Jeff asked her, feeling ridiculously formal.

"Ah, no."

"Oh," he said. "Why?"

She considered. "When you go away it will hurt more."

One passionate moment they broke from a long kiss, and he removed her hair from his mouth and felt her heart beating like sunshine within his, and he said, "Do you love me?"

"I. Ah —"

"Do you love me?"

Bian Fu leapt up and threw her hands wide. "Always you are asking do you love, do you love me? You are worse than a Chinese woman! Yes, I love you. I LOVE YOU!"

"Because I think I love you," he said.

She laid her head on his chest and breathed. Jeff lay aware that this was preposterous; he was leaving soon. He had been in love before. Never had it been so miserable.

Beijing glared at them as they walked stunned through the myriad city — its taxi drivers and their rear-view stares, its *bing-qie* saleswomen with their concentrated disapproval, the strolling summertime couples, the parks filled with kids, the asphalt shimmering in silver waves. They visited Lao He Gong, the Tibetan Buddhist temple, and gawked and gaped at the golden fifty-foot Buddha, where monks in their orange robes milled around and lit incense with a resigned metronomy. The Chinese had turned the temple into a museum; it was hard to imagine the traditional monastic life that had once taken place there. But of course it was continuing, thought Jeff: a truly enlightened Buddhist monk would have seen the occupation of Tibet and the resultant suffering as illusion. As were the fantastically carved eaves of the temple.

As was Bian Fu in white high-heels, sucking on a Popsicle.

The prayer flags hung motionless from the ceilings. They knelt before the Buddha, side by side, clasping sticks of burning incense, and made their separate wishes. In this he felt intensely artificial, as though he would bow before anything to reduce uncertainty, yet remain aware that uncertainty persisted. He had not told her he was a Muslim; he thought it unnecessary; one more complication in an already complicated liaison. What if that was too strange, too foreign for her? Privately he wondered if he truly was one: all that remained of his observance of Islam's pillars, despite his earlier religious spell in the South, the prayers, giving to charity and the rest of it, was the sense that God existed, the bringer of fate, poser of problems that tested and refined.

Outside the gates, an old man pressed his calligraphy into Jeff's face. It was the character *Ai* —

"Love!" the old man said.

"Yes, I know what love is," Jeff said. "I don't want to buy it."

Bian Fu snorted.

One evening, they met at Tian An Men Square. There was a huge countdown scoreboard for the return of Xiang Gang. Chinese tourists wandered the vast plain of smooth concrete. Pot-bellied fathers held the hands of their daughters; mothers in summer dresses fussed for photographs. They had come by bus from the hotel, and got out early to buy *baozi* at a particular hole in the wall. "My mother likes this woman's *baozi*," Bian Fu said. In the middle of the square they sat on the flimsy Chinese foolscap she always carried for such purposes. They were the only two without cameras. It was a balmy evening, with kites — grasshoppers, eagles, and, of course, butterflies — high in the dulling blue sky.

They ate and talked, and, despite the interested stares of a man on a blanket, Jeff felt completely at home. They chatted about nothings, how they had met, their walk to the Chao Bai River; she put her head on his shoulder. He enjoyed hearing her laugh. Still she did not mention her family or the boyfriend.

At dusk they walked back across the Gate of Heavenly Peace. He noticed, near the subway station, the red rice paper balloons floating above the temple with its upswept eaves, the McDonald's on the far corner, and, returning his gaze to the temple that had mounted in the mind as it lost form in the twilight, the swallows. A line of an old Chinese poem came to him: "Swallows that once flew into the roofs of nobles now fly into the lives of commoners," he said.

She nodded, but he couldn't tell if she knew the poem or not. "They are birds." She smiled. "Like you."

They caught a bus.

Bian Fu pointed out a woman under a streetlight, "Look, she is wearing traditional clothes-es. I think women should not wear them until they are about thirty. Me, I like very modern, very beautiful clothes-es. I wear them very well."

She reached into his pocket, and he gently removed her hand. "Ah-ah." The precious *jiazi*, his gift to her, was tucked in there. It had acquired the cachet of an engagement ring.

At the corner near her sister's apartment, she took his hand and they entered the *hutong*s. A group of men played cards on an overturned box, squatting and slapping the cards down, and their talk, high-pitched, wafting and wowing in that bombastic way Jeff loved about Chinese, faded out, then they heard the traffic again.

They passed a stand with white yogurt bottles and red Cokes lined up in stripes. A couple of kids with backpacks sucked on Popsicles. Smells of shao kao rou and charcoal and fried peanuts; the huge movie marquee with the overblown faces of a man and a woman, about to kiss, the woman's lips an unlifelike red. They zagged again and couldn't hear the street anymore, just a faint whirring. The source was a brilliantly lit basement apartment, the door open, with numerous wigs of all colours set on broom-handles with fans drying them. Another turn, and they were in a radically darker passage, with wooden slats overhead, the moonlight barring their faces. Garbage smells from somewhere, sweet orange peel, urine. They stood against a brick wall with tattered movie posters; near them a parked bike with an attached flatbed holding indistinct sacks. He touched her waist. She put her arms around his neck. He took the jiazi out of his pocket. "Bian Fu. This is for you."

"*Xie xie.*"

"Let's go meet your sister and brother-in-law."

"Oh, I go see if they're up."

And she flitted around the corner.

He stood there, breathing. He stood there. Breathing. There was someone else breathing in that passage, in the complicated moonlight.

One of the sacks stirred and a face lifted — an old face, a male face, a small saga of shot teeth. Then it sank and went out.

She was back. "They are all sleeping. Do you know the way out?"

He took her in his arms and kissed her for a whole minute. His heart was pounding.

#

Jeff asked her at lunch the next day, "How are things going with your family?"

"I do not want to talk about it right now," she said, pouting. She took it out on the waitress. "Xiaojie, xiao *jie! Yao cu, wo jiu yao cu!* I can't believe this, you know, a restaurant and they don't have the brains serve vinegar with *leng mian*, what is this, *bu hao, xian zai ba cu zai zhuo ya!*

"Can you believe it — *leng mian* with no *cu?*"

His last evening in Beijing they went to JJ's disco. "It is really the best way to relax, don't you think?" she said. "That buh-buh-buh," and her fists mimed the throb of the speakers. They danced for a couple of hours that night, trying, again, to ignore the attention they drew. Jeff laughed at the music: an incredible remix of Dan Hill's "Sometimes When We Touch," incredible because as the song's speed increased the oh-so-sensitive lyrics became irresistibly funny; then the *Star Wars* theme was played as complicated machinery on the ceiling moved grandly across it, lights flashing, and dumped glitter all over the dancers; the DJ, an Australian, threw fluorescent plastic bracelets into the crowd at regular intervals; the romantic waltzes were Carpenters oldies; and it was deliciously hilarious for Jeff to see hundreds of young Chinese men flailing their arms around to "Y-M-C-A" with no idea of the song's social context. He explained this to Bian Fu, who shook her head: "No! No? *Shi ma?*"

And then, at the far end of the dance floor, the curtains drew back on a stage, and ten tall guards, their eyes fixed, stood with their arms crossed, facing the crowd as ten young women behind them, in feather boas, bathing suits and pumps, cavorted briefly to Jerry Lee Lewis' "Chantilly Lace."

It was all sort of a reader's guide to American pop.

During a waltz, it hit her. Bian Fu leaned against him and he felt her entire weight, her sudden lack of energy, her cling. He whispered in her ear. He comforted her. He told her he would come back to her. She gripped his shirt with her fists and her shoulder blades shuddered.

The next morning when she showed up at the hotel, her facial muscles barely moved. Jeff asked her to write her address in characters on some envelopes; she did this, taking a long time to make the *hanzi* clear.

"You know I love you." He gently stroked her back. "I will come back to you."

She did not respond.

Finally, in the cab to the airport, as they were passing San Li Tun's Hard Rock Cafe, its Fender Stratocaster and Cadillac on the roof, she spoke. The summer had gathered in a moody cloud that pushed down on the apartments, the overpasses, the six-lanes, the billboards. Everything pulsed with that sick green light, so common before storms, that brings out deep brown from cement and fatigue from the human face.

"I am not very good at expressing my feelings," she said. "I have been trained not to show them. I hope you understand that, because I love you."

"I understand," he said. "I love you too. And I will come back to you."

Then they were standing in front of the airport terminal.

"You take care and I will write you every day," he said.

"Jeff. When you come back?"

"As soon as I can."

They kissed. "Okay. I will go now." They kissed again. She walked off, she stopped, confused. She came back.

"It is the wrong way to the bus," she said.

He hugged her and lifted her feet off the ground, pressing and pressing her ribs and tasting her lips deeply; he wanted to get inside her. She started to shake. When her feet touched the ground, she brushed his cheek with her fingertips and said "*Zai jian.*" She disappeared down a stairway.

Then it hit him. His heart fell in.

All the way to Canada in his cramped seat, her lovely image played before him. Her hair, her eyes, her slim waist. He saw her very clearly.

Part Two

Putonghua

普通话

The Common Tongue

Chapter Four

I am living in a walled compound here, thought Jeff.

He had been back in China two weeks.

Even to enter Jian Hua University required dismounting from your bicycle at a stone gate and passing the scrutiny of the silent policeman on a pedestal. At the corner of Jeff's dormitory road, the workers from the country were building yet another wall and a new speed bump, squatting in all weathers among their bricks and mortar; through yet another gate, a door, and past the desk where the *fuwuyuan*, the service people, were wont to observe who you were, who you were with, the time of day, and took this information down for the police; each day after classes he would lope up the stairs to the same rooms the foreigners had lived in for years — the foreigners, a commodity to be watched, with their desirable language and their inscrutable T-shirts.

The wall, studded with glass shards, surrounded the university. In the early morning he'd sip coffee and watch the bicycle pilgrimage pass outside the wall — students, mothers with children on their rat-trap carriers, bicycle-wagons hauling neat piles of the many-holed cylinders of coal, cheerful middle-aged men talking on cellphones, young men pumping like hell, standing on the pedals. There was neither end nor ebb to their frequency, their panoply.

One morning he saw a singular figure, balanced on the lip of the ditch, as if gathering resolve, black windbreaker, black turtleneck, black pants, black gloves and (of course) black hair. He was running now, a balanced lope across the many lanes of traffic, dodging through the bikes. He plunged into the far ditch, surmounted it, and ran flat out, his black windbreaker flapping behind him until with a long leap he stopped in front of the huge earthworks, the ridges of dirt and mud turned up by the caterpillars, and he stood still for a moment. Then he pliéd, and with his one leg cocked up, the other extended, he began the motions. Black figure, black earth. Hands making clouds. Grasp the sparrow's tail. Snake strikes. His shoulder collapsed in a fluid arm-plunge away from his torso, his hands forming the moment and eliminating the last moment; he was contained; each element of gesture came from a time and returned to it, as if there were nothing in the world that could add to the shapes he made.

Everywhere in the city they unfolded their grace, the *tai qi* practitioners, in resignation and relinquishment of the nightmare of Beijing: on campus in the shade of willows; outside apartment buildings; in children's playgrounds. They described the force in the universe: *qi*. The force was everywhere, and so were they. It was in weather reports and the tires of your bike. It was in your body. It rose in you, fear, anger, *sheng qi le*. So potent was *qi* that it needed tempering: in the early morning, in intense cold, with heavy clothing.

Time to get to class.

It took him about fifteen minutes to ride to class: the campus was huge, with its own traffic. Outside the dormitory compound there were the identical blue supply trucks, idling or trundling along, caparisoned in oil-smoke. The odd taxi bearing a single dignitary. As he neared the academic centre of Jian Hua, the road began to fill with students on their bikes, from outright beaters to expensive mountain bikes. He wove in and out. The pleasure of overhearing the students' Chinese conversations occupied him. Words at this point: he was picking out words, phrases. The old man with his horse-drawn trash cart gentled the horse beside the dumpster. On the island in the middle of the water lily pond older women were ballroom dancing to curiously martial music. The bikes became denser; students stood on their pedals and cruised in and around the slowing bike jam. On the main boulevard leading to the teaching buildings, a big character poster suspended above reminded everyone to build a socialist state with Chinese characteristics. The vendors had already pulled their carts of cigarettes, notebooks, biscuits and soft drinks out into the road, for it was never too early to begin haggling.

There was, predictably, no place to park his bike. Along the road, between the trees, bikes were lined up trunk to trunk. Whoops and yells suddenly, arising from a thunderous clatter. One bike had fallen over and dominoed down the whole line. A couple of students, laughing, began to pick these up, while the bike attendant, an old woman wearing a laboratory coat and a surgical mask, shouted instructions.

Jeff's two months back in Canada had been mostly spent finding, setting up and taking apart an apartment, and playing with his eight-year-old daughter in the park. Melissa had fallen in love with swinging on the rings and had set herself the task of skipping two rings, and Jeff had watched her earnest delight as she swung, missed, fell, swung again. Her hair turned the colour of corn silk in the sun.

In the middle of the night a phone call from Jian Hua University came, offering him a foreign expert's position. He was not sure where they had gotten his name: he had *guanxi*, he supposed, connections. Perhaps Mark. Perhaps from the teachers in San Tiao.

He accepted the offer immediately.

The letters from Bian Fu had come twice a week, and vaguely indicated that she was in trouble with her family. Her mother, she said, had been urging her to reconcile with her boyfriend. She didn't mention her father. When you come back? When you come back? she wrote. *Wo xiang nian ni.* I miss you.

Inside the teaching building it was dark and crowded; students thronged through the doors with their backpacks and Walkmans. He felt the slight panic that always unnerved him in a Chinese crowd. He knew a proverb: *ren shan ren hai*, human mountain, human sea. Everyone walked slowly and politely up the stairs, squinting, taking half steps. Someone had already been on the fourth floor and turned the lights on in the classrooms. Jeff's class had over forty students, hardly ideal for a conversation class. On the blackboards, the class monitor had already written advice on how to act in a *wenming* or civilized manner. Some were reading English articles on software or CD-ROM brochures in the dim fluorescence.

He began writing common adjectives on the blackboard. There was chalk all over the lectern, his desk and the chairs. It was cold.

Everyone kept their jackets on, preparing not necessarily to speak, but to absorb English through their pores, to benefit from contact with him, the foreigner, who asked the day's first question, "How was your weekend?"

Too personal a question, perhaps.

No one answered. The students in their rows, tensely formal, were prepared to sit in silence for as long as it took.

In the middle of these comatose listeners, there was only one student who truly seemed to pay attention, Wang Fang, with a dreamily calm expression, her hair loose and long, playing with a pencil. Jeff had noticed her, wasn't sure why. She strove in all things to be soft-spoken, to not attract attention, to be studious, but her eyes twinkled; she was no doubt full of fun and games elsewhere. Her front teeth were broken, her lips cracked by the winter cold.

As Jeff paced and lectured on his platform, perhaps she was composing the bizarre English sentences that would show up in her first essay. She was from Inner Mongolia, from a concrete city of snow and smoke and then, beyond the walls, sheep, miles upon miles of sheep. She put this far more idiosyncratically: "Prairie-born and prairie-bred, I have never seen a pretty Mongolian girl, honestly!" She described the politics of Mongolian university cafeterias, where, she unconvincingly claimed, the fights — occasionally fatal and always involving knives — were all started by Mongolian students, incensed at not getting enough food. The Mongolians attacked the pacific Chinese students.

"Why do you want to learn English?" Jeff asked the class.

A young woman in the back, who rarely spoke, stood up and said, "English is a tool, which we will use to master your technology, and then we will surpass you."

Forty heads with black hair gazed at him, waiting for a reaction. Jeff opened the textbook. "Turn to page forty-three…"

Jeff had flown back to Beijing on the eve of the Moon Festival. The week before, Bian Fu had sent him a drawing of the moon, its lower curve darkened with scribbled ink.

When he first caught sight of her, she was hopping from one foot to the other, trying to see over the crowd at the airport gangway. She was dressed simply in corduroy pants and a turtleneck and had her hair up in a bun. He told the money-changing *fuwuyuan* to wait a moment and walked out to meet Bian Fu. When she threw her arms around his neck and kissed him, he stiffened, surprised to be kissed in public by her. He awkwardly returned the kiss, but the reunion was botched.

"Jeff!"

"Bian Fu! I just have to change some money. Be right back."

In the taxi to the Tiantan Hotel, she said little, just clasped his hand and clasped it again, sat churchlike on the lobby couch while twenty yards away Jeff had the same argument with the *fuwuyuan* (Yes, I only want to stay one night. No, I do not require the mini-bar) he'd had in the summer. Upstairs, they silently suffered the attentions of more *fuwuyuan*, who rushed into their room to gather up the drinks from the bar, tidy things they just couldn't put off, and stare at her derisively.

Finally they were alone.

Jeff undid her *jiazi* and let her hair fall, slipping over his fingers, deep black, hidden chestnuts, blue forbidden coves. He nuzzled in and smelled her.

"Ai ni," she said. *I love you.*

"Shen ai ni," he said.

They undressed each other in seconds, and he was in her, her smell around him, their mouths hot together. He came too quickly, and her hips continued to drive into his, until he said, "I'm finished." Her lower lip pulsed in disappointment.

"I had a long flight," he said. "Sorry."

"*Mei guanxi.*" *Don't worry about it.*

They lay in each other's arms. She had brought *bing-yue*, moon cakes with sweet bean paste, and they nibbled these as she curled into him. Cars honked below on the streets.

"Tell me about your childhood," he said, breaking their silence.

"My childhood. Ah…" She propped herself up on one elbow; Jeff could see her thinking, selecting what she could communicate

in English. "I was a tomboy, can I say? At that time in China there
was nothing to eat. My parents were off working elsewhere and I lived
with my aunt and my grandmother; there were children from two or
three different families in the house. I do not remember very much
from then, but I was not sad. Not, can I say, not unhappy. We were in
the city once and I remember…the Red Guards lined up beside a long
ditch and I know something has happened but I do not know what.
Maybe something burning…a fire. They tell us to move on. I am very
frightened.

"No. I cannot remember it very clear.

"There were roses in my father's yard in Bing He. There were so
many. Lovely."

He nodded and nodded.

"I was a member of the Communist Youth League. Everyone was.
They told us people in America starved their old people to death."

Jeff laughed.

"Oh, Jeff! Once a gang of we went out and stole vegetables from a
neighbour's garden. Carrots, *shu cai*, I do not know the English name.
When my grandfather found out he was very angry. He took me out
in the yard and with a stick he drew a large circle in the dust, and
told me to stay in the circle for a whole day." She faltered then, as if
the strength to recount these things had ebbed. She brushed her lips
against his chest, curled into him, snuggled.

"I am a woman, and you are a man," she said.

"That's a good story," he said.

"I want to know about your family."

"I don't have many. A mother in Winnipeg."

"You should send her money."

"And my daughter in Victoria."

"And your *qianqi*, your last wife," she said, frowning.

"My daughter lives with my ex," he said. "I live alone."

She considered this moodily. "That woman will cause a trouble."

Below they heard motors and horns and all the importunate
sounds of transit. All Beijing surrounded them, its uncountable
souls and lights, eons of pastry-eating ceremonies, firecrackers and

giggling children. They felt shy within an alien quality of their love,
how in coming together they were neither here nor there, intimate yet
lonely.

"I want to know you," she said simply. "I want to know your joy
and your pain."

"Me too," he said.

"I never want to be apart from you again."

"Yes," he said.

In a while she got dressed and said she was going to her sister's.
As soon as she was gone, Jeff fell asleep.

The next morning, jet lag overtook Jeff in the long taxi ride to
the university; the cab crawled through the city in the fabled golden
autumn air; bicycles surged around him as he dozed. Thrown awake
by a gush or clot of traffic, he sensed Beijing's endless reconstruction
of itself, the millions of faces pouring forth from the side streets. The
faces amazed him. He had the delicious feeling he'd had before when
travelling, of the face that, once seen, triggers an awareness of the
earth's greater neighbourhood, the family member long forgotten,
the soul's deep address book. After being given a room, key, receipt,
after being greeted by the Assistant Head of the Foreign Languages
Department, who shook his hand forcefully, looked noncommittally
at his one suitcase and backpack and left, he fell deeply asleep, again,
safe in Jian Hua's willow leaf and stone fortress, dreaming of Bian Fu
in a shower cap.

The phone woke him. "*Wei*," he said.

"*Ai, ni hao*," a male voice said, "this is Li Tongzhi, Wang's
comrade, Wang Xiaojie's comrade, I want to meet with you."

"Who? *Shi shei*?"

"I am a friend of Miss Wang's," the voice repeated. "You are an
English teacher at Jian Hua. I want to meet with you. When can we
meet? It is important that I meet with you. I will come and see you."

"I don't know you, *bu renshi*," Jeff said quickly, and hung up.

With an almost imperceptible hush, the Lazy Susan slowly
revolved with sliced pork and green onions, Beijing duck, pancakes,

caramelized potatoes, the dreadful crispy-rice-puffs-with-gravy dish, fish with sweet-sour sauce, all the dishes glistening and moving away before he could get at them, distracted by chit-chat, while the shot glass of *baijiu* stayed in front of him. He was at a banquet that same evening for all the foreign teachers. Jeff turned to flirt a bit with Tabitha, the violin major from Princeton, and snagged a slice of the Beijing duck. Qiang Bei Uan, the department head, was raising her shot glass and saying something about all the work that had to be done; Jeff could barely hear her. A demure girl in a green dress slid from the wall and refilled his glass of coconut juice. They all drank.

He wondered if he could stomach another one of those crispy-rice squares with gravy. He found that he could.

Among the other foreign experts around the table was Robert, a Canadian who had been in China four years and spoke fairly fluent Chinese: this put him in the position of court translator, and he blushed deeply when he didn't know the meaning of a word. Now, Robert listened red-faced to He Jing, an affable sort, thick-necked and full of cheerful contempt, who was telling them something about Ha Er Bin, his *laojia* or hometown. Ha Er Bin, where men are men and women wear five pairs of underwear in the winter, Jeff thought. Where breakfast is mushy rice soaked in one-hundred-eighty-proof alcohol. Where being Chinese merges with being Inuit, O Western Han, O Eastern Han. Jesus, this baijiu is stern stuff.

Grinning, grinning and loving it, He Jing filled the shot glasses again and urged them to drink, *Gan bei!*

Evelyn was a motherly sort who was half-blind, and came from some American Midwestern university; she researched cognition. And Bruce was also from Princeton. He was chatting up Li Li, a stunning middle-aged beauty whom Jeff liked instantly because she had heard of Don DeLillo. She nodded and nodded at Bruce, whose eyes wandered to her breasts as he described a road trip to New York he took last year.

Robert stood up and proposed a toast: Jeff didn't catch it all, but the last words were "*zuihao piaoliang de xiaojie,*" the most beautiful girl. His face was livid. The serving girl looked directly at her shoes.

The Director raised her glass and didn't blink, but five minutes later, she was heard to say, "I think He Jing, if he wishes to drink at these department functions, should start paying for the *baijiu*."

The serving girl departed for some other function; they picked at the rest of the revolving plates; and then they were in the lobby of the campus restaurant, doing up jackets, going over the class schedules again.

"I overheard that you play basketball," Jeff said to He Jing. "Mind if I come along and play?"

"Nice to meet you," he said.

Back at the dormitory, Jeff invited Robert and Bruce into his room for coffee.

"So, checking out that Li Li, eh?" said Robert.

"Not too bad, not too bad," said Bruce.

Jeff laughed nervously.

"Dong Bei woman, northeast woman. Pretty tough, pretty fucking tough. She'd grind it out of you," Robert said.

Robert took a good look at the picture of Bian Fu on Jeff's bookshelf.

"Hey, Robert," said Bruce, "you read Chinese, don't you? Let's go to my room. I've got something to show you."

Bruce's room was a showroom of cutting-edge Japanese electronic appliances: video, stereo, mini-fridge, computer, fax. There were pinup posters plastered to every vertical surface.

Bruce produced a bundle of letters from Korean and Chinese girls, from his previous year teaching in Nan Jing, passing it under Jeff's nose, and handed it to Robert. Robert read parts of the letters out loud, managing to convey that Bruce was badly wanted by every college-age female in Nan Jing. "I was in your class. Do you remember me?" Gold-digging letters to the rich foreigner.

"This handwriting actually isn't bad at all," Robert said, "it's not that cursive."

"So what should I say?"

"Tell her you'd be glad to see her when she is in Beijing."

"But I'm seeing another girl right now."

Robert rolled his eyes, overwhelmed by the American's failure to grasp a simple principle. "Look, why close that door?"

They leered at each other, and another letter was pulled out. "Now this one, I can't remember her very well, I think she was in my third-year class. This one says she wants to study abroad…"

They laughed. "So what else is new?" said Robert.

Jeff was silent.

Robert went to his room and brought back a well-handled Kodak folder; the shots were of a fashion show. The women were all around twenty and displayed themselves *en compagnie* on a runway or individually at little tables laden with sweet drinks.

"These girls didn't speak English or even want to learn very much, and I didn't care."

"They're beautiful women," said Jeff.

"Got a Chinese chick yet?" said Robert.

"No," said Jeff.

"Hey," Robert said to Bruce, "did you see those two at JJ's last night?"

"What, dancing together, like she had those leopard tights?"

Jeff refused a beer.

"Yeah, the one with the great tits."

"Really acting up, eh. Attracting a lot of attention. So…?"

"Nope."

"'Cause you knew it meant another two hundred kuai, eh? 'Cause that's what it would have taken."

Bruce grinned.

Suddenly they realized that Edward, the other American teacher, who had not been at the banquet, was standing in the doorway.

"Are you guys American?" he said to Jeff and Robert.

"No," said Jeff.

"Yeah, well, anyway. I was playing soccer this afternoon with a bunch of Chinese guys. They were so fucking chippy. Finally I challenged them all to a fight. Twenty of them. They backed right off. Ha!"

No one said anything.

When he had gone, Bruce said, "How embarrassing for those Chinese."

"Boy, is he lucky they didn't beat the shit out of him."

"Can you believe that?" Robert said. "I'll tell you my lousy story even though you're not American and can't really appreciate what a homeboy I am?"

"Oh, chill," said Bruce.

"Jerk."

"What were we talking about?"

"You should see this article I saw in *Asia Week*," said Robert, slurring his words, "how Vancouver is totally Chinese now. They were talking about a shopping centre in Richmond and the only white guy mentioned was a clown handing out balloons."

"No way."

"Don't you think, I mean, really, the Canadian government ought to get tough? What was it you were saying about being able to take exams in BC in Mandarin? Let's get real, the only way we can have a society is if we agree it's an English-speaking society. Those people coming over from China they've got no interest in speaking English. They just want it to be a Chinese society, it's the same old game. They always buy up all the downtown centres in our cities and you can't even talk to them. I mean, you don't know how frustrating it is to try and learn Chinese in China."

"Yes, I do," Jeff said. Exams in BC in Mandarin? Where did he get this stuff? Jeff thought.

Robert ignored him. "If you came to Canada to learn English, I mean, people would speak to you in English on the streets. Here, why, just the other day I was reading some Chinese on a blackboard in the department and a couple of students were standing right next to me looking at me like I was a freak."

"I hate that," said Jeff. "The thing I can't stand is when someone asks to take a picture with you and his friend because his friend has never had his picture taken with a foreigner before. I mean, what am I, some kind of anatomical curiosity?"

"You just have to know how to make that work in your favour," said Bruce. "Come on, I'll show you some more pictures."

He met Bian Fu at the West Gate of the university the next day. She carried a huge plastic bag on the handlebars of her bike.

"What's in the bag?"

"When I learn that you are hungry, I bring food and quick when I can."

They set out looking for a park to eat in, a near-impossibility in Beijing. For there was no privacy: even in the parks, or, more correctly, the scenic marshalling grounds, they were always within ten feet of someone else. It drove Jeff crazy. But he was happy to be in the sunshine walking beside her. Bian Fu was not tall; her head could nestle against his collarbone; her hair went beyond black to a radiant blue; her legs made him dream of outdoor badminton. And in her eyes he saw mountain flowers springing up everywhere, *bian di kai hua*. Above all he loved her speech, her giggles and emphatically held aspect-particles at the end of sentences. He paid bright attention to her questions (*ma*), stirred himself at her summons (*ya*), perked to her instructions (*ba*), sympathetically agreed with her inclusive inveiglements (*ne*), and felt excited when she simply stressed a point (*a!*).

"How was the Moon Festival with your family?" he asked.

"We ate and ate and ate," she said.

Finally they found a triangle of dusty grass, a shortcut between streets, and he spread his sweater out. They sat. Bian Fu took out cold dumplings and twenty or so *yuebing*, moon cakes stuffed with red bean paste, and they munched away.

Jeff noticed a group of Chinese at the corner observing them. He made eye contact; they all turned, pretending they weren't looking.

"Hey, some guy phoned me and said he was your colleague and wanted to talk to me. You didn't give anyone my phone number, did you?"

"Ah, no."

"Weird. He was really urgent about it. Maybe it was just a wrong number."

"No, if he phoned you, there must have been some purpose. Tell me your dream of our future life," she said suddenly, laying her head on his lap. Jeff checked: the group of Chinese were openly staring now.

"Uh, we live together in Canada. Maybe we will get a house there. But first we live here in Beijing for a while."

"We should get an apartment in Beijing."

"Well, maybe we will. First things first, eh?"

Bian Fu licked off her fingers.

"So, if we get married, where would you like to get married?" he said.

"You tell me where we should."

"I think we should get married in your hometown and then we should go to Canada and do it again."

"*Xing a!*" she said, All right!

"When can we go and meet your father? What does your father do?"

"My father is a doctor. Now he runs a Chinese medicine clinic in Bing He. When I returned to my *laojia* this summer I was helping him prepare the herbal medicines and he was very delighted."

Jeff absorbed this — he had noticed that the question was unanswered, and an anxiety began to rise in him. She seemed to retreat from him when they talked; it was subtle, but there.

"So when can we go there to meet him?"

"I will phone and arrange it."

"So how is your family taking all this?" he said

"They still upset, can I say, upset? But they hope us very happy." She leaned back on her elbows and smiled.

The next day she met him on Jian Hua's grounds, under a willow tree.

"Ah, I was standing here thinking how stupid. Here I am, under a tree, waiting for a man." She was drunk. Her head lolled around; it was difficult to tell what she was feeling or thinking. They sat on a picnic table outside the dormitories. He tried to kiss her and she moved her head away.

"So, where were you drinking?"

"I went out for lunch with a male friend. He took me to this place, special vegetable dishes. We ate and ate. Oh, I was telling him how I need money. Maybe you should come work for me, he said.

You could be my secretary. Ah, I need money but I don't need it that bad, I say."

She went on to describe how much money he made, with particular attention to his cellular phone: in fact, supplied a complete breakdown of pricing structures in the cellphone industry. Jeff was silent. Eventually, he steered her toward the dormitory; he caught a quick glimpse of the *fuwuyuan* watching as they hurried up the stairs. They made hurried love, but as soon as they untangled, regarding each other confusedly amid the rucked-up bedclothes, Bian Fu blurted out a little rhyme, counting on her fingers, "*Yi, er, san...*"

Jeff smiled uncertainly.

She flew into a fury. "Buh! You, you do not even know *yi er san*. You cannot even understand that, and us Chinese we all — aaaagh. Look, maybe I just should just phone my friend and get him to pick me up, *hao bu hao*."

"*Da ba*," he said. "Go ahead, phone him."

They glared.

The sun was going down. A small wind came in the window and lifted his taped-up characters away from the wall. Bian Fu waved her hand at them. "Childish!" she said.

"You can leave any time."

But she didn't. She lay on the bed and drank a cup of tea, and an expression he would become familiar with came over her face, pushed out her lower lip and narrowed her eyes. Her nostrils flared. She was deeply alone. There was a horrible insufficiency in the world, the look said, and it pained her nobility of spirit to discover it again and again; her next move would prove this and transcend it. Jeff knew the look well. It had crossed his own face many times.

Jeff read to his class from a textbook by one of the Chinese English teachers. "I shall always remember my time at Oxford University, because it is such a hallowed institution." The final exam was based on this stuff. The students composed and repeated responses to questions concerning the advantages of Beijing living, what makes a good marriage, and whether it is possible for men and women to be friends, as opposed to lovers. This was a subject they were deeply interested in, or perhaps they were deeply interested in his barbaric opinions on the subject. The women said yes, the men no. Jeff pretended to have no opinion.

"Husbands and wives have to have secrets from each other," one of the men said.

"What kind of secrets?" he asked.

"Dark secrets!"

"Deeply secrets!"

Murmurs of agreement; truths.

"About what?"

He stood there in the silence for a few minutes. Nothing. So he circulated in the classroom and tried to prod them into speech. "You, you break up with your girlfriend and the next month you run into her on Wang Fu Jing Avenue. What do you say?"

"Say?"

"Yes, would you say, Excuse me, can you tell me where the McDonald's is? Would you say, How nice to see you?"

"I say nothing."

"Okay, you're at the McDonald's and you see your old girlfriend come in with a guy. You leave and go see your best friend. What do you tell him?"

"I think we would study English together."

Occasionally the students said something that they meant. When discussing what a good marriage was, Wang Fang's seat mate said, "In a good marriage two people get to know each other very well. They become imitate —"

"Intimate," Jeff said.

"Yes, *intimate*. Sorry. Then they can experience tenderness."

"Yes," Jeff said.

Wang Fang looked at her desk.

Jeff had read that the Chinese believe earth is a reflection of heaven; thus the king, Wang, is the man who can connect heaven, earth and the people, and the ideograph, Jeff thought, surely showed this. Tian, Heaven, is a man standing beneath the sky.

That autumn, Jeff knew that heaven and earth were well-aligned. Golden light filled his days and the edges of Beijing, birdcages, boulevards, lanterns, were gilded. A strange beauty in the multitude, that torrent of brown arms after the blistering summer. He had bought a bike and, though it cost about twice what it should have and the seat was forever loose, twisting under him on tight turns, and the tires forever needed repairing, it served, and together he and Bian Fu rode all across Beijing, visiting temples, museums, noodle shops, bookstores, bars — wherever. They had long conversations riding companionably side by side, and for a while he lost interest in studying Chinese; he didn't want to work hard. He wanted to pedal and coast.

Beijing was organized around three huge ring roads, radiating outwards from Gu Gong, the Forbidden City, and broad expressways connected these; everything was on a scale so grand minibuses and bikes seemed to inch across the city. The medians were strewn with paper and plastic garbage. The farther from Gu Gong, the more their pace outstripped the car traffic. Jeff saw an old, scrawny man with ten computer monitors on the back of his bike. The farther from Gu Gong, too, the less likely that Bian Fu would want to hold his hand. And the sweet potatoes for sale, slowly cavitating on the top of oil drums, were worse and worse, barely edible, charred, woody.

Jeff studied the faces. Women in padded cotton jackets, laden with shopping bags, viewing the crowded streets with calm derision, their teeth blackened or missing. They shuffled. Young men with a splendid focus to their gaze cruised past, refusing to make eye contact or return a smile. And the schoolgirls in their ponytails and knee-length skirts held hands and skipped and sang out in bright giggles, as schoolgirls will. The leaves began to fall along the broad boulevards.

"So how are your friends at school?" he shouted at her in Chinese, above the traffic.

She looked worried.

"Bian Fu! How are your friends at school?" he repeated.

"Oh, I thought you asked me if I could play the piano."

She pedalled on for a block, before she said, in English, "I do not think you would like my friends or approve of their ideas. They are very young. All they care about is going to the clubs and spending money. They are very rich."

"So why not let me meet them and find out for myself?"

A half mile later she said, "I have to be careful about the *fuwuyuan* at Jian Hua. If my parents find out we *shui jiao* together, they will never approve of our marriage."

"You slept with your boyfriend. How traditional can they be?"

Bian Fu pedalled on.

Jeff bit his lip.

On campus, he was starting to see the ghosts, the vestiges of what he imagined as an older China. The ghosts showed up in the dormitory corridors and took a month to scrape a wall of plaster; they watched him, toothpicks in their mouths, their hair white with dust. They squatted Pakistani-style on their breaks. There was an old man, slightly addled, with almost no teeth, who handed out tape recorders in the teaching building; he shuffled amid stacks of defunct seventies equipment, unfailingly polite, a pleasure to say nothing with. And Jeff's students: so many came from deep peasant country — the only village student ever to leave, now at a metropolitan university. He could only guess at their stories. They had made incredible journeys. One girl's father was a fisherman from Shandong province. As a child she would help him mend his nets. Another told him his mountain village was so steep there had never been a car in it. Jeff sensed that beyond the city, with its bright, moneyed pockets of internationalism, lay a huge, strange world.

They were lying in his bed, and suddenly Bian Fu's weight on his chest became noticeably heavier, clinging; he shifted and she burrowed in his hair and would not look up; her shoulder blades were moving up and down as she silently wept.

He nudged her chin and she finally raised her head. His chest was soaked with her tears.

"What's the matter, Bian Fu?"

"I am sad. All the time I would tell him, What's the matter with you? I was so mad at him I could hardly speak. All he do is work, work, work and watch football."

"Yes?"

"I used to say to him I want to study abroad and all he would say is, 'No, my parents need me.'"

"Uh-huh." Jeff did not want to hear this, because she was not talking to him; she was talking to her memories.

"What is the matter with him? I am thinking. Thirty years old and he does not make his decisions for himself, he just do what his parents want him to do. His parents always interfering with us. They used to get so angry when we slept together."

"Well, he was your boyfriend, what did they expect?"

"They want us to wait until we were married."

"There, there. Don't cry. Okay, cry. But isn't this traditional Chinese culture?"

She paused. Then she started weeping again. "He hurt me badly."

"So why don't you work it out with him? Go back to him and solve your problems." Jeff didn't know whether he meant this — it just came out.

"Ah, no. I have nothing more to say to him. He would come when you were in Canada and talk to me for hours but I would say nothing, just listen. And my mother, she talk like this, Your boyfriend love you very much. He is supporting your life. He has been with you three years. Does three years equal one month? I don't think so. Besides, foreigners say they love people all the time. He will go and love another. And my boyfriend say, Bian Fu, he will need another woman and then he will leave you. I just listen and say nothing."

He rode Bian Fu back on his bike. They arrived at the crossroads near her mother's place, and he pedalled as slowly as possible until he lost balance and stopped. It was stinging cold, the air one part wet mist, one part coal smoke, with a trace of roasted corn. Bian Fu hopped off.

"Stay on," he said.

"Is there a policeman?" she asked. Bian Fu was virtually blind at dusk without her glasses.

"Why? Because you're riding on the carrier? You seriously mean to tell me you're worried about riding double because of the police?"

"There is a fine," she said.

Jeff realized that they were being stared at, listened to, speculated about; they were that monstrosity, a foreigner with a Chinese woman, and had therefore relinquished their rights to privacy, to civic togetherness. Some stared openly, but wouldn't meet his eyes. The lovers were silent, enduring it. One man drew up and asked Bian Fu, "What country is he from?" She tucked her chin down. All around them, the eyes registered clear disapproval and disgust. From the crowd the two syllables Jeff hated drifted out, *lao wai,* the contemptuous label for "foreigner."

Once they crossed the boulevard, Bian Fu said, "We have to say goodbye now."

"Why? I'll ride you home."

Her eyes filled with fear. "Where my mother lives, there are no foreigners," she said, "and we haven't told her that we are coming. It would be impolite."

"Oh."

"*Zai jian,*" she said, and squeezed his hand, and began walking away by the roadside into the smoky reaches of her mother's neighbourhood. All right, he thought, all right, this is still difficult. When was it going to get easier?

When he got back to his dormitory, the *fuwuyuan* told him that his Chinese was very good.

Once a week, in the late afternoon, Jeff held office hours in the teaching building. A light was necessary; the campus was absorbing light into its treetops and the dull red tile roofs. Jeff was annoyed as he listened to the few students, correcting pronunciation. Again the head of the department had sidestepped his request for a university e-mail address. "It will take time," she said, and bent to her appointment book. The previous time she had said, "What kind of account was it you wanted?" Internally, he was fuming. Why didn't she just say no?

The office hours bored him. At first many students had shown up, and Jeff had difficulty managing the group. He taught them words from popular songs and explained what the songs meant. The students asked the same questions over and over again about Canada. Many of them, without a text or model sentences to go by, had trouble understanding him. He could hear a shadow personality of his emerging — one that repeated things at maximum volume and minimum speed.

Wang Fang showed up every time, and so did Li Ruang Yun, who was not in his class, but was from the South, now in Beijing studying for some test so she could go to North America and do an MBA. They seemed reassured to have the same conversations with him week after week. Then there was Zhuan Chen, a myopic, burly engineering student who sat there listening intently. Often he would stay when the others had gone.

"My name is Chen Zhuan," he reminded Jeff.

"What is your research about?" Jeff asked.

From the structure that Chen Zhuan drew, he gleaned that it had something to do with heat and molecules.

"Inside, and this outside. We make heat here on outside, and try find out what molecule is doing on inside," said Chen Zhuan.

"What is this for?"

"Heat buildings maybe."

Jeff looked out the window. Below, on the pavement, one of the *fuwuyuan* with a mask on was slowly sweeping the boulevard with a fan-broom.

He turned and said, "Do you mind if I ask you a question?"

Chen Zhuan nodded.

"You might not like it."

Chen Zhuan did not blink. "You may ask, *Lao shi*."

"Why do Chinese people lie all the time?" Jeff sucked his breath in. There. He had done it. Chen Zhuan said nothing. What was he thinking?

"Chen Zhuan?"

"I am thinking."

"Did I offend you?"

"No, it is okay."

"You don't have to answer. It is an unfair question."

"I will answer. You do not understand, teacher. Because of the Cultural Revolution. People had to lie or be killed. So they learned to lie. Their children learned it from them. Please understand," he said, and it was horrible for Jeff to witness his embarrassment and see behind Zhuan's deep brown liquefying eyes the ghosts, the real people, the liars and the sufferers, his relatives.

"Oh," Jeff said.

"People in Canada tell lies too," Jeff said.

"Sometimes," the student said, "sometimes they are just trying to be polite. Just polite. They do not want to disappoint you."

"Thank you," said Jeff. "I appreciate your explanation."

"Take it easy, *Lao shi*," Chen Zhuan said, and packed his books up. "See you next week."

In the resultant silence, Jeff realized that even if his question were offensive, Chen Zhuan would never had said so. He rode back to the dormitory in the dusk, sad in the smell of noodle soup from the student cafeterias.

Bian Fu's mother's neighbourhood was called Ti Yu Guan, "Athletics Park," for a nearby soccer stadium, but Jeff called it Kick Fish County, because, with his limited vocabulary, and ignorance of the tones, that was what he made of the first two syllables. The only "Ti" he knew meant "kick," and the only "Yu" he knew meant "fish." He was happy to get the fish in there. Kick Fish County was a maze of dirt alleys and brick one-storey homes off a blacktop road in northwestern Beijing. It was almost a month after his return before he was allowed to visit; it took Bian Fu that long to convince her mother to meet him.

They pedalled down a long shadowy lane beside the canal. There was a sweets-seller on the corner. Trucks bright with oranges leaned on the shoulder, parked in front of restaurants, corner stores, the countryman always kneeling among his pile of tangerines, the wife in the cab. Brown faces, eager, charging him no more than four or five times the Chinese price. There was a small factory selling its Buddhist statuary in its yard, shiny casts of Shakyamuni and Kuan Yin on long tables, dust blowing against them. At a *shao kao rou* stand, the vendor bent, turning and turning the kebabs over the coals, sparks going out at his wrists. The road opened on one side and between well-spaced willows there were fields of cabbages, turned earth, strong yellow pyramids of straw. Low fires smouldered in the furrows.

"I'm nervous as hell," Jeff said.

"You don't have to use bad words," Bian Fu said. Another crossroad, and suddenly everything was brick, not cement, not tile. Red brick. Tattered awnings limp over storefronts. The tea shop with its big, fluorescent green *cha* character. They turned and entered the *hutong*s, which twisted and turned, disorienting. Children ran away from them, chanting, *foreigner, foreigner.* Occasionally an iron door to a siheyuan, a courtyard, was open, affording a glimpse of a private life. Laundry draped over a bicycle; someone stirring a wok.

They pulled their bikes up at an iron gate, parked them, and a middle-aged woman and man turned from a long low table in the courtyard where they were chopping leeks, and raised their arms.

"*Ni hao.*"

"*Ni hao,*" he replied.

Bian Fu said simply, "Jeff, *wo* Ma, Ma, Jeff."

They went inside.

"Sit, sit, sit, sit," said Bian Fu's mother.

Jeff presented his gift: seven peacock feathers. Bian Fu's mother said *Xie xie* and tacked them to the wall. He showed the mother some photographs. They were of Victoria, and she was deeply appreciative of one, a shot of a beach.

"There must be much fresh air there," Bian Fu translated.

Bian Fu's uncle continued cooking. The other family members arrived. He was introduced to her brother, an engineer from Bing He. He regarded Jeff with the deepest suspicion, a stance he did not relax from throughout the evening. Their toddler, Er Bao, pointed at Jeff and cried, "*Guizi! Guizi!*" Ghost, ghost!

The brother shushed her, and offered Jeff a cigarette. Er Bao began shouting, *Chir ma da, yao chir ma da,* I want to eat locusts. Much effort was expended explaining this. Jeff tried some locusts. They tasted like hardened french fries.

He helped them set up a table in the small room. There were only two rooms. The brother politely answered his questions, yes, he was an engineer, yes, they lived in Bing He, yes, thank you, his daughter was cute, but did not ask him any.

The meal began at seven and lasted until almost ten. Their plan was to render him immobile by force feeding. The table was colourful with dishes, plates half-covering plates, beef dishes, pork dishes, fish, gummy macaroni-like vegetables, stir-fried cabbage, spicy strips of tofu, shrimps.

Her family soon tired of Bian Fu and him talking in English and tired even sooner of his attempts at Chinese. "I know about two hundred characters," he said. Very good, they said. "When I first came to China all I could say was Ni hao." Really, they said. Bian Fu dutifully translated. Jeff couldn't remember later what he had asked them — probably innocent questions that here represented the height of rudeness. He dutifully supplied them with statistics concerning Canada: population, size, and, of course, its dissimilarity to America.

"America is very disorganized," said Bian Fu's mother.

A group of boarders passed through the living room. One of them stopped and made a comment, there was laughter, and Bian Fu, grinning, said, "He says he has studied English for seven years and now, when there is a foreigner in front of him, he can't think of a thing to say!"

The topic of wheat and Canadian farms was brought up and abandoned. Eat, eat, they said. Soup was produced. Bian Fu had to get up to answer a phone call.

Everyone noted his panic, alone with the alien Chinese. They shifted uncomfortably on their chairs, abandoned with this strange guest. They plied him with more food. "*Bao le, bao le,*" he pleaded. I'm full.

They grabbed his bowl, gave him more.

"He isn't a child," said the uncle.

Jeff stared in amazement at the uncle.

Later, they all walked him out to the gate and he mounted his bike.

"*Xiao xin,*" they said. Take care.

"*Xie xie,*" he said.

"*Zai jian,*" they said.

"I'll call you," Bian Fu muttered. "My mother thinks you are very romantic."

Jeff had tears in his eyes. He knew that the evening had been a complete failure. They would never accept their relationship.

"Bye-bye," said Bian Fu.

As he rode back to Jian Hua University, he kept seeing the dark eyes of Bian Fu's brother, and knew he was her father's emissary; he doubted the brother would give a positive report. He doesn't speak very much Chinese, he would say. He is a lustful wretch who keeps touching Bian Fu.

He dresses like a peasant.

Chapter Five

The next time Jeff went over to Bian Fu's, the place was a shambles. Five of Bian Fu's mother's friends had shown up from Bing He to help her install central heating. They planned to run heating pipe from the coal stove into the bedroom and into the next apartment for the couple with the newborn baby. In the bedroom, furniture was pulled into the centre, with drills and tools scattered everywhere, the unassembled radiators piled on the desk. The crew took turns hammering away at an eighteen-inch spike with a sledge, slowly biting a hole into the brick wall for the pipe. Incredibly, in the midst of all this clutter, dust and noise, Er Bao had gone to sleep. Bian Fu leaned back on the bed, stroking Er Bao's forehead, and said, "It is very hard for a man in modern society, but not for a woman, I think."

The men worked for four days. They were rough, their hands swollen and scarred from their jobs, tradesmen fallen from their former status as engineers.

At supper they asked Bian Fu, "What sort of person is this? What language does he speak?" They approved of his appetite for chili-hot dishes. One of them asked, "Does he know about the Cultural Revolution?"

"Why are they asking that?" Jeff said.

"All of their lives have been affected by the Cultural Revolution. Terrible things have happened to them. They are really very kind-hearted people."

"I know they are; they showed up here to help your mother. They must be kind. Why would I think otherwise?"

"The language barrier," she said.

"Yes, I know about the Cultural Revolution," he told them. "In the West, that is practically all we know about China. Many many books have been written about it."

"The West doesn't know what went on," one said through Bian Fu.

"Hold it," Jeff said, "I know plenty about it. It lasted from 1965 to 1975. China was supposed to be completely revolutionized. It began with a staged event on the steps of the Great Hall of the People, when Mao met a fifteen-year-old girl and asked her, *Yao wu ma?* Do you want violence? And she answered *Wo yao wu a!* Yes, I want violence. The idea was to found modern China on the image of the peasants. People were criticized and beaten in the streets because of their 'incorrect' class backgrounds. Mao and Jiang Qing, his wife, established the *Hong Wei Bing*, the Red Guards, to instill the appropriate amount of terror in everyone. Intellectual activities in China were completely shut down, books banned, the only art was stern revolutionary operas and movies. Before they closed the colleges, a seventeen-year-old refused to write his college entry exams, claiming he should get in because his family was peasant class. Handed in a blank paper. Got in anyway."

Bian Fu and the men listened to him, but Bian Fu didn't bother translating — either because it was too difficult or because his commentary on their history was plain rude. Jeff didn't know himself what caused him to make such a speech. He expected at least one of them to say, "Okay, he knows a little." But their troubled eyes said, "You don't really know, you can't know." They remained polite, but their talk flattened into asking if wanted another apple and saying *Hao* when he helped them after dinner. "How thick is the wall?" he said, about to attack it again with the spike. "A foot," one said, "but if we do our very best, we will succeed." His hands rang until tender on the sledgehammer's handle.

By early October, Jeff's visits centred on Er Bao. He enjoyed playing with her, and he no longer thought that Er Bao's making strange with him was xenophobia. Not entirely anyway. Rather, he thought it was the customary shyness of all small children. Jeff thought it strange that love for a woman would produce this extra affection for a two-and-a-half-year-old child, who wore the same paddy-baby clothes every day, was seldom washed and craved attention like sugar. Jeff missed his daughter; Er Bao missed her mother and father in Bing He. When her mother had gotten a new job at a factory, Er Bao was forthwith delivered to her grandmother, Wang Fu Ren. Er Bao was often in the courtyard of the *siheyuan* sucking on a piece of string.

Her grubbiness had been her first attainment in life and she powerfully wished to retain it.

Bian Fu called her *"xiao zang zhu!"* (dirty little pig!). Er Bao would pout, and bleat, "Wo *bu* shir" (I am *not*), the *"bu"* all trembly and indignant. She was fascinated by the hair on Jeff's arms. *"Mei you,"* she'd say, plucking and picking at his forearm, twisting the hairs together, pinching. When Er Bao was napping, Bian Fu showed him the dark down on the child's back. "It will disappear," Bian Fu said.

Once a visit, Er Bao would fall — off a chair or from the sofa — injuring her reserve, and she'd erupt into stiffening sobs. Her accidents were not entirely random. They would never occur, for instance, when she played with knives, which she enjoyed: they were sharp, they had heft, and they were superior toys. She had few others. She wore Bian Fu and her mother down.

Very early in Jeff's courtship of the Wang household, Er Bao had gleefully surveyed him, and said, "Auntie has picked up a ghost-person."

Wang Fu Ren crossed her arms and grimaced. *"Bu li mao,"* she said. *Not polite.*

Er Bao hated it when Jeff and Bian Fu spoke English, which was virtually all the time, Jeff's Chinese not practiced enough to deal with anything except the simplest concepts. Once, Er Bao said, "Why do you talk like that? I listen but I can't understand." Then she left, off to play with the outdoor knives. Bian Fu was amused: she approved of Er Bao's stormy and sulky repertoire. Jeff got the idea that Er Bao's stubby little legs, elegant long eyelashes and rotundity were the perfect, pleasing summation of Bian Fu's earlier girlhood. Defiance was essential to her. It was no surprise, then, when Er Bao kicked

over the chamber pot in a fit, that Bian Fu and her mother laughed
and Bian Fu said, "What did I tell you? She's going to be an annoying
person."

The lovers role-played a possible conversation with Bian Fu's
father, who was still declining to meet Jeff. Bian Fu sat on the bed in a
straight-backed solemnity.

"He is very stubborn and traditional," Bian Fu said.

"I hear you are a very intelligent man who has written three books
comparing Chinese and Western medicine," Jeff said in Chinese.

"Thank you," she said.

"I want to thank you for inviting me here to your home; it's very
kind of you."

"You're welcome," she said.

"I really love your daughter, and I know you do too."

"Since I have been doing that for twenty-seven years, and since
I have the greater experience with doing that, I think that is how I
should prefer it to remain," she said.

"Hold it," Jeff said, his role slipping, "is he really going to be like
that?"

"Oh, yes. Perhaps much worse."

Er Bao wandered in and climbed up on the bed, ending that
discussion.

Occasionally, Bian Fu would turn sulky, and criticize Jeff in a
carping manner that he didn't like.

"Why do you wear those old clothes?" she said. "It does not look
good."

"I have my own style," he said. "It's a little sloppy. So what? Why
should I look like everyone else?"

"A person should live in society," she replied. "Not outside it. In.
Look, if there are two sets of clothes, one nice, one not-nice, which
would you buy?"

"The nice ones, I suppose."

"See?"

She stopped at this ultimate proof.

During his time alone on campus, Jeff tried to keep busy. He diligently worked his way through a dull grammar book, and taped more characters on the wall. He wrote letters to Melissa. His eyes would blur and sting in the afternoons, and he'd nap. As he drifted off, he was swarmed by fantasies that strangely elongated themselves into dreams.

Chen Zhuan lifted his chess piece in the teaching building. Their game had lasted for hours — the campus was drowning in dusk. As they played, he slowly explained the network of students that was patiently bringing about political change in China. Using many aliases and swiftly drawn and crumpled maps, he made Jeff see the conspiracy which stretched like a web from Beijing to the farthest flat sands of Xinjiang, to the tropical stilt houses of Xi Xuang Ban Na. Then he described the ecological damage to the river skirting his *laojia*, submerging with Jeff to show him mutated fish with stunted legs and the strange vegetation that had sprouted blue crystals, unexplained. Then Chen Zhuan made his move. Jeff countered with a sudden intuition. Zhuan smiled. "Chuangzi said the way that can be pointed to is not the way. It may seem that Chinese society is fixed, written, but the spirit of my people is strong, and we will never succub."

"Succumb."

"Succumb, sorry." Zhuan placed his knight and the board revealed its next dimension. Pausing to acknowledge Jeff's smile of defeat, he pocketed the pieces and folded the board. He slid another map across the table and left.

Jeff dreamed the famous actress Gong Li called him.

"Jeff, Jeff, there's a big party tonight at the Jing Huang Hotel, penthouse party, I meet you there, okay? I can't stop thinking about you."

"Gong Li, if I've told you once, I've told you a thousand times, I'm engaged."

"Not even a nightcap?"

Was this what he was missing? He tried to sleep.

Guo po shan he zai, he recited, *Cheng chun cao mu shen*. The country is broken, rivers and mountains remain, springtime in the city's lush…

The real phone rang. It was a Canadian journalist, returning his call. Jeff had been digging around for extra work. There was none. Jeff asked him how he liked reporting in China.

"It would be okay if they at least let you do some journalism," he said. "The other day we went to the Three Gorges. It was maddening. First you wait for weeks by the phone. Then they tell you you're going the next morning, and they load you on a bus and you're there — six miles from the actual project. They tell you who you're going to talk to and tell you what you're going to write, and it's boring as hell, and then they load you on the bus and send you back. What's the matter with the Chinese? Oh, I know, I know, many of them are just as aware of their problems, but nobody can actually do anything about them. You know what I think? It's stupid Mao when he said he didn't care about the bomb, it didn't matter because they could afford to lose a few million. That affected the thinking. Now they're drowning in themselves. That was a blockhead —"

"Hey," Jeff said, "for sure this phone is bugged."

"I don't care. What's another ten thousand villages, we'll just relocate everyone to Xinjiang and everyone will be happy. And everyone is happy. All ONE POINT TWO BILLION are happy. What can we do? There are only one point two billion of us. Jesus. Listen, I need a shower."

"Right."

"I'll let you know if anything comes up."

"Cheers."

Robert was standing in Jeff's doorway with a miserable grin. Jeff half-dreaded seeing him; Robert had had a lousy time in China and was determined everyone else would too.

"Did you talk to Doctor Wu?" Robert said.

"I did, and he was just a shadow of the man that I once knew. Come in."

Dr. Wu was the manager of an English school where Robert sometimes taught; Robert was trying to ensure that Jeff got the classes he didn't want to teach himself. Though Jeff was mildly interested in making more money, at another level he didn't care. He wasn't going to do it unless they paid more — one hundred twenty kuai an hour sounded good until you factored in the three hours travel time in taxis that played incomprehensible *xiangsheng*, crosstalk comedy routines, at maximum volume. Jeff had already told every cab driver in Beijing that he had a seven-year-old daughter, was divorced, and, no, he wasn't a rich man. And he wasn't getting any richer talking to Robert.

"What did Doctor Wu say?" Robert said.

"He said one twenty was it. Possibly a thirty-kuai taxi allowance. Which would get me halfway there."

"And…?"

"He seemed reluctant to commit to the Saturday class."

"Oh, I told him you had a Chinese girlfriend you saw on Saturdays."

"You *what*?"

"Uh, I guess I shouldn't have said that. Sorry."

Jeff breathed deeply and let it go. It was done. "You know what Wu did this time? He pulled out his lousy company magazine and asked me who was on the cover. Gong Li, I said. If you teach this class, I'll introduce you to the editor of this magazine, he promised. What a sleazebag. Does he think we all came to China to meet Gong Li? Well, he's right!"

Jeff started to laugh hysterically. Robert took a step back.

"Furthermore, look at this fucking rag. 'Cross-cultural Tips for Business Etiquette.' Here it says if a Chinese employee makes a mistake and you reprimand him, he will smile, and the article takes care to point out that this is because he's nervous, not because he thinks it's funny. Helpful, eh? *Not* because he's figuring out how to get you."

Robert smiled nervously.

"Or look at this: '*Wo jia le yi ge zhong guo nan ren.*' 'I Married a Chinese Man.' I was a teenage *lao wai* chick. You notice something about this article? Well, two things, one, we will never see an article by a foreigner called, 'I Married a Chinese Woman' because the readership would find this so reprehensible they'd cancel their subscriptions, and two, *there are no pictures of the man in this article because he would lose face.* But that's not the pièce de résistance. Look at this baby, 'The Helicopter Cult of the West.'"

There were pictures of statuesque women with blonde, close-cropped hair, wearing leather jackets, standing beside a helicopter, each with one foot on the landing floats, as if dominating slain game. Predictably, one was talking on a cellphone. Robert had a good long look.

"Oh, yeah, right," he said. "That's so like my lifestyle in Canada. Just call up a friend and take the helicopter to a party. We partied in helicopters all the time in T.O. It was a thing we did. Are you busy?"

"Let's go for a bike ride," Jeff said.

Once they got off campus and were cruising down Stone Bridge Avenue, Jeff cheered up. It was a beautiful fall day, everything interesting and vivid. He watched a crew of city workers repairing asphalt; they ambled behind the asphalt spreader with their rakes, happy like bored employees everywhere.

"I used to do that," he said. "It was hot in the summer."

"I could hardly make ends meet in Toronto. And I could never get a date because of that. I figured I was better off in China," said Robert.

"Hey, do you remember the T-shirts they had in Vancouver in the late eighties? NO, NO, NO, YES, NO?"

Robert looked puzzled. Then he got it. "Oh, yeah, the questionnaire on the back of the Unemployment Insurance forms."

"It's great to have a shared culture, isn't it?"

But Robert refused to be happy. "I went to the Canadian embassy get-togethers a couple of times in San Li Tun, and everybody was speaking French. I mean, that just takes the cake. I couldn't even work for the Canadian embassy, though I speak Mandarin, because I don't speak French."

"It's a tough world. Let's go in this shopping centre."

They wandered around on the jewellery floor, a repository for all the glitter and outsized precious stones in this corner of Beijing. Jeff kept his eye out for opals; Bian Fu's birthday was coming up. Robert was pursuing his theme again; Jeff had started to tune him out. "Most of those language schools in Toronto only paid twelve dollars an hour; here I can party and save some money. I just don't want to be back in Canada on welfare. Why did you come to China?"

"To learn Chinese."

Jeff laughed. "My favourite is the taxi drivers who talk to you like this: Ni...ren...shi...bu...ren...shi...zhong...guo...ren...jiao... lao...bai...xing? Like, fuck...right...off," said Jeff.

But Robert's attention was wandering. Jeff saw why. A couple of stunning Chinese women, one in a red turtleneck and leather skirt, the other in tight jeans and T-shirt, were strolling through the jade pendant section. Where had Jeff seen them before? Probably the jade necklace section. They passed; the taller one returned Jeff's casual smile with a look smelted on the dark side of Mercury.

"Did you see that?" said Jeff.

"Yeah, not bad, eh?"

"No, I mean her look. Challenging and angry or what?" The word Jeff was looking for — and came to him as he looked again — was *contemptuous.*

"No, I didn't get that at all. C'mon. You can practise your Chinese."

"I'm getting tired of this mall. Did you want to buy something? What are you looking for?"

Robert was staring at the two women, who were over by the necklaces now.

"Oh, something," he said. His eyes were glazed. "Not always available."

Jeff left him there.

When he got back to the dormitory, he phoned Dr. Wu. "Two hundred kuai," he said. "That's my final offer."

"Jeff." Dr. Wu's voice was velvety. "You know I can only go to one hundred twenty kuai. Those are the rules. Everything is a game," Dr. Wu said. "Everything has its rules that you must play by. If you teach this course for me, I will introduce you to the editor of that magazine I showed you."

"I don't want to play the game," said Jeff, and hung up.

"*Xiaojie!* XIAOJIE!"

Jeff and Bian Fu were halfway up the stairs. It was the *fuwuyuan*, waving a newspaper at Bian Fu, summoning them back down.

"Just ignore her," Jeff said. But Bian Fu had already tucked in her chin and started back.

"*Xiaojie*, you can't go up there. You have to register at the desk," the *fuwuyuan* began.

"What do you mean, I can't go up there? I am his Chinese teacher," Bian Fu said. Jeff flinched. "I have been there several times. We are having a language exchange."

Bian Fu was adamant, for she loved to argue. However, with the *fuwuyuan*'s next question, her demeanour changed utterly; she hung her head and listened, her eyes darkening as she regarded the counter in front of the fuwuyuan.

"Who are you? Where are you from?" said the *fuwuyuan*. And then the conversation flew out beyond Jeff's Chinese ability.

He tried to say a couple of things to slow down the *fuwuyuan* and give Bian Fu time to think, but she ignored him. They both ignored him; this was a Chinese matter.

Bian Fu turned to him. "Come on, let's go. I want to go away from here."

"What was that about?" he said when they were outside.

Bian Fu looked trapped. "She want to see my ID."

"So why didn't you show it to her?"

"I do not have Beijing *hukou*. My ID is from Hebei province. You do not understand. It is a Chinese thing."

"So show them your student ID."

She said nothing.

At the West Gate she said, "If my parents find out I come to visit you here, they would never accept our marriage." He knew instantly this was a lie.

He smiled, and squeezed her hand. She was profoundly ashamed, and he knew it was useless to press her for an explanation. Jeff was humiliated. The woman he loved had secrets. It was a Chinese thing — what could be more important?

In the next couple of weeks they could not make love anywhere. Bian Fu would not risk getting questioned by the *fuwuyuan* again, and there were always others around at her mother's place. For Jeff, this was another layer of the constant surveillance they were subjected to. It was uncomfortable, tiring. A small distance opened up between them, Bian Fu acting bored when they were together, Jeff desirous, but also embarrassed that this prohibition could grow to assume such importance. Surely there was something else to their relationship?

The nights were colder, the wind whistled through the cracks in the window mouldings, and the trees were resplendent with reds and yellows, then slowly transparent as they dropped their leaves.

Jeff realized he hadn't seen Mark for months, and figured Sandy would be back in Beijing, that they'd had their baby and were now parents. He phoned. He was right — Mark and Sandy were "doing the diaper thing," as Mark put it. Jeff suggested they have lunch together.

They were supposed to meet at Beijing Xirfen University, but Mark and Sandy didn't show up and Bian Fu and Jeff ate lunch alone. He tried to talk about her family and when he might meet her father — she evaded the question.

"Spring Festival would be a good time to get married," she said.

"Bian Fu, I might not be here second term," Jeff said. "I'll have to let them know later on in the term."

They picked at their lunch and avoided looking at each other. They were walking out of Beijing Xirfen's neighbourhood when a car honked and slowed down. It was Mark and Sandy and their baby, Tara.

"Hey, sorry we missed you. Nice to meet you. Hop in, let's go for tea."

Mark looked Bian Fu up and down, and she smiled shyly, and then busied herself in the back seat with the baby, smiling at her, going Buh, buh, buh, and Coo, coo, coo. Mark meaningfully looked at Jeff and said, "How's your Chinese?"

"Getting better," he said. Better than yours, he meant. "*Wo shuo hanyu, shuo de bucuo.*" I speak Chinese not bad.

"I can only speak Chinese when I know what they're going to say," said Mark.

Sandy said nothing.

They found a *canting* with outdoor seating and Mark and Sandy busied themselves with the car-seat, blankets, comforter, and then diapers, for Tara was wet. "Sorry we missed you," Mark said. "We waited, but Tara started fussing, so we had to walk her. Why don't you go and order tea for us?"

But Jeff and Bian Fu had been on time. Jeff started to say something, then decided against it.

Bian Fu and Jeff went into the *canting*. Away from the autumn sunlight, a wild-looking man with frizzy hair was stirring and stirring a foul pot of viscid broth. "Can we have tea?" Jeff said. With expansive gestures the man said no.

"He says there is only mutton," said Bian Fu, with a big grin. Jeff brightened. "Don't be nervous," he said. "Mark and Sandy are nice people."

She nodded.

"No tea," he reported. "What kind of soft drink would you like?"

"No tea?" Mark said. "Yeah, right. You mean they're too lazy and can't be bothered to put the kettle on for the foreigners. Okay, I'll have a Coke. Sandy?"

"Oh, I don't know about that. They seem like nice people," Jeff said.

"I'm sure they're nice people, but they're not about to get off their butts to serve a bunch of foreigners."

Bian Fu made a spider with her hand and crawled it across the table for the baby. She didn't look at Mark and Sandy.

Jeff went back in and got the drinks and paid for them.

When he returned, Sandy was nursing Tara and Mark was interrogating Bian Fu. "Thanks. Did you pay for the drinks, Jeff? And where are you from, Been Fu?"

Bian Fu's demeanour had changed. She leaned forward, with a strained smile, her hands locked together. Jeff touched her arm to reassure her.

"I am from Bing He. It is in Hebei province. It is a very old city."

"Yeah, I was reading about Bing He some time ago. Isn't that the place where — I read this in a journal our school gets, or was it the *China Daily?* — it seems some Chinese found a bunch of tombs that may have been the tombs of an Emperor of the Warring States dynasty or was it the Han dynasty? I always get those two mixed up, there are so many dynasties, don't you think? Anyway, these tombs they found are very old and they started to carbon 14 date some of the artifacts and brought in an international team of experts tops in their field to begin the work of archaeological reconstruction but it will take them many years to do this. Is that Bing He?"

"Bing He is a very beautiful place," said Bian Fu, then turned to Jeff for help. Sandy and Mark were waiting too. How to translate? Jeff thought. Tombs? *Fengmi,* as in *Jiehun shi aiqing de fengmi,* Marriage is the tomb of love.

This did not seem a promising way to start. He gave up. "I can't translate that," he said.

Bian Fu was sliding down in her seat. Sandy was nursing the baby, watching, pity in her eyes.

"It would take about an hour and a good dictionary for me to translate that," he told Mark. "Sorry."

Mark looked as though he had proven something. "What do you do?" he asked Bian Fu.

"Study English."

"And what do you want to be doing in five years' time, say if you go to Canada?"

This Jeff could translate. Bian Fu was twisting her hands now, and Jeff felt a rising anger that he tried to suppress. She couldn't think of the words. "*Xue jingji,*" Jeff said softly. Study economics.

"I want to study economics."

"And how about you, Jeff?" Mark said. "How are you doing? Can you make a living, support yourself?"

"Yes, I can support myself. I can live on my salary from Jian Hua," he said.

"Well, you've got a direct telephone line instead of an extension," Mark said, "so you can't be doing too badly."

"How are you two finding life with the new baby?" Under the table, he took Bian Fu's hand and stroked it gently. Her attention was wholly fixed on the baby, and that topic extended the conversation a little longer, but not by much. Jeff said they had to catch a bus.

"You're sure you paid for the drinks?" said Mark.

"Yes."

"Well, keep in touch."

"I wish you much happiness with your family," said Bian Fu.

When they were around the corner, she said, "He is like a policeman."

"Who? Mark? Yes, he's very conservative. Look, I'm sorry."

"*Mei guanxi.*"

But Jeff was angry. "Fuck, imagine that, *Can you make a living?* How insulting. Just because they make forty grand a year they think —"

"You don't have to swear."

"Sorry."

"Yes, you are very different from them."

He tried to take her hand, and she shook it away. Finally she said, "I don't know if I want to go to Canada."

"Jesus. I mean, Bian Fu, Canadians aren't all like that. What do you mean, you don't want to go to Canada? Just because —"

"You don't have to get angry at me," she said. "I said I wasn't sure I want to go to Canada. I am very nervous around foreigners. I can't tell what they're thinking. This is my true feeling. I tell you my true feeling and you get mad. *Sheng qi le!*"

He bit his tongue.

They walked a couple of blocks and caught a minibus. "I am sorry," he said.

"Me too."

"I guess they're not really my friends after all."

"I do not understand foreigners."

"I am not a foreigner, I am a human being."

"YES, I KNOW YOU ARE A HUMAN BEING. Don't be so childish."

"Childish?"

"Yes, childish." She started crying, bent forward so no one could see.

"*The Elephant Man.* It is a movie," he said, slowly. "In the movie there is a man who has a horrible disease. His body swells up and is all ugly like a monster, like a *guaishou*. He looks like an elephant, and people come to see him. They won't leave him alone. Everybody wants to look at him, touch him, because he is strange. They call him the Elephant Man. He cannot take it any more, so he yells, I AM NOT AN ANIMAL, I AM A HUMAN BEING."

She was processing this, then her lips parted and broke into a delighted smile. "'I am a human being...'" she giggled. "Oh, yes, it is excellent! You are not a foreigner, you are an elephant. I am not a Chinese, I am elephant! Yes, it is very fun! We are both elephants!"

"*Dui ya.* My beautiful elephant!"

"My elephant with the *nan de bizi*, with the difficult nose. Oh, I like it!" She extended her own nose with her arm. "I AM NOT A CHINESE PERSON, I AM AN ELEPHANT."

But they both knew that he was a foreigner and she was Chinese.

And so the next weekend they bused it to Xiang Shan, the famous mountain just outside Beijing where the Chinese customarily went to admire the turning autumn leaves.

Bian Fu took out her little packet of serviettes she always carried and blew her nose. People were chattering around them. "They say that someone had their wallet stolen," said Bian Fu.

At each bus stop Chinese pushed and shoved and straight-armed each other to get on, and then wedged against each other. The adults endured the ride, said nothing except to discipline their children; the students and the children were far more voluble. At the stops, more passengers were in long queues confined by the railings along the curb. These crowd-control features chilled Jeff; they reminded him of the cattle chutes at Canada Packers in Winnipeg. He idly imagined a significant part of driver training was how to stop the bus so the doors aligned with the breaks in the railings; otherwise, an outbreak of clambering and leaping might be fatal.

At Xiang Shan, they laboured up steep stone steps in the last of the autumn sunshine, among hundreds of people, some very old, sweating and suffering and all pressing upwards. The steps were strewn with trash. Xiang Shan's turning leaves were disappointing. The neighbouring hill was a pallid, edgeless red within the haze that lay over the valley and extended to the fringes of Beijing — factory stack after factory stack spilling sulphurous smog.

At the top of Xiang Shan, they found a patch to sit. Bian Fu wiped away a tear, and then another. He looked up from his notebook. He was writing a letter to Melissa which she read over his shoulder.

> *I miss you very much. Always remember, Melissa, that you are my daughter and I am very proud of you. I will always return to you. Your mother tells me that you are doing very well in school. Would you please send me some of your work? I love you, Panda. Here is the Chinese character for love. You can see that it is a friend under a roof. You be a good girl and I will see you soon...*

"What's the matter, honey?"

She wouldn't answer.

They were just off the main path for descent — even Xiang Shan was tightly organized as to where you went — and Chinese family after Chinese family took their turn to stare and huffily move on. Teenage boys clambered over a rope barrier to take pictures of them. Women looked and sniffed. The middle-aged men were the worst, ogling Bian Fu's body with disdain, as though in an inferior shopping district.

Bian Fu snuffled and stared straight ahead.

He jotted down more.

> *I have found here that many people are not very interested in us Canadians — or in people who are different. Maybe you will experience this when you get older. It is too bad. But if you are open and try to be friendly, you will always meet people who are glad to know you.*

Hugging her knees, Bian Fu was crying.

"What's the matter?"

"I was reading your letter."

They sat amidst discarded Evian bottles, broken pop bottles, shreds of newspaper, plastic bags, Popsicle sticks.

"A letter to Melissa, yes."

"I have acted very selfishly."

"How so?"

"Asking you come back."

"I made the choice," he said. "That was my decision."

"I was very selfish," she said.

She had to go to the washroom. While Jeff waited, a smiling Chinese man and his wife approached him, the man offering a cigarette. "Where are you from?"

"Canada. Western Canada."

"Vancouver?"

"Near Vancouver." Jeff warmed to the simple conversation.

"*Jianada, Jianada,*" he said. "*Jianada* is bigger than China, more beautiful, perhaps?"

"It is bigger, but not more beautiful. China is a very beautiful country."

"Does it have many mountains and rivers?"

"Very many. Where are you from?"

"Bing He. In Hebei province."

"No kidding, I have a friend who is from there."

Just then Bian Fu returned. The man and his wife took one look at her, politely said Ni hao, and walked away, the woman laughing with her husband, pointing once at Bian Fu, casting an admonitory look backwards at Jeff.

"Come on, let's go," said Jeff.

Halfway down, the crowds thinned and the afternoon sun mellowed; they caught its warmth through the sweeping shadows of pines as they strolled hand in hand down a series of stone-paved switchbacks. Two lovers passed them, absorbed.

"That couple," said Bian Fu, pointing, "he was saying to her, When we have a baby, the baby will have your hair, and she was saying, He will be intelligent just like you."

"If we have a baby, it will have your eyes and smile, and your nose like an elephant," he said.

"Oh, it is terrible," she laughed, and then the shadow of another thought crossed her face. Jeff knew instantly what it was. Last week, they had been preparing supper with Bian Fu's mother, who had started to like Jeff, and Bian Fu had said, "She says if we have children they will be beautiful. I cannot believe she said that."

"Thank you," Jeff said.

Bian Fu's mother had her hands on her hips, with a mysterious smile.

"*Xiu, xiu,*" she said.

Bian Fu laughed. "She says Guilty, guilty, thinking about children and you are not even married yet." Bian Fu stopped laughing and lifted a piece of eggplant stuck on the wok and meticulously turned it, and then another, intently staring at the chunks of eggplant.

This all came back as they descended Xiang Shan together. The idea of non Han-Chinese children was unappealing to her, something she had not considered.

Er Bao had hopped up on Jeff's lap and he stared at his face in the living room mirror, then moved, so there was no face in the mirror. He talked lowly to Er Bao, "*Gu dian shihou you yi ge nongmin zai ta de di faxian le yi jian gu tongjing.* Once there was a peasant who in his fields discovered an ancient copper mirror..." He slid his face back into the mirror, and Er Bao squealed. He did it again. She bounced on his knees. Bian Fu was still stirring the eggplant, lifting each done chunk from the wok onto a plate. Her mother chided her at close range.

Bian Fu said nothing.

She came and sat beside him. "Mother says she knew a Chinese woman who married a Thai man and they had beautiful children."

"I don't want to hear about it," he had said.

They continued to walk down Xiang Shan. Clouds had gathered and it was getting chilly. They passed a couple of women, who said *lao wai.*

"Typical," he said.

"They said it because you are good-looking."

They ran a little way, to relieve the tension.

"You," her mother had said in the kitchen, addressing Jeff, "you have a beautiful daughter. I don't know what you see in mine. She is useless. She will just go off with another man someday."

"No, she's not. No, she won't."

"Yes, she will. Why do you waste your time? She is completely useless."

"I love her. *Wo ai ta.*"

"She is not worth the trouble. She is completely useless. Another man comes along and she is gone."

"Well," he began, and Bian Fu had to translate this, for it was turned and considered, "If you're right, and she does go off with another man, then we two can have the pleasure of agreeing with each other. If you're wrong, then we can all be happy."

Wang Fu Ren considered this. "She is useless."

"*Wo ai ta a!*" Jeff said.

"Bian Fu," he said on the bus back from Xiang Shan, "I have something to say to you."

"*Ni shuo ba.*" Her eyes were fixed on her knees.

"Look at me."

She did, and his throat caught, seeing her worry.

"I think we should spend some time apart, so we can think about this. So we can decide if we really want to continue. I think we shouldn't see each other for a week."

She said nothing.

They collected their bikes at the bus stop. A chill wind was mounting, and they shivered. "I will see you next Friday, okay?"

She straddled her bike and slumped over the handlebars. "Next Friday," she said. "Why don't you come for dinner at my place tonight? I am making *baozi*. I —"

"I will come to your place next Friday. Then we can talk about this."

The wind whipped newspapers across the parking lot, dishevelling their hair, making it more difficult to part. He held her and kissed her. She stroked his neck. "I love you," she said.

"Next Friday."

He pushed off.

The wind fought him all the way back to Jian Hua. He was gasping with the exertion of pedalling against it, breathing in huge grey chunks.

In his room with the heat full blast, rubbing his hands, something Bian Fu had said once rose in his mind, *A person should live in society. Not outside it. In society.*

But which society? And how to live?

Across the hall, Tabitha sawed away at her violin, its timbre a forlorn creaking, far away, beyond his fatigue, his difficult feelings, as he fell asleep.

Chapter Six

What do you love about Bian Fu anyway? he set out to ask himself
that week. He began by making lists.

She has at best a complicated relationship with the truth.

She has racist attitudes.

She is manipulative and selfish.

*She is not interested in sharing her language or culture; culture is
trotted out to rationalize behaviour.*

She expects me to choose all our activities and pay for them.

She gives me little idea of what her real life is like, who she is.

*Her mother is not wholly wrong about her. She is perfectly capable of
lying on the couch.*

She loves you, Jeff.

Talking to himself. Haggard. His shoes had holes.

He had fallen in love, and the thought of reversing that gravity
was enough to keep him attached. Love was like that, he reasoned.
It drew you in over your head, despite your objections. Still, the
objections remained. He was uncomfortable; their liaison was
awkward. He didn't like his reliance on her to translate and explain
when they were off-campus. He didn't like their non-existent sex life
now that the *fuwuyuan* were making it so difficult. Dusky brides on
bewildering shores. His fantasy of marriage to her persisted, oddly,
but he could not bring himself to form any conclusions about their
relationship. No. He formed them, but didn't accept them. He liked
the idea of bringing her to Canada, but realized that meant he wanted
to be in Canada. It was confusing.

When he ventured out beyond campus, his hands were getting
colder on the handlebars, and he had to stop more and more frequently
at the repair shack near the gates with the yellow, caged canary to get

his tires or seat fixed, for his bike was a hopeless lemon. The repairman insisted he was Japanese, with a nasty irony, and studied Jeff for his reaction. He found this a lot funnier than Jeff did.

His wife sidled out and said, "Where's your friend?"

"My friend?" said Jeff.

"You know, your very very good friend," she said, and he recoiled from her insinuation. The two of them were laughing as he rode off.

Beijing was uglier and uglier. Its gleaming international hotels appalled him. Its acre upon acre of building sites where one-storey homes were knocked down to make way for apartment buildings and more gleaming international hotels appalled him. The vendors with their rapacious smiles and pitches, *I only charge you this because you are my pengyou,* my friend, bored him. Standing astride his bike near the Xi Zhi Men subway station, near an intricate system of overpasses and underpasses, overlooking a black garbage-clogged canal, ignoring the Chinese stares, he watched the ceaseless traffic flow and thought, I might as well have gone to Toronto. And his Chinese was stuck at a certain level, a spare playground of free-standing characters, without aspect or nuance, a language to ask for second helpings and simple directions with.

He repeatedly remembered an evening in his room. He was going over the different uses of *zai* (to be, to exist, to be in a place); Bian Fu was quietly studying the map of Canada above his bed — perhaps too quietly. She was reaching up, touching the map. Her hair-bun bobbed as she discovered more about this strange land across the Pacific. Jeff enjoyed the companionable silence.

"Jeff?"

"Bian Fu?"

"Is Victoria very cold?"

"No. It is one of the warmest places in Canada. It hardly ever snows in the winter, maybe one day a year. Beijing is much colder. *Beijing bi Victoria dou leng.*"

He kept reading.

"Jeff?"

"Yes?"

"How many people are there in Victoria?"

"About three hundred thousand. *San shi wan.*"

"Jeff, are there Chinese people in Victoria?"

He disguised his irritation. "Yes, there is a small Chinese community in Victoria, perhaps ten thousand people. There is a Chinatown downtown. Of course," he said, "they are Canadians."

He looked up. Bian Fu was squinting at the map, the white uninhabitable part.

He joined her on the bed. "Bian Fu, that's *Victoria Island* you're looking at. God, that's near the North Pole! Try down here."

And he showed her Vancouver Island, and Victoria's yellow metropolitan blob, and showed her the route through the Gulf Islands to Vancouver; here, he said, there were many many Chinese people. She was so relieved she visibly shivered. "I thought you were going to take me to live up here," and she put her hands around the wholly white island, fjord-fringed, sixty-five below.

Jeff chuckled. "There's nothing but dogs and polar bears up there."

"Polar bears?"

"Yes," and with a studious look on his face, he galumphed toward her on his knees. "Polar bear, a huge white bear."

"Ah — *qie-e!* We will live with the polar bears and the dogs! Oh, it is wonderful! *Qie-e!* We would eat snow!"

"If we were lucky!"

"We would teach the polar bears *zhong wen!*" She threw her arms around his neck and kissed him.

"Oh, my little polar bear." He started to tickle her and she squirmed and kicked and kissed him again. They laughed and laughed. She curled up against him, and said, "You are the polar bear I love."

But recently, when he had to pass the hostile stares of the *fuwuyuan,* he could not help but repeat the small print in his contract with Jian Hua, *Party B shall agree to do nothing to violate the morals of the Chinese people.*

Li Ruang Yun, the girl from the South, regularly ate with the foreign teachers in the cafeteria, presumably to practise her English, for she was preparing for her GMAT tests.

She ate with a picky, pissed-off concentration, at length pushing the tray away from her. "Terrible food!" Often she would remain silent while the foreigners babbled their fabulous argot, preferring or pretending to listen. Or preferring to think her own thoughts.

"I looked up your name in the dictionary," Jeff said. "Ruang Yun, this is a beautiful name. Soft Clouds."

She looked quizzically at him. "Thank you."

"How is your studying going?" he asked her.

"I am studying hard. It is boring. I want to go to sleep in the afternoon. I am very tired."

"*Shi dongtian,*" he said, hesitantly, "*Ni xihuan dongmian, shi bu shi?*" It's winter. Perhaps you want to hibernate?

"*Shi de!*" she said.

Jeff didn't say anything else during the meal. He realized he'd been flirting.

The next evening she showed up at his room with a notebook, a pencil in her mouth.

"Excuse me please, Jeff, could I ask you a favour? I have all these universities on this form, see, could you tell me about them and show me where they are?"

"Sure."

While he made her a cup of Nescafé, Ruang Yun hopped up on the bed and began to study the map. He joined her and went down her list, Queens is here, a good school, a very snobby school.

"Snobby?"

"Students from Queens think they are better than everyone else. They certainly think they are better than Carleton students. I went there. It's in Ottawa."

"I thought you went to UBC?"

"I did. That was for my master's."

"I have a master's too. In economics."

"What did you study in undergraduate?"

"Sorry?"

"Your first degree?"

"Oh, engineer. I worked for five years engineer. It was very boring. Mostly designing bridges."

"What's the South like?"

"Oh, everything is money all the time. Always making money, money. My friends, they all talk about stocks and bonds. It is very boring, and very ugly and crowded. You could get a job there, make a lot of money, but it is very hard to enjoy life, I think. There is no culture. Beijing — it is the capital of culture in China. There is so much music and art."

She was waving her hands around indolently.

"Really? Culture?" Jeff said.

"Oh, yes, it is not like the South. Though the food is better in the south, there is more seafood, things are fresher." She got down from the bed and started looking at the pictures on his bookshelf. "Who are these people?"

"My mother. And this is my daughter, with her dog."

"It is too big."

"What, the dog?"

"I am afraid of dogs. Do you like to eat them? In Canada?"

"No, we never e —"

"Who's this?"

"My fiancée."

"Ah —"

"The person I am engaged to."

She took a step back. "Very pretty," she said. "When?"

"I don't know."

She asked him a few more questions about McGill and Calgary, and then left, politely thanking him for his help. Jeff flushed. He had been flirting with her. Definitely.

Bian Fu phoned that night. "What are you doing?" she said.

"Studying Chinese."

"My neighbours have, I mean, they are having a party," she said. "They are naming their baby, and they have invited you. Do you want to come?"

He paused. "Yes, I would like to come, but you remember we are supposed to be thinking. I need time to myself to think. So I cannot come. Sorry."

"I understand," she said. "Friday? I will see you Friday?"

"Yes, I will see you Friday."

"Come to my place for lunch on Friday."

"Okay," he said.

"*Wo ai ni*!"

"I love you too," he said. He hung up, numb in the realization that he wanted out.

He was glumly copying characters into his notebook when he heard excited voices in the corridor. He went out to see. It was Tabitha, having a panic attack. It seemed the *fuwuyuan* had demanded money because she had allowed a couple of American friends to stay with her. Moreover, precisely to avoid this payment, she had snuck them in; they had not signed in with the *fuwuyuan*. "Why should they pay?" she said.

"Absolutely," said Robert, to the rescue. "Why the hell should you?"

For your safety, Jeff thought, but didn't say anything.

She was distraught; her face had turned the colour of wok-fried pork, and she raked her fingers through her hair. What was she going to do? She was going to get Robert to help her, because his Chinese was the best. Jeff tagged along. Robert had issues with the *fuwuyuan*, as they had made his quest to get Chinese women into his room at night after the bars closed well-nigh impossible lately; consequently, he had been forced to spend far too much time with his Mongolian girlfriend. Since she didn't look Han, the *fuwuyuan* couldn't care less. Robert was delighted with the prospect of tackling Tabitha's problem.

"Let me talk to her," he said. "Which one, the fat one?"

The *fuwuyuan* sat behind the counter, watching them descend. It was curious, Jeff thought, it was difficult to think of one *fuwuyuan* instead of all of them, the *dan wei*, or work unit, since their lives seemed so hopelessly entangled. They rode to work together, they talked with each other all day, they helped each other with parcels and hot water; perhaps in the evenings they had *dan wei* meetings where they studied the restrictions on foreigners in light of Party principles. All of them were, naturally, sick and tired of the corner-store Chinese they had to listen to. Well, this would be a change.

Jeff drifted to the far end of the counter while Robert, Tabitha at his elbow, exchanged salutations with the *fuwuyuan*. Robert made a point of translating loudly after each exchange. He began his argument with the dubious proposition — Jeff almost laughed — Is This Dormitory Not Our Home?

"Yes, it is your home," she replied.

How on earth is he going to get from Is This Dormitory Not Our Home to And Cannot I Bed As Many Bar-girls In It As I Want? Jeff wondered. And how was he going to help Tabitha, who just wanted to save herself a couple of hundred kuai. The *fuwuyuan* eyed Robert with practised patience. "Now, My Friend Here Had a Couple of Friends Staying With her for a Couple of Nights in her Home. Why Should She Have to Pay for Them?"

"She should have registered them at the desk," said the *fuwuyuan* in an even tone. "Because they are guests, we charge a certain rate for them."

"But One Does Not Charge One's Friends To Stay For A Night, Is This Not True?"

Robert was pumped up. He was leaning over the counter and his second tones — rising, rising — were skimming the *fuwuyuan*'s forehead. She had hunkered down, but was prepared to Party Line it with the unruly foreigner.

Robert started in on the concept of home, of *jia*, arguing that "Home Must Surely Include One's Guests, And Responsibility For Them Surely Is With The Welcoming Friend."

Tabitha started to look around, realizing this was not helping.

And Home Must Also Include Those We Find Helpless and Unsheltered In The Local Bar, And Who Are Opposite In Sex, Jeff thought. This was futile.

"All guests must be registered with this desk," said the *fuwuyuan*. "And this is done —"

"You Are Not Going To Say For Our Own Safety, Are You?"

"— for your own safety." A smile phantomed in her face.

The male *fuwuyuan* with glasses shuffled out from the back room in his slippers, where he had been waiting to fulfil his function in life, that is, waiting to hand out the bicycle pump, and surveyed this international incident, whose roots lay in the sum of twenty-four dollars Canadian.

He shuffled back in.

"You Mean To Tell Me You Are Going To Charge Her For Having Friends Over For A Couple Of Nights."

"*Dui!*" she said.

Then Robert lost it, started banging on her desk, and shouting, "You Chinese are always trying to make money out of us, restricting our freedom. You Chinese —"

"What's going on?"

They turned. It was Tudi Fu, one of the overseas Chinese in the dorm.

"A dispute," Jeff said.

Robert turned on her. "I don't see how you can pretend to this great cultural knowledge when you know bloody well that these people are just trying to rob us blind."

"This has nothing to do with culture," Tudi said. "It has to do with body language. All she can see right now is you pounding on her desk. She's frightened of you." And it was true. The reason the *fuwuyuan* didn't show it was thoroughly Chinese: she was saving face.

"Please stop, now. Let's just walk away right now, please," said Tudi. And they did, in various states of embarrassment. Robert went straight to his room and slammed the door.

He began Friday morning alone in the cafeteria, munching on his three meat dumplings, sipping his sweetened milk. Simply show up, tell her she is a wonderful person, but you have to end the relationship, he told himself. Don't explain it. Teach your class, pedal your bike over there, buy a few oranges as usual, say hello to the relatives, go for a walk, break up with her, ride home.

The ground was frosty. His bike, which he had left out front last night, was now buried amid a hundred bikes. It took him a good ten minutes to clear a path and lift it out.

He passed the *fuwuyuan* riding in a tidy line through the gate, their scarves and toques touched with white. "*Ni hao!*" They ignored him. He told himself, turn left, ride past the athletic fields, where the overly disciplined do push-ups in the frost, take the bridge, skirt the willows, lock your bike, teach your class, speak clearly and slowly, break up with her, get back for lunch.

"Today we will study different uses of the semi-colon," he told the forty-odd students in their parkas. "I wonder if I could get a volunteer. I am prepared to wait several hours for a volunteer. Okay, you, write a sentence on the board explaining why you don't want a part-time job while you're studying."

The student began writing. Wang Fang flipped through her textbook with a panicky look.

"Wang Fang!"

A couple of other students snickered, because they knew that Wang Fang's was the only name Jeff remembered.

"*Lao shi?*"

"It isn't in the textbook. Watch the board, please."

"Yes, I am happy to watch the board. Thank you, thank you."

> *I do not want a part-time job because I need to study English very hard, but I don't have money, therefore I need to work, so I look for work, but there isn't any work, and my parents needs money, but I have to study hard and I don't have any time, so I decide not to have part-time job.*

Jeff stared at this sentence. The perpetrator stared too, in eager anticipation. Jeff forced himself to think. *I don't have any money and I don't have a part-time job, but I want to study Chinese, yet my daughter is in Canada, but I love her, but it is too difficult and we need money to get married, so I can return with her to Canada, but it will take time, and her parents need to get rid of me, so I ride over, slip out the back, Jack, forget the part-time job, period.*

"*Lao shi?*"

"Let's break it into two or three simple ideas," he said. "As we recall, semi-colons join what kind of clauses?"

"INDEPENDENT."

"*Ting hao.* So: let's try this."

> *I have to study English very hard; my parents need money badly; I looked for a part-time job for a while, but there weren't any; I returned to my studies.*

"What's the difference?" Jeff said.

The student said, "My sentence says the same thing as yours." Then he changed his mind. "No, my sentence is better. My sentence, I can say, expresses how complicated."

I'll say, Jeff thought.

"Yes, but what is the difference between the sentences?" (*I was poor; she had no job; her parents hated me; we broke up.*)

"Use semi-colons," somebody said presently.

"My sentence still better."

"Look," he said, "take this first sentence. Somebody want to count the conjunctions in it? How many? I'm trying to show you how by using the semi-colon you can make these simple, elegant connections without using a whole bunch of conjunctions!"

"Why is my sentence not better? My parents needed the money; I wanted to study; there was no job anyway; I returned to my studies."

"THAT'S IT!"

"*Lao shi?* Hemingway is very good American writer, yes? Hemingway sometimes use 'and' ten and eleven times in a sentence. This is not good?"

"It's a matter of style. I'm trying to give you different tools you can use. Okay, everybody write three sentences using the semi-colon."

Wang Fang stuck her pencil in her mouth and began to suck on it.

When autumn came, the leaves fell from the trees along the road leading to Kick Fish County, and they made a pleasant sound as he rode

over them, and the vegetables on the stands the old man with the sad
face sold were not as good as in the summer, and he rode by the brown
vegetables quickly, and she was waiting at the corner, and blinked her eyes
from the shao kao rou smoke, and he said Hi, and she said Ni hao, and he
said what he had to say to her and she listened, she listened well, and when
he stopped she said goodbye and walked away into Kick Fish County, and
he pedalled hard, and harder, back through the dead leaves on the road,
and when he got home his friend said, What's up?, and he said, Shut your
fucking mouth, and walked over and selected a magazine with Gong Li on
the cover, the actress who had so amused the Beijing crowds —

The bell was ringing.

It took ages to get down the crowded stairs. Inching, inching. On the second landing, Wang Fang stood with her hands lightly touching the railing, gazing through the big sunny windows. She saw him looking. He kept moving.

Just as he was unlocking his bike, a pair of students from Fujian province caught up with him, the big ugly one who could barely speak a word of English, and his smarter, smaller friend. "Excuse me, sir. My friend offers you this present as token of friendship, and thanks for your wonderful lessons. You might ask, what is it?"

It was a jumbled mass of roots and spiky green leaves wrapped in wet Kleenex in a plastic bag.

"This flower is a Fujian *hua*, a Fujian flower. It is very beautiful and it often given as token of friendship so that friends remember each other very well."

"Thank you."

The big guy was smiling and nodding.

"My friend is on a fast-track program get his PhD and has not very much time study English. You say we must talk five minutes English in Christmas exam. My friend want to discuss why it is better to live in the country than the city. Please you tell him this is okay."

Jeff had stipulated that the oral exam topics were to be random, chosen from those they had already discussed.

"You will agree to this, please. Here — take the flower. It is a gift as token of —"

"Put the flower in my basket," he said in Chinese. "I'll think about it."

"*Xie xie, xie xie, xie xie...*"

He started pedalling. It was a beautiful fall day. The bright clouds did not move above Jian Hua University as he exited the West Gate, passed the public park where they had eaten moon cakes not long ago, made a difficult turn across two lanes of traffic, and, pumping hard, shot past the other park where they had groped each other in the twilight, and hit the canal road in a fury of legs. He was almost there. He would park his bike, play with Er Bao a little, ask Bian Fu to go for a walk, take his bike along, stop on a corner, tell her he was breaking up with her, comfort her, and ride home. He stopped at the Kick Fish crossroads to buy a small bag of sweets. Upon pocketing his three-hundred-per-cent profit the vendor told him his Chinese was very good.

Er Bao sat in the siheyuan gateway stabbing a plastic bag with a stick. Her tiny face beamed. "*Jie Fu jiu lai le!*" she squealed. Jeff's here!

Bian Fu's mother rushed out to greet him. "Come, come, come, come," she said. "Sit, sit, sit, sit."

Inside, the uncle balefully tapped his cigarette in the ashtray as he watched a dull documentary about an ethnic minority in a far-flung province who spent their days cleaning rice and dancing in circles.

"Bian Fu is on her way from school," Wang Fu Ren said. "Tea?" She was in the kitchen chopping vegetables. "Have you eaten?"

"No."

"You must eat!"

"No, I...okay."

He hunched on the couch and lit a cigarette. You will eat lunch, suggest to Bian Fu that a walk would be nice, no, a bike ride, go for coffee with her, tell her adamantly and decisively that you are ending the relationship, wish her well, go and kick the shit out of some dead leaves. The uncle looked like he hadn't slept for a week; Bian Fu was always saying that when he was a young man he was very handsome, like a movie star. This would have been in the fifties, during the Great

Leap Forward. A movie star? Well, Jeff could imagine him hanging around a dance hall with those eyes. Dance hall? Try he was an inspiring work-unit boss at an improvised steel smelter.

"Beijing must have changed a great deal since you were a young man," Jeff said.

Uncomprehending stare.

Jeff repeated the sentence slowly and deliberately.

When was Bian Fu going to show, so he could thank her for the lovely memories, wish her well, go back to sleep?

"Ah," the uncle said, "yes."

"There are many more cars now, *shi ma?*"

"Yes."

He tried another tack. "When you were a child, where did you live?"

"Here," he said.

"In Kick Fish County?"

"Here," he said, and pointed to the couch.

Then Bian Fu entered, hunched forward, eyes shining, wild; in one motion she grabbed teapot and cup and set it in front of him and poured and took a letter from her pocket, "*Ni hao.* I wrote this last night." She sat next to him, their lips touched. "Read! Read!"

She had not taken off her parka yet. Her lower lip held all the sweetness of the earth. She lifted her cup to her lips and smiled, and the room went inside out and he lifted up, seeing himself small inside the crazy labyrinth of *hutong*s and all their arms pointing inward at the coffee table, his bald spot bent over this small square of paper and the little letters that swam. *We love each other very well...I am a woman, you are a man...god bless us, very one...sleep, and I hope your dreams are full of Wang Bian Fus...*

"I write this three in the morning," she said.

His heart boomed once and the room returned as something drained from it, and something filled it, flickering in his blood.

"I love you," he said.

That afternoon in his room he told her he would always love her. She fell asleep in his arms. She was exhausted. She had had quite an argument with the *fuwuyuan*, who had relented. Jeff stayed awake and listened to her breathe, shifted when her body shifted, overwhelmed by the smell of her silky hair.

#

"I think foreigners protect their women differently than Chinese men do," Bian Fu said.

"Do you think so?"

They walked along Ba Jin Qiao Lu, oblivious to all around them, the scarves and gloves and padded coats, the freezing throng.

"Yes, you are very different. You know, usually I never talk to other people on the bus, I just read my English book."

"Of course, that's what I noticed," Jeff said.

"I think by the Chao Bai He, when you said, I am a fish and you are a bird, that's when I knew we would love each other."

"No, when I wanted to touch your vaccination mark, that's when I knew."

"When I cook eggplant."

"When you gave me the leaves on our walk with Han Xiu Ling and the other students. Was there any meaning in that?"

"Ah, no. I just wanted to give you a leaf."

A pattern developed — she would either come over to his place for supper, which he bought at the Jian Hua market, usually meat dumplings and noodles, or he would go to the *siheyuan*, close with the smell of coal now, and eat with her family. When she arrived from the cold and from another argument with the *fuwuyuan* about the validity of her ID, something that just had to be endured now, a ritual, her cheeks were red and she would press the back of her hand into his neck, then warm her hands under his collar. At her place, the family were uninvolved, but polite. They didn't extend conversations beyond one-sentence replies, and after supper, Bian Fu and he would go into the family bedroom and study together, turning often from their respective grammar books to enjoy each other's eyes.

"Often I can't remember the characters. I keep having to look them up."

"Yes, I have the same problem with English words."

Jeff's efforts to speak with her family were frustrating. He couldn't hear their tones, they couldn't hear his. So Bian Fu would translate. Often she repeated exactly what he had said in Chinese to her mother, who, of course, instantly understood. He was sure the family had the sensation of watching a seal at play as they followed the slowly bouncing ball of his *Hanyu*.

Then, one day, a small voice saluted him at the West Gate. "*Ni hao, zheli bu shir Yi He Yuan, shi ba? Zhe shi yi zuo daxue, shi bu shi? Yi He Yuan zai nar?*"

"*Shi de, ni shuo dui le*," Jeff said. "*Zhe, shi Jian Hua Daxue. Dan shi Yi He Yuan bu tai yuan. Zai nali*," and pointed across the street. The peasant had asked him if this was the Summer Palace, the famous park, and if this wasn't some sort of university. Jeff stared in befuddlement at the clearly visible sign above Jian Hua's gate, wondering... Of course. The man was illiterate. Jeff repeated his directions and wished him a good day. The peasant was short, and buck-toothed, obviously from a village. His clothes were torn, filthy; on the back of his bike was a case of serviettes and cheap soft drinks.

Jeff hadn't intended to say anything — just reacted.

He could speak!

Bian Fu pulled up on her bike, got off, and he tried to tell her.

"*Bu haoting*. Don't say *Yi wei nongmin*, it is very bad Chinese. Look at that man with a cellular phone. My classmates call those sort of men *nongmin*, with their *nongmin dian huas*."

"The farmers with the farmer cellular telephones?"

"Yes. Your Chinese is very good."

He tried to kiss her, and she pushed his face away.

"What's the matter?"

"I do not like that in public."

"It's because I'm a foreigner, isn't it?"

"*Bu shir!*" She started walking faster.

"Okay, let's not talk about it."

"*Hen hao!*"

They got on their bikes and started off.

When they stopped in a park, Jeff tried to soften her irritation with a few Chinese sentences. "I love your eyes, and I love the funny stories you tell, and the way you touch me, and I love that you have the courage to break some of the rules, and I love the way you put salt into eggplant, and I love your intelligence — you are very smart — and I love your indirect way of telling me things, and —"

"Ho, this is very bad Chinese."

"You're making fun of my Chinese when I'm trying to tell you my true feelings?"

"I am not. It is simply very bad. It is just a bunch of words, not in sentences."

Her eyes were trained down, but he saw they brimmed. Jeff did not understand. She did not speak again until they said goodbye that afternoon.

Jeff had to mark papers. He was treated to many tortuous attempts to explain the making of *baozi*; if followed literally, the directions would result in badly burnt hands and mangled dumplings. He suffered through the description of a Formula One auto race which amused him because of the unlikely verbs the student was prone to insert between careening prepositions — "among forwarded behind the car left beside catched in to try, and win" was a fair example — in his effort to keep the cars on the track, in what must have been a contested waste of gasoline.

Prepositions are difficult in any language. Please note my corrections. You might try reading Sports Illustrated. *Next.*

He pinched his eyes. The idea of a series of rubber stamps — BU HAOTING, AWKWARD, SHENME?, WHAT?, BU DUI!, WRONG!— to blast out quick responses to this dreck was appealing, and yet he was the one encouraging them to read *Sports Illustrated*. They couldn't get their hands on anything contemporary worth reading — the English section of Beijing bookstores stopped at Hemingway.

Jeff liked the paper of one student whose first essays had been disasters, but now wrote about being posted to a dull job in Xinjiang province where he was only permitted to do routine transactions, and he extrapolated from this to comment subtly on his country's global position. "No taking chances, no meaningful interaction with the world, no growth and no development," he wrote. Jeff was surprised at this thoughtful analysis and told him so. "What was wrong before?" Jeff asked.

"Oh. My family had to leave where we were living, so I was spending all my time looking for another apartment."

Jeff nodded. Finding an apartment in Beijing was indeed difficult.

"So I just finished negotiating with the landlord last week. Finally we are all moved in."

"It is getting cold outside."

"It's warm inside." He smiled.

"Why are you studying here? I mean Jian Hua's specialty is not literature. Why don't you go to Bei Da? It's the literature university, isn't it?"

"They wouldn't take me. So I was offered a position studying literature here."

"Why wouldn't they take you? If you don't mind me asking."

"I failed Marxism-Leninism."

After marking papers, Jeff lounged on his bed and watched the strangest interludes on late-night TV: illusive signals of the essential acquisitiveness of the culture.

They were long infomercials. Sometimes they slow-motioned past five and pushed seven minutes, the soundtracks an ethereal texture of beat and mesh. Sometimes in black and white. Couples, always couples, would arrive at intervals to tryst in time-lapse. There would be two chairs, one occupied by the female, attending nothing, her neck pale and long, open to scrutiny, then the second body, male, would materialize in the waiting chair. The heads were often cut off when the camera shifted. So they sat, headless, making mating gestures to each other. A hint of narrative — one picked up a cellphone. The camera came close, revealing brand and features. There was then much attention to the woman's jewellery: her *jiazi*, her *xiangliar*, her bracelets, her rings. She was a nest of diamonds, of curlyworked gold. He had a fine leather jacket and watch and tie-pin to show. This went on interminably. Their bodies were beautiful. The woman's hair shimmered. Perfume, pearls, cigarette case, beeper.

The models were unimportant; they were merely mobile plinths for the accessories. The screen emptied again. A jump-cut to blue sky, cloud. The couple beamed down in lounging robes. Next to a dragon-carved screen. They fished for sunglasses; the camera moved to accommodate their heads.

An astral parade of products.

If you change the channel, Jeff thought, it's either Beijing opera, the rapid-fire news, or an interview with a villager.

The villager, then.

He was typically filmed walking in his fields. Hands behind his back, as though expecting handcuffs or to find a polished copper mirror. He pointed out crops — this barley was his mother's people's. Father's over there. His brothers and sisters all live in the village. Did he have a family? The reporter asked the question a few times — "*Mei you.*" No family, no wife, no children.

Where do they find these people, willing to be followed around all day by a Beijing cameraman and a polite reporter? The only unmarried peasant in Hebei province, sneered Jeff.

The reporter nodded and nodded as the villager, skinny and knotty at the joints, nearly toothless, started to talk about a big fire in the field that was put out. He was telling what everyone in the village did. It became clear that the reporter could not understand him; he was too enthusiastic, not speaking clearly, jabbering, really. Someone at the TV station got his dialect, though, because the Mandarin subtitles were floating across the bottom of the screen. Occasionally Jeff could match a word (somewhat) with the peasant's excited utterances.

Now they were in a dirt-floor kitchen; his sister-in-law slicing mutton skin thinly. Garlic and coriander hung in huge bunches. In the corner, the obligatory chicken picked a fight with the infant.

Back to the fields, always sloping downward, following some hidden river, the camera moving over the landscape at the shaky ministrations of an illiterate man's bony hand.

The film ended.
The next feature was a tour of a textile factory.

They were walking down Chang An Avenue on Bian Fu's birthday, hand in hand. Jeff had a simple gold ring hidden deep in his coat pocket, the gift box wrapped in many layers of tissue paper, on which he had painstakingly drawn characters. Bian Fu was telling stories:

"Once there was a mouse who had a very beautiful daughter and he loved her very much. Many many mice came to visit asking to marry the mouse-girl, for she was the most attractive mouse in the city. The father mouse he had to think about it a long time. Finally he decided he would marry his daughter to the fiercest and the bravest of all the suitors. That was when the cat showed up to propose. The father saw that the cat was clearly the bravest and the fiercest, so he agreed to let his daughter marry the cat. And the cat ate her."

"That's a good story," he said. "What are you trying to tell me?"

"What do you think I am trying to tell you?" she said.

"Maybe that you think or your family thinks I won't take care of you. Maybe you think that. I don't know."

"It is a story about a mouse and a cat," she said.

In the pedestrian underpass there were several vendors selling human hair, and a blind woman singing a mournful song about a long-lost *pengyou.*

"God, what a corny song," Jeff said.

"That is a sweet song," said Bian Fu.

They kept walking. "Where are we going?" said Bian Fu.

"Oh, I don't know."

"Tell me a story."

"Okay," he said. He recited the lyrics of Leonard Cohen's "Suzanne."

"That is a very sad story," she said. "What is its meaning?"

"You know, people in my country are still trying to figure that out."

"*Zhen chiguai.* Very strange."

They ate a bag of dumplings on the street corner, then, still licking their fingers, entered the chandeliered and plushly carpeted lobby of the Beijing Concert Hall.

Bian Fu was delighted.

Once they were seated, she touched his finger. "Honey," she said, "I think a Western woman would express her happiness much differently; she would say, 'Oh, Jeff, I love you so much. I love you taking me to the concert; I am very happy.' But my way is different, I am very, oh, how to say, implicit."

"I like your way."

The concert was a blend of traditional Chinese and Japanese music with musicians from both countries. Jeff loved the music, loved the names of the Chinese instruments, *hu-qin, pi-pa,* he loved the wandering but unerringly placed motifs, the shivers of crystal that broke inside the melody, loved the formality of the musicians, men in tuxedos, women in the long red *qi pao*s embroidered with golden dragons. The *er-hu* solos were particularly lovely: a banshee and a river's mist from a simplified violin stole inside the heart and tore and lifted it inexplicably.

Halfway through the concert, Bian Fu whispered in his ear, "I am so proud: Chinese music is so wonderful; we have five thousand years of history. Thank you, dear."

He was proud himself; he had made her happy.

She said she had to get home by eleven — which presented him with a problem when the concert was over. How to give her the ring?

"Do you want to go for a drink at that hotel?"

"No." She was walking briskly. "We have to get to the bus stop."

"Why?"

"If I get home too late, my family will lock the gate and I will have to wake them up."

"It's only ten."

"Please, we must hurry."

They passed several drunken men who scowled at Bian Fu because she was with a foreigner and therefore a prostitute.

"Please, can we stop somewhere?" Jeff squeezed her hand.

"Why?"

"Because I have a present to give you."

He took her hand and led her over to the steps of a shopping centre, and sat her down under bright banners advertising upcoming sales. It was cold.

He handed her the wrapped box. "*Sheng ri kuai le*," he said, "Happy Birthday."

She removed the first layer of tissue. "*Nan-nu*," she read. "Yes. I am a woman and you are a man."

"Go on."

"*Shuang xing fu*. Double Happiness. Yes, maybe, if we are lucky, I think." She looked like Er Bao peering into the mirror. Prettily enchanted.

"*Nande bizi*. Oh, that is you. You have the difficult nose, not me."

"What are you doing?" a voice said.

It was a security guard. He loomed above them.

"Giving her a birthday present," Jeff said.

"*Hao*." He walked off, but kept his eyes on them.

"*Da xiang*. Yes, we are both elephants."

Finally she got to the heart-shaped box, which she opened and took a quick look at the ring. "*Xie xie*," she said. She snapped the heart shut and put it in her pocket. "Come on, we have to catch the bus."

"Don't you want to wear...?" He stopped. She was a half block out in front of him.

The ticket taker, bundled up in her platform near the bus's back doors, kept staring at them, then looking away, as they rode home.

Finally Bian Fu said, "I never did such thing before, open a present on the steps of a shopping centre."

He didn't say anything.

The floorboards of the ramshackle, proletarian hulk of a bus shook and shook and shook.

Chapter Seven

Chen Jie, the servant-girl, was from a village in Anhui province. She rarely spoke, or, more correctly, would only speak at the end of the day, when her work was done and she was allowed to fill a bowl with cold food and pull up a stool at the coffee table to eat. The family often interrupted her and she stopped talking immediately. She watched. When Chen Jie had finished cleaning up after supper, Bian Fu's mother would hand her a piece of knitting and bark instructions, not that she needed any. She was the fastest knitter Jeff had ever seen. Her nimble hands flurried as she yanked more yarn out of the ball tucked in the corner of the couch. Whenever Anhui province was shown on TV, she would stab at the screen with her needles, as if to say, That's me! The family smiled politely.

"My mother take her on," said Bian Fu. "She is really a good-hearted woman. Chen Jie make some money to send home to her village. She will go back there and get married, I think."

"Marry who?"

"Someone from the village."

Jeff felt Bian Fu's mother's eyes on him. She left off stirring the *chou*, crossed her arms, and asked him, "Don't you ever get homesick?"

"I love your daughter," he said.

"Your hometown, you do not miss it?"

"Wang Fu Ren, in Canada I do not live in my hometown. My hometown is Winnipeg. My family is far away. I miss it in a way, but families often live very far from each other in Canada."

"In China too," said Bian Fu.

Wang Fu Ren returned to the *chou*, a complicated worry in her eyes.

Often when he arrived at the *siheyuan*, Chen Jie was crouched in the courtyard in her puffy winter jacket, crouched over a basin of cold water, scrubbing away at the family's clothes on a plastic washboard. Or cutting vegetables on the door laid over trestles that served as a kitchen counter. She always wore the same clothes. When he greeted her, *Ni hao*, she would grin crazily, only permitting herself to return the greeting and laughing so her whole, compact body convulsed when Jeff spoke Chinese.

She thought Jeff was the funniest thing ever, and Jeff suspected that included cartoons.

Late one night she was washing socks. She asked Bian Fu if Canadian men washed their wives' socks. Bian Fu didn't know, so Jeff volunteered to wash hers, making a point of sniffing the socks to make sure they were clean. Bian Fu thought this was good, and scrunched her nose up as if she heard a mosquito.

"*Hen haowanr,*" said Chen Jie. Very funny.

They shot a couple of comments back and forth in Bing He dialect.

Chen Jie was alternately ignored and bossed around, as befit her station. Jeff tried to include her in conversations, which the uncle found strange. Whenever she spoke, the uncle would immediately set her a chore. Jeff knew his presence upset the pecking order. And there was a strain permeating the *siheyuan*. The family's actions were carefully tamped down; only Chen Jie, reacting to Jeff with brazen amazement, seemed animated.

"Your family is very polite to me, but I don't think they want me around," he said in English one evening.

"They will accept us once they have no choice," said Bian Fu. "Don't get angry — it is just your imagination."

"Don't you understand, Je Fu, that my daughter is useless?" said Wang Fu Ren.

The uncle groaned and handed him a cigarette.

They were watching a teledrama in which a Chinese family, upon hearing bad news from a relative, perched on their expensive furniture in deepening gloom, waiting for the patriarch to speak.

After he did, successive family members stood up, made dire speeches, and sat back down. It was the most static TV show Jeff had ever seen. He reread a paperback of *Tess of the D'Urbervilles* he'd found in the dormitory.

But Bian Fu's family loved the show, because they too were inside a four-walled *siheyuan*, watching another family within their four-walled *siheyuan* scrap for some advantage. Even though the TV family had Persian carpets and Wang Fu Ren had scarred linoleum, there was reassurance in the TV family's patterns of attack and strategic manoeuvring. The males rose again and again and issued edicts or announced vengeful intentions; the females listened and, when the males left to perpetrate honour and decency, confided in each other. None of them owned an outfit worth less than five hundred dollars American.

Suddenly Chen Jie spoke.

Just as abruptly, she stopped.

No one responded.

"What did she say?" said Jeff.

Bian Fu whispered, "She says that she became a Christian and that God and Jesus and Mary are her parents."

"That's very nice," Jeff said.

Chen Jie returned to the kitchen to wash the dishes.

"Bah," said Bian Fu. "She is a little crazy."

One of the neighbours often showed up in the evenings, trailed by his obnoxious kid and his wife, who could talk about shopping for hours. The kid carried a plastic machine gun and always aimed it at Jeff, in some murderous patriotic junior fantasy. The neighbour was a taxi-driver, so had some experience with Europeans — he said they were more casual than Chinese, meaning they wore shorts and exposed their legs to others. This he demonstrated. Westerners also had lots of money, and were suckers. He had made a bundle the other day taking some Germans to see The Great Wall. The neighbour was likable, always chattering; there was no way Jeff could understand him, but his meaning occasionally leaped forth. "Blah blah blah blah DAO!"

Jeff flinched.

"He says if those tourists go into those restaurants at Chang Cheng it will be like they are attacked with a KNIFE!" said Bian Fu.

"Yes, I got the knife part."

"*Lao wai, lao wai, lao wai,*" the little brat was chanting.

"Blah blah blah blah blah blah blah blah *bo-wu-ling*?"

"What?"

"He wants to know if you ever go bowling. He goes every Tuesday and Wednesday. He has his own uniform and *bo-wu-ling* ball."

"Sure, I'll go with him," Jeff said.

"He wants to know how much money you make in North America."

"Tell him I am a lineman for the county, and I make one hundred dollars a year and I have to work with polar bears."

"You should be polite," said Bian Fu. "This neighbour, he is a relative of my uncle."

Jeff couldn't concentrate. He had witnessed something on the way over. Riding through twilight along the canal, he'd heard voices up ahead. He saw figures twinning out of each other: a throng. He got off and walked his bike. The crowd was gathered in front of an apartment building, jabbering; a scene of some import had transpired. There were children clinging to their parents' legs. Men pointing and waving their arms. There were police. On the second-storey balcony, a couple of women clung together so tightly they seemed joined, one creature who shrieked down at the onlookers. A policeman asked them a single question; they lifted their heads together and howled into the sky, howled from a source black and far and ancient, beyond the realm of senses. Jeff looked at the ground and walked his bike past them. He had no idea what it was all about, but his heart pounded and he swung up on his saddle and got the hell out. It had not even occurred to him to ask. He did not want to know.

Bian Fu began pumping him that evening about what their life in Canada would be like. Jeff said, "Look, *ai ren*, we don't even have a plan for when we're going to get married. Don't you want to get married?"

"Yes."

"Well?"

"Spring Festival would be a good time," she said.

This made him even moodier. His contract with Jian Hua was only for the first term — sooner or later he would have to decide whether to extend it. He didn't have the money to go back to Canada for the spring break, visit Melissa, and return. Which he would prefer over a maybe wedding.

"Look," said Bian Fu, "this program is about Bing He."

Lost in his funk, Jeff let the Chinese chatter go on without him, and thought of the ostentatious Christmas decoration store on Government Street in Victoria. And the busker with his trumpet who was terrible — after five years he could summon neither tone nor timbre, but would shout *One Love, My Man, One Love* at Jeff when he passed. And the silver trays with paper doilies at Murchie's, and the bonbons and hazelnut mice. And the retro hippie styles of the grunged-out young, their toques and bell-bottoms and tie-dyed shirts and the rings and studs in their ears, their noses, their lips. And the hours spent in the bookstore, pulling down random poetry titles and taking the message for what it was:

> *There's a certain slant of light*
> *On winter afternoons*
> *That oppresses, like the heft*
> *Of cathedral tunes*

And leaving just as twilight encroached. Most of all he thought of his daughter: how tall was she now?

"I'm tired. I'm going back to Jian Hua," he said.

He rode back feeling oddly hurt, because though the meal had been good, it had not been made especially for him; they were going to eat anyway. All this was just politeness — they did not want him in their family and were waiting for him to go. Again the sensation of not knowing what was going on, as if his life with Bian Fu were dependent on some action he had to take, but he could not figure out what it was.

And he was broke. Months of paying for Bian Fu — concerts, discos, drinks, meals — and long-distance phone calls to his daughter at three hundred kuai a shot had depleted his paltry savings. He had just made it to the end of October on his salary.

He kept seeing the photographed face of Bian Fu's father, a stern face, a proud face, a face that would play the angles, wait him out, a face reflected in Wang Brother's when he had come to inspect the *lao wai*, a face that Bian Fu's face was distinct from but formed from; a face that kept its distance, clever, complicated, compromised. It irritated him deeply that the father would not meet him.

That night Robert came to his room. He looked meek, teetering around in his outsized sweatshirt. "Can I talk with you?"

Jeff purposely offered him the chair facing away from Bian Fu's picture.

"Do you remember my girlfriend?"

"Yes."

"She's in jail. I just found out. I just got off the phone talking with her mother. We talked for an hour. Give me some of that coffee. Thanks. She's in jail."

"She what? Christ, that's terrible. What happened? What did she do?"

"Her and her friends rolled a foreigner, some American guy, he was drunk, and the cops caught her. They went and put her in jail. I hadn't seen her for a couple of weeks and I just figured, oh well, she had bigger fish to fry than me. Her mother has been looking for her. We had a long conversation — it turns out she doesn't have any siblings."

"Sorry?"

"She told me she had a sister and a brother. Nope. She's the only child. I was very careful during the conversation, using the word *qin* because it means blood relative."

"You just phoned the mother out of the blue?"

"She phoned me. She was worried. She found my number in one of her schoolbooks. So she doesn't have any siblings, that's lie number one. Turns out she isn't going to school, either. She told me she was going to Art College. Nope. Her and her friends were roaming around San Li Tun picking up foreigners. Her mother said she doesn't know how long they will hold her. I met another girl."

"Hold it. So what else did you find out about your friend?"

"The mother thinks she's on drugs. Nobody could figure out where she went. She had the whole neighbourhood out looking for her."

"Why didn't she go to the police?"

"Look, if you have a problem, the last people you go to in Beijing are the police. If there's no problem, they'll invent one and make you pay for it. You know those little scraps of paper Chinese women fill out when they come to visit us? Those all go to the police. Someone checks them over. They look for patterns. They're checking for prostitutes, for girls outside Beijing visiting many people at many places. It doesn't matter how little evidence there is, they will make somebody pay."

Jeff didn't say anything.

"So this girl I met, I took her out for dinner. The second date she starts telling me she was living in Shanghai last year and she went to a pub. Before she knew it — it was late at night — she was surrounded by guys and they started to threaten her. Pushed her around. Talking like they were going to rape her. She got out of it somehow but then couldn't go back to any of the places she used to go. She was frightened. She didn't want to go to the police. So she came to Beijing to stay with a relative."

"Is she paranoid now?" Jeff asked. "Sorry, I mean, how is she acting now?"

"She wanted to tell someone her story, but I don't know. I don't know. I don't want any part of it."

"Do you like her? I mean that's the past. So she tells you about something that disturbed her, frightened her. Don't you have any compassion?"

"I don't want to get involved."

"Fair enough."

Robert took off his glasses and wiped them. He began talking again, as though the story he had just told didn't exist. "I went to San Li Tun to look for my friend. But I couldn't find her. I went to all the bars I know, but nope, I couldn't even find her trashy little buddies. So they've been rolling American guys. It just goes to show — you think you know these women, and there's always some surprise. The mother wouldn't let me off the phone. She was angry at *me*. She thought I had something to do with it. Shit, I've been giving her money to support her."

"So why date all these women if you don't want to get involved?"

"I want to get married."

"Well, you get married, you're involved."

"I want to have a kid; there's no way I could do that in Canada. Here, I work. Here, I get another couple of teaching jobs, I'm making seven, eight thousand kuai, I'm rich by Beijing standards. But I can't meet any nice girls."

"Someone gets attacked in a bar and they're not nice?"

"All the nice girls have their time taken up by Communist Party meetings. There's so much social control, we have no idea. The nice ones go from classes to meetings to their family; they're not going to have any time to meet —"

"Foreigners," Jeff said.

"So how's *your* friend?"

"We're getting married."

"When's the wedding?"

"Don't know yet. The family is not onside. I haven't met the father yet."

"Look," Robert said. "The family's already made their decision. If you haven't met the father, forget it. You don't make enough money. Or they don't like the way you treat her. Or something. It's up to you guys, or it's not going to happen."

"Yeah, maybe it's not going to happen. But we were supposed to go to Bing He to meet the other relatives. It hasn't happened yet. I'm being patient."

"You're wasting your time. You should check out Li Ruang Yun. There's someone who's at least getting to North America under her own steam. That's what you should be thinking about — whether this friend of yours is actually going to be able to make the transition. I mean what's she going to do in Canada — work for some Chinese businessman?" His tone was decidedly suggestive.

"I love her," said Jeff.

"Good luck!"

There didn't seem to be much else to say, so Jeff didn't.

"I just know too much about the pragmatic nature of the Chinese," Robert said. "You've got to be more aggressive. If you really want her."

"We'll see." Jeff had closed off. This was none of Robert's business.

"I was wondering…" said Robert.

"Uh-huh?"

"Do you think you could introduce me to your class of graduate students?"

"I'll think about it."

When he had gone Jeff looked out the window at the university wall, thinking. Robert spoke reasonably good Chinese; he was a beginner. To move forward in this society you had to be focused and fierce; it didn't hurt to have massive *guanxi* behind you either.

He had to move forward. Whatever it was, he had to pay the price.

The next morning he spent an hour in a taxi to the Canadian embassy, where he laid down sixty kuai for a certificate, signed and sealed by the Canadian attaché, that stated a marriage was to be solemnized between Wang Bian Fu and himself. This was the first step in a long process of necessary documentation for the egregious act of a foreigner marrying a Chinese.

I am a Canadian citizen.

I am not currently married.

He showed the attaché his divorce certificate.

"Just passing through?" the attaché asked.

"I work here."

I work for Jian Hua University. My local address is such and such.

He signed it. "I'll get you some change," said the attaché.

He felt giddy-happy. The people passing on the Dong Zhi Men sidewalk intensely interested him; they did not seem sinister or complicated. They were holding hands with children. They were going to school. They read newspapers and ate pancakes and meat dumplings for breakfast. They had everyday lives.

On his way out of the embassy, the security guard hailed him and they chatted.

"Hey, your Chinese isn't bad," the guard said.

But when he showed Bian Fu the cerificate later that day, she did not greet it with the happiness he expected; instead, she frowned, and squeezed his hand, and said she had to read it over.

On a sunny Saturday he took Bian Fu to the mosque. Beijing sparkled as he rode through the Kick Fish crossroads to pick her up. People's eyes shone with the foreknowledge of snow. Old couples walked together laden with *baixin* and bok choy in net bags. Garbage can lids brimmed with pistachios and peanuts. The vendors sat cross-legged on their carts and weighed their goods with the funny tippy scales that they held in one hand and tapped with the other until they balanced or until their patter convinced the buyer. In huge parked trucks there were bales of children's clothing being picked over by mothers, the kids climbing onto the flatbed to roll and shriek in the multicoloured nest.

He waited at the crossroads.

In Chen Jie's puffy moon-man jacket, struggling to propel the bike that was too small for her legs, Bian Fu was beautiful, with her elegant nose and high, thin eyebrows and iridescent hair that shifted on her shoulders. Yet other facets swiftly rose in Jeff's fantasy of her. She was anybody's sister on the way to market, schoolmate off to the library, a daughter and denizen of Kick Fish County, floating out of the crossroads, from among the peddlers and their illicit bottles of *baijiu*, she was neighbour to the man in the restaurant door doing jumping jacks in the cold, the *shao kao* wizard turning corn on the coals.

He rode beside her and admired her face.

She rode beside him and enjoyed his admiring of her face.

She was the girl he had travelled thousands of miles to see because he wanted to marry her.

"Do you have the map?" she said.

He touched his pocket, "Got it."

They passed Er Wai, where she went to school. There was a huge satellite dish atop another school. "That is the Broadcasting

University," she said. "They are all stars there. All of them are very beautiful. Maybe you should teach there in the future. Very beautiful students. You will marry all of them."

"No, just you."

She liked this sort of teasing. It made Jeff nervous. "What do your parents say about us?"

"They wish us happiness, but they are very traditional. Maybe see us at Spring Festival."

He stopped smiling. The weight of his decision — stay or not stay in Beijing — bore down, but he shook it off. It was such a beautiful day. Their bikes gleamed, the city coalescing around them as they rode through Chang Ping Kou, the building sites knocking and thudding away, grey apartments giving over to mirror-windowed office towers, Baskin and Robbins and Pizza Hut franchises, myriad English signs advertising Internet access and fax services; then peddlers of sweet potatoes and candied haws giving over to bike-rickshaws and curb-cruising taxis. "CD-LOM, CD-LOM," cried importunate men, boxes crooked under their arms. A billboard with a signature moustache announced a Yanni concert.

"*Yanni haokan ma?*" she said. Isn't Yanni good-looking?

"*Yanni hen haokan,*" he grinned. "He makes my heart go pitter-pat."

"Really? Oh, you Westerners are so strange. 'Pitter-pat?'"

"Thump-thump."

They stopped by the canal near the International Post Office for a snack of candied haws — sickeningly sweet. Men were fishing in the black water.

"They will never catch anything."

"People don't go fishing to catch fish," she said. "Tell me some more about our life in Victoria."

She cleaned the haws off the stick with the same alacrity she had stripped a duck's foot the other night. They could see their breath but the sunlight quickly quelled it.

"We get up in the morning and take a walk in a huge park, and then go down to the ocean and watch the sun rise. I work at a job, and you work. We cook big meals together, we go to see movies, we go out dancing at the bar, we have my daughter come over and stay with us on the weekends…"

She was nodding prettily.

"All my friends want to meet you, and we go to my hometown in Winnipeg to meet my mother. Eventually we save enough money to go travelling again, and we go to Africa to visit our other relatives the elephants. What do you think?"

"Hmm, not bad. Go on. *Ni shuo ba.*"

He realized he had not talked to his mother for months — since his father's death. "It's difficult to see the future. Maybe we have a child and maybe we don't. What do you think about our future?"

The sunlight was directly behind her and this startled him; her silhouette shone so blackly — dark willow, waving hair — that he turned and looked across the canal where, trundling along the walls of Beihai Park, several Chinese families, dark cutouts, strolled with their children, the men straying from the tight groups intermittently to cuff the children, and then regrouping.

"What do you think?" he said.

"I don't know," she said. "I don't know if I want to go to Canada sometimes. I don't know if I can live outside Zhong Guo." She started working on another candied haw. "It sounds good, I think. When I get old I will probably want to live in China. I don't know." Her lip came out.

She pulled a strand of her hair across her cheek and began to suck it. "I think if you leave China and our love doesn't work out I will have a deep feeling of shame. I never have this feeling before. Maybe I will just leave and go to South China, leave my family. I never have this feeling. Oh! You know, there are many Chinese men, all they want is sex. We Chinese women can tell. With you I cannot tell, the signs are not there."

"Let's go visit the mosque," he said, frustrated.

Once they were inside the gates, the mosque appeared exactly like the one in Dali, and he was seized by a powerful melancholy and a somewhat patriarchal insistence that Bian Fu put on the *hejab* he had asked her to bring.

"Really? I have to put on this head scarf?"

"In the mosque, yes."

At the end of the courtyard were the red, wooden doors, exactly as in Dali, and the huge, golden Chinese characters above the door instead of Arabic. There were the cedars lining the courtyard. And there were the rows of two-storied wood homes encircling the mosque. A couple of barefoot children chased each other in the sunlight. A woman without a head scarf carried a bucket of water towards an old man smoking a pipe.

"She's not wearing one."

"She's not in the mosque."

He went into a room just off the courtyard to wash his feet and hands and rinse out his mouth and wet his hair. Bian Fu poked her head in. She looked worried.

"She says I don't have to wear the scarf because I am not *hui ren*."

"Okay, I'm wrong. In Arab countries you would have to. Sorry, dear."

But he didn't like the way she said, I am not *hui ren*. Everything else we do, we have to do a certain way because you are Han, and the Han have rules, but you…oh, forget it, he thought. You are not here to argue about rules, you are here to show her the mosque and to make your prayers.

They stepped through the doors into the marvellously musky-smelling mosque. It was empty, and not as vast as the outside led him to believe; perhaps there were meeting rooms behind this part. The carpets were thick and numerous but disappointingly factory-made, with blocky representations of the Grand Mosque at Mecca and the *Kaba'a* on some of them. He explained these things to Bian Fu, who was quiet. His voice took on a parental quality among the pillars and the several slanting beams of sunlight that penetrated the holes in the window-shades. Here is the *mihrab*, it faces Mecca, the *laojia* of Muhammad, where Islam started. Here is the *minbar*, where the *imam* gives his *khutba* or sermon. He showed her the large *Qur'an* beside the *minbar*, whose calligraphic style surprised him a little; instead of the flowing, multifoliate curves and flourishes, the expected and delicate play of combination and elongation he loved, and the many precise super and subscripts, this was a blocky, angular Arabic, the consonants recognizable but with a stiff, carved quality, reminiscent of Kufic script but bereft of its formal perfection, a writing painstakingly learnt by the men in tents in the sandy wastes of Western China, perhaps, taught in village after village by the one old man who knew how to make the letters, and replicated stiffly by small boys wearing fur hats.

"It is very strange," said Bian Fu, nodding. She looked worried again.

He laughed. "It is a little strange to me, too. I have to make my prayers."

He performed his *salah*. She stood waiting, listening to him.

"I felt strange," she said outside. "When you make your prayers. It was a very bad feeling. I think there is no way I can understand you. I do not know this language. And you — you, you will just leave and go to another country, learn another language, meet another woman. I think there is no way I can understand this man. And I have a memory. My school friend she once have a friend who is *hui ren*. She visit her friend's home and the mother gets very angry when she learns that my friend ate off their dishes, so she starts washing the whole kitchen in front of her, saying she is unclean, she is dirty. This is very cruel. But you are not like that, I know."

"No, I'm not." But he knew what she was talking about. He knew well how it was for Muslim Chinese here: he had seen the rundown buildings on the outskirts where all the members of a community lived, the one building that would be kitchen, garden, mosque, school, cemetery, all within one encircling wall. He could understand the need to close oneself off, to resist the Han, to marry your children to other Muslims, to do business only with other Muslims.

What he said was, "Tell me your true feeling."

"I think this is something strange in you I do not understand. Tell me, do Muslim men treat their women badly?"

"Some of them do."

"Always make them wear the scarf?"

"Some of them do."

"I do not like it."

"There are Chinese men who treat their wives badly. They have affairs, they hit their wives, and so on."

"Ah, no. I am very proud our Chinese men. What men do this? How do you know this?"

"Look, you said yourself you didn't like the way you were treated."

She was brooding.

"That is different. I am very proud our Chinese men."

Jeff was seized by a strange sense of artificiality. What was he doing? He rarely practised his religion; except for Dali, when his father died, he had not been in a mosque for years. He had brought her here with some sense of occasion, but now, in the sunlight, faced with her worry, it seemed insignificant.

"Look," he said, "this is not so important. This is only a small part of me. At home I never go to the mosque."

"I thought you believe this religion."

"I do believe, in a way. It is like you, do you believe in Buddha?"

"Yes, sometimes."

"Well, that's like me. Sometimes this is just part of my life, that's all."

She was silent for a while. They stopped again at Beihai Park and crouched on the sidewalk.

"I always learned," she suddenly said, "that there are two types of men you must never marry. One is Korean men, because they leave the women to do all the work and just go out drinking. And the other was Muslim men. I admit it. I was prejudiced. I have felt prejudice." Her eyes fell in shame.

"Let's ride home."

Halfway home, she started calling out, "You know, I love you. It is true, I love you. It is the truth. I don't care my boyfriend any more." He shivered; he thought *he* was her boyfriend. "He must face the truth. Everyone must face the truth. I love you, I love you."

When Bian Fu uttered those magic words, at such a volume, he almost blushed. Perhaps he was becoming Chinese.

That evening Bian Fu showed him her ceramic antiques in her room, a Qing dynasty bowl and spoon set. She did this slowly, unwrapping each from its tissue, and presenting them to him. Her fingers traced the delicate line of each spoon, the scalloped rim of each bowl, and she smiled shyly, her eyes meeting his and dropping, meeting, dropping. She pointed out the creamy colour, the simplicity of form. When he had seen them all, she meticulously smoothed each piece of tissue and wrapped each piece up and put them away in her desk, where she had put away all of his presents, and his letters, and the wildflowers he had sent her from Canada. She breathed out, completely satisfied. She had unwrapped her heart and showed it to him. Now she could make tea.

The fight between Bian Fu and her mother started the next afternoon, shortly after the neighbour left with her baby. They been discussing the white flakes of skin that had started to develop on the baby's scalp and tongue, and the women had gently washed the baby's skin with weak ginger tea. The fight began after Chen Jie lifted the sheets of kelp off the clothesline and Bian Fu had started to press them out with her slender hands and carefully cut them into thin strips on the coffee table; they crackled as she cut.

Wang Fu Ren entered from the courtyard and grimaced at Bian Fu.

Jeff pretended interest in the TV, where a Chinese family was hilariously debating whether it was better to have a lot of money or a whole lot of money.

Wang Fu Ren lowered coal into the stove with the tongs, and fired the first shots in an aggrieved mutter. No response. She poked her head out of the stove-room and repeated her comments louder, as if he weren't in the room. Bian Fu said something brightly appeasing, and concentrated on the kelp.

If you have a whole lot of money, you can get a whole lot more, went the TV.

Ah, yes, but if your pile of money is this big, you have to have somewhere to put it.

There is always somewhere to put it.

The studio audience cracked up.

Wang Fu Ren wheeled out into the living room and raised her voice and aimed at her daughter. Bian Fu laid the cleaver on the block, edge then haft, and gathered kelp strips in her hands, purposely turning her back on her mother and filling a bowl with water, laying the kelp in the water and flicking a few overhanging strands into the bowl. She brushed past her mother on her way into the bedroom, where she picked up a hairbrush, came back out, and began brushing her hair in the large mirror.

Wang Fu Ren incredulously watched her come and go and brush. She established dominance in the living room, hands on her hips, and uttered a long, long bitter sentence with plenty of aspectual *Ah*s thrown straight into Bian Fu's shoulder blades.

Bian Fu separated out a strand of hair and rubbed it over her lower lip, her eyes retreating to protective depth.

"*Ai wah!*" spat Wang Fu Ren, disgusted. Halfway back to the coal stove, she looked apologetically at Jeff and then was mauled by an emotion so potent it whirled her around and yanked her head forward and her tongue leaped from her mouth and started flicking at her teeth. Words streamed from her, rich, biting words, words she would never be able to take back, her fleshy arms thrashed before her.

"*Zhen de ma?*" Bian Fu said. Really?

"*Shi ba?*" Bian Fu said. You don't say?

"*Bu shi!*" Bian Fu said. I am *not!*

Her mother fumed and stomped her feet.

Silence.

Er Bao and the neighbour's kid came in, bearing a plastic knife and gun, sized up the situation, and fled into the bedroom, the neighbour kid stopping briefly to fire a couple of imaginary rounds at Jeff with a xenophobic vigour that was always annoying coming from someone who had not yet learned how to blow his nose. Jeff followed them.

The voices resumed their practised violence, though Bian Fu was keeping a lid on it. Back and forth. Their steps circled the coffee table, into the kitchen, back out. Bian Fu stuck her head in the bedroom, said, "Hey, Jeff, she is angry the ashtray got broken, the Qing dynasty ashtray, so I said to her, if it's so valuable why do you use it?"

"Right," he said.

He wadded up pieces of notepaper and tried to interest the neighbour boy and Er Bao in a makeshift game of volleyball, because the kids were frightened; their eyes were round and brown.

Wang Fu Ren's next comment froze Bian Fu in the doorway and a filmy, snake-like sheen played in her eyes, then she whirled and stomped back at her mother. She was shouting now. Now they were really at it.

"No," he told Er Bao, "hit the ball like this."

"I don't want to play with you," she said. She crawled under the bed. Sensible, he thought.

Bian Fu and Wang Fu Ren had started to slip out of Mandarin and into Bing He dialect, Jeff could tell: the words flew with the rapidity of the unconscious, the drama of the churning heart. The women were gripped with an atavistic fever, and their speech became folkloric, the Bing He accent frothing with ornaments of rich derision, a verbal texture full of snakes and hens and pigs and straw and shit and lazy husbands and faithless wives and frozen rivers and hard-luck Han tales of the misery, the poverty, the ignominy, the broken eggs, the leaking roof, the mud and blood, the remember this, remember that, the village idiot and the idiot village until the apartment was spattered with their volleys and salvos and nobody listened because they'd heard it all before and why would anyone with any sense try to talk to someone like you, you shrew, you dog, you sheep, you rat, you get me up in the morning and never let me rest, you —

"Keep cool," Jeff yelled at Bian Fu. "KEEP COOL!"

She looked at him as if she had never seen him before.

Then she straightened, stood tall.

She went and drained the kelp and rinsed it.

Wang Fu Ren muttered something further and sat down on the couch, exhausted. She began to rub her legs. Her shoulders heaved.

Bian Fu brushed past Jeff and gathered up Er Bao and the other kid in her arms on the bed, and the children stroked her hair. A tear traced her cheek.

He told Bian Fu he had better leave.

The next evening had started out pleasantly enough, with a meal of noodles and *baozi* in his room. They started to ride back to Bian Fu's place. It was another damp, cold evening. "So when are we going?" Jeff asked.

"When are we going where?"

"To your *laojia*."

"I am not certain when you wanted to go."

"Remember we talked about October? It's December now. Did you ask your father?"

"It is very difficult for me to remember. I will phone him and ask him."

Once home, they started watching TV with her mother.

"I would really like to go to Bing He. When can we go?"

"I am not sure when you wanted to go. Please tell me the exact time." Bian Fu's affect had become more and more mechanical as she registered his growing anger.

"I want to meet your father."

"Yes, he want to meet you too."

He got up and made for the door.

"Keep *cool!*" said Bian Fu.

The mother shrank behind her knitting.

"I have to go," he said.

"You should stay," said Bian Fu.

He apologized to the mother.

"*Mei guanxi, mei guanxi,*" she said.

"She is just a mother," Bian Fu said. "She wants to see which man love her daughter very much."

"I do love you very much, but I don't like being lied to."

She called him the next day after his classes. "I have to talk to you."

And so they met in the Dunkin' Donuts franchise in Tiyuguan. Bian Fu drew a ripped-out page from her pocket and handed it to him, her eyes down.

"This is from my diary, Jeff. Jeff? — you must promise not to be angry with me."

> *I feel terrible. I did not mean to hurt Jeff but when he said if*
> *I been married he would not go near me I got scared. Some*
> *people think it was not a true marriage because there was*
> *no marriage ceremony yet, but I must admit, it is a legally*
> *registered marriage...*

He stopped reading. He folded the note and smoothed it on the table, patted it once, breathed. He looked into her eyes, and looked outside at the rows of bikes, and he got up and he sat down.

"So what do we do now?" he said.

Chapter Eight

"Everyone has to face the truth, eh?"

They were drinking coffee in a café. She was silent. Jeff was in his third day of ranting and raving. How could Bian Fu have been so deceptive? Was there anything else he didn't know? How long did she have to wait for a divorce? For a divorce — shit, what was he doing? He was going to marry this woman? He left his daughter and came five thousand miles to court a married woman?

"No wonder your father doesn't want to see me," he said.

"Yes, it is a very difficult situation," she said. "And it is all my fault. They really put a lot of pressure on me when you went back to Canada last time."

"That's no excuse. Did it ever occur to you that if you told me the truth there might have been a different way to solve the problem? If we get married, is this the way it's going to be? One version for your Chinese relatives and one for me? Dammit, YOU'RE USING ME!"

"NO, I AM NOT USING YOU."

They glared at each other.

"Want more coffee?"

"Okay."

A foreigner — obviously a Chinese language student — came in and told the waitress if she wanted to bring him dishes she must wash her hands.

"If I was her I would say, Cheeky devil," said Bian Fu.

More coffee came.

"When you get mad like that," she said, "it reminds me of a cartoon character I know."

"Cartoon character?"

"But I like that cartoon character…"

"Okay, listen, Bian Fu. Is there anything else I don't know? If we're going to move forward at all we've got to be completely honest with each other."

"There is one thing. When you were in Canada, my husband come over all the time and beg me. He say, 'Don't you want to marry me? You said all the time you wanted to marry me.' And I would just listen, say nothing."

"Hold it. I thought you said you were legally married to him."

"It is true that we legally registered the marriage. That is why we live together at his parents' place. That is the non-traditional part of it. But many people think it is not a real marriage until you have a wedding ceremony. That was supposed to take place in October."

He winced. Her early curfew…the evasion of his requests to go to Bing He…Bian Fu's mother screaming at her…it all made sense now. Jeff shivered — he was lucky to be alive, he thought. He had better watch his back. Then he thought, don't be so melodramatic.

"So you were saying there's more to it."

"Do you remember when I wrote you and told you 'my boyfriend' ask me to do something?"

"Uh-huh."

"He ask me to wait get a divorce until he can get an apartment for himself, which he need my cooperation, and I agreed. So I am waiting for him to get the exact information on the apartment, then I will be free."

He sputtered in rage, then he smiled, calmed, oddly, by his — and her — naïvety. It was a brilliant chess move. And no doubt the rest of the family were making their moves too, afraid they would have to spend the rest of their lives in close contact with a *lao wai*.

"*Ming bai*," he said. "It is very clear. Anything else?"

"My father like my husband very much."

"Sure, he's a great guy. Fuck! You told me he didn't treat you so well."

"You do not have to swear."

He breathed.

"Yes, I remember that very well," she said. "My father likes my husband, he think he is very sensitive man. He is very difficult to communicate with about this; when I went to visit him in Bing He he said, 'You are a rebel. The family will lose face.' Then he said, 'If you love him, Bian Fu, I will not stand in your way.'"

"And you believe him?"

"He is my father."

"Anything else?"

"He said, 'If you marry Jeff you will have to work.'"

She was moving the spoons around.

"Yes, that's true. And?"

"He offer me thirty thousand kuai to marry the man he want me to marry."

"Bian Fu, *ni bu shi mai de dong xi, wo shuo dui le, dui ma? Dui ma?*" Bian Fu, you are not a thing for sale, am I right? Am I?

She lowered her eyes so he would not see her fear.

"I make a very big mistake lying to you. There will be no more lies. I leave the marriage, and leave the marriage make me feel pain, because I loved him. But I love you. I love you now, and I will get a divorce. I can do this thing very well. Everything I do I have done so we can be together."

"Oh yeah, and who paid your tuition?"

"My family."

"And what do you talk about when he comes around?"

"Talk about divorce."

"And?" He stopped. She was crying. In public. This was no good. He wiped her eyes with a serviette.

"It's over," he said. "The worst is over. We will find a way."

"Way."

"Don't cry."

"I give up everything," she said. "I give up wedding presents, the *hui men* he gave me, I give up money, clothes, property. I even give up my Song dynasty painting — it is very lovely."

"I'm sorry. I was angry. I'm sorry."

"When you go back to Canada I did not know what to do. He come visit me every day. All my friends say you would leave me. My mother say, 'Bian Fu, you are very naïve about life. Your husband is supporting your life. You will hurt yourself and two men as well.' I never face such thing before."

"Look, how long is it going to take you to get a divorce?"

"Sometime new year."

"And the apartment?"

"I am waiting for the exact information."

"Let's go for a bike ride," he said.

"I tell you the truth because I love you."

"Don't forget your mittens."

He blasted through marking essays all evening. Let go. He would look up from his marking and stare out the window. Let go. Why can't you let go? Around midnight he finished the papers and fell into a shallow sleep. He heard the phone ringing.

"Daddy!"

"Melissa."

Her voice was very far away, at the end of the world.

"I lost a tooth!"

"No! Which one?"

"My front. Mommy said, 'Wait.' And it wouldn't come. She said, 'I'll pull it out.' I said, 'Eeeeeeeeeeeeeee!' It fell out."

"Congratulations! I miss you."

"I miss you, Daddy. What time is it there, Daddy?"

"It's three in the morning."

"Are you walking around in the dark with everyone?" she said.

"No, we're sleeping."

"When are you coming home?" she said.

"Soon."

"Oh, good."

"You be a good girl," he said. "I miss you. Bye bye."

Jeff took stock of the class from his platform. This was Jian Hua University after all; these were China's future leaders. Soon they would be vying in the Communist Party, addressing their colleagues in work-unit meetings, sealing, signing and stamping official orders. They would also hold sway over new technologies — the Internet, interactive TV, fibre optics, holography — which they would employ to improve the Middle Kingdom. How much had he learned about them? If they had children, they were officially dedicated to them. They were always glad of the chance to describe their home towns. A clear majority of them found beauty to be an insufficient quality in a marriage partner. All spoke of this nervous need they had for China to be a developed country and yet were also convinced that China was the most civilized country on earth, incomparable. Perhaps there was so much they perforce had to forget to maintain this illusion that it all fell away easily, and the TV vision of China the Progressive, its devoted scientists in lab coats, its kung fu rock videos where armies of young bucks shadow-fought en masse amidst time-worn symbols of the Ancient Kingdom (an old man's fiery head sticking up above the ground, the body buried), and its military saints, rescuing children the length and breadth of the land, became irresistible.

Perhaps he didn't know a thing about them.

They liked it that way, too, he gathered.

He paused by Wang Fang's desk; she was deep in an English conversation with another woman. He looked out the window and listened.

"We are fighting all the time."

"What are you fighting about?"

"My boyfriend and I, we have been seeing each other since high school. This has been going on so long I can't imagine anything else."

"But what is the problem?" Wang Fang spoke in her gentlest voice.

"Now my boyfriend is a businessman. He is always in situations now that I cannot accept. They are quite strange to me, but he doesn't listen to my objections. When I try to talk to him, he just get angry. I—"

Wang Fang had turned her eyes on him. Reproach. He excused himself. They continued their conversation in Chinese. Jeff wandered around the room. Half the conversations were in Chinese. He decided he had better teach.

A strange thing happened: Bian Fu's mother let him sleep over, in the living room. She said it was because of the cold.

After they had used the chamber pot in the kitchen, there came upon them a quiet, and they sat within the winter night, breathing; a settling-down period. The last tangerines were shared. Er Bao finally fell asleep in Bian Fu's arms and she was carried into the bedroom and covered up. The uncle ceased his voluble spirit of reverie and went inward, working within the weight of the *baijiu* he'd drunk, a last strategy before sleep. Bian Fu absently cracked *guazir* between intent teeth and spat out the shells.

Jia, he thought. Family.

They, the Han, sat cold in their four-walled home, digesting, *mi fan* clinging to their stomach linings, sensing each other's fatigue as they drifted towards sleep.

"What is this on TV?" Jeff asked. "It just seems to go on and on and on. Song after song after song after dance after dance..."

"It's called *All-Night Dance Party*," said Bian Fu.

"Oh."

Chen Jie swept the floor of peels and butts, of shells and bones. They carried around bedding, shifted furniture.

Bian Fu stretched, got up and loaded the coal stove with the long tongs.

"You should learn how to do this," she said to him.

Chen Jie began weeping, complaining, weeping, complaining, inconsolable about some injustice earlier in the day. Bian Fu and her mother scoffed at her. This took Jeff aback. They would have none of it. Wouldn't even countenance her complaints. They just mocked her. She gathered up her bedroll and, still sniffling, crept into the other room. The uncle lit the last smoke of the evening and watched it burn towards his fingers. Outside there was the wind and the scrape and bang and thunk of someone in the compound locking the metal gate.

A few days later, Christmas dawned, overcast and stinging cold. Jeff bicycled through the outdoor market. He did not see three ships come sailing in. He bought a casserole for Bian Fu's mother, a bottle of *baijiu* for the uncle, and a snakeskin-patterned scarf for Bian Fu.

When he arrived, Chen Jie was lugging garbage bags across the courtyard and dumping them at the gate. The bags were full of soft toys and clothes and she was off to sell them at the market. Wang Furen was going to make a *jingli*, a businesswoman, out of her yet. Chen Jie snickered, predictably, when he greeted her. Bian Fu was at school; the uncle was sitting around watching TV. The uncle was always sitting around watching TV. Bian Fu's mother was in Bing He. It did not feel like Christmas at all.

There was a TV drama on. There was always a TV drama on. This one was no sillier than the rest. Bian Fu bustled in from the cold, pecked Jeff's cheek, and went back outside to cook. The show took place in Moscow and was cleverly filmed so it appeared that the sole denizens of that northern city, secure in their vans and their padded jackets, were Chinese. They held tête-à-têtes with the Kremlin in the background. They argued about money in their warm apartments.

The uncle lay back on the couch. He would soon have to leave for his cab-driving job, Jeff knew.

A landscape painter, exiled rebel in a jean jacket and sideburns, painted an Orthodox church in a Western style; in his soulful eyes there pulsed a Bitter Mile Affliction. Jeff wondered what the other Foreign Experts were up to this Christmas, then remembered — they were drinking their faces off in the bars near Bei Da University.

Bian Fu came in and offered him something glutinous, hot and moundy-mushy in a bowl.

"What's this? It smells like chocolate."

"That's what you bought yesterday," Bian Fu said, "I had to cook them for a half-hour."

"I thought you ate them raw."

They weren't bad. Chewy-chocolate-sugar balls in rice mush.

Meanwhile, on screen, things were heating up.

Two Chinese in parkas by a roadway talked very seriously, so seriously their faces hardly moved. One handed the other some money. This caused a rebuke. In the next scene, the older man handed the money to a woman in her bedroom; she went crazy, hurling the bills across the room and weeping inconsolably. She looked a little like Chen Jie.

"She doesn't want the money, she wants him," he managed to communicate to the uncle, who sat up straighter, as if now fully convinced of Jeff's stupidity.

"*Dui*," he said, and Jeff studied his eyes. Would the uncle agree with Jeff's application of this moral to his, their situation? What did that *Dui* agree with?

When the uncle left for work, he looked at Jeff balefully, expecting him to leave too, then at Bian Fu, and they didn't budge. The uncle shrugged. The lovers will spend the afternoon together and there's nothing I can do, he seemed to be thinking.

In place of carols they had the English Beijing FM station, which employed Australian DJs to announce Michael Bolton songs; in place of family, he supposed, they had each other, and the strangest Christmas he had had in a long time began to unfold.

Bian Fu unwrapped her scarf and admired it, modelling it at the full-length mirror. Then He Dao from next door came over with her baby, and showed them the soft, white flakes on the baby's scalp and tongue. He Dao asked for old tea leaves she would steep in warm water and use that liquid to wash her baby's tongue. The baby struggled with its perception of the ceiling. Jeff liked the baby — it was unlikely to notice he was a foreigner. They sat. Morning's dull cold was giving way to a warmer afternoon but the *siheyuan* retained the chill. He Dao fed her baby and asked Jeff several questions about Christmas, without any interest in the culture of Christmas, no questions about Jesus or Christmas trees. She wanted to know what foreigners did on Christmas. "They eat," Jeff said. "That is just like us Chinese," she said. Of course they were, thought Jeff. What else was there to be? In spite of his slight annoyance, he liked He Dao; she had the natural ability to be in a room with people and demand nothing from them; her talk was always rapid but offered purely, for the sheer joy of the exchange; but he wanted time with Bian Fu and wished she would go away.

She did.

Bian Fu shut and locked the door.

She turned the TV off.

She unpinned her hair, let it fall.

Their hands made a moist knot as they went to the bedroom, locking that door too.

He ran his tongue over her full lower lip and the beseechment in her eyes blossomed deep, burnt brown. She pulled on his ears as he unbuttoned her shirt. "*Lao gong, Lao gong*," she whispered, Husband. As they lay down, the sweets-seller in the street was far away crying, *Yi kuai wu, yi kuai wu le.*

In the aftermath of Yunnan cigarettes and peeled mandarins, Bian Fu took out a small photo album. She touched each page, and appeared sad, almost in tears. She spent a long time looking at the pictures, saying nothing.

"What's going on?" Jeff said. "I'm interested in what your feeling is."

Not until after she had gone through the whole album did she hand it to him. It was a series of pictures of her and her family: standing outside a police cruiser wearing winter clothes, Bian Fu with her head on her father's knee, Bian Fu looking unsure of herself outside Bing He University with a graduation cap on, cross-legged on the carpet in the family home with Wang Mei Hua, her niece. In all the photos the absent husband was to be inferred behind the lens.

As he pondered how to respond, a tape of student folk songs was still playing.

Yin wei yi ge ren, yi ge jia
Ah, bu tai rong yi...
Because one person, one home
Ah, it's not so easy...

"I don't understand your feeling about your family. Are you worried that you will lose them? I don't understand how the Chinese traditional family works. You will have to explain."

"I miss my *jia*."

"Are you missing your husband?"

"Bah! No. It is my home."

"Home is very important," Jeff said, "and you haven't lost that. Your family still loves you."

"I thought you wanted to know something about Chinese culture, Chinese traditional culture," she said.

"Yes, that's true."

"Well, here's your chance."

He adopted what he hoped was an attentive attitude.

"Even in the village with peasants in China the feeling is the same. First people build a home, and then they have a family." She sat up. "It is reasonable for me to think about wanting an apartment in Beijing."

"Yes, it's reasonable, but we have other things to think about first."

"Before I met you I was used to one kind of life; now I have to learn a whole different way of life. You don't expect me to not be Chinese? Do you?"

"No, I don't. But I do expect you to consider our circumstances."

"Many many beautiful Chinese women have to face this issue of being loved or choosing an easy life. If you leave China I know I will have a deep sense of shame. I will leave Beijing — maybe I will go to *Nanbian*. In Guangdong there are many beautiful clothes-es, and many young Chinese women do not have to work. A rich man will pay for them to live. There are so many of them. In Guangdong it is said, *san san bu, bie mei nu.*"

"What does that mean?"

"Walk three steps and there's another beautiful woman."

"So why don't you go? Go now. If that's what you want, go now."

"Ah — no."

They noticed they were both staring at the same wad of one-hundred-kuai notes on the bedside table.

"Oh, gee," she said, "I wonder whose money this is?"

She took back the photo album. "Here I was a very different woman. This was after my first boyfriend left me. Always he said I will never leave you and he left me. I did not know what sort of things to say at that time."

The picture was a summer scene of the Wang women at a feast of some sort — Wang Furen, her sister, another aunt. Their arms were brown and their plates were loaded with melons and grapes.

"You know I cried when I first left my hometown."

Right then, he was aware of his deep fatigue. He was thousands of miles away from his own family. His daughter was tossing and turning in her excited expectation of Santa Claus, and he was missing it; he was far away in a strange land, listening to someone else's disappointments. He kept this to himself.

Bian Fu blew her nose.

"What do you want me to do, promise you that we'll have an apartment in Beijing and one in Victoria? We can't afford it and you know it. Not if you're not working."

"It is very hard for a young Chinese woman break the traditional."

Bian Fu turned over onto her stomach, and slid the photo album away. "Tell me your dream of our future life."

"We get to know each other better. We marry and love each other deeply. Maybe we live here for a while, maybe we live in Canada, with my daughter. Maybe we have our own child." He knew it by heart.

"Yes, maybe."

"Maybe you should get divorced first."

Her bottom lip came out.

He went into the kitchen to get another tangerine. The tape with the students singing their earnest dreams of returning to their *jias* had clicked off. He felt a dreadful hiatus; it was that part of the early evening in Beijing when the fog, the cold, crept out of the walls. Move forward, Jeff thought, we have to find a way to move forward; it is what humans expect, day becomes night, narratives move forward, when you get on a bus you will arrive sometime, and then you will shout *Dao Le!*

But they seemed to be stuck there in the *siheyuan*.

As he turned in the kitchen searching for the bag of tangerines, a motion in the outer wall stopped him. What he *thought* was the outer wall. He regarded it closely; it had the form of a human limb. This disoriented him. Yes, there was a shape. A head shape. There was crouching or sitting on a bed going on in there. There was a *person* behind the screen, which overwrote his idea of the total privacy they had been sharing. The screen was painted over. There was clearly another apartment he had been unaware of. Their conversation was mostly in English, so being overheard didn't seriously bother him; it was the revelation of something basic, totally overlooked, that shook him. He found the oranges and returned to the bedroom.

"I never knew there was another apartment here," he said, handing Bian Fu a tangerine.

"Yes, my mother rents that part of the *siheyuan* to some young people. It is very small. I think they are students. We never see them." She laughed. "They spend a lot of time in bed."

She had turned on the radio again, with the Australian DJs introducing bad MOR muzak. Jeff imitated the DJs. "Hello out there on this do-right Christmas day in swinging Bei-jing...good on ya, Zhu Rong Ji. Got a call in from Roger in San Li Tur, wants to hear 'I Saw Mommy Kissing Santa Claus.' No worries, Roger. Here it is..."

Bian Fu stood on the bed and shifted her hips, fingers in the air, and shook her bellybutton go-go-girl style. Then she changed the station.

"Today on *English Hour* we are going to listen to one of the most popular and enchanting stories of the English-speaking world, *Cinderella*. Now, Cinderella was a good little girl who was always helping her family with the chores around the house; she had two ugly and unkind stepsisters and a wicked stepmother who were never satisfied with what Cinderella did. Every day from sunup to sundown Cinderella had a lot of work to do. She had to wash the dishes, scrub the kitchen floor, carry water from the well, cook the morning, noon and evening meals, and mend her stepsisters' clothes..."

"This is my favourite story," said Bian Fu. She hugged her knees and settled in to listen.

"Oh, it is, is it?"

"Yes, I heard the story a long time ago and it has always been my favourite."

"Would that be," he said smugly, "because a man comes along and solves all of Cinderella's problems?"

They stared at each other.

"Ah, no. It is my favourite story because the Prince and Cinderella love each other. They get a chance to be together. They love each other!"

She was furious.

He left shortly thereafter, long before coach and four became pumpkin and mice.

He stopped at the canal to have a smoke with a group of Beijing policemen who were chatting in a circle in their huge winter coats. "Merry Christmas," he said. "So, you guys busy tonight?"

They all laughed. After a minute, they lost interest in him. Who was this guy?

Who else but a foreigner would seek out the police for company?

In the days that followed, Jeff dithered. He did not know what to do. He phoned the Department Chair again and said he needed more time to decide, went back to his room and made out elaborate lists, looked intensely at the pictures on his bookshelf, went for walks around the campus with his head full of contradictory and extreme notions. He saw himself and Bian Fu eating an apple dangling from the ceiling, as in the Chinese marriage celebration; he saw them walking hand in hand in downtown Victoria. There was nothing to do in Beijing; the divorce would happen or not: he could not influence it. He refused all contact with the foreigners on his floor, offering only the most perfunctory of greetings; he ate alone in the cafeteria and could not sit still for more than a few minutes; he paced around in his room, but finally he decided to go back to Canada.

When Jeff told Bian Fu, she didn't say anything at first. They were in the courtyard at her place; she was unpinning frozen sheets and shirts from the line. She took the news without expression, as if she knew already.

"I expected too much from you," she said finally. "When you leave, I will have to face a lot of things on my own."

"Yes."

"It is not easy being a beautiful young Chinese woman. Beautiful young Chinese women have to face this issue — to love or to have easy life."

"What's an easy life?"

"In Bing He I work at the hospital. Very easy. I live at my father's house and have enough money for myself: I just buy books I like and some beauty cream."

She gathered the washing from the line and went in and dumped it on the bed and collapsed face down in the stiff sheets, her shoulder blades heaving. She did not mention his decision again for some time.

Not long after, despite or maybe because of their impending separation, he had one moment of absolute bliss in Beijing. It came after Western New Year's Eve at the pub near some technical institution. They had gone for drinks with Jin Zhong, Bian Fu's friend, and Jeff had gotten slightly drunk. They listened to indifferently performed Chinese folk music and chatted with Jin Zhong until midnight, when they raised their glasses and brought in the New Year. Then it was time to go.

On the way home, they walked the bike through a large park, all blues and shades of black, two figures joined in the litmus of willows. They found a bench and sat in the comforting curve of the lake, the moon bright, their breath twinning and disappearing in the cold. Neither spoke. He put his arm around her; she let her head rest on his shoulder. Jeff felt all the weight of all the lovers who had ever met there, and then it lifted, as though the lovers had never been, and Bian Fu stirred and kissed his neck.

The road beside the canal was limitless ink as he pedalled, fatigued, towards Kick Fish County. Bian Fu's arms slipped around his waist and her head rested between his shoulder blades.

This was his woman. They were on their way home.

Everyone was sleeping when he dropped her off.

On the way out of Kick Fish he had to piss, but when he came out of the public outhouse at the end of the alley, two bright lights were hovering, which lowered, and a male voice said, "*Shei ya?*"

Well, who was he?

He touched his nose. "*Wo?*"

They were two policemen, an older, stout one, frowning, and a younger, slim one, smiling. "Who are you?" Stout repeated.

"I work at Jian Hua University. I am a Canadian."

"Do you have your passport?"

"No."

"What are you doing here so late at night?"

"I was accompanying my friend home from the bar."

"Boyfriend or girlfriend?"

They were clearly at a new level here. He hesitated, and they saw him hesitate. He didn't want Bian Fu involved in this, but he was out of his depth. With his limited Chinese he could hardly lie to them convincingly. And why should he lie to the police? Which was, come to think of it, a distinctly un-Chinese thought.

"Girlfriend."

"Let's go see her," Slim said.

"Okay."

"You must get off your bicycle," said Stout.

As they walked back through Kick Fish, Slim was convivial, "You're not from Quebec, are you?"

"No."

"I knew some Canadians from Quebec once."

"That's nice."

They got to the door.

"*Shei ya?*" He heard Bian Fu's voice.

"It's me, and a couple of friends," Jeff said.

Bian Fu didn't blink on seeing the two cops. They started grilling her in Chinese, and he could make out New Year's Eve, near Bei Da, my friend, bicycle. It all sounded quite reasonable.

Then they were entering the Wang household. Thank God her mother's not here, Jeff thought. The uncle sat up in his blankets, eyes wide. Chen Jie slunk out from the bedroom.

"And who are you?" Slim asked Bian Fu.

"I live here, this is my mother's place."

Jeff felt cold. He was an ID card, a lousy *hukou*, away from going to jail. The policemen were obviously suspicious, perhaps thinking Bian Fu was a prostitute. They asked her, "Where is your mother? Why were you out so late?"

"New Year's is a very important festival to Western people," said Bian Fu.

Jeff offered Slim a cigarette.

Chen Jie cringed in her comforter.

"Let's see your ID," said Stout.

Jeff's eyes focused on nothing. Wang Bian Fu. Place of Registration: Hebei Province. Marital Status: Married. Husband's Name: *Han Han Han.*

She went back in the bedroom and returned with her student card. Slim barely looked at it.

"Let's go, there's nothing here," he said.

"You — we'll escort you out of the neighbourhood," said Stout. He waved his torch.

"Talk to you tomorrow," Jeff said.

"*Zai jian,*" said Bian Fu.

"You know," said Stout, wheeling at the door to address them all, "a number of people have been killed in this neighbourhood lately. Everything we have done we have done for your safety."

"For our safety," they all repeated.

They took him to the high-road and told him to be careful. And that his Chinese was very good.

They were holding hands and walking their bikes on a sunny afternoon, snow glinting in the roadside fields, not saying much, as if all the circumstances that made their love possible had dropped away, were done with, and a truer feeling had emerged; their hearts could touch and there was less need to speak. Or there were more things to keep to yourself, Jeff thought. In any case they were not unhappy. They did not talk about his departure or her divorce.

That's when they ran into her relatives from Bing He.

They came trundling out of a *hutong*, their arms linked, improbably whistling a tune together, Mom and Dad and Cousin Wang Xue Nian, the perfect family out for a Sunday stroll, in identical windbreakers. They were so happy to be out with their son, newly come to study in Beijing and stay at Wang Furen's, that they beamed. The kid was rangy and wore glasses.

Bian Fu started waving and yelling.

Jeff was shocked. Wang Mom and Dad greeted him with genuine interest and friendliness. Wang Dad shook his hand and looked him up and down, laughed at the odd tension, for he knew that virtually anything he could say wouldn't be understood, but told Jeff, "It's a nice day, isn't it?" and, still gripping his hand, clapped him on the shoulder with manly force. Bian Fu and Wang Aunt were already tittering and giggling. "They want to know if we would like to go shopping with them," said Bian Fu.

So they backtracked to the commercial district of Kick Fish, locked the bikes up, and entered a multi-storey *zhongxin*. Why is it the two characters the Chinese choose to represent "shopping centre" with are "centre" and "heart," Jeff wondered. The floors thronged with other families linking arms and poking noses at, pointing fingers at the makeup, jewellery, knick-knacks, calendars (the Year of the Tiger was fast approaching), candy, ties and belts, purses, woks and pots and pans, ladles, dishes, bikes, bike accessories. All these things. Bian Fu and her aunt stopped to sample Maybelline lipstick. Wang Xue Nian stayed close by his father. The ladies decided on colours, and Wang Dad pulled out his wallet, stuffed with one-hundred-kuai notes.

Then they stopped at a table where a short but energetic fellow was holding a jug of water at a dramatic height, pouring it into a glass. A crowd had gathered as he spilled water onto the table; his voice was loud. "Friends!" he yelled. "Water! Wet, wet!" His hands were very quick. He yanked forth a chamois and, rolling and unfurling it repeatedly to show its compactness and stretch, suitable for any apartment kitchen, he sopped up all the water with a series of short, sharp scrubs and then reached behind him for a bottle of soy sauce. "And that's not all!" He scrunched up the Wonder Rag and made it rear like a cobra, then twisted and wrung it so all the water splooshed into the glass. He held out the rag like a bullfighter's cape, then twirled it away. He shook soy sauce onto the table. People were transfixed. This was the living end of kitchen miracles. Jeff started to giggle, because he wouldn't have paid a second's attention to this kind of demonstration in North America, but here he started to enjoy himself. What an interesting guy. What *chutzpah*. Sooner or later, he'll be selling Miatas.

"*Kan yi kan, kan yi kan*," he chanted, "Look here, look here. With this soy sauce I'll now perform another everyday function of Wonder Rag — anyone want to step forward and verify that this is indeed the obnoxious stainer known as soy sauce? Very good there. Tai Tai, thank you very much. Sauce it is? Lick off those fingers. Thank you…now, Wonder Rag to the rescue." He rolled the rag like a strip of *baozi* dough, stretched it out, pizza'd it up in the air, and flicked it over the soy droplets. He displayed the stained rag. Then he dunked it vigorously in the water, scrunched it up, and wrung it out. Wonder Rag unstained. Virgin. Water murky. "Let's hear it now for Wonder Rag. *Fei chang hao ji le, shi ba?*"

Bian Fu tugged his arm; the others wanted to go look at clothes.

Up the stairs they went, Wang Aunt clutching the Wonder Rag that Wang Uncle had bought her.

All these *things!* Skeins and balls of wool from the Number Three Wool Manufacturing Plant in Changsha. Big colourful quilts hanging beside dowdy padded housecoats. At the skirt section Bian Fu pulled out a corduroy mini and held it to her waist. "Like it?" she asked him. His hand was on his wallet. "Hah!" she huffed and thrust it back. "*Bu haokan*. I don't." The things were multifoliate, infinitely cheerful. Then he saw it.

It was an anomaly among the propped-up saxophones and velvet-cased flutes and silver-stopped oboes in the music section, but it seemed to sing to him from its stand. It shone in the direct centre of the milling crowd, the urgent voices, the green-jacketed *fuwuyuan*, hands always in their pockets, suppressing their yawns. It was a blue guitar. His mouth moved sideways. A blue guitar. Things…the family had started to move off; he grabbed Bian Fu's arm and struggled to say what he suddenly had to say to her; he was ridiculously happy. Things...

"What is it, dear?"

"I feel suddenly very happy, Bian Fu. It is, just, the shopping around, it is like everyday life. It is normal. And I just saw that!"

She was concerned; perhaps he was feeling sick?

"No, no, no. That!"

"It is a guitar."

"It is a blue guitar! *A blue guitar.* Everything is fine. We are together now and having a nice time. Everything is just as it is."

She studied his eyes.

"You see, there is a famous poem by an American poet. It goes, '*The man replied things AS THEY ARE,/ Are changed upon the blue guitar.*' And everything is as it is. And we are shopping. And there is the blue guitar. And everything is fine! I love you. I am very happy."

"Do you want to buy it?" she asked.

"No, no..."

"Come on, Wang Xue Nian need a pair of blue jeans."

The blue guitar got obscured by the throng for a second, but was still there, a bright, robin's-egg blue, as Bian Fu and Jeff moved away. Tears welled in his eyes. He squeezed Bian Fu's hand.

"There are things in the blue guitar?" she asked hesitantly.

"I am happy," he said.

"You are very special," she said. "Come on."

That evening they made *baozi* in the apartment. They got out the huge cutting board and dusted it with flour. With chopsticks, they mixed and mixed and mixed the ample bowl of ground pork, ginger, scallions, sesame oil, and soy sauce. Wang Uncle smoked, his cigarette hanging over the bowl. Then Bian Fu hefted a bo-wu-ling-size ball of dough onto the coffee table and a *baozi*-making bee began; they ripped off chunks and rolled them with their hands into arm-width sausages; then sliced these into cookie-rounds, which they in turn, using miniature pins, rolled out into pancakes a big as a hand. A pile grew and the others set to tweezing a lump of meat mixture onto each palmed pancake. They fluted the dough around the meat with swift tucks and finished each dumpling by pinching the top shut. Jeff's first efforts were not so elegant; they resembled mashed perogies.

"Why is it so difficult for a foreigner?" said Bian Fu.

All this time the conversation turned around Canada — how big? how many people? and yes, how many Chinese lived there? Yes, China was much older than Canada, it had *five thousand years* of tradition. Canada was relatively young; the United States was bad, very, very bad; it was difficult to convey in a few words how bad it was, but those words seemed to do just fine.

"What do you guys do?" asked Jeff.

"Computer company," said Wang Uncle. "She teaches piano. Our son here is a student, study computers."

Wang Furen arranged the *baozi* in bamboo steamers and carried them into the kitchen and placed them over boiling pots. The men lit each other's cigarettes. The women chatted with the women, men with men. "How much does a car cost in Canada? A computer? How much do you make in Canada? One hundred and twenty thousand kuai you make? *Feichang hao...*"

"But, look, it is very expensive to live," said Jeff.

"Yes, like Beijing."

"My mother and Wang Aunt are discussing how much they love their children," said Bian Fu.

"Hmmm."

"My mother just say, All is fair in love and war."

"Yes, um. Do you believe that? I don't believe that."

"Ho, it is true."

"True for you, maybe."

She pouted.

Wang Furen, her hands and arms swaddled in oven mitts and towels, returned bearing *baozi*. Bian Fu scuttled for the bowls of vinegar and soy sauce and chopped garlic. A great cry rose from the Chinese: *chir baozi ba!*

Mouths munching through meat and sauce and pastry.

"Where does your family live?"

My family is very complicated," he said, and Bian Fu kicked him under the coffee table. "Very traditional," he said. "I have a mother in Winnipeg and I — ouch!"

"Jeff says he is very happy to meet you all!"

Wang Bian Fu smiled and offered him more *baozi*.

"The Canadian dollar, is it seven to one *renminbi* or six?"

"How many years you go to university?"

Jeff was fading. Another steamer was plonked before them.

Wang Furen said something. Bian Fu yelped with glee and tugged on his arm. "She say you welcome come to her hometown at Spring Festival!"

He fished around for garlic in the soy sauce. "*Xie xie*," he said politely.

"Except you are not going to be here during Spring Festival," said Bian Fu in English. She picked at her *baozi*. Then she laid down her chopsticks and picked up her knitting.

"What do you think of China? Is China very beautiful? What Chinese cities have you seen? Have you seen Shanghai? Shanghai is very beautiful."

"Bathroom, have to go to bathroom," Jeff managed in Chinese.

He felt woozy. In the *hutong* the mist hung close to the brickwork, about to freeze to it. Several men passed, then turned to stare. He leaned against the wall, and his heart reverberated once, and it spoke, once, in a small, penetrating voice from deep inside him — No — and as he clung to the wall, breathing hard but hardly breathing, he saw one book spine, then two book spines, then shelves and shelves of variegated sideways titles, ramifying, until his lungs were full of the entire contents of a bookstore he'd frequented in Victoria, thousands of miles away, best-sellers and coffee table, literary and new-age, display books face out with their gold medallions for the awards they'd won and remaindered titles in haphazard bins with black marker slashes across the cut-pages, and at Jeff's core, in the middle of this warehouse of type, the word repeated — No.

He sucked in all the charcoal in the *hutong*, coughed, and shook it off.

Back inside, Wang Furen was saying he worked at a university.

"I must go," he told Bian Fu.

"No," she said.

"I'm tired."

"These people are very important to me. When I was a little girl I used to stay at their place. You have to stay for a while."

"I have to go. I'm exhausted."

She said nothing.

Finally he stood up and shook everyone's hand.

"*Xiao xin,*" said Bian Fu when he mounted his bike, "take care."

She was furious.

A week later, Bian Fu's mother had gone away, her uncle had gone away, the relatives had gone away, Er Bao had gone away, Wang Xue Nian was off studying with friends: there was just Jeff and Bian Fu in the *siheyuan.* It was approaching midnight. On TV, a panel show, "The Most Famous and Respectable Young People in Beijing." All couples. There was a cadre and his wife, a policeman in uniform and his wife (not in uniform), a professor and his wife, a businessman and his wife. The natty host asked questions about China's development. The men answered all the questions.

"Young people?" Jeff said. "Some of these people look like they're forty-five."

"Yes, they are about your age," she said. "Why don't you stay over? It is very cold outside. Come on, stay over."

He hesitated.

"Look, what if the other people in the *siheyuan* say something?"

"They won't say anything. Come on. Ah, I can hear my Mother — 'What! *Shui jiao?* I go away and you sleep with him?' And I will say, 'It is not so terrible. It is a very good feeling. You should try it.' Come on."

Forty minutes later they had not moved from the couch, and were slowly kissing.

"I might as well," he said.

BANG BANG BANG.

"Who's that?" said Jeff.

And that is precisely what He Dao, the neighbour, suddenly shouted, her voice ringing through the walls: "*SHEI YA!*"

"Li Hua An," said a small and humble voice.

"That's Li," Bian Fu whispered. "That's my husband."

They sat still.

"*TA MEI ZAI,*" said He Dao.

"She's telling him I'm not in."

"I see," Jeff said. There was no way out. Her husband was on the other side of the door. It was late. Perhaps he was drunk. Perhaps he had a knife. Or a gun.

Jeff's right leg was shaking and shaking; he clamped his hand on it, quelled it.

They heard the husband's back shush along the door and his rear end sit down hard on the step. They heard him breathing. Shifting.

"Come into the bedroom," whispered Bian Fu. A smile played about her lips.

Jeff tried to stand, but his leg was shaking again. "Shit, shit, shit," he said through his teeth, and he took the leg and stamped it on the floor until he could stand. Bian Fu watched him. Then they went into the bedroom and sat on the bed.

"Maybe I let him in and you stay in here."

"No way."

"I can control him. I know how to control him."

"No! Shit, Bian Fu, yes, you've been doing a wonderful job of controlling him. Very, very clever. How many times have you told him not to come around, it's over, and he's still showing up in the dead of night?" He paused, because the answer, None, occurred to him.

Faintly, they heard Li Hua An shift against the door again.

Jeff continued: "Look, if there's trouble, if there's a fight, guess who's going to jail? He's your husband. I'm in trouble, I'm the one going to jail. Not him. Me. No way. It's too volatile a situation."

He lit a cigarette. "Volatile?" said Bian Fu.

"Risky."

"Maybe he brought the documents for the apartment we agree to," she said.

"Maybe he's loading his gun."

"I can control him."

"No!"

They looked into each other's eyes. She lay back on her elbows. After a while, she said, "Jeff, we are in here doing our best, and he is out there doing his best, because none of we has any other way. *Mei banfa.*"

She seemed very pleased by this.

He looked around the room anxiously. It all came to this. The tangerine peels on the desk. The wardrobe stuffed with clothes that nobody wore. The pile of quilts on the bed. The pale flower pattern on the radiator-shield. This was where he was going to die. He saw Melissa five thousand miles away petting her dog.

Suddenly, he sat up on the bed.

"Bian Fu, okay, open the door."

"No, I think we should wait."

"No, open it. I want to see this guy."

"He is doing his best, but you shouldn't worry. I love you, not him. We are doing our best, kind of adventure, all doing our best. *Tian ah,* I'm tired." She yawned. "Come here and hold me."

Bian Fu's eyes opened, then closed.

"He's gone," she said a while later.

"I'm going."

"Wait, wait a while, please."

Her hand was smoothing and smoothing his shirt on his shoulder.

"Okay," she said finally. "*Ai wah,* I have to go bathroom." She searched for toilet paper under the bed, found it, and they went to the door.

The courtyard was quiet. The knives lay gleaming on the food-prep table in the moonlight. As they swung open the metal gate, their breath bloomed enormous before them.

"I'll talk to you tomorrow," she said.

"Do you feel safe?" he said. "I'll come with you to the washroom."

"It's okay," she said.

Jeff got on his bike. When he turned, she was standing in the *hutong*, sleepily waving, the loose end of the toilet paper twirling to the ground.

The Year of the Tiger imminent, the shops and stalls outside Lao He Gong, the Tibetan temple, burgeoned with posters, calendars and stuffed tigers of all shapes and sizes. Bian Fu and Jeff wandered around the temple grounds, just as the Tibetan monks wandered in their saffron robes. It struck Jeff that he and Bian Fu, and the monks, were in their shuffling circuits both answering the question, How long to wait? — for a free Tibet, for Bian Fu's divorce — with As long as it takes.

They lit incense and kneeled before the Buddha, side by side.

Outside the gate, a vendor pounced on Jeff thrusting a scroll with the character LOVE in his face.

"I've got it," Jeff said. "Love. *Ai.*"

"Why did you want to come here again?" said Bian Fu, clinging to his arm.

"To pray. To pray in a Chinese way."

"Pray for what, *ai ren*?"

"I'm not sure," he said. "A normal life?"

Chapter Nine

The full force of Beijing's winter descended on the Jian Hua campus. The *fuwuyuan* sat behind her desk in a duck-hunting vest. Jeff's tires were perpetually flat. The meagre snow, filthy with coal soot, lay over the hard earth, and the trees were stark and suspended from the heavens from etiolated twigs. His gloves were useless as he rode to class. His hands ached. He required four or five dumplings in the early morning, and two glasses of hot, sweetened milk.

There they were, the Han, thought Jeff, dancing on their frozen island in the early morning, wielding swords and banners, the Han, their paper lanterns, the dead snakes at the bottom of eighty-eight-ounce demijohns of *maotai*, how splendid, the renewable armature of the Beijing opera performers' poses, the deep magic and binding tremors of being Chinese. Everything frozen in the gesture of identity — manners, food, family relations, but somehow ever undulant, the stomping Reeboks underneath the rippling, rearing, many-manned dragon.

They're just people, thought Jeff. People doing push-ups in the morning. Save your clichés for Canada.

Lighten up.

In his dormitory room, the wind infiltrated the considerable gaps between window and frame. His sheets of Chinese characters broke from their flimsy tape moorings and drifted onto the floor. The sun set shortly after four-thirty, in a chemical roar, having sucked the blasted breath out of fifteen million souls for its eerie combustive red; in its wavering depths Jeff sensed the stuck-on-one-station flicker of their infantile faith in it. He waited patiently for the hot water to come on, he marked papers, he went for short but tiring walks around campus. The workers in overalls, toothless, patrolled the lily ponds in flat-bottomed boats, breaking up the ice, and fished the stinking, black mass of lily-dreck out of the ponds; it would be recycled, plowed back into the earth. Nothing was wasted. The cabbage on the dinner plates in the *shitang* retained yesterday's gloss. It was amazing what a little oil could do.

He spent a great deal of his time eating. Digesting.

Robert was not around. A couple of the other foreign experts had gone travelling. The dormitory hall floor shone like a tomb. And Tabitha was depressed.

He sat in her room and listened to her agonize about her teaching.

"I can't seem to get them to talk."

"It's cultural, Tabitha. They're not used to talking. It's not you."

"It's a total failure," she said. "I'm not a good teacher."

"Do you go to class?"

"Yes."

"Do you try?"

"Yes, I try. I guess." Her eyes were red.

"Then you're not a total failure," he said. "Look, it's an interaction, right?"

"I should have prepared better. I should have thought more about it before I came. I'm letting them down. I'll never be any good."

"You're doing a good job," he said.

But he felt like saying, "Everything we *lao wai* are doing here is a total failure, because we persist in our notion that we have something to teach. We have nothing to teach these people. Their own experience has taken them to the human depths and the human heights. Our experience has been padded by shallow luxury. They are not learning from us, they are practising their English. We must relinquish our CD collections. We must give up our Gap apparel. Only after we survive the levelling humilities of the village will we ever have an effect on Chinese life. Thank you. I have managed to construct these thoughts without the benefits of Princeton. I shall still be available to rewrite your lecture on 'Ode to the West Wind' on short notice, because you are my countryman, sort of."

Instead, he patted her shoulder and told her to come see him if she needed to talk. She nodded mechanically.

As for his own students, Wang Fang and her crew trooped up to the raised platform one chilly morning and performed a miserable farce in which she, the insistent housewife, talked her "husband," and three or four others, into quitting smoking. She lectured them through her giggles. Smoking was not good healthy. It cost too much money. Maybe if we quit, said the "husband," we will have more money for drinking. Ah, no!

This was great fun. The other skits had similar structures — the comic Chinese family, hectoring *lao pu* and useless, intractable *lao gong*, had a conversation on:

1) vacuum cleaners, their excellence and many features.
2) their child's education, spare no expense.
3) whether it is better to live in the village or the city.

And Jeff enjoyed these skits immensely. This was more like it. Instead of running around the classroom pleading with them to talk, here was vitality, here life, here laughter. He caught himself smiling. Was this China? This was China.

Outside the campus wall, the dark-skinned people with sooty faces crouched near the bus queues, their clothes tatters, their teeth a legend, their palms upwards. They sang, they played fiddles, they talked to themselves. They had no place: the city was vast but miserly towards them; when they were told by guards and police to move on, they did, heavily, as if they bore between their shoulder blades a fatal mark stamped on them from birth, far away, long ago. He smiled sympathetically, finding in them a remote and holy silence, a hunger alien to him, what he would never know, for he was leaving.

He rode more energetically to Bian Fu's place; he was going back to Canada; had to see her as much as possible. He blasted through crossroads and swerved out from behind trucks; he yelled out "AN QUAN, AN QUAN" as he parted the bands of student cyclists; more than once he narrowly avoided head-on collisions with the more sedate Chinese riders in the narrow *hutongs* of Kick Fish County. He had learned a few tricks: how to regain balance by pushing off the brick walls. Nobody paid any attention to him. As a foreigner he was allowed a wide margin of behaviour. Anything short of carrying a gun was considered probably a North American custom, and dismissed. Bian Fu's uncle actually waved and greeted him with a big smile now that he knew Jeff was leaving.

"How was your father?" he asked Bian Fu, for she had taken a couple of days and gone to Bing He.

Bian Fu was sullen. "He say, 'It will be hard for you to marry the foreigner.'"

He laughed. "Come on, let's go to my place. I give up."

"When you leave I will have to face many things."

"*Xing,*" he said. "Yep."

The *fuwuyuan* ignored Bian Fu now; they were simply aware of her passage up the stairs, above their knitting, their newspapers. Jeff and Bian Fu were in bed once and there was a knock on the door, and a paper slid underneath, then the scamper of many feet and a furious giggling.

With a great groan he went and got it. Bian Fu said, "The notice, it say we are using too much heat."

Like a nincompoop he looked at the heater settings.

"It is their Chinese way, their nasty little joke," said Bian Fu. She was crying.

"Honey, it's okay. Okay, okay. Look, we got used to it, didn't we? All those people staring at Xiang Shan? It doesn't matter any more."

"It is unfair. We don't have any other way. We never have another way."

She sobbed. She touched his eyebrows, his cheekbones. "Jeff? What if we had a baby?"

He sighed. "Bian Fu, we don't know one another well enough yet to have a baby."

"I guess not. I accept it."

The hot water gurgling in the pipes, the blast of taps throughout the dorm because it was four o'clock and the sun was setting.

"The baby would have your difficult nose and my hair," she said.

"What would you call him?"

"Xiang Ye, Fragrant Tea Leaf," she murmured, and fell asleep.

Jeff showed up one evening and Bian Fu was in a dither, rushing around looking for clothes-es to wear — she had an interview for a job that her sister had set her up with. "That's great. Why didn't you call me? I would have stayed at Jian Hua and marked papers..."

"You can stay or you can go. It's your decision." She was distracted, hardly looked at him.

She came back four hours later — she had gotten the job, and a beeper, which she showed off as though it were an extension of her personality. Wang Furen made her sit down on the couch and replay the interview.

"And was he good looking?"

"Ah — no," said Bian Fu in a clenched way that strongly suggested Yes.

"And how much money does he make every month?" Wang Furen said.

"Ten thousand kuai."

"That's very impressive," Jeff said. "Can he read and write?"

They ignored him. She was telling her mother about the interview: some quiddity about the sisters' names, a bit of Chinese chat-up. He went out for a piss.

When he got back, Bian Fu was resolutely smoking a cigarette on the couch, and her mother was looking on in mixed amazement and reproach. Bian Fu never smoked cigarettes in front of her mother; she almost never smoked in front of Jeff. Her legs were crossed and her face defiant. Her mother looked like a migraine was setting in — her daughter smoking a cigarette? In front of the foreigner?

"See, I told you," Jeff said, "she's not a useless person. Congratulations, Bian Fu, you got a job."

Bian Fu nodded, as though he were an unnecessary postscript to a highly satisfactory moment.

"See, Wang Furen, your daughter is very clever. *Ta shi hen congming.*"

Wang Furen's eyes narrowed. She looked her daughter up and down, and muttered, "*Hen congming, ai wa, hen congming...* Yes, very clever, all right," with such intense irony that Jeff recoiled.

Wang Furen returned to the grand theme of Bian Fu's uselessness.

"Well, you know her," said Jeff.

This fired her up. "Of course I know her! I gave birth to her! I ought to know her!"

"Okay, so you know her."

"Look, Je Fu," her voice lowered, "you have a lovely daughter in Canada."

"Yes, thank you."

Then he, ignoring Bian Fu, reached out and tapped Wang Furen's knee. "*San Cong Si De*," he said smugly. He was pleased to have remembered the Confucian maxim denoting the three rights and four responsibilities of females to husbands and other related males; and he knew its male counterpart, *San Guan Wu Chang*.

Bian Fu's mother was surprised, but gathered herself with a resolve to further browbeat her daughter. She loved it; she was reminded of something so powerfully true there was no need to repeat it, but repeat it she did, because it gave her strength and purpose. "*San Cong Si De!* " she wagged her finger at Bian Fu. Then she turned the finger on him. "*San Guan Wu Chang!* "

Bian Fu filed her nails.

Bian Fu said, "*San Cong Si De!* Bah. I never did this thing in my marriage; why should I do it now?"

Jeff just looked at her. And looked at her and looked at her.

The last morning before exams he strode into class and said, "Look, guys, one of the students in my other class wrote an essay about the cultural differences between Chinese students and North American students. I would like to hear from you guys about these differences."

There was an embarrassed silence.

A materials engineer stuck up his hand. "*Lao shi*? I have seen Western people movies, Western people always say *love*, they love this person, they love that person. In China we almost never use this word."

The student paused, thinking, "We use the word *love* to describe love of country. 'I love you, Mother and Father.' This is a sentence I have never uttered."

Jeff surveyed the silent faces.

Then a student at the back of the class said, "You believe that there is a difference, and we believe that there is no difference, and perhaps that is one difference."

Jeff flinched; maybe it was true.

"Okay, class, everybody sing out loud, let them hear you in Hebei province," he pointed to the blackboard.

> TRAILERS FOR SALE OR RENT
> ROOMS TO LET FIFTY CENTS
> NO BOOZE, NO PHONE, NO PETS
> I AIN'T GOT NO CIGARETTES

"Is he bragging or complaining? Why does he talk about what he doesn't have?" came the first question.

"I'm glad you asked that. Many wouldn't." Blank stares. "He is describing a way of life. He is romanticizing it a little. Do you know romanticize?" He wrote *lang man* on the board — romantic. This was not quite right. *Lang man* might describe young men in China who don't have jobs and wear their hair long and tied back and usually have guitars. Perhaps Jeff meant something closer to *liu mang*: a ruffian, a hooligan, someone in a soiled suit with a concealed knife.

"There is no woman in the song. How is this romantic?"

Wang Fang's head bowed instantly, eyes on her pens, hair brushing the desktop.

"He is making his life sound more romantic than it really is; it is a philosophy of pride in a way, simple pride, he has nothing but is proud of it because he has his freedom, and yet he is conscious of what it has cost him," Jeff said.

"Trailers?"

"A trailer is a portable house."

"He carries a house with him?"

"No. This is used to portray a way of life. This is the only type of house that this man can afford when he is in a town."

He was boring himself. Surely the song was not that deep.

"Shall we go on?"

AH BUT TWO HOURS OF PUSHING BROOM
BUYS AN EIGHT BY TWELVE FOUR-BIT ROOM
I'M A MAN OF MEANS BY NO MEANS
KING OF THE ROAD.

This verse brought a flurry of questions. They scribbled in their notebooks. Pushing broom was easy enough — but Jeff thought of the moss in a Chinese poem he vaguely remembered, moss so thick the lover's footsteps remained in it and could not be swept away.

"Excuse me. He means and he does not mean? What is his meaning, exactly?"

"It is a play on words, a pun, a bit of the irony of language. A man of means is a rich man. 'By no means' means 'in no manner of speaking.' There is no way we can describe him as rich, and yet he is the King of the Road, *Wang Da Jie*. It is a paradox. The song invites us to examine the meaning of richness. It calls out to those who are comfortable to examine the so-called richness of their lives. It plays on the human longing for travel, recklessness, wanderlust."

There was no way they could say he was not filling their scribblers, he thought.

It is a Kiwanis Club wet dream, he thought.

It is a mangy bit of Muzak.

He saw the road-crown in the Manitoba winter, snow blowing over it, the boarded windows of an old prairie hotel, a public park in Istanbul as autumn was growing colder, a guitar laid on a bench in a German train station.

He shook his hair out.

"Excuse me, *Lao shi*? In the other verse you say he takes trains from place to place. He has no home, right?"

"That's right."

"He is a peasant?"

"In a way."

"He is a peasant without a village, is this true?"

He paused.

"Yes, that's true," he said, "he is a peasant without a village."

"How can this be? All peasants have villages."

"He doesn't."

"*Zhen chiguai*. Very strange." The student shook his head and put away his notebook. The bell rang. Jeff stood on the platform a long time, gazing at his chalky fingerprints on the lectern.

Jeff ruminated in his room, studying his return plane ticket: How Chinese, to return to the homeland. *Lao wai.*

Then he rode over to Bian Fu's. He did not see the eyes as they stared, the fingers as they pointed, or the voices as they cried out in his wake. When he got there, the whole family was in the living room, anticipating a hotpot feast. They were shifting their feet in the cold apartment, waiting for him.

He settled in on the couch beside Wang Xue Nian, the cousin. As soon as he did, the cousin was told get up off the couch now and do it, and so Wang pushed his glasses up and fetched the propane tank, which he set beside the coffee table. "Now get it going!" yelled Wang Furen. She came out of the kitchen bearing the hotpot casserole, half full of water, and showed him where to attach the tank. Bian Fu was patiently chopping bok choy.

"Can I help?" said Jeff.

"No, no, no, no."

Chen Jie entered, struggling with the garbage bag of toys she had failed to sell at the market; or perhaps this was the garbage bag of toys she had traded up to by ridding the *siheyuan* of old baby clothes; it was difficult to keep track of the commercial strategies Wang Furen put her up to at the market.

"Chen *Jingli, ni hao*," Jeff said.

Everyone howled. She blushed. He had taken to calling her Chen Big Businesswoman, and could never tell if it embarrassed her, her nature was so cheerful. Bian Fu handed her a half-frozen bag and told her to go out in the courtyard and prepare the squid. Wang Uncle, cheerful because Jeff was leaving in four days, and he would no longer have to stay up past his bedtime explaining dumb soap operas to him, sat with a cigarette in his mouth, slicing lamb into thin wafers. The dishes came out: heaps of onions, bigger-than-usual shrimp, *sui choi*, *baixin*, oyster-mushrooms; the coffee table vanished under the food, the hotpot started to boil. Then Er Bao rushed in and tripped over the gas line, nearly overturning tank and table.

Han-demonium, Jeff thought. Voices began to vie, to carp, shrill and joyous in their practised ire, they assigned blame and pointed fingers, tongues flew, suggesting more strategic arrangements of gas line and chairs. Everyone enjoyed the chance to yell. Jeff never understood their need to yell at each other, so kept silent. And there was another reason: he had a low-grade headache, probably because of the ever-present coal smoke in the *siheyuan*.

Bian Fu, one hand on hip, was telling her mother something that had probably occurred years ago.

The uncle calmly sliced away. The things in Beijing had the final word, Jeff thought: all the edges and corners of the apartment gleamed hard against his aching eyes, and they summoned further shapes — bicycle seats forever loose, the TV's occult behaviour, revenge of the sputtering hot water tap — as though these reified their time together, deeming these Beijing people things themselves, the transitory flotsam in the slow lanes, making them more fully human, bought and sold.

He shifted on the couch. Things in Beijing. He liked that. He liked its tinny ring.

The subways, the buses, the plastic-coated couch.

The tigers grinning from the ends of canes.

Bian Fu's two frontmost teeth had notches in them, from enthusiastic childhood *guazir* cracking and splitting. She was washing cabbage now, hands wet, shining.

Er Bao brandished her plastic knife. She called the baby next door *nankan*, difficult to look at, ugly. She up and called a one-month-old *nankan*. She jabbed an apple with the knife.

All these things we carried, used, slouched around on, our bodies got along with. We would get by with each other, no problem. You had to watch the things, though. The full-length mirror leaned against the wall.

Bian Fu stood close to the mirror as she prinked and drew fine lines along her eyebrows, and poked with her pinky at her lipstick, her face, as usual, a study in concentrated calm. Then she went into the bedroom where Wang Xue Nian sat waiting with the brush; he stood behind her in the darkened room and brushed her hair out. It was what they did, *jie* and *di*, older aunt and younger cousin. They were devoted to each other. The brush was purple, with plastic antennae. The *jiazi* he fastened for her was a glittery swirl, a silver leaf in torque, and her hair fell from it, weightless in its black splendour, unrainbow. Now Bian Fu was ready to get dressed.

As he slouched, gazing around the apartment, he realized: this was all there was. This cut-out-sheet-metal coal stove. These many plastic hangers. When winter had begun, the uncle had plunked down four bags of rice in a corner of the kitchen; they grew immensely symbolic in their corner. This was the winter supply of rice. Sometimes others in the *siheyuan* came to bargain for it; and were allowed a portion if Bian Fu's mother approved. One neighbour showed up once too often with her kid when she didn't feel like cooking and mooched food. The derision flew from Bian Fu and Wang Furen's knitting needles the next day. "The lazy cow." "Too lazy to cook for her own child. *Ai wah!*" Resources were limited: only idiots wasted them.

A Turkish tablecloth, a cassette tape of Anup Jalotha's *baijans*, a red plaid shirt, a pocket Chinese-English dictionary he'd given her. "These things are for our *jia*," he said. She nodded and put them away in the cupboard.

The hand-drawn *hanzi* on the paper playing cards drawn by Wang Xue Nian, scattered and shredded by an out-of-control Er Bao, that ended in contradictory positions across the coffee table, couch and floor: thief covering emperor, chief justice in the ashtray. A game with feudal underpinnings, just like Western card games: king, queen, knave. They never got to play. Er Bao ate a chocolate bar and set to merrily shredding and scattering the cards.

Beijing's things.

Five peacock feathers, their quills jammed between the heating pipe and the wall, the plumes curving outwards as the quills dried out: a fan of sorts.

"Why didn't you buy my mother flowers?"

"I thought those were beautiful."

"They are. But don't buy my mother any more pots, like at Christmas. That she thought strange indeed. *Zhen chiguai!*"

The *shaguo*, the pot. A pale flower and leaf pattern, tan glaze. Ordinary enough. He had bought it from a street vendor on the way to Bian Fu's Christmas Day. "What is his meaning?" the mother had asked when she returned from Bing He. "He gives me a pot? *Shenme?*"

"You see," said Bian Fu, "we Chinese never give kitchen things like pots unless someone is moving out or getting married."

One evening Jeff decided to make a joke about the pot. "I'm looking around for another *shagua*," he said.

There was a silence.

"Who?" said Wang Xue Nian.

"Bian Fu's mother." He grinned.

The family stared into their bowls of rice and *yang rou*.

"What's wrong, Bian Fu?" he asked, panicky.

"Well, Jeff, they thought you said *shagua* instead of *shaguo*."

"And what does *shagua* mean?"

"It means a foolish woman, Jeff."

"Oh."

He attempted to explain his mistake. Uneasy doubt shifted from face to face. Surely the foreigner realized that such a mistake was not, strictly speaking, *explainable*.

The motion of the uncle's cleaver brought him back. Cigarette hanging from his mouth, the uncle calmly sliced away at the lamb.

The first vegetables and lamb slices and squid were thrown in the boiling water, along with soy and two packets of chili sauce.

"*Chir ba, chir ba!*" everyone yelled.

Bian Fu handed him *kuaizi* and a bowl. "What's the matter, Jeff?"

"I don't know."

"*Chir ba, chir ba.*"

Er Bao started to scream, "*Yao chir made, chir made!*"

"We don't have any locusts," Wang Furen said.

"*CHIR MADE BA!*" she yelled.

His right leg started to shake uncontrollably. Then his left leg.

"What's the matter, dear?"

"I don't know."

Everyone was hunched over their bowls. Wang Furen attempted to give him more lamb. "*Chir ba, chir ba!*"

He felt woozy.

He looked around the table. No one said anything.

"They are all worried about you," said Bian Fu.

"I feel cold."

Wang Furen sprang up; she filled a large pot with hot water and told him to take his shoes and socks off. He put his feet in the water and sat there shivering. She went into the bedroom and returned with a thermometer, thrust it under his armpit.

"She was a nurse, you know," said Bian Fu.

"*Fa shao le,*" she said, squinting at the mercury.

"She says you have a fever. Are you sweating?"

"*Mei you.*" He wasn't.

"She says if your temperature does not go down in one hour you must go to hospital."

Wang Furen draped a leather coat with fur trim over his shoulders. She told him not to eat meat, then, forgetting her advice, put more lamb in his bowl.

He concentrated on the warmth in his feet. Time passed. The tremor in his legs began again, subsided, then his hands shook violently.

Wang Furen checked his temperature: he still had a fever.

"WEAR THAT COAT!" Wang Furen shouted. Somehow, though he couldn't remember moving his legs, they were in a cab speeding through the brilliant winter mist of Kick Fish County. He was breathing slowly, and leaned into Bian Fu for warmth. "Take it easy, *bao bai,*" she said. By the way she was sitting, stiff and still, he knew she was worried. "Bian Fu, Bian Fu, it's probably just a bad cold."

"I don't think so."

The hospital was dank and brightly lit. It smelled of disinfectant and blood and something more disturbing. He sat on a bench, still not sweating, in a calm trance, as Bian Fu ran around with his wallet from wicket to wicket collecting the tickets and slips one must have before seeing a Chinese doctor. The sick and wounded, supported by stunned family members, hobbled in from the Beijing night. This was the evidence of their grievance with the world: they had arms that could be broken, fingers crushed, skin that slit and bled, went puffy filled with pus, turned blue, teeth that rotted, and inside more confusion, fungal scuppers and drains, badly stuffed cases of meat and blood, schizoid tubes and tendons. No one had to talk about it, this inner mess, and indeed no one did: one could see it in the eyes.

In a draughty room a woman doctor told him to take off his shirt.

"Why, I hardly know you." He laughed.

Bian Fu frowned and helped him out of his shirt.

The doctor prodded his chest, took temperature, commanded him to get an x-ray.

He kicked up a fuss when they had no lead shield; Bian Fu looked like she wanted to kick him in his genitals. "Keep cool," she said. "You're sick. I worked in the hospital before; we do this all the time; the percentage of people sick by x-ray is very low."

Back in the waiting room, to atone for his bad behaviour, he started offering everyone his chair.

"*Fa shao le*," Bian Fu told everyone.

"Jeff, just sit down, okay?" She was beside herself. She squeezed his hand and gently moved his hair back over his earlobes: her doing this in public shocked him so much that he immediately became subdued and sat down.

Everyone was staring at them.

The doctor told Bian Fu that Jeff had *fei yan* and, after much fumbling with the dictionary, Jeff found out it was pneumonia.

And so they spent their first whole night together, Jeff propped in bed with an antibiotic drip in his arm and Bian Fu in a bedside chair. An old couple were talking quietly to each other at the other bed. The wind was howling outside. Jeff had to talk.

"If I die," he said, "I want you to know that I have never loved anyone as much as I have loved you. I want you to know that. I need to tell you that you are the most loving woman, the most beautiful woman, the most tender woman I have ever known. No one has ever been in my heart the way you have. If I die, I want you to know you have been loved. I love you. I really love you."

"Oh, Jeff, you should sleep."

He awoke in the night. Bian Fu had pulled her chair snug to the bed, and leaned across him, her head on his chest. He awoke again near dawn. She was sitting up, praying. He clutched her hand and smiled.

As he staggered out into the parking lot in the morning, still wearing Bian Fu's mother's coat, groggy, Bian Fu said, "Now that's more like a married couple. We got through that and we keep going."

For the next three days he slept in the *siheyuan*, in the bedroom he had thought he was going to die in not long ago. Bian Fu clung to his recovering body. Her hair got in his mouth and nostrils. Or she sat in the lotus position beside him, her eyes slits of fire in the darkened room. They heard people moving in the next room, but the family kept their respectful distance, as though they attended the recently dead.

And they found themselves, once he recovered, at the Beijing Airport. Jeff, dizzy and still tired, hardly heard the airport clamour; the announcements came from far away, from some reverberant empyrean realm.

In the lounge he counted out and gave Bian Fu twelve hundred *renminbi*. "This is for you, if you need it to get a lawyer, or whatever."

When she took it with a scowl and curtly said "*Xie xie*," he realized his *faux pas*. The Chinese businessmen at the next table greatly appreciated it. They jabbered away, laughing, looking away, laughing.

They went outside the terminal.

"I love you and I will return to you," he said.

A tear streaked down her cheek. They kissed for a long time.

"Showing everybody your deep feelings," Wang Furen had said to her daughter, in front of Jeff, earlier that fall, "Shame. What's the matter with you? You must be shallow." He watched her absorb this, say nothing.

When they parted this time, just outside the terminal doors, she cried and held him very tightly.

"You will write me?" she said.

"Every day," he said.

They kissed. She took a *qi pao* button from her pocket and tied it around his neck with a shoelace, kissed him again. She walked away, then stopped, as though she thought she was taking the wrong route, and had to turn around. She skipped back into his arms, and they clung together, turning and turning, in a hungry waltz. Then he let her go and she touched his face once and strode away, purposely brisk. He knew she would maintain that manner as long as necessary.

He picked up his bags.

How quiet the plane, lifting above the din of Beijing, city of mouths, the voices rising into the warped sun, gone now, the *cha*-sharp chop and punch of Chinese, fragments of meaning in a sea of phonemes, sealed off behind the plastic airplane windows. He was leaving the Middle Kingdom, the centre of the Chinese world, his love. When the shadow of the plane drifted over the Great Wall, the stone containment that plumed and snaked among the hills of Hebei province, those folding contours, it filled him with a single thought, You are outside the wall now.

Uplifting reveries followed, of barbarian attacks, flaming arrows, smoke rising nobly from the watchtowers. He was hurtling over the fearful vastness, the north that would become the west, the brown and rudely stoned land that at the end of the Wall would join the desert. Where the horses come from, where the winds are fierce, where the bride sits by the river in the evening. Where the birds are still. Where the husbands go.

He was returning to a world he had heard little about for months. The silence was round like the discs of coal used in China, with holes in it. But you couldn't lift the silence with tongs and burn it to a papery grey ash. You couldn't touch it. It was everywhere and hence nowhere. What is the sound, after all, of someone keeping his mouth shut?

He sat next to a Beijing businessman who was flying to visit relatives in Vancouver and spent much time selecting gifts from the in-flight catalogue. Bracelets, rings, perfume, purses, wallets, silk scarves. That done, he turned to Jeff and said, "Your Chinese is very good. But you should really marry a Beijing girl, you know. If you don't, your accent will be all screwed up."

"*Xie xie*," Jeff said.

They soared, racing the sun. Over Ohtosk and the curving, amoebic gleaming rinds of shore and river and black earth, the first movie started showing. It was called *Double Happiness*.

Part Three

Chengyu

成语

Established Speech

Chapter Ten

Crammed in with underwear and socks, in his carry-on suitcase, a number of books and study materials accompanied Jeff back to Canada. There was a weighty Chinese-English dictionary in a cardboard sleeve with big characters, which he loved for its sheer volume of unintelligible signs and closely printed tables of the characters' radicals. There was a pocketbook edition of *Fun with Chinese Idioms*, with its cartoons and pithy sayings. A grammar published by Beijing Foreign Languages Press in 1986, featuring the dumpling-fed and thoroughly wholesome adventures of Gubi and Palanka, two Soviet students visiting Beijing. A Penguin edition of *The Analects of Confucius*. And, wrapped in a Jian Hua sweatshirt, *150 Song and Tang Dynasty Poems*. In that book was a particular poem by Li Bai; in that poem was a young woman's waiting, changing face.

He was exhausted upon landing in Vancouver. The customs queue.

"What were you doing in China?" asked the customs woman.

"Teaching English. And studying Chinese," Jeff said.

"Which was it?" she said.

"Teaching English," he said.

The wait for luggage. The cart with the stuck wheel. The first cigarette in twelve hours. The long Vancouver layover, coffee sustaining him, the short hop to Victoria. It seemed forever before he landed in Victoria and strode through the rain towards the terminal.

The electric doors slid open. He heard a piercing shout — "*Daddy!*" — and his daughter shot towards him and leaped into his arms, her eyes as wide as he had ever seen. "Melissa!" he said. They were hugging. And he dropped his bag and spun her around among waiting travellers who were bored and ignoring similar reunions. Melissa was taller than he remembered; she had lost some of her small-girl pudginess, seemed leaner. Heavier.

Annette, the ex, waited, smiling; Jeff avoided getting too close. He shook her hand. The flight was fine. She didn't ask any questions about Bian Fu. Never mentioned her. Jeff was staying with her and Melissa until he could find a new place.

As they drove away from the airport, he turned in his seat to look at Melissa; she was straining, fidgeting, beaming — he had not seen joy like that, not for a long time. The weight of the thought suddenly tired him, and his chest felt heavy. He turned back to the front, replying to the ex's questions with short answers. Despite the double espresso he'd had at the Vancouver airport, he knew sleep was only a couple of hours away.

The conversation with Bian Fu about his ex came back to him —

"I have a very bad feeling about her. I think she will come between us. She will do something that will prevent us from being together."

"Let's just worry about what we do," Jeff had said.

"And you are going to stay with her. No. I do not like this. I cannot accept this…"

"It is just to save money, until I can find a place."

"And how you feel I sleep with Li because of the money? Bah!"

"I'm not sleeping with her." He was tired of arguing.

"I said how is Bian Wang Fu," the ex said, looking across from the steering wheel.

"Wang Bian Fu," Jeff said mechanically. "Last name first."

"Of course."

"She's doing all right, Annette."

The ex looked at him hard, expecting more, and he avoided her eyes. They swept home on eerily silent, rain-blackened streets. It was late afternoon and the streetlights were on. Melissa strained at her seat belt and kept saying Daddy, Daddy, as though she had been prohibited from saying it before. She brimmed with tidbits from her days. "Daddy, I did a headstand, a whole ten seconds, and this week we're learning cartwheels."

"That's great, honey."

"She's in gymnastics Tuesday, Thursday, Saturday morning," said Annette.

"Mommy says next year we can get a dog. I want a big fluffy dog."

"Daddy, we went to see Santa Claus at Christmas. It was really fun."

They arrived, and Jeff lugged the backpack and suitcase inside the house that he had left years ago; as usual, stepping into it unnerved him, as if he were expecting to see the former marks of his inhabitancy. But there was little. The same living room furniture was cat-clawed. Out back the fence he had put up one summer still leaned. Melissa was tugging on his arm, "Come see my room, Daddy!" There was a sign on her door, "Melissa's Room — Death Trap for Parents."

"You're sleeping in there with Melissa," said Annette.

"Fine," he said.

Melissa's room was festooned with pale phosphorescent stars on the walls and ceiling, and every inch of available surface was covered with stickers. Her bed was piled high with stuffed animals. There was a single foam mattress on the floor at the foot of Melissa's bed.

"Thank you for agreeing to put me up till I get a place."

"First thing you should do," said Annette, "is make an appointment with the GP, make sure about your lungs."

"I got treated in Beijing."

"With antibiotics?"

"Yes, and."

"And what?"

"Some sort of Chinese medicine."

"I'll phone in the morning. Melissa has gym tomorrow. Can you take her? And maybe you'd like to drive her to school. I've got to get back to work. You can have the car for the day."

"Sure. Hey, Melissa, let's go to the ocean."

He walked her down to the waterfront, about a block away, a stony cove. She insisted on a shoulder ride, and Jeff hoisted her up. When he swung her down at the water, he coughed, then almost fell off a rock he tried to balance on. Melissa was delighted to hold his hand and delicately inch out to where the low, skimming waves touched and darkened the smallest rocks below the tideline, and jumped back when a thin white crest of foam nearly touched her runner. She tried to imitate him skipping stones. She wound up and released, her arm floppy, laughed at the plop in the water, and whirled around in a giddy circle.

Jeff was watching where the clouds covered the peaks of the Olympic Mountains across the strait. "See, honey, over that way is China."

"You were in China, Daddy. How far is it to go?"

He smiled. "About the time between when you get up and when you get home from school, a little more, till supper. By plane. What did you tell your friends your dad was doing in China?"

"I told them you were holding tiny baby pandas."

Jeff laughed, partly to cover a tiny stabbing he felt.

"Did you see any baby pandas?"

"No, honey, I didn't."

"Are there baby pandas there, Daddy?"

"Yes, there are, I think a couple in the Beijing Zoo."

"Did you go there, Daddy?"

"No, I didn't. I was teaching English."

"You're very good at teaching English, Daddy. I know you are."

He fell asleep when they got back to the house, and woke, disoriented, under the pale glow of the phosphorescent stars glued on her ceiling.

He found Annette at the kitchen table. She was writing on bills and clipping them together — he knew she was aware of his presence. Scribble, clip. Scribble, clip. He saw she was tired. Whatever hair was not gathered in her pony tail hung limply over her cheekbones. She may have been waiting for some ceremony: greeting of the miscreant ex. Jeff cleared his throat; she indicated a chair.

He had loved her, once. Whatever had made him leave — his restlessness, his resentment of his sharply diminished importance yet greater responsibility once Melissa had arrived, his sense that there had to be more than this four-room house and its chattels, all heavily subsidized by Annette's family — didn't change that he had once loved her. He reminded himself of that as she, characteristically, finished her task and hung the clipped-together bills up before any talk could happen. Jeff knew there would be an argument; he didn't know its size or shape but it was palpable.

"So you're back."

"Melissa seems fine."

"She was up at six this morning asking, 'Is it time to go to the airport yet?'"

"I missed her."

"You missed her. You go away for six months and you missed her."

"Well, it's true."

"Do you want tea?"

"I'm fine."

"What happened? Are you married?"

"No, I'm not."

"I thought you were getting married."

"I did too. There were problems."

"So are you still with her?" Jeff wasn't sure what she wanted confirmed. He didn't want to tell her anything, so he said, "We're communicating, yes."

"How nice. You're communicating. To what purpose, may I ask? Are you going back?"

"I don't know."

"How long are you staying here?"

"I don't know. Look, Annette, I just got off the plane, I just had pneumonia, a lot of things happened I need time to think about."

"Such as?"

"The — look, I don't want to talk about it."

"Your daughter's going to ask you, you know."

"I'll deal with it when I have to." Frustrated, he pushed back his chair. "Look, what do you want me to say? I'm never going to China again?"

"No, I didn't ask you to say that, but I would — we would — appreciate some sort of plan on your part."

"Life's not like that."

Annette stared at him.

"Okay, Jeff, let me spell it out for you. What are you teaching our little girl? That she's worth one week's notice for you to go to the other side of the world, and all her time with you, that she builds her world around, is turned upside down. Let me ask you this. Suppose you had gotten married. Would you have stayed for a second term in Beijing?"

"I don't know."

"Well, were you planning on it?"

"I — it didn't happen that way."

"What I'm saying is that little girl loves you more than Fu Wang ever will. She —"

"Bian Fu."

"— deserves a father in her life. Your love, that's got to be there for her, like a rock."

"I've spent time with her every weekend for five years, Annette. Something comes along and I want to develop my life, I'm supposed to say no because you've got this comfortable life here?"

"All I'm saying," she said, "is you start including her in your plans."

"So why do you think I'm back here?"

"Well, that was my original question. Why are you back here?"

Jeff smiled, acknowledging her logic, and the circular nature of arguments. Annette went to bed. Jeff stayed up sitting at the table. It was two in the afternoon, Beijing time.

When his first unemployment insurance cheque came, he got an apartment, a one-bedroom in Fairfield, not far from Beacon Hill Park, close to the ocean. His friend Terry loaned him his truck to fetch his belongings from Annette's basement, where they perched at angles on the outcroppings of rock: books, stereo, desk, futon frame, what little he had. He had no more than a student and he was almost forty. Annette made it plain that she wished this were the last time she would see him move, or at least be involved. "Look at this chair," she said, "it's toast. When are you going to get rid of it?"

"When I have money to buy a new one." He managed to keep his voice emotionless.

"And these records. Do you even have a turntable?"

Jeff tuned out and concentrated on packing the truck as compactly as he could, so he only had to make one trip.

She stood with arms crossed watching him. "So have you found any work yet?"

"Still looking."

She went inside with Melissa.

She came back out. "Remember Melissa wants to be involved in setting up her room. She's picking out the stuff she wants to take over."

"Bring it Saturday," he said.

He got in and started up the truck, then turned it off. He walked around the back and got Annette's attention by rapping on the doorjamb. "Melissa?" he said.

"She's in her room. Take off your shoes. I just vacuumed."

Melissa was absorbed in pinning buttons on a teddy bear. He looked closer: a five-star red Chinese flag, a silhouette of Mao: Bian Fu's gifts.

"You think it looks good, Daddy?"

"Sure, honey."

"Bian Fu, will she come and play with me?"

"I… I don't know, honey."

"You said you would marry her."

"Yes, we want to."

"When is she coming, Daddy? I want to see her. Can she speak English?"

"Yes, she can."

Melissa gave a disappointed smirk, and snapped her fingers. "Rats! I wanted to teach her."

"Oh, you probably will teach her. Some words. I'll see you Saturday, love."

They had agreed that Melissa wouldn't stay over until he got the place set up, which took him the better part of two days. He dawdled. He turned and turned among strewn boxes, a speaker wire in one hand, a pillow in the other. He set up a shrine of sorts on top of a speaker, where he laid the pictures of Bian Fu, the *qi pao* button, which had started to irritate his collarbone, and her letters. Already three or four had arrived at Annette's. He had not gotten around to deciphering the Chinese parts, but contented himself with the simple English paragraphs expressing longing. When he got fed up with arranging his new apartment, he went for walks.

He phoned his mother in Winnipeg, who sounded mildly surprised to hear from him.

"Thought you were in China."

"I was. Mom — I met a girl there."

She clucked. "So have you gotten a job yet?"

"Mom, we're engaged. We want to get married."

"Oh, is that so? I guess she's Chinese then." She sounded preoccupied, as though Jeff had interrupted her favourite TV program "Well, let me know. And you better look for a job."

"Yes, Mom. Mom?"

"Uh-huh."

"Are you okay?"

"Oh, don't worry about me. I'm getting by."

In Victoria, the very space around him was preternaturally silent. There was laughable space. He stood on the Cook Street sidewalk in the January twilight. He heard everything — the chickle of a ten-speed's gears, cups against plates in the outdoor café, conversations between strolling lovers half a block away, and at evening the diminishing shrieks of the seagulls. No longer overwhelmed by the glut of noise in Beijing, his ears opened. But there was little to hear; along Dallas Road the space and silence was voidlike. A trick surely. When he got past this section of the path and its overhanging tree-tunnel, he would come upon leek-pancake sellers, hordes of bicyclists, a white flurry of schoolgirls — their sheer, black hair making their stiff shirts whiter — hands linked — a lifting cloud of laughter But no: a single old person, on a scooter. A young woman walking a chihuahua.

Were the changes so huge, or was he still recovering from pneumonia? He was tired, his lungs were heavy; perhaps his lungs

were shocked and hyperventilating, now free of both the illness and
the coal smoke. He walked by the sea, fragments of conversations
with Bian Fu playing in his head.

He was angry. He had wasted four months. He read through
her letters quickly, searching for evidence of further treachery;
he perused the predictable phrases of affection and separation,
smugly convinced that they elided some further gamesmanship on
her part, some hidden trick. But the letters were sweet in tone and
hopeful — Bian Fu was looking for work, again. She said nothing
about Li and the apartment, the divorce: the subject was him. When
was he going to return? Please tell me when you are going to return. I
wait for you to come back China.

She decorated the margins of her letters with drawings of comic
birds and fishes. He smiled in spite of himself. Their pet names for
each other.

He wrote back to her saying that of course he missed her as well,
he missed her very much, he loved her, but he would not return until
she was divorced and she had the required letter from her parents
stating they were aware that she was marrying a foreigner. She did not
respond to this demand. She simply restated hers. When you come
back?

He asked her how her family was.

On Saturday Melissa arrived, with her plastic play-table, chair
and three boxes of stuffed animals. She pronounced the apartment
"Cool!" and ran into their bedroom. Annette stood in the front hall
and issued instructions as to what Melissa would like to do, said that
she was "off" garlic and other spices, repeated her bedtime twice, and
left.

Jeff carried the box of stuffies in to her. "Here's your friends."

She was bouncing, on her bum, on the bed. "I like it, Daddy,
but...could I sleep by the window, Daddy?"

He laughed — his daughter's feminine tact, coming out already.
He lugged the mattresses and box spring around in the cramped
space while she herded her stuffies out of the way. After he'd set
up her bed again, Melissa carefully lined up the stuffies against the

wall: a red bulbous dog called Ralph near her pillow, innumerable versions of bear and rabbit, beetles and plush velvet snails and fishes and spiders, their plastic eyes looking in on her. A jumble of multicoloured furs.

"Who's your favourite?"

"Ralph. He's my feeling dog."

"Oh, how's that?"

"Mommy said when I have bad feelings, tell them to my feeling dog. He listens and my feelings aren't so bad anymore." She hopped up on the bed and hugged Ralph. She turned on her belly and made a wave through her shoulders and her hips, her toes kicking the mattress. "I like doing the worm, it's fun!"

He laughed. "You set up your other things while I do some stuff out here."

He arranged his cassettes on top of his turntable-minus-stylus. He emptied boxes of books and set them on shelves, drifting into a daydream of a future apartment — when? — where Bian Fu's Chinese books and his would sit in separate bookshelves, or perhaps all jumbled together, for by then there would be no language difficulty. He saw her selecting one, finger on her nose, her locative of "I," just as his was hand on heart; she glided around this imaginary room, eyeing wallspace for a Qing dynasty painting she wanted back and he had never seen, for it was still the property of her husband. Distracted by his fantasies, he left the books and started hanging a scroll from his students in San Tiao. Melissa came bounding out of the bedroom. The scroll was typical: the *shan shui* vision of a rural southern China, with a journeyer (and umbrella-toting servant) skirting a bread-loaf mountain typical of the region, red maple leaves on the trees. Traditional house in the mid-ground, built into the mountainside, and the traveller taking forever to get to the house, which one assumed was home. Though dwarfed, the humans seemed indelibly dominant over nature in the print.

"How many people are in that picture?" Melissa asked from behind him. She was fond of this sort of discovery puzzle.

"Two."

"No, Daddy, look." There were several, cleverly concealed along the mountain trail, waiting on the house's verandah, fishing in the lake.

"Cool, honey. I never noticed them."

It was a bad print. The red of the leaves drifted from the actual outline of the leaves, as though the cloth had slipped during the screening process. The calligraphy was written so cursively and, again, badly transferred, that he could only make out a few of the characters: mountain, heart.

"Silly Daddy," she said.

Jeff barely heard: he was thinking of another print, the sort of poster that's sold in Western gallery gift shops; it hung in Bian Fu's mother's apartment in Kick Fish County, on the coal-stove room door, which was usually open, so the print gave on to the wall, unseen. It was a while before he noticed it.

She was a nude in the oil-painting tradition, fleshy, fully mammalian; perhaps from the seventeenth century. Rubens came to mind. Just hanging there. With a look that said adore me, and yet was indifferent. Her body and her look. "Who painted that?" he asked Bian Fu.

"Ah — I do not know. It has been there forever. I don't know who bought it."

"Why does your mother keep it there?"

"Because it is beautiful."

The nude kept gazing into the wall, unseen. Adore me.

Now, Jeff refocused on the scroll: the traveller did not get home. He hung there with his valiant horse among the render-wandering leaves. Jeff blinked and asked Melissa if she was hungry, but didn't hear her answer. His eyes still floated in that dream-like gorge, disembodied, in company with that traveller, diminished in scale by what loomed around him.

My feeling dog.

And what feelings, exactly, had Melissa told the dog, in the night, when he had been in Beijing?

"So, are you hungry?" he said.

"How come you're not married?" said Terry. "You didn't answer my letter. No word from you. I knew something was up. I figured the Triad gangs were slow-roasting you somewhere. You started a business renting your foreigner's body out to movie-production companies. Something. What the hell happened?"

"I —" Jeff turned on his futon couch to stretch his cramped legs from th coffee table, over which his friend was leaning, as he crushed and fluffed several large buds of Vancouver Island pot. "It doesn't have to be the perfect spliff," Jeff grumbled. "Roll it — it's been four months."

"You didn't answer my question. And I'm sure your brain can wait a few more minutes before your unit, once again, tastes the awesome depths of —" he poked the dope, a fine efflorescence filling their nostrils, "— crystal on these fuckers. So what happened?"

"She's married," said Jeff. "She will need to get a divorce, if. If *we* are going to get married."

Terry whistled, and licked the end of the joint. "Trust issues, then. How'd you find this out?"

"Trust issues! Jesus. Language issues. *Race* issues, not-knowing-what-the-fuck-was-going-on issues. A mess. A fucking mess. Gimme that."

They shared the joint, Jeff initially sucking hard, holding in the smoke, letting it creep through his body until he could feel the tingle in his fingertips.

"I wasn't prepared for any of this. I thought we'd have a few weeks of romance and then off to the family home, wedding, start dealing with the immigration process."

"Which would leave you about where you are now. What's the waiting time anyway? Two years, three years? You sure there weren't some other reasons she wanted you? I'm sure there are lots of Chinese who would love to get out of China."

"Damn it, you think I don't know that? I wanted to be sure about that."

"And what rigorous test did you devise to make sure? Did you see if she could stand you plunging your cock into her? Oh, she goes to the disco with me — that must mean she loves me. Hark, I hear a moan that issueth from this young maiden. Proof positive of true love. Face it, Jeff, you wanted it to be easy."

"Is that so bad? Something easy?"

"Boy, you need — I don't know what you need. Hmmm. You need to listen to about a quarter of a million blues records, is what."

"I was so blind," said Jeff. "At first I thought I wasn't getting it, that she'd changed her mind, that she'd met someone else, even."

"Which was true — she met him when they were changing the bed sheets. '*Oh. Are you who? Husband, maybe?*'" Terry minced around the coffee table, the affected accent surprisingly close, in its mocking way, to Bian Fu's.

"You don't understand. How little I fulfilled the role of Chinese husband she had in mind. Everything turned around money, was I paying for this and that. Other guy's well-off. That was always on her mind. I was only making three thousand kuai a month."

"What's that?"

"About five hundred Canadian."

Terry said nothing for a moment, thinking. "What does money have to do with it? That would only be a big issue the way I see it once you established yourself as a couple. How the hell could you do that in your situation?"

"Yeah, you're right. But something got established."

"I'll say. You got addicted to her pussy."

Jeff stared at his friend. He wanted to lash out, to defend himself — and Bian Fu — but he was tired. "Oh, I don't know," he said. "It wasn't just sexual."

"In the first stages, tell me, when is it ever not just sexual? How often did you screw?"

"At the beginning it was even difficult to do that. We had a hard time getting past the guards at the dormitory. And her place was right out. For weeks we didn't have sex."

"But it didn't stop you trying."

"We did it when we could."

"And tell me, was she a good lover?"

"She is the best lover I've ever had," said Jeff, and meant it.

"Lots of playful names for body parts and such?"

"I don't want to tell you."

Terry clasped his chest and tilted sideways. "Oh, I offend him, verily I doth. Fine. But, look, what I'm trying to tell you, is at first there's this big strong physical connection, but all the time a woman is considering you as a mate, so naturally she sees you as a means of financial support, or at the very least, sees whether you're going to fit into all the other supports in her life. I'm talking your typical case. That's what's going on, slut-boy. And you better be prepared for a few realities. Now that you're out of the picture, her husband over there in the Land of Exotic Knock-offs is going to try and reattach. You prepare your heart for that." Terry sat back, and picked up the roach, brushing it, deciding if it was worth lighting again; he tweezed two big buds out of the baggie and began rolling another.

Jeff got up and rummaged for a cassette. He put in one he bought at a night market in Kick Fish County: soft Taiwanese rock. He stood swaying as the woman's restrained, soft voice swelled into the first chorus.

> *Ren zhen de zuiqui ni bu dong xin teng*
> *Wo jiu shi xing fu de zhu ren…*

Yes, he thought, to sincerely woo you without knowing heartache, then I'd be a happy person. That would be sweet.

"What is that shit?" said Terry. "Jesus, I can just hear the repression coming off it like summer from asphalt."

"Gao Hui Jun," Jeff said. "She's Taiwanese." One hand on the speaker, he turned. "But what about love?" he said, aware that even if he was not actually blushing, his voice had choked up an octave; he was about twelve years old. "What about companionship, and tenderness, and just being fascinated by another person?"

"What I'm telling you is, all that's first-stage theatrics. I know you don't want to hear this. No, you don't like the messy details, my friend. Oh, shut up for a second. I'm saying you've got a strong romantic streak. Always the unattainable goddess-chase with you. 'And what about love?' the erotic conqueror doth enquire. That *is* love, all those bothersome things you don't want to consider. Money, money, money. Her family. Your daughter. Jesus, suppose you did get married. Where were you thinking you were going to live? Here? There? What about Melissa? Last time I looked there weren't very many dry places between here and Beijing."

"You think I don't know that?" Jeff waved the joint, which had gone out. He lit it. "Why do you think I'm back here now?"

"You missed Starbucks."

"Powerfully." Jeff let himself laugh. The talk made him uncomfortable, but he was enjoying his friend, the predictable things he said, because Terry knew him. "Another couple of months in Beijing, I wouldn't have been able to avoid Starbucks. Shit, there was a Dunkin' Donuts near the university."

"No shit, eh? Did the police frequent it?"

"No, they hang out on street corners. So what's going on with you?" Jeff sat back to listen; he had evaded something; things he didn't want to tell. He would tell Terry sometime.

Terry had bought a new truck. He struggled to find time to paint. His kids were in French immersion. The light was past dim now, the cars rushing past outside — Jeff hadn't noticed when he took the place how busy the road was. The late-evening convection wind stirred leaves from twigs and branches from trunks. He clawed himself upward from a deep slouch; in the last minute, he had gone inward, was weaving purposefully towards a blurry green light, around which dark figures were milling. His brain sizzled with *shao kao rou* smells against dark brick walls, with a fug of car exhaust, and then the green light leaped out: it was the character for tea above the shop at the Kick Fish crossroads, a magical gateway. A man slurping tea from a jar stood in front, regarding him, then pushed plastic ribbons aside and disappeared into the shop. The electric *cha* character sputtered, flashed, flashed, *shan-yi-shan*, limning his face in the Beijing dusk. He blinked at Terry, who was talking, may have been talking for minutes, surely had started talking at some point.

" —the kids to the Okanagan, and I said, no way, I got a business to run here, but she goes and does it anyway, that's real female thinking, you go and do it, see who follows, but I wouldn't go, get everyone else signed up and then the principal player's gotta react, but I'm not into it, if it weren't for her whole family going it'd be different, but I gotta bear down now, I can't fuck around with these graphics projects I got going, Jesus, this is my last kick at the cat, you know what I'm talking about. But on the whole she's fine, she's fine, she's got the kids doing a million things — and let me tell you I know about it, I get the bills, I see the credit card statements, say, Carol, what the fuck, you're five thousand dollars over your fucking budget."

Jeff remembered, he had asked how Carol was.

"Slow down, man. I just asked you how your wife was. Christ, you're giving me an audit!"

"And just what do you think marriage is, if it isn't that, O plunderer of the female heart? Sooth! It *is* an audit. Marriage is a long, slow audit of the other's expenditures, and you can interpret that on whatever level you care to, my friend, 'cause it's the truth. It's the deadly boring counting out the pennies of your sweetheart's purse. The necessary asking of the basic questions. To wit: how are we living? Can we afford it? What's next? Gotta happen, gotta be done. And I'm one of the underpaid, quasi-professionals that gets to do it, bloody shame though it may be, the whole world's turning depends on these questions of spousal management. Depends on average guys like me, fools that we are, see what's in the bank account, at least on a semi-annual basis. World needs us too, stay-at-home, do-a-job, sex-on-Friday, willing to stay put, slug it out, and still get a hard-on now and then. Just as important as athletic sex with exotic maidens on distant shores. What the fuck is this guy singing about anyway?"

"He's telling his friend to live for the day and drink more beer. He's telling him about his hometown and someone named Mei Li. Has to study for four years."

"Sure there's not something in there about the local girls?"

"Pretty sure." Jeff could make out only a third of the meaning of this cassette, though he had heard it fifty times. "It's your standard Chinese hymn of longing. To be followed by the standard song of resolute promises."

Terry looked unsurprised.

"You still want to marry her, don't you?"

"Yes."

"I think," Terry said, "that you're not so sure. You will have time to think it over, and that's good." He paused. "You think I don't understand. Been in love myself, you know. I think you want to be loved. That's not so bad. No, don't hang your head. Hell, I've done everything that everyone's ever expected of me, and I'm not going to hang my head. Nothing wrong with wanting to be loved. But I tell you, marriage, you go looking for it in that form and watch out."

Jeff said, "I guess I'll have to think about it." He struggled to preserve his passion, especially faced with his friend's sadness, for there was a sadness, he knew that, despite the bluster. His own passion, he knew, would rise again.

"You want some of this?" Terry dangled the baggie.

"If you can spare it."

"Fuck, I've got garbage bags of the stuff. Here, keep it. I've gotta go."

Jeff played the cassette over again by himself. He rolled another joint and sat on his prayer mat by the sliding glass door to the balcony. A cold February night. Inside him the green *cha* sign flashed again and was gone in the obscuring night. The cassette thrilled him less now; he could no longer hear Bian Fu's breath, informing every beat, each lifted note. He heard the music as music now, not as accompaniment, and like all pop music it impregnated and birthed its possibilities quickly, kaput. He did not understand all the lyrics, but he could hear that the songs were not wholly Chinese. In one tune's steely weeping guitar, the shadow of the Eagles. Another chorus said Beatles, chronic la-la. He had no idea where to place these student folkies within Chinese traditions. He had heard of, but never heard, the Chinese rock-rebel god Cui Jian. Half-familiarity was breeding, if not contempt, at least puzzlement.

He walked out on the balcony.

He had listened and listened to Terry.

Why had he not talked and talked about the marvellous adventures he had had in China?

Must make a point of that.

Adventures.

Sex and television. And four months of eating another family's meals. He went to his desk; piled in a printer-paper box, her letters, which kept on coming.

In the afternoons he turned to her letters, and then to his Chinese grammar books, in a state of dogged curiosity and longing. Bian Fu made her situation sound like penury. Up early, go to work, which was, he gathered, as a low-level salesperson for a Chinese medicine company. He could see her taking those creaky, crowded buses, hands in her pockets and hair tucked under her collar among the tri-wheeled bikes, the backfiring, rapidly filling minivans, the dust-caked groups of construction labourers at the Kick Fish County crossroads, and on into the choked-off streets, the greater city.

He eyed her latest letter. He made coffee, laid out his dictionary and grammar book, anticipating — yes, correctly — that half the letter was in Chinese. He sipped, began to translate.

By the second sentence, he was in trouble. Only two characters eluded him, but the verb was pivotal. "We always —— —— love together, and we…" Feel? Experience? He flipped through the radicals in the dictionary. A good five minutes got him *ji de,* to remember. The effort needed to uncover this basic sentiment was disproportionate; why did he have such a hard time remembering "remember"? He thought back: in Beijing, often, when he had forgotten something, he would cry out in Chinese, "I did not forget," meaning the opposite, yet certain he was right. He realized, staring at the sentences yet to translate, that Bian Fu was doing the same as he, using the simplest words that would summon at least the ghost of her meaning. There was nothing nuanced about them; they were solid blocks of emotion. And something else: he compared the fluid, looping glyphs of her signature, written without thinking, to the painstaking, stroke-by-stoke completeness, the rigid angularity of the text he was slowly parsing, and he realized how much effort it had taken her to write the characters so he could recognize them, and look them up if necessary. She probably had not written her language this way since the third grade.

Love was an effort to consider, he thought.

Onward. A series of four characters in the next clause threw him completely. *Tian*? *Hai*? Day or Heaven? Something. Ocean? Something.

Bian Fu, what on earth do you mean?

His fingers felt out for the baggie of bud, as though for elixir.

Her language, if only he could grasp it, utterly. Eyes red, he tracked down the characters. They made no sense. He looked outside; people were walking, biking home from work. The ubiquitous backpacks. The bulky running shoes at odds with long skirts. The briefcases — but no briefcase looked like a briefcase anymore. Everything was soft and zippered, like backpacks, as though work were athletic self-improvement.

He hadn't gotten any interviews yet. He licked his finger and touched the edges of the joint so it would burn evenly.

Tian Ya Hai Jiao, he made out.

They said you needed only a thousand characters to read a newspaper. He knew, what, three hundred? Four hundred? He checked, the dictionary held ten thousand. Surely some of these were obsolete. He ran his eyes down the forbidding rows. And phrases, it would seem. He peered at one of these — he recognized the first and last character. *Men dang hu dui.* "Families who are equal in economic and social status are well-matched in marriage." How did they get all that into four characters? It beat him all to hell. He riffled through the dictionary and sampled another: *shou zhu dai tu.* Stand, stump, wait, rabbit. This alluded to a farmer who saw a rabbit brain itself on a tree, so decided to wait for the next free dinner. Of course he starved to death, Jeff inferred, earning his place in the history of Han foolhardiness.

His hand and eye flew back to the listing for *Tian*, and there, near the end of a list of nearly a hundred entries, was the phrase *Tian Ya*

Hai Jiao — "limitless, endless, to the ends of the earth." She loved him to the ends of the earth.

And here we are.

With something like passion he spent the next two hours copying out these idioms. Were they what Bian Fu would have told him regularly, if he could understand? Were they the source of her canny thinking about life's predictability; where she drew her sense of the possible or probable? Would he understand her better if he penetrated this layer? Or was there another layer, less folkloric, the idiom of world-weary songs in karaoke bars to consider? Of course there was, he recalled:

> *Qing ren mei you qian wo bu ai*
> Young man, no money, I won't love
> *Lao ren mei you qian wo bu jia*
> Old man, no money, I won't marry

When his eyes started to blink from the smoke and strain, he put down his pen, made grilled cheese sandwiches, ate them and lay down.

In his bed, under the mildly stinking sleeping bag, she came to him naked, her nipples red and hardened, brushing his chest as she straddled him, his hands grabbing her ass, and he came into his hand and lay there sweating.

It was noon in Beijing; he had said he would phone her on Spring Festival, Chinese New Year, which was four days off.

Terry rang him near midnight. "Come on, time to play. Stiff as Nails is playing at the Box. Let's go."

Terry's new truck was an SUV of some picaresque naming. Wanderer, Plunderer. It was idling, contained bass thumping away inside. It was mint, shiny in the streetlights. The interior was more battered. A stick of incense fumed in the ashtray, which held a few roaches. Something sticky had marred the dashboard. Take-out coffee containers rolled on the floor. It smelled as though Terry had been partying in it all week.

"Whaddya think, homeboy?"

"Terry, I don't know. Didn't this cost a shitload of money?"

"You bet your Beijing booty it did. Twenty-eight grand."

"Shit!" Jeff peered at the dash, wanting to lower the bass by a throb.

"Money's a tool," Terry said, taking a thin joint from a throat-lozenge container, lighting it, toking, passing it over, pounding on Jeff's knee. "Thirty-six months, I can carry it, all systems are go, space for the kids, and we're tooling around. Someday you'll see the beauty in money. Solid eight percent on my funds, beating the bushes for contracts, dog's world, keep rolling that credit limit over and over, it's all there is."

"What does Carol think?"

"Christ, what's she gonna say? We need another vehicle."

"What's this? You look up people's registrations with this, or what?"

"DVD player. Perfect for the long haul. Kids watch videos; we argue about the route."

The Box had recently been renamed, as all nightclubs in Victoria were every six months. It used to be The Swank. Their hands stamped, they bought beers from a liberally pierced woman who drew the bottles from ice in a galvanized tub. The walls of The Box were painted a high-gloss, galactic black, seeming to recede infinitely; the ceiling shone with fluorescent purple planets, swarms of stars; on the walls, hanging at indeterminate depth, were killingly silver nuts and bolts, callipers, French curves and compasses, and test tubes of variously realistic sizes. A projection of Albert Einstein raising a bemused, didactic finger by the bar. The patrons, easily fifteen years younger than Jeff and Terry, stood bouncing in their platforms and flares, cargoes and tees, as the music, a mesh of rapid, repetitive drums and synthy whine with ornamental sax fills, looped on, spicing holes in all recognized space.

As they toured the tiny tables, Jeff was not unconscious that they were ignored. Women regarded the surface of their drinks; men struck their tough, stony faces. A gallery of poses and styles. Nostril studs were common; forearms bore greenish-blue tattoos of Chinese characters. These were typically AI or PING AN, love, peace, metaphysical nostrums in the new age of tranquillizing noise. He would have to tell Bian Fu.

"Thought you said there was a band," Jeff said.

"What?"

"BAND. Where's the BAND?"

"TOO EARLY. Let's play POOL."

They took half an hour to play a single game of solids and stripes, their coordination laughable.

The band members wandered to the stage and dutifully attended to their monitors and instruments, clipped howls and banged chords, broken beats from the drums, a plangent bass run. Terry and Jeff stood at the edge of the dance floor, Terry hopping, Jeff swaying. A brilliant flash went off and Jeff saw a pretty, red-haired woman still at her table, straw in her mouth, bored. The band, after a few perfunctory remarks, kicked straight into some punishing staccato yelling. Jeff was fascinated by a projection above them that seemed to be an amoeba, distending, engorging another radiant shape, swimming at the limits of its form, when a hand touched his leg just above his knee and slipped across his thigh, around his ass, and then left with a friendly push of his tailbone. By instinct he followed the hand's path. A garish wash of light swam over a slender female back, a shifting single braid of hair; she was slipping away between the punching arms and hips, in no great hurry, but then gone.

The song had ended, and the gallant lout was slicking back his hair as he angled towards the microphone.

"WHY DON'T YOU ALL COME...COME, A LITTLE CLOSER."

Jeff, paralyzed, let out a single, lame whoop.

Bian Fu picked up on the second long bleep. The line broke her *Wei* in half.

"*Ni hao,*" he said.

"*Ai, ni hao. Chun jie kuai le!*"

He returned the greeting. "Happy Spring Festival."

They savoured each other's voices.

"How is your family?"

"They are all laughing at me," she tittered. "Yes, they have fun, a lot, can I say? They bother me I get up six in the morning wait for your call."

"Why?"

"I did not know when you would call. Oh, Jeff. Miss you. *Xiang nian ni.*"

"Me too. So what's going on, I mean Spring Festival — are you partying all day?"

"Sorry."

"What you do all day?" He was aware he was leaving out words, like her.

"Today we eat a great deal. All my relatives are here. Even my grand —"

"— said, *Shang kang,* and you hopped up —"

"— here."

"— her bed."

Jeff pressed the receiver into his ear. Interruptions didn't work: the satellite delay.

"We tell stories and, Jeff?...they like the spring clothes you bought me."

"So what else is happening?"

"Er Bao eat too much. She threw up."

"No I mean."

"My job is okay," she continued. "Every day on the bus, and work, and on the bus home back. I never do such thing before!"

"I'm proud of you."

"Ah, Jeff. What you do in Canada?"

"I'm looking for work," he lied.

"I wish you luck. Sooner you find work, the sooner you come back China."

"Yeah, if," he said. "So what else is happening?"

"Xue Nian did well his exams."

"I mean with you."

"Good to see my father."

"And Li? Did he tell you about the apartment yet? How's that going? When are you and he getting divorced?"

"Sorry."

"HAS LI TOLD YOU WHEN YOU'RE GETTING DIVORCED YET?"

"I do not know your meaning."

Jeff held his breath, tried to think it through. She's there in her uncle's home; maybe she can't, or doesn't want to talk about Li.

"How is your father?" he said.

"He is good. He say, Jeff, oh, he say, 'You young people are too untraditional and us old people, too traditional.'"

"Anything else?"

"He say to me, 'If you love him, I will not stand in your way.'"

"I love you."

"Yes, me too."

"You'll let me know, Bian-Bian, won't you?"

"It will take time," she said. "This problem must to be solved in a Chinese way."

"I'm sorry," he said. "I ask about all these things, I want all these answers. Sorry." He sounded like a non-native speaker himself, his sentences so spare.

Her voice was careful, picking her way through the English, a proper, lobbing cadence. "No, I understand. If you are Chinese, we could say these things so indirect. But we are not. We have different culture, so we must say them very clear."

"*Ting de dong*," he said. He understood.

"Jeff, what are your days, you not work now?"

"I study Chinese, study your letters."

"Keep going! There is, how I say, in Chinese famous saying, '*Jianchi shi jinbu*.' It is, persistence is success."

"I will keep trying." Jeff had his wallet out and was touching the small picture of her.

"Why you not find job?"

"I don't know."

"You must find job."

"I *must*?"

"Jeff."

"I'm not sure what kind of job I want."

"Jeff, you must try and build better life for yourself. For me. For us. Not all day sit read book, and smoke, smoke, smoke."

"So you work on getting a divorce and I'll look for a job. Take it easy."

"You are angry."

"No." Then, out of nowhere, he said, with a nervous laugh, "*xiang fang xiang cheng.*" Things that oppose, also complement each other.

She laughed too, sarcastically. "Oh, *chengyu*. You study *chengyu*. Is very famous, in China. Yes, things that are, can I say, not like, they go together. Yes, maybe. But it is a proverb, very old. I want to know our future."

"Look," he said, "you don't get divorced, there is no future."

The satellite transmission bleep was intense.

"Bian Fu? It's just. I just got back, I've been back and forth twice, it's all a little exhausting. I'll find a job, Bian-Bian."

"Yes, I am listening."

"Have you thought of getting your parents involved in this? In the divorce. They could help you."

"Um, no, I don't think so. I want to divorce a man my father think is sensitive, very nice. You do not understand how shocked they are I leave this marriage. And they do not know you. It will take time."

"*Ting de dong.*"

"It is my business," she said. "I can do this thing. I can do it very well."

"I should let you get back to your family."

"Why don't you want a job, Jeff? How will you live?"

"I'm doing all right." He could not think of a way to explain unemployment insurance to her, not on the phone. He glanced at his watch.

"Don't you want to work?"

"I — sometimes I do, sometimes I don't. I don't always like work."

"A person should live in society," said Bian Fu. "Not outside it, inside. Why do you struggle so much?"

"I don't believe in society," he said. "Society is people, just people."

"Fight, fight, fight, fight."

"I don't fight it," he said. "You know what Laozi said, 'He who does not fight cannot be beaten.'"

"You always say, 'What about you?' 'What do you want?' 'Why think about your family?' I have to think about my family. They are part of me."

"Laozi said, 'He who knows others is wise; he who knows himself is enlightened.'"

Boring himself.

"Bah, Laozi," Bian Fu said. "He sit around all day and people bring him meals. All day he sits, does nothing. He got to know himself very well."

Jeff yawned in the morning cold; Bian Fu kept talking; she was trying to tell him about herself. "All the time I am young, I go to *Gong Chan Dang* meetings, youth meetings. They tell us many bad things about America, and I believe them. My parents were caught up in this when I was a little girl. At first they have a nice time, but then my father get sent away to work, and he have to leave my mother, and before that she have to lie and lie to prevent him to be killed. I heard this from other family members. They never tell me whole story. All this time I still do not understand why my parents separate. Why they keep a marriage there is no love in it? And yet this is the Chinese way. We have a feeling for China you do not understand. You do not understand me very well. You love me, not understand me."

He realized she had paused. He did not know what to say, but he said, "And yet I like your *yangzi*, your way of loving me."

"Yes, I like yours too."

Jeff rubbed his eyes. This is where he wanted to end the conversation. "Bian Fu. Please take care. I love you. Say hello to your mother."

"Yes, I will. Oh! Jeff — how is Melissa?"

"*Hen hao*. She is good. She wants to teach you English."

"Yes, she will be a good teacher. Not like Er Bao."

"Okay, bye, I love you."

"*Wo ai ni,*" she said.

Then he hung up.

Her way of loving: he saw Bian Fu at his Jian Hua door, peeling off a mitten and laying her hand across her red cheek, the skin turning white around her hand, then touching his neck — see, how cold? Her eyes dancing. The way she said Bah — disgusted — and drove her fist into the space between his shoulder blades and tugged back each shoulder, then pushed his butt in with her knee; scolded him into standing upright. Or: She in the front row at his one public campus lecture, when he displayed sarcastic annoyance at the plants in the audience who asked him the predictable questions about Tibet. He did not answer them. He asked them where Tibet was. Afterwards, in the bleak hallway of the teaching building, she said she was proud of him for not answering their stupid questions. She tousled his hair, whispered in his ear. Her habits of loving were part instruction — which he secretly took pleasure in but outwardly resisted — and part physical tenderness. She loved to play with the hairs on his forearms. He rubbed at his lip and thought of the richness of her lower lip. Glad he could still remember its shape, he set about making coffee.

Later that Chinese New Year's Day, he stood in drizzling rain in Victoria's Chinatown. The grocers had their produce out on the sidewalks in cardboard boxes, as usual; the vegetables more vital, brighter than the pallid faces. Under the Gate of Heavenly Benevolence, among a gathering of local Chinese, he watched the painted lion rear and shake and swoop around — four sets of Nikes prancing underneath the ceremonial cloak, a shocking, rippling long blend of greens and reds, colourful, not necessarily traditional. A group of sullen teenagers whaled the shit out of some tom-toms. The lion made its way from shop to shop, reaching up and plucking the bundles of money wrapped in lettuce hung above each door. Why lettuce? Jeff wondered. Firecrackers sputtered and went off, crappy, yapping bangs.

He said *Chun Jie Kuai Le* very loudly to a woman standing next to him. She did not reply. He repeated the New Year's greeting. She slid off in the crowd. The lion was drawing applause outside windows full of livid barbecued ducks. He went into a store. In front of a wall unit of the typical blue and white rice bowls, an old man smoking unfiltered cigarettes was talking with a younger man wearing the most nondescript windbreaker Jeff had ever seen. *Chun Jie Kuai Le*, he said to them. The old man looked at him, turned and said something rapid and edgy to the young man. "Happy New Year," Jeff said again, "*Wo bai nian ni!*" I give you New Year tidings! "*Chun Jie Kuai Le.*"

The old man returned the greeting unemotionally and swivelled on his stool to resume his conversation.

Jeff listened. They were speaking Mandarin.

He felt like an idiot. He pretended to feel the horsehairs on the calligraphy brushes in the plastic bins, and then he left.

He missed Bian Fu's smell. As he moved towards sleep, addled by more than one joint, rolling himself into different positions on the hard futon, listening to the momentary sweep of wet tires over pavement, the smell returned with pungent fierceness: her neighbourhood: coal smoke, dishes of congealing pork in the fridge, dumplings, the oily dampness between her ear and neck, cheap knock-offs of famous perfumes she wore — and the smell of her as she emerged from the four o'clock showers they luxuriated in at Jian Hua, the caressable soft yellow-brown of her skin, her arms open, belly twisting with desire. He lay there and visualized a single mole on her left leg. They had compared the shape of their eyes once, whispering to each other in his room: at close range significant difference disappeared as breath dispersed over skin; they pronounced each other beautiful, and merged.

"*Lao gong,*" she would whisper, inculcating him into her mysteries, "*lao gong.* Husband…"

Her next letter smacked of anxiety.

> *I want to know what is your true feeling our future. I see a video of true story at my friend's place. It is about a Chinese woman and an Australian man, they married twelve years. One morning the man say he is leaving. There is another*

> *woman. I do not understand this. Twelve years and the relationship is over. When I see this, I frightened. You write about passion. But I am wondering. Passion does not last. After a few years there is no passion, just everyday chores. Does this mean in the West the relationship is over? Please tell me your true feeling.*

Jeff sucked hard on his pen, confronting what he would rather not think about. He wrote a paragraph, reassuring her that he loved her very much, but ripped it up, realizing that it hardly answered the question. He started again.

> *I am pleased that you want to know my true feelings. I have no idea how we will feel about each other in twelve years. Right now we are dealing with our feelings of being separated and trying to solve our problems. I must make some money and you have to get divorced. That is what is before us now. I know many people in China feel this about the West, that our marriages break up very often. I have left a marriage, <u>and so have you</u>.*

He wrote out the same paragraph again, without the underline, and continued.

> *I think maybe you are right: great passion in a relationship does eventually fade. But I hope it can change into a deeper love based on respect and mutual understanding. And common goals. So it is good that we are seriously thinking about this right now. I will tell you one thing: I will not return to China to marry you unless two things happen, one, you get a divorce from Li and two, you get that letter from your parents saying that they understand their daughter is marrying a foreigner. Because that is what we need. Without those things, we don't have a chance.*

He sealed the envelope. He returned to his reading: now it was Confucius. He took a quick toke and skimmed the passage again: the potted definition of *ren*, the ineffable quality that Confucius did not claim to possess and scarcely defined, but knew was out there, latent in everyone, or at least in those privileged enough to be instructed. It was something like "humanity" or "goodness" or "compassion" but not exactly any of those. As Jeff understood it, *ren* could only be approached through the observance of *li*, or ritual, the myriad correct ways to handle situations based on the past's example. He dimly understood the deep sense of propriety in Chinese culture. The suffocating-to-him idea of correct behaviour towards family members, elders.

He thought Confucius a fool. His unwavering devotion to the ideas of the deep past. Especially ridiculous was his veneration of the demigods Yu and Shen, who were buried so far back in antiquity that their achievements, agricultural reforms, irrigation and damming, had no tangible human reality. The annals may have said that Yu ditched and dammed tirelessly, but for all Master Kung knew, these men were slave masters. And indeed, the general picture Jeff formed of the Confucian base of Chinese society, everyone in their place, going through the polite motions, filled him with bitterness at how he had been treated in Beijing. He thought, Bian Fu's family never gave him any indication of their disapproval. They simply tolerated him, didn't owe him any truth. And had he fulfilled their idea of a courting lover? Probably not. He simply showed up for meals, too broke to take her out often. Yet they had taken care of him when he was sick; he was grateful. Were they obligated by custom (*li*) or was it evidence of their goodness (*ren*)? He grew confused. He remembered Bian Fu's mother frozen in his spontaneous hug when he left: social awkwardness or distaste? What was the truth? From this welter of simplistic cultural notions, Bian Fu's deception stood out, and it rankled. What was really going on in Beijing? Was she trying to get divorced, or weighing the outcomes with a pragmatic eye? She was certainly expecting a larger commitment from him. Did he trust her? He regretted having left: no, that was a greater hopelessness. He could not influence the situation.

He read further.

There was room for a condescending fondness for old Kung. He was a bit of a loser, shambling from kingdom to kingdom trying to get a Prince to buy into his ideas. The old philosopher was unwholesomely canny, duplicitous. The passage where Kung turned away a visitor he did not approve of, saying he was ill, but then Kung deliberately snatched up his zither and strummed merrily away at the visitor's departing back, so he would realize that Kung was hale. Now there's a great example of behaviour, thought Jeff. Way to go. The *old* philosopher? Jeff suspected he was about the same age as Kung in the book. "If a man has not been heard of by forty, then I grant there is no reason to pay him attention." And there was reason to feel sorry for Kung: a man so in love with his ideals that his pledges to contribute to the state — "All right, I am going to serve!" — rang hollow. Jeff sensed that Kung knew his efforts were futile, but he persisted not so much because he knew he was right, but because not to do so would mar the pride Kung had salvaged from antiquity. Kung was in a rut.

Jeff found one concept fascinating, that of cessation or yielding, doing by not-doing, or *wu wei*. In this he saw all sorts of possible explanations for the Wang family's behaviour, and Bian Fu's. Maybe this was how she planned to get her divorce and lure him back to China; to stick to her decision like an impassive emperor from the storied past, ruling the state by merely sitting in majestic attitude, facing south.

He sat, miming a great inaction within himself.

This is just a book. What about reality?

Terry's voice in his head. REAL WORLD, my friend, REAL WORLD.

Before he closed the book, however, he chanced upon this passage: "Marry a girl who has not betrayed her kin, and you may safely present her to your ancestors." He laughed out loud, got up, stretched. He put the book away. Melissa was coming over: he had to get groceries.

"Find a girl who has not betrayed her kin, and you will spend a great deal of time talking to your ancestors," he said out loud, pleased with his wit. But he was not pleased. He was twisting and turning inside; a way in, a way out. He did not know what he sought.

Jeff considered his finances. He did this as he perched on the edge of the couch, making beef dumplings, everything spread out on the coffee table. A big bowl of ground beef, soy, cilantro, garlic, ginger. Stack of wonton wrappers. He didn't dare attempt the dumpling wrappers from scratch. Ashtray full, curved ash leading from the filter balanced on the edge. Big glass of Coke. Bag of weed. Cigs. Bank statement. ATM transaction records. Last UI stub, which read: ATTENTION: YOU ARE NEARING THE END OF YOUR CLAIM.

He pawed up a half-handful of stuffing, plunked it in a wrapper, and began folding and pinching all the way around. Stopped to light another cigarette. Had to wipe pink meat off his fingers. His dumplings were irregularly shaped and the wrapping tore in small slits, exposing the filling. *Why is it so difficult for a foreigner?* Money in bank: about a thousand, what remained of his travel fund from before he met Bian Fu. All last fall, he had dipped into it when his Jian Hua salary fell short. Still a couple of UI cheques, but then what?

He inhaled and let smoke stream out his nostrils.

Expenses were looming. Return to Beijing: about twelve hundred. Immigration, should they get married. The application alone was a thousand. Landing rights, five hundred. He placed another dumpling in the steamer, whose slats, fastened with crisscross strips of bamboo, were starting to loosen.

What had he expected? A short-term stay here and back to China? *Ain't gonna happen.* This divorce, however it proceeded, would take time. He hadn't even thought about jobs back in China. Well, there was only one — teach English.

He raked in the bowl and formed the last dumpling. The water was boiling: he set the steamer and cover on the pot.

He tried to relight a gummy joint, gave up and swallowed it, shivered as it went down. Outside, a couple rode their bikes past. His eyes returned peripherally to his apartment — the battered bookcases, second-hand paperbacks, ten-year-old futon with coffee stains in two places, mismatched kitchen chairs at the one serviceable table, coffee table where he ate most of his meals covered in papers and dirty glasses.

All this could be stored, he thought. At Terry's. Not Annette's again. When did the moving stop? He saw himself in Wang Furen's tiny Beijing apartment, trying to explain why he had not found work. The thought stopped him. To be out of work in Beijing, a foreigner. He had not considered that. He supposed Jian Hua would laugh if he applied there again. The department head said to him one day, *We hear you are dating a student.* If he went back, he had better change his conduct. Separate the private and the public. Another image claimed his attention — the even tinier apartment where He Dao lived with her baby. He went to the kitchen and stared at the steamer, the damp darkness of the lid. He Dao had ushered him in one day to see the baby, the one room with its filthy lino floor, the radio set on the couch's arm. Calendar on the wall. With her hand, she shifted the hanging plastic strips that created a bedroom and shyly indicated he could enter. There was a bed made of empty jute rice bags and a single sheet, and diapers in various stages of cleanliness, some draped to dry, some soaking in vinegar. The brownish baby, lolling happily in strewn blankets, blinked and blinked at the light bulb. Whole place no bigger than his kitchen. He measured. Okay, somewhat bigger than his kitchen. Throw in the entranceway. He Dao cooked outside on a hotplate.

Hen piao liang, he had said of the baby. Very pretty.

He Dao's husband showed up once a week, often less frequently, commuting from Hebei province where he sold something, computers maybe. He was cheerful, his smile always on, given what he had to do to make it all work, the punishing ride on the bus to and from Beijing. He would stay one day and then head back. That was how he lived.

Jeff started and turned the steamer off.

As soon as he had set the plate of dumplings on the coffee table, the soy-and-stuffing aroma wafting up and making his eyes tear, an equally strange picture of himself took over. He was on a lectern-stage, making some sort of summary statement, and then, when his voice stopped, the whole arrangement of desks erupted into action, students gathering books, and then, their babble rapid, thrown back and forth, rising in volume and tone to envelop him, helpless, no longer the focus; they left him, streaming out of the classroom, their speech incomprehensible, save snatches. Wang Fang with her shy smile exiting too, and he remained, with his farewell in his mouth, *zai jian*.

They had passed out that door to their greater lives, having fulfilled their forty-five-minute commitment to English, code of the trade-mad world, and abandoned him to his stage of adjectives and the proper use of the semi-colon: ghost-person, intangible, hardly there at all.

Wang Fang. Odd that he remembered her and she was not the one he loved.

He rolled a joint and got back to *Song and Tang Dynasty — 150 Poems*. He skimmed — wandering scholars, unrequited everything, species of martial longing: "I dreamed of frozen rivers crossed by cavaliers." He found that line remarkable. The severe limits of the poetic forms interested him: five characters or seven characters a line, exacting rhyme schemes. One poem by Li Bai kept drawing him into its mournful but complete world. "Chang Gan Xing" — Jeff made this out as "The Immense Journey"; he was already vaguely familiar with the poem from another, freer translation by Ezra Pound, "The River-Merchant's Wife." At the centre of the poem was a bereaved woman, of a class and society he could barely imagine, whose husband went away on a business trip and did not return; the poem was her recounting of the stages of their relationship, from childish games to endlessly suspended longing, and more, Jeff sensed, through the half-meanings of the characters in their spare, locked progression — hair, flower, gate, bamboo horse, lowered head, wall — the sublime creation, reification, deification of an ever-faithful, ever-changing countenance, that humbled face clearer and clearer in the mind as the poem explored her grief. He read it over and over, trying to connect the characters he didn't know with the rhyming, archaic translation on the facing page, "We children twain," indeed.

Their entire life in thirty lines. Their courtship as children in a riverside village, their betrothal, their fuller commitment, eternal vows: fourteen, fifteen, sixteen years old. He could not connect with this. But there were two lines he chose to apply to Bian Fu:

> *Di tou xiang an bi*
> *Qian huan bu yi hui*
> Hanging my head, I'd look towards the wall
> A thousand times I'd not answer your call

Though he understood this, dimly, as a prescribed pre-marriage ritual, reinforcing the bond with the family giving her up for marriage, and emphasizing her subservience to the necessary waiting — waiting being the activity that would consume her whole life — Jeff turned it around and imagined Bian Fu's lovely face, the moonish bloom of her cheekbones, trembling lips, her complicated eyes fixing on some nailhead or brick chip in the Bing He family home as her mother, father, her innumerable relatives, held forth in increasingly shrill voices against her desire to be with him, Jeff, the unknown quantity, the foreigner. Hadn't he seen her still herself as her mother let fly at her, hunkered down in a timeless, stubborn cavity as Wang Furen, hectoring, pleading, tried to knock her loose from her conviction? Hadn't she told him they had all been relentless the first time he was absent? At least a thousand times she'd not answered their call.

He turned the book over and said, All right, I am going to revise my résumé.

By noon the next day he had distributed ten copies, and had made more copies, aware that these pages, full of the necessary yet vague verbs to be traded for monthly cash — facilitated, organized, edited, liaised — represented at best five stints of lacklustre performance in short-term government contracts: hardly the cv of a rising bureaucrat. Yet in Victoria what was there to do but apply to government? He dutifully revisited the dull floors of endless cubicles, uttered bright-sounding affirmations in the face of bored secretaries more than a decade younger than he. Though he wore his best dress pants, a white shirt and a tie, he felt rumpled, stiff, as he drifted past the offices where earnest faces studied computer screens — oddly, these people were in jeans — and hallways where young men in suits too big in the shoulders (perhaps they would grow into them) chatted imperiously on cellphones. Reminders that he scarcely existed in certain worlds.

He had only one interview, with a Bill Somebody, who, after "I got nothing right now," impatiently flicked at his résumé, spun it, the signal for Jeff to speak.

"I've done some writing and editing for government. The communications basics. Press releases, backgrounders."

"Huh. Jian Hua University. What the hell do they teach there? That's in Beijing, right?"

"Actually it's quite a well-known scientific university. The best in China," he said.

"That so? Taught English. Can they learn English? What's that weird language they speak — Mandawho?"

"Mandarin."

"Right."

"Er, many of them have studied English since they were teenagers. So many of them speak quite well. Their writing," he put in, "was not so good."

"I guess not with those picture-thingeys they use."

"The characters."

"I was in Hong Kong last year," Bill Something said. "Absolutely nuts, crazy the way those people live, all crowded together. Had to plug my ears, all that jabbering — don't those people ever change?"

"Well, the language — the use of the characters, that is — has actually changed a great deal," Jeff said. He did not want to be too contradictory, so he let it rest.

"That so? They all look the same to me. Tell you what. I'll keep this on hand, let you know. Might be a contract I could toss your way."

"I'm available. Thank —"

"So what did you think of the Chinese women?"

Jeff paused. "I don't know. The students seemed nice." Bill Something wanted more, his hands knit together. "What did you think?" Jeff said.

"Some pretty gorgeous women, seemed to me. Went to a few clubs. Some babes, willing to go, know what I mean? They really wanted to get out of there. Could have had our pick. Some pretty gorgeous pussy."

"Really?" said Jeff.

Bill's eyes were drifting to his monitor, which was emitting e-mail bleeps.

"Well, thanks for your time," said Jeff.

"No problem. Bei-jing, eh? Glad to be back?"

"Absolutely," he said.

"Had one. Had to get rid of her," Bill said. "Couldn't have been more than nineteen. I'll be in touch."

Back home, Jeff glanced at the *Times-Colonist*, his head aching. Full of jobs for which he was not remotely qualified — web page designers, mostly, and jobs that were barely worth having, the ten-dollar-an-hour slavery of hotels and restaurants.

Another letter from Bian Fu lay unopened.

Melissa and he walked by the ocean, she urging him to walk only on wood, on the beached logs and smoothed-down sea-drift, and she ran, balancing and leaping, far ahead. It was a dull day, windless, the ocean stretching towards the Olympic Mountains, Port Angeles invisible behind low-lying clouds. Where did the incessant lap at the beach's edge come from, exactly? He lost his balance on a log and plunged onto pebbles. Melissa shrieked: "You lose, Daddy. I'm on wood, you're not." He laughed. Then she wanted to collect rocks, and the smooth pieces of green glass.

"I like these green rocks, Daddy, here. Here."

His pockets were already stuffed.

On their way back, she ran ahead up a long staircase in the cliff, then did a quick cartwheel on the Dallas Road walkway. A friendly setter ran up to sniff her, and she began to pet him, then a collie bounded up and nudged her, and Jeff ran to protect her. He was always frightened of dogs. But Melissa loved them: she rubbed their necks and snouts, banged on their backs with her small hands so Jeff flinched. The owners collected their dogs and Melissa waved goodbye.

"I want a dog, Daddy."

"In an apartment?" he said. "I don't think so."

They crossed into Beacon Hill Park, and set out across an immense crushed-gravel soccer field. They plodded through that grey waste, moving towards a distant border of oaks.

"Just a small dog, Daddy."

"You will have to ask your mother for your place."

"Will you get a car, Daddy?"

"I don't think so. Not yet."

"When, Daddy?"

"I don't know."

Halfway across the field his stride had lengthened and Melissa lagged a few steps behind, then farther. He slowed his pace, thinking immediately of two disparate memories: himself, an early version of him, trying to catch up to his father; and an older Chinese couple he had seen jogging in Victoria one morning, the woman dutifully running in choppy imitation of her husband, ten steps behind. Jeff turned around and swept Melissa up and gave her a shoulder-ride all the way home.

That night she came into the living room and said she could not sleep. "Will you snuggle with me, Daddy?"

"I'll come in in a few minutes, see how you're doing," he said.

"I want you to snuggle. I can't get to sleep."

So he did. He balanced on the edge of the bed and rubbed her back.

"It's just that I want to sleep, Daddy, but I can't sleep. If I can't sleep, I will be tired, and I don't want to be tired, but I can't sleep," she sobbed.

"There, there, sweetheart. Don't think about it. Think of something else, something nice."

"I try, but I can't sleep, Daddy." He could feel her breathing getting bigger in her tense back ; he gently stroked her hair. "Is that better?"

"Yes, but I don't like it when I can't sleep, Daddy."

"Think of something different," he said. "Think of China. All those little pandas over there."

"How big is China? Is it very big, Daddy?"

"As big as Canada, or nearly as big. Pretty big."

She turned and grasped his hand.

"Will you go back there, Daddy?"

"I might," he said. "I might go back to marry Bian Fu. But not now, honey. I'm staying here for now."

"But will you always come back to me?"

"Yes, I will always come back. To you, you little panda. Are you ticklish?"

"No, Daddy. I need to get to sleep."

In a while her body relaxed and his back was stiff from maintaining his position. He listened to her breathe. He slid out and left the door ajar.

He opened Bian Fu's letter.

> *I have bad news to tell you, Jeff. Last week my boss he say I should help the company. And help myself, he say, by doing things with the clients I do not want to do. He say it very clearly. I tell him I will not, what do you think I am, a bad woman? He say I should be practical and do this, go out with these men. I refuse. And so I have losed this job recent days. Now I am looking for a new job and wish me luck. This is a terrible thing happened. I do not understand what this man think I am. My mother tell me not to give up and try to finding other work.*

> *I do not like this. I am angry he think I will go with these men.*

> *When I think of you at night I feel safe.*

> *I think about your health, is it good, Jeff? When I think this way I know my feeling is love.*

> Xiang fang xiang cheng *is not the same meaning I think you are meaning. Do you think we are not the same feeling, not like each? We are, can I say, against each other, is that your meaning? Tell me your true feeling.*

> Wo ai ni,
> *Bian Fu.*

Chapter Eleven

In June it invariably rains in Victoria, and the Juan de Fuca Strait separating Vancouver Island from Washington State is a grey morass. Only rarely are the mountains seen; the broad Pacific Ocean is a distant rumour. Walkers at the sea-edge are few. Cars pull up at the lookouts and park, their drivers staring out at nothing.

The last week in June brings the sun: the blue-white peaks of the Olympic Mountains stand out clearly, surmounting all; Mount Baker stuns, like the reappearance of a god; all along the beach and sea-paths, the humans roam, finding in themselves new energies. Arms and legs are bared. Even the laziest break into trots. Dogs congregate in shaggy communion. All along Cook Street, a double row of chestnuts are in white flower, their leaves touching above the street. Bikes gleam, newly washed and oiled. Their riders lounge in the competing two large cafés on either side, a fabulous Spandex array of coloured shirts and sleek shorts; they wear sunglasses until the streetlights come on.

Jeff sat in the café, smoking a cigarette.

His attention was inward: a blinking green sign: *cha, cha, cha.* And then the Beijing film running, the echelons of dark apartments above him, the clanging, ringing and squeaking of bikes slowing to turn at the crossroads, swerving to avoid the vendors' carts, the entrance to the alleyways, the *cha* sign blinking. He effortlessly understood the chatter around him. "*Yi kuai wu, yi kuai wu le.*" A kuai and a half. "*Lao wai.*" Foreigner. "*Nai-nai, Je-Fu jiu lai le.*" Granny, Jeff's here.

He missed her.

There was no word about the divorce. She had recently got a new job — teaching English to *tu er suo* students, kindergartners — at a large company. She did say that Li had almost got the apartment.

Jeff was sullen; he had found work too, at a communications office in the government. He went in at 6:00 a.m. and listened to radio news broadcasts, producing a summary of each story that might affect the government. It was repetitive and he had to work quickly. He strained to hear any news of China, which was rare. He noted that Zhu Rong Ji signed an international declaration of human rights and the very next day arrested all the leaders of alternative political parties. Jeff supposed if he were to return, it would be in September, when the new school term started. The grounds of Jian Hua, drooping willows and stone ping-pong tables, rose in his mind, died.

Terry set the lattes down.

"Let's go sit in the sun."

As they did, a flash of red hair caught his eye. Blue eyes.

"Hi," he said.

"Hi," she said. Neutral. She returned her eyes to her book.

Terry was craning at their streetside table.

"Did you see that one? Thank God for rollerblading. It's the best thing to happen for legs and ass since, since… Help me out here."

"Since what?"

"Never mind. God, the women are beautiful. Look at that one. What do you say, homeboy?"

"She looks nineteen, that's what I thought of that one."

"Tits," Terry said. "Spring and a young man's fancy. Turns and bounces up and down. Look! Near Mac's. Sucking on a slushie. It's love, no question. And forsooth — I a married man."

"So's she."

"Huh?"

"She has a ring the size of a ping-pong ball."

"Oh-ho. Not that it's ever stopped you, my friend. How goes the hapless romance?"

"She got a new job. No word of divorce. Shit."

"Yeah, you were saying, her last job."

"What do you expect? Chinese business. A fucking whorehouse."

"Wanted some extra duties out of her, eh? Never happen here. Place's so PC it makes my head spin."

"Here's not there. Should have seen her last letter." Jeff lit another cigarette. "It's like she hates that shit but she totally buys into it too. She has this fantasy that she'll go to South China. You know why? Because if you're a 'beautiful Chinese woman,' there are plenty of rich men 'pay for you to live.'"

Terry shrugged.

"Doesn't that kill you?"

Terry shrugged again. "Maybe that's the reality, bucko. Question-begging time, what are you gonna do about it? Are you saving any money?"

"Pretty tough on the four, five hours a day I'm working."

Terry made to say something, then looked away.

"What? What?"

"Nothing. Let's go for a walk."

They didn't speak until they were on the ocean path. Two Chinese women passed; Jeff tried to catch their words. "Hai tan hen chang... Shi de." *The beach is long... Yes.*

"More to your taste?" said Terry.

"Just listening to their *zhong wen*."

"Just parting your legs, ma'am, to attend to your *zhong wen*," said Terry.

"Oh, shut the fuck up."

"Let's fire one up," said Terry.

They passed the joint back and forth. The broom was out in brilliant yellow along the cliffs; two lovers walked hand in hand on the beach far below.

"It's how she negotiates," Jeff said. "She's playing on my insecurity. She's trying to get me back there. It's how she was raised. They're so pragmatic. Everything with its price. If I don't come, who knows what she'll do? This South, rich men stuff, is just a lure."

"It appears to be working."

Jeff said, "Shit."

"You ever thought she's just as impatient as you are? That she wants some finality out of all this? I mean, let's be realistic. Sure, you had some hot times, but how long can that last? You either get back together or you don't. It's not going to go on forever. How long before your pecker starts wanting some trim?"

"You think that's what this is all about?"

"I *know* that's what this is all about."

"I love her."

"Then you better be clear," said Terry, clapping Jeff on the shoulder.

"How clear can I be?" said Jeff. "I don't even know what's going on. I go back, there's no guarantee. Things could be completely different — I mean, from what she —"

"That's your fear," said Terry.

"— what she tells me."

"You better get over that. Look, how long was it before you started noticing other women? Try twenty minutes after you got on the plane. Oh, his eyes flash with the passion he can barely stand. Am I right? I'm right, aren't I?"

"Give me that joint," said Jeff.

"All I'm saying, you want her, you got to have a plan. I know you love her." Terry turned in a circle. "I know what you're going through."

"You don't know what it's like over there."

"No, I guess I don't. But that's why you need to know how you're going to get on in Beijing, if you go back. And that includes Melissa, how you keep in touch, how often you visit. You gonna get Fu Wang over here?"

"Bian Fu," he said automatically. "I'm gonna try."

"How?"

"Don't know."

Jeff stopped and squatted. He was breathing fast. He stood up. Terry scanned the ocean.

"It's always a great fucking confusion, how people come together. You try this, you try that. Everyone's got their own ideas of how it should be. A fucking mess. It was that way with Carol and me. Parents, where do we live, borders, boundaries. And then something gives. You just let go, and all the decisions, they're already made. Look at us, ten years later, we still can't agree on how to set the table, even. Yet on we go."

"But you and Carol, you were in the same place."

"Well, now you're talking reality at least. Shared reality."

"*Wu wei,*" Jeff said.

"Woo what? Come again."

"To act without acting, it's a Chinese philosophical term. I don't do anything right now: I wait. I see where things go. I move with the flow."

"Is that what she's doing, or you?"

"Just an idea. An approach."

"Things don't seem to be moving you two together," said Terry quietly.

"Not now," Jeff said.

They were almost at the breakwater.

"You *wu wu* too much, you'll end up paralyzed," said Terry.

Jeff said, primarily to himself, "Laozi said the sage pays great attention to details, thus in the end he is free of them."

"I go with Laozi. How's the job?"

"Boring."

"My friend, you've just described ninety-nine per cent of all jobs."

They continued walking, two figures among many on the stone breakwater that hulked out of the brilliant sea.

When Jeff took Melissa by bus to gymnastics, he felt like an outsider, if not a pauper. He could not precisely explain this; it was no particular thing anyone said to him; but he hurried through the parking lot, to avoid all but the most perfunctory conversations with other parents. Who pulled up in their minivans, their Lexuses, their SUVs. The women, drivers for their yelling broods, wore sweat pants and T-shirts. Their figures in decline. A sad reckoning as they locked their cars, to issue commands, to scold and chide, and saw their kids outstripping them, grubby hands already on the gym's glass door. The women's eyes were controlled; their inner selves filed endlessly through anticipated costs and driving arrangements. He could not for the life of him think of anything to say to them. His hellos and how-are-yous were returned, but all connection died in the volley of shouts from the gym floor.

The men were fewer. They simply looked tired, obviously just off work, in white shirts and ties. God knows what the men thought about as they waited. Sex? Hockey? Radial tires? All gathered in the viewing area to hunch in plastic chairs and wave at the kids as they learned the basics: the cartwheel, the headstand, the swinging on uneven bars, the popular bouncing on the trampoline. Badly drawn cartoon characters shone on the walls.

Jeff was merely the messenger: he got Melissa suited up and sat among the other parents, saying nothing, reading. He got up occasionally and looked at the signs for bake sales, T-shirt sales, parent committees, none of which he was involved in. A faint resentment stirred in him, of being the one who takes his kid to things his ex-wife's family has paid for. Sometimes he had conversations with the other parents.

"So, where you working?"

"BC Systems. Been there for ages. You?"

"BC Communications. Just started. I was in China before."

"What was that like? Crazy, I'll bet."

"It was okay."

"Mine's the redhead down there."

Jeff could picture the man's house, with sports equipment and fading plastic toys all over the yard. "Mine's right there, on her head," he said. "The blondish girl. I had some good experiences in China. And I was studying Chinese."

"That must be difficult."

"It's not too bad once you get the tones down. That's the major part, first year, you can't hear the tones." Jeff would falter, the conversation palling.

More typically, he would leave the gym, his *Song and Tang* poetry book under his arm, and walk a few blocks in the rain, past biker bars and insurance companies and carpet and furniture warehouses, to sit for most of his daughter's lesson in a half-empty mall food court, gulping bad coffee. Sorry for himself, because he realized the only person he shared anything of substance with, about Bian Fu, about China, was Terry.

He was a loner, a loser. No cars, no colleagues, no houses, no family around him.

He was engaged. Therefore he should be happy. Was happiness long-term jobs, houses, so on? Surely not. But to be in love: this was happiness. Wasn't it? He felt no delight. Where was it?

His conversation with the man in the gym returned. "I had some good experiences. And…" And what?

And he had some bad experiences.

It followed.

Didn't it?

He would open his book and try to forget his uncertainty. The River-Merchant's Wife's image rose fresh from the page, equally from the simplified characters and the English. He could not see her hands, and doubtless her feet were bound, but Li Bai's words made her face, raised in hope, ambit slowly around an ancient walled city. Her eyes were haunting. "I was fifteen when I composed my brow / To mix my dust with yours were my dear vows."

He closed the book and walked back in the drizzle. He couldn't see the future anymore; he had no idea. He had to keep going. It was not just the woman in the book: those images merged with Bian Fu's serious face beside the hospital bed in Beijing. He picked Melissa up and heard her, without paying much attention to her, recount the lesson.

The birthday parties were worse. He couldn't remember this many from his own childhood; Melissa's friends seemed to have a birthday party every weekend. These involved searches for appropriate presents in malls, and excruciating waits while Melissa selected a gift — how many different stuffed animals were there? — when all he wanted was a cigarette. Her endless fascination with the obnoxious Rita's Boutique, with its carousels of costume jewellery, bright plastic purses, Day-Glo knick-knacks with the faces of the latest teen stars, stickers, bracelets, pocket diaries, earrings…it overwhelmed him and, simply to get her out of the store, he would invariably agree to whatever she coveted for herself. His apartment filled up with rub-on tattoos, spangly hairbands and clips, items Melissa adored for a week and then let fall; they ended up under her bed.

To get to the birthday parties they took long bus rides through progressively more expensive suburbs, duplexes giving way to discrete yards separated by hedges and catalogue fences, giving way to yards like golf fairways. Jeff made Melissa ask for transfers and drop the coins in the farebox. I'm teaching her how to ride the bus. She'll need to know this, thought Jeff, but was instantly reminded of how useless this instruction was, as her mother had a car. "When are we going to get a car, Daddy?" she would ask, fidgeting on the seat, trying repeatedly to stand up when he gently forced her to sit down.

"I don't know, honey, perhaps never."

When they arrived the hostess would say, "And you must be Melissa's dad," as if there were some other possibility, and they would be led into an acreage of carpet, huge TV screen, gleaming kitchen appliances on a waste of tile, so that Jeff was ashamed of his tiny apartment. He could not imagine having seven kids at his place — where would they play? On the balcony?

Would he like a beer?

You seen my new minivan? Pretty good mileage.

So you've been at Communications two months.

He could never figure out why he felt stupid when he accepted a ride back to his place for Melissa and himself.

"When is Bian Fu coming, Daddy?"

"I don't know honey. We just have to be patient."

"But why, Daddy?"

"It is hard to leave China."

"But you went there, Daddy."

"She is trying to come here, honey."

Was she? Her letters angled for another direction. Always it was, "When are you coming back?"

"Some day Bian Fu and I will get married, sweetie, and we will all get to know each other."

"Daddy, Mommy says you won't get married. You just have one girlfriend after another."

That stung.

"Why do you have a girlfriend in another country, Daddy? You don't get to see her."

#

Chang cun bao zhu xin
Qi shang wang fu tai
Rather than break faith I declared I'd die
Who knew I'd live alone in a tower high?

In Jeff's mind, the woman in the poem — who had Bian Fu's features, the round face and cheekbones, the beseeching eyes, but none of her verve — grew more and more sickly, barely mobile as he read her tale over and over. The husband stayed away, four months, five months. The screams of monkeys rose to the high heavens. She pined in a dreary room, feet tucked beneath her as she leaned over a bare table, occasionally touching her face with a fingertip. She went to the door, on whose sill moss grew, and she studied the imprints in the green: her husband's footprints. Six months. The moss grew deeper; Jeff saw her in the doorway, absently holding a broom, sickened resolve on her face. She shuffled back inside and laid the broom down. The moss glowed around the inconsiderable house.

Jeff was standing before a banked row of spinach and romaine.

He selected the spinach, pushed his cart forward.

"Hi."

It was the redhead he had seen at the café.

"You seriously gapped out there by the lettuce," she said.

"I was thinking."

"It's a serious decision."

"Pardon?"

"The spinach or the lettuce."

Jeff hesitated. She seemed to be inviting him.

"Jeff. Jeff Mott." He extended his hand.

She gave him a pleased smile. Shook his hand, hard. "Samantha."

She was not much shorter than he. Green eyes.

"I've seen you around," he said.

"Moka House. The hangout."

They were both gripping their shopping cart handles.

"We should. I mean, if you want…"

"Zucchini?" She laughed.

"Have coffee, I meant. At Moka. If you're not, if you'd like."

She swept her hair off her shoulders. "Great."

Jeff flushed and looked away. Spinach, cucumbers, green peppers, carrots.

"So, when?" she said.

They agreed to meet the next evening at Moka. She had classes.

"Eat your spinach!" she said, as he wheeled towards the dairy case.

Jeff spent the next few moments on two per cent or homo. As he crossed an aisle, he saw her at the cashier; her hair shifted as she chatted; her hands rested on the counter, offered her bank card. He was dizzy.

At work the next day he could not wait to get through the morning routine of lead news stories, repeats, fillers. The Minister of This said that. The Minister of That said what he had said yesterday, with slight enhancements. The opposition critic howled. The lobbyists howled. Men and women on the street, unused to the microphone, responded pleasantly, then got used to the microphone, and howled.

"Jeff," his boss said at the door, "there's a problem with the 9:30."

"Huh."

"You have the Minister of Health saying that the program is efficient because the program is efficient."

Jeff laughed. "That's one of the more reasonable things he's —"

"Fix it, would you? He gives figures. Put them in."

Jeff got through the shift.

At home, he managed to study Chinese for a half hour before he had an urge to clean the apartment. He applied himself, scrubbing the toilet and the tiles around it where his piss had splattered, got down on his knees to work away at the nodules of hair and macaroni between the stove and the cupboards; he used two newspapers, enjoying the squeaking, on the nicotine-coated windows. The papers came away a toffee-brown. He balled up his sheets, which were semen-stained and smelly, and stretched a clean sheet over the mattress. He opened the windows to air the place. He had a couple of tokes on the balcony, and continued. He straightened his desk, stowed Bian Fu's letters in a drawer. Then he removed her picture from the speaker, and the lock of her hair: in the drawer. After a long bath, and a shave, he tried to reapply himself to his Chinese. He shut the book when he came to a sentence: *Yinwei ta shi yi ge wai guo ren, wo dui ni jianglai you guanxin: Because he is a foreigner, I have some concern about your future.*

He saw the River-Merchant's Wife looking at him sideways, more out of interest than reproach, through the filtered green light of her venerable world.

Nonsense, he thought. A simple coffee. With a friend.

Bian Fu was just now waking up in Beijing. She was placing a pot of tea on the coffee table. Her mother was up too, carping at her. Bian Fu was drawing her hair up in a bun.

"… no idea what my students were thinking, most of the time. I think they thought I was pretty strange," Jeff said.

Samantha laughed. "Were they right?"

"Yes, maybe so. It's a weird situation. You realize halfway through that you know nothing about them. And they know it. Some of them had their own weird sense of humour about it. I remember one. She got up one class and said that English was a tool that they would use to master our technology. Then they were going to surpass us. Something like that. I was shocked. Halfway through the term I realized that she was joking, and the whole class was laughing at me, at my stunned reaction. Of course they didn't laugh out loud. But I'm sure they enjoyed it."

"I can picture that."

"I found it quite chastening. You realize so many things after the fact in China."

"I like the idea of you being chastened," Samantha said. "Did you travel around much?"

Jeff smiled. He liked her.

"Just Kunming and a couple of other places down south. I was busy teaching most of the time."

"Would you like to go back?"

"Some day. I — I don't know. No immediate plans."

"So you speak Chinese," Samantha said. She played with a coin on the tabletop. "That must be difficult."

"It was. It is. I think China is the most difficult place in the world to learn Chinese."

"Oh? That's weird. It'd be all around you."

"Well it is, but most people won't talk to you. And the students of course, they all want to speak English — that's all they want. The peasants actually, the people running the small shops, they'd talk to you, for a few minutes anyway. They were curious. Some of them had never seen a foreigner before."

"Did you feel lonely?" she said.

"Sometimes, very."

They talked in the shadows of the chestnut leaves outside the café. It was warm. Samantha wore a green top with a scooped neckline. Jeff was aware of her freckled collarbone and her fine, red hair around her quizzical face. She opened her hands.

"I remember feeling some of that in Quebec. I did a couple of months of immersion. God, I would get so tongue-tied." She laughed. "I was dying to speak English to anyone! A three-year-old!"

"Well, there were other English speakers around. The other teachers. All of them obsessed with how they were treated by the Chinese."

"Like you."

"Obsessed?" Jeff was surprised. "Well, yes, I guess I was. I never, okay, I did sometimes, but I never really thought of myself as different, and then you're in a place where everyone considers you strange and —"

"—and you're just being who you are, right?"

"Well, no, it's more complicated than that. Sometimes you acted differently because you knew that being yourself wasn't going to work. But it's funny. I mean, what was I thinking? That everyone was like me? It doesn't make sense."

"I know exactly what you mean," Samantha said.

She looked dreamily at the street.

"More coffee?"

"I'm kinda coffeed out."

"Do you want to…?" Jeff motioned.

"Walk, let's go for a walk," she said.

They slipped away from the café and its many conversations into the silence of the sidestreets; they passed the blue flickering TV-lit windows.

"Beacon Hill Park?"

"Sure."

He heard her breathing as they flowed into the park, in darkness up a long path between great bluish fir trees into a children's playground, and dallied for a while on the swings, Samantha dangling in small arcs beside him. Her runners scraped the ground. He touched her arm. "I wonder what the ducks are doing."

By the edge of the pond there were no ducks, only the long willow fronds touching the water, and moonlight coming through the treetops, making the water silver.

He slipped his arm around her waist.

Her head settled against his shoulder, and she turned into him; they kissed.

"Nice," she said, "that's nice."

He was floating with her. His voice seemed to occur some distance from him; his knees trembled.

"I could walk you home. Or."

"Or?"

"You could come to my place. For a tea."

"Sure."

He was tracing her palm lightly with his forefinger.

"I like you."

She giggled. "I don't like you."

"Oh?"

"Yes, terrible, terrible man. Come on."

He ran after her back the way they'd come. He caught her, mock-tackled her. Happily entangled, they went to his place.

The tea got made. It sat on the coffee table, cooling during their longkisses. His hand counted her ribs, rested on her breast. She shifted, pressed into him. She kissed him again, her eyes open, searching his face; her hand started playing with his neck, his collarbone. Then one button came undone.

#

"You were talking in your sleep."

Her hand was on his hamstring, stroking, soothing. She cupped his buttock. "You're beautiful."

"Talking?"

"Yes, yes. Some other language. Is that Chinese? I couldn't make it out."

"I don't know. *Ni ye shi hen mei li.* Like that?"

"No."

"That's Chinese."

"What's it mean?" She rested her head on his chest.

"You're beautiful, too."

"Oh, I bet you say that to all the women you sleep with."

He didn't say anything.

"Some, then." She chucked his chin. "Well?"

"What?"

"Did you sleep with any Chinese women?"

"Why's that so important?"

"It's not. Come on, I'm just curious."

"One."

"And was she very beautiful?"

"Yes."

"I'll bet she was."

"You?"

"I have never slept with a Chinese woman," Samantha said.

"Men."

"Not so many." Then she tossed her hair and laughed. "Oh, my God, I'm doing it. I said I'd never. With guys I've found you have to downplay the number you've slept with. Keep it to three. Or some guys think you're a slut. Isn't that silly?"

"Three, eh?" They were both laughing.

"Three and a half." She touched his cock, then rubbed it around her labia. "Three and three quarters."

"Four," he said, with a thrust.

When they finished making love, he turned and she snuggled against his back, kissing his neck. His fist was clenched against his belly when sleep took him.

#

When he set his backpack inside his door, home from work, the first thing he saw was a gold glint from the top of the speaker. The *qi pao* button. He picked it up and rubbed it.

Walked into the bedroom.

He smelt Samantha on the bedsheets.

He walked back and set the button on the coffee table. Rolled it back and forth. It wobbled, its complex, knotted surface unbalanced.

Asshole.

Samantha was coming over for dinner.

He slept with her. On the first date.

I love you and I will return to you.

She of the red hair and the smile that drew him towards her.

Tell me about our future life.

He started to pace. It was too much, too much responsibility; he had no control over what happened in Beijing. That was why he had done it. A release. From all that will-you-take-care-of-me onslaught he had to face, week in, week out, in Bian Fu's letters.

Yet Bian Fu's reproachful eyes were on him. As he muttered to himself in the kitchen, the bathroom, on the balcony, Bian Fu's eyes measured his endurance, gathering their brief past together, and their wishes for the future. Her arms folded, she had no need to repeat his many promises. He felt sick. His apartment was full of voices, like bats' cries.

Wo xiang nian ni, lao gong. I miss you, husband.

Rarely have I met a man in whom the desire to be good was stronger than sexual desire.

Let's see this. Then: oh, I love the little hairs around it. Let's…
Lowering my head, I'd look straight at the wall /
A thousand times I'd not answer your call.
The Chinese, they're so pragmatic.

Were they? To leave a marriage with a well-off oil company employee and camp out in her down-and-out mother's tiny flat in a neighbourhood of Beijing more resembling a village than a city, accepting the most student-like, immaterial proofs of love from a man whose everyday life in another country was unknown: this was pragmatic?

Tian Kang had said, *A girl like her will do anything to get out of China.*

Samantha's skin, warm, smooth against his in the night.

He had to choose.

The *qi pao* button was clenched in his hand. He crouched on the balcony, smoking. Samantha arrived when the light started to fade and a moody equilibrium quavered between the apartment, a couple of candles burning, and the darkening leaves and roofs on the corner. Samantha cradled a bouquet of tiger lilies. He buzzed her up.

They kissed tenderly, and she pressed the flowers into his hands.

"They're beautiful," he said.

"Aren't they? I wanted lilies or glads. I like the spots — see? — touch them. They're so soft inside."

He touched them and went and put them in a mayonnaise jar, filled it with water, and set them on the table.

"Nice vase." She laughed.

They stood very close, and she took his hands, fingered his palm. Her hair was down.

He touched her neck below her ear.

"I'm hungry," she said. "What'd you make?"

"Chicken curry," he said. "I'll get it."

As he turned to do so, she sat and crossed her legs; his eye was led by the curve of her leg up into her skirt, and she was aware, but studied his books.

"You've got a lot of Chinese stuff."

"Have a boo," he said. "I'll get the food."

He set it out: the rice, the curry with chopped coriander, little bowls of chutney. Juice, water. He served her, and she leaned over the table and kissed him fiercely.

"Thank you for cooking," she said.

He was working the spoon around in the rice.

"We don't know each other very well, do we?" she said.

"I think you're great."

She smiled, tilting her head.

"Obviously, I'm very attracted to you," he went on. "You're very lovely."

"Is this," she said, "a serious talk? I need to know if this is going to be one of those serious discussions. Because I have this urge. Shall I tell you?"

He didn't know what to say.

"I have this urge to play with the hair on your chest. Right now."

She got up and planted herself, one leg at a time, over his lap. The closeness of her smell and her lips, the fresh passion, kept him quiet. He kissed her within his knowledge of kissing; as though he would not explore anything new. She stopped presently, her eyes still merry.

"Your urges are complicated," he said.

He kissed her eyes and undid her buttons and placed his hand on her breastbone; she moaned; his mouth found her nipples and licked full and hard and he began to suck. She gathered her breasts in her own hands, offering them, and he carried her into the bedroom and set her with a great lurch on the bed, began tugging at her panties. She had her hand on his cock. In a moment he was in her.

"Chutney," she said, "chutney."

He fetched a bowl and smeared her belly with the sticky mango-syrup and when he had, working downward, reached her pubic bone, dolloped more on the insides of her thighs and began to lap it; and then his tongue found her clitoris, urging, darting against it, and he could not tell if his tongue or his jaw or her legs were shaking. She pushed him off and settled over him and he rolled over onto her and they made love until he came in a great, howling shudder so his elbows buckled and he gasped at her neck, and her hands clutched his ass.

"Is it so serious?" she said, when their breathing had stilled. "Unh?"

"You are a great lover," he said.

"Happy?"

"Unh."

She got up to pee. When she returned, he was sitting on the edge of the bed. He patted the sheets beside him and she sat. She ran a finger down his spine.

"You sit up straight now," she said.

"What do you feel?" he said. "I want to know your feelings."

"I feel warm. And happy. And I feel I am with you. Now," she said.

"Nothing more?"

"You know, asking me about my feelings isn't the same as talking about your own," she said.

"My feelings are."

"Yes?"

"Oh, my feelings, the hell with my feelings."

She said nothing.

"I mean, why can't it be enough? But it isn't. Because I'm not giving you enough. Because there is another part of me that. I don't know, there is another feeling... I am going to have to. Just say it. I love another woman."

Again she said nothing.

"So I don't know why I...I did."

"We did," she said.

"I know we did. She is far away. She has been far away for a long time. We are engaged. We want to get married. And here, I... But it's not that I don't want you. I want you very much, and I like you, and I'm sorry that we have to... That... We have to, but."

"Where is she?"

"Beijing," he said miserably.

"So go to her."

"She is not available yet," he said, after a while. "I keep waiting, and that comes down to I get, I got lonely, and it's not fair to you. It's not fair."

Samantha lay back on her elbows. He touched her hair.

"I don't know what to say, Jeff."

"No."

"Do you want to hear what I'm thinking?"

"Yes."

"I'm not mad at you or anything, you know. I'm not terribly happy you told me either. It just is. It is, Jeff. Jeff, you're not one of those, are you? I mean those guys who feel every time they make love with someone they have to marry them. Because I'm not like that myself. I just enjoy you. It's that simple. But you...you must know something else. Does she love you? Are you sure?"

"I think so. I don't know what kind of guy I am."

She waved that away. "And yourself? You — Jeff — you love her?"

"If you say you do," he said, "then you do, isn't that the truth? Your having said it puts you in the position of doing it, you are in doing mode. Yes, I do."

"But how do you do that? How do you love her here and not there?"

"Well, that's it, isn't it?" he said. "I — that's how come." He let his hand open over the bed.

"I can understand that."

"Can you?"

"I'm leaving Victoria, Jeff. I'm going very soon. I made these plans months ago. I'm sorry."

"No, don't. Sorry?"

"I'm going to study back east. I didn't think to tell you. But being with you, it's good. I haven't thought beyond that. I haven't thought yet what it might be like to not be here. Or — "

"You lost me."

"— or what staying would be like. I mean what could be wrong with us sleeping together?"

He looked at her, took her hand.

"I can't comment on you and her," she said.

"I know. That's me."

"So I'm not the one you could have had. Instead of. Or anything like that. I'm just me."

"Will you keep in touch?"

"No, I don't think so."

"So, we're just sex."

"Oh, Jeff."

"No, come on, I thought you liked me."

"I do like you. But you don't get it."

"No, I don't."

"Why do you want this to be a good thing or a bad thing? Because that's what you're getting at."

"I don't want."

"Sure?"

"I don't want, no. I don't know what. I didn't know what I wanted anyway," he said. "Why should I expect you to?"

"I think we understand each other."

"Really?"

"Oh, yes."

"For myself, I feel this is bad," he said.

"Give it time."

They were lying in each other's arms, again.

"Hungry?" he said, after a while.

They ate the rest of the meal in bed.

"What's it like?" she said.

"What?"

"Loving someone so far away."

"I'm not sure," he said. "Mostly it's remembering and hoping you get the chance to have more time together."

"Don't you have a plan?"

"I can't talk about it," he said.

She woke him in the night with kisses; he responded; he remembered sweat in the small of her back before dawn, and her sounds as she rose above him, her eyes for which he supplied the colour; and then her breathing again.

The alarm woke him. She was gone. He checked the apartment: nothing.

There was another letter from Bian Fu when he returned from work.

> *At work we have a big meeting, and the boss asks us why we are working there. I tell them very clearly. I am working because my mother always says I am useless. So prove to her this is not true, I came to work. Also I say I am here because my boyfriend beliefs. He knows what true love is. So I work and think of him.*
>
> *Jeff I want to know how your work is going. And our plans of marriage, how do you think of them? We will achieve the goals together. I am certain.*
>
> *Love you much,*
> *Bian Fu*

He thought of Master Kung a lot in late August, making his way through the swaying willow-shadows of the park at night. "Never have I seen a person in whom the desire to be good…" Give it a break, Kung. Never had you the chance to do otherwise, so let me walk freely in my own cage. Kung would smile and let him rant. Kung frail in his robes. The picture of politeness. Hardly satisfied, Jeff stopped by the duck pond, sat on a bench. None noticed him, but sometimes the incurious, bright eyes of a raccoon would accidentally light on him. The nights were chillier. He drew deeply on tightly rolled joints. He heard the footsteps of lovers sometimes, and enviously surveyed them as they passed; how did they have the right to be happy, to be together; by what process had they become so? He had the sense that Bian Fu was beside him; he felt this as a kind of weakness in his ribs, the thickness of a shadow. He knew what she expected of him — to be joined in her desires and dreams, and to fight to realize them. It was what she required of a man. There could be no discussion of their months apart, or of any real feeling, until they were together again.

He no longer wished to know what her days and nights were like in Beijing. He knew already. She would help her mother with Er Bao; she would pull all the furniture out into the courtyard and wash the floor. She would stand out in the midst of uncountable others (his lover's conceit), walking down the Kick Fish County high road, with the characteristic pout she'd learned to shield her beauty, assailed by the male eyes that would assess but not entreat, for to do so would be a loss of pride. Out with her friends from the language school, all dressed in space-boots and minis, she would act smarter and older than they in the glitzy nightclubs, where she would spend money he would never know she had. He considered that her allure and power consisted wholly in being separate from him: he did not know her life, only thought he did.

The family from Bing He would come and go. Not so much by direct comment but more often by the studious refusal to comment, they would unanimously condemn his presence and absence, act as if Jeff and Bian Fu's love, even if it took place in residences they themselves inhabited and paid for, did not exist. He shivered on the bench. Was this what his endurance was destined to overcome? Er Bao would now and then cry out *Guizi!* Ghost person! But the family would ignore it. The significance of that idiom: ghost person. Only a sliver of her family's reaction slipped into her letters, second-hand: "Wang Xue Nian has come recently from Bing He. He says that we cannot expect any support for our marriage."

How often, thought Jeff, had Li shown up in Bing He for an audience with her father, for some commiseration: the emotions of females, my son, so unpredictable, swayable even by a foreigner, the outlandishness. He saw Bian Fu's father pulverizing his medicinal herbs intently, unbothered by the unruliness of the blood that he himself had loosed on the earth. The chaos of unfilial children. He saw her grandmother pondering this, sitting up on the heated *kang* it was her fate to inhabit until death.

He was a moody pool of resentment. Pouring over the curbs, alighting from the minibuses, slurping in the noodle houses, the Chinese who surrounded her were part of her life in a way he knew he could not be. He desired that again — the transport, the immersion. He also knew he could not act, yet. This tension threw him in impulsive directions. Downtown, overhearing Chinese teenagers at a display window of shoes, he would hang behind them, following their chatter, until a yes, *Dui!*, burst from his mouth in imitation. He tore a phone number from the bottom of a sign in Chinatown: Mandarin lessons. The language had been roiling uselessly in him for months, filling him with unsaid sentence patterns, stories of crafty peasants, measured prognostications on developing economies, the earnest qualities of work-unit leaders, malicious tricks by foxes and dogs. He needed to speak. He resolved to call the number.

In the meantime, *wu wei*. He would do nothing and watch the universe, for as long as he could. He realized that his daughter was growing up. On the side of his bookshelf, there were pencil marks, begun even before he had gone to China, measuring her height. There were more marks now, inches, questions.

"Will I be as tall as you, Daddy?"

"I don't know. Probably somewhere in between my height and your mother's."

"I want to be as tall as you. How tall is Bian Fu?"

He indicated the top of his neck.

"Will you have more children, Daddy? Like me?"

"Not like you, honey. You're one of a kind."

Annette had to work in the afternoons and so Melissa was dropped off to him at lunch. They went to the playground on Cook Street, and Melissa returned to her mastery of the bars and rings, her favourite features of the jungle gym. He watched her swing, sipped coffee, tired from his early mornings. The cries of the children rose up through the leaves toward the sunlight. He watched how his daughter made friends, drew kids to her with her smile, joined in games. She protested loudly when it was time to go. The summer had passed, the grass more lovely in the slanting afternoon sun. He visualized the woman in the poem crumpled in her ruin, drenched in the rain at the end of a promontory, the sun sinking, birds caught in their cries of changing destination. She turned toward him to speak, "*Gan ci qie shang xin/*

Zuo chou hong yan lao. Sitting alone my rosy cheeks would fade/ My heart break and I'm afraid." In the background he heard Master Kung's mumbling counterpoint, "It is not that I do not love you, it is just that your house is so far away." Jeff hung his head at the thought of his own unfaithfulness, but the picture of the sage and the bereaved lover did not waver. They were in touch with him constantly at the edge of every wand of sunlight. The children fell from the jungle gym and spread across the grass, their legs flashing in great swift cartwheels.

The woman he started taking Chinese lessons with was short, precise in her habits, and polite. She met him each time at the door, tilting her head a little to say, "*Qing jin.*" Come in. As he removed his shoes, he studied her detailed shopping lists on the fridge, with weeks of dishes preplanned. He tried to cut through the kitchen to their study table, and she stopped him, indicating he must walk across the living room. That he never understood. The table always the same: a single sheet of paper and a pen, precisely centred. When he started talking, she would pick up the pen and begin twirling it; she had a trick, learned at school in Taipei, of revolving the pen swiftly so it sprang back between her thumb and forefinger. Her eyes flashed. She was bored with his stupidity, he knew.

On the way to her place he had whole conversations with himself in Chinese: sentence followed sentence, cities rose and fell in simple nouns and stunningly placed adjectives; when he sat before his teacher, his mouth struggled with, attempted to budge, a single stone buried in his throat that was holding up the words.

To help him, she threw off her boredom and revolved the white paper, drew a couple of characters, revolved the paper back to him, and pronounced.

"*Ni juede shenme?*"

He stared at the characters.

"I don't recognize them."

She drew two more.

"Oh, *jue de.* To feel. These characters are different."

"*Zhe ge,*" she pointed, "*na ge,* this and that, *tong yi ge,* mean the same. Written differently."

"Why?"

She pointed again, beside herself with his obtuseness. "China. Taiwan. Simplified characters; ancient characters. Now, tell me again about Jian Hua University. Describe it."

He peered at the characters, realizing another level of ignorance opening up, a chasm.

"What about it?" he said.

"Tell me," she said, her face perfectly still.

"Okay. Jian Hua University. I there taught. Very big university — very big. Has, there is, possible one ten thousand students."

"Good," she said, tilting her head. "Continue."

"In Jian Hua inside is ponds and little parks many-many, which ponds beside is trees. Many students walk-walk."

"Did you teach in the ponds?" she asked.

"I am not."

"Go on."

"Old buildings cold," he said, a panic coming over him, though a clear film ran in his mind: the throngs of bikes, the vendors, the smell of chalk dust, Wang Fang sucking on her pencil, but he could not get any of this out of his mouth.

"Jian Hua China's universities, the best, one of," he said.

"Good. Next week?"

He paid her twenty dollars for the hour. They set the time for the next lesson and he rode the bus home, abashed.

The afternoons with Melissa continued. She had progressed from the handstand and the cartwheel to the front roundoff, the front walkover. Her small body bent and unlimbered with a grace that made him ache. She flaunted her skill. "Daddy, can you do the splits?"

"No."

"Come on, try."

He got into a back-piercing position on the grass and tried to push his legs to spread farther. They wouldn't go. He smiled and spread his hands.

"Daddy, it's easy," she said. "Look."

And she bent her head to the ground, precisely between her outspread feet.

They went shopping for school supplies, which Melissa loved, and she begged for extra stickers so she could cover her notebooks. School starting. The days were filled by a softening, lazy light, contained by the cold of the mornings and evenings. He couldn't think why this was important.

He was wakened one night from a deep sleep. The phone. He ran. It could only be one person.

It was.

"Jeff! Ah, Jeff!"

"Love, what is it?"

"It is me. I got a divorce. I am free. Li give me a divorce."

Chapter Twelve

Jeff opened Bian Fu's package and breathed. Here it was, the fruit of their e-mail discussions. He had tried to imagine her typing in English in one of the storefront Internet cafés near Jian Hua. It was Bian Fu's application for a six-month tourist visa. The package was thick — many sheets of closely printed application forms, mostly unrecognizable characters, spaces for seals and signatures. It struck him as appropriate that the Chinese government wished to communicate primarily with other officials, the Chinese consulate in Vancouver, the Lieutenant Governor in Council of British Columbia. All they wanted from Jeff was a one-page letter stating he was willing to pay her expenses while in Canada. Bian Fu had gone about this task swiftly; she said her father had helped her. This surprised him. He knew she was reluctant.

> *I am not sure this is exactly how we are proceeding correctly. It would be easier you come back China, Jeff. Why don't you come back?*

He replied:

> *I think this is better. This way, you get to see what life is like over here and what my life is like. You will get to meet Melissa. We can make other plans once you come.*

She:

> *It is very hard, and I think maybe it is not such a good chance. But we will try. I want to see Canada and know you very deeply.*

He:

> *When you come, we can go for long walks on the beach here. And in the park. You will be surprised at how few people there are, and how much space there is.*

He brought Melissa along as he collected the many signatures the forms required. It was tedious. Often he had to drop the documents off and pick them up a day later. Melissa was confused.

"When is she coming?" Her hand tugged on his.

"I don't know yet, honey. We have to get all this paperwork done."

"Why?"

"Because of the Chinese government."

"Does she live with the Chinese government? Not with her parents?"

"She has parents, like you," Jeff said, "but the government of China has rules. They have to have all these papers before they let her leave her country."

"Did you have to when you went to China?"

"No. It was much easier."

"Weird," she said, with a look meaning that she didn't understand yet and would have to think about it.

Finally he sent the package back to Bian Fu, with a queer, unsettling relief that a matter so personal was in someone else's hands. A series of officials would stamp, seal or not stamp and not seal the documents and she would come or not come. The feeling unnerved him: he did not know what to do with it. It was either the strength to accept fate or a weakness, the relinquishment of control.

In any case he steam-cleaned his carpet.

He relegated half his clothes to a wire basket in the closet so she might have half the hangers.

On the weekends he and Melissa went swimming at the Crystal Pool, an activity he dreaded on some level. It was attention-intensive, beginning with the walk there. She dawdled and complained. "How much farther is it, Daddy?" It was plain that the ten blocks exceeded any distance her mother expected her to walk. When they arrived, there was the difficulty of supervising her undressing, making sure she stowed her stuff in the lockers without strewing it on the wet floor, and the further difficulty of her using the men's locker room. He did not dare let her go by herself into the women's. He remembered an infant swimming class when she was two: it had taken him easily a half hour to get her into her bathing suit, working feverishly against her wriggling, scared she would roll off the bench and crash to the floor.

But when Melissa got into the pool, she was all action and energy, and he had to keep alert to her every movement, as she was only at the floating stage and could not be trusted by herself. Thus he forced himself to trot behind her on the deck, as she verged on running, which was forbidden. In the water, he struggled to shake her off various flotation mats, which caused her endless delight. Finally she would let go, shriek, and plunge off, then Jeff would float her back for another ride.

He thought of Bian Fu in a bathing suit. Would she like accompanying them on these father-daughter outings? The only rest he had was in the kiddy-pool, shallow and several degrees warmer, a dreamy environment of seahorse sculptures spraying water from their mouths, and giant mushrooms raining down on the shrieking children, where he leaned back on his elbows and watched her frolic. The kids bounced weightless beach balls off each other's heads. Babies bawled on the brink of the mini-waterslide, let go, and swooshed into their parents' arms.

But the pool's big attraction was the super-waterslide. The announcements — *attention, the big green waterslide will be opening in five minutes* — encouraged kids to worship it as a sort of grail, or a scarce resource. The slide, looping several times up to the ceiling in huge plastic coils, attracted long lineups down its painted metal stairs that stung the feet.

He half-ran over to the slide, Melissa and her latest friend well out ahead of him. Melissa had recently learned to ride the slide herself, which spared him the back-stiffening ritual of cradling her between his knees all the way down, and lifting her out, heavy now, after they washed into the slopping end-chute. He lagged behind the girls when they skipped ahead in line. He saw Melissa's legs flashing up the stairs. His attention had wandered to the huge domed skylight, when a shout startled him.

"Jeff! Jeff! Melissa's hurt."

He took the stairs four at a time. On a landing near the top, Melissa crouched, hand covering her mouth, blood all over. He stooped to pick her up and she resisted him; she would not be held, so shocked and suffering was she, weeping, "I slipped," and howling at the outrageous unfairness.

"She slipped," said the lifeguard.

"Let me see it, honey."

She moved her hand away. The underside of her chin, where she had struck the step, was slick with blood. A gash. Jeff could almost fit his pinky in it.

"She shouldn't have been running," the lifeguard said.

"Yes, we know. Where's first aid?"

He led her down the steps. She wouldn't let him carry her. In the first-aid station a more sympathetic lifeguard offered her a grape Freezee and her crying slowed. The lifeguard gave Jeff an ice pack and told him to apply it. The bleeding stopped, but the gash was raw and pink and wide; stitches were going to be necessary.

"What are stitches?" Melissa said.

Jeff looked up from the accident form he was supposed to fill out, a form whose principal purpose was to exonerate the pool from any responsibility. "They're like little sewing stitches," he said. "We're going to go to the hospital now, and a doctor will sew that wound together in your chin so it will heal better. Now come on and we'll get changed."

On the bus to the hospital, she leaned into him, held his hand, and asked him more questions, frightened of the stitches that lay ahead.

"Will I always have them in me, Daddy?"

"No, they will be taken out later, honey. They're just for a little while."

It didn't take long. They were in an emergency room, and the doctor stepped in. "All right, who's hurt?"

"She is, my daughter."

"What's her name?"

"Melissa."

"Melissa, do you want to lie down here on this table?"

She did, her eyes wide as dollar coins. She arched her back and blinked at the bright lights, extended her arm stiffly, and clutched Jeff's hand hard. The single stitch took but a few seconds, the doctor swiftly threading it up and through, and Jeff felt every clamour of her nerves as it happened. Her brow was damp.

On the bus back home, she repeatedly asked if she would have to have this black stitch under her chin for the rest of her life. Over supper she was drained, picked at her food. Around seven, she announced that she was tired and asked to go to bed, without the usual struggle. She gathered her animals around her and closed her eyes. Jeff kissed her good night. He sat on the bed until her breathing was regular and she let go of his hand. He was exhausted.

The visa application fell through. Bian Fu told him by e-mail, and the next morning he was on the phone, calling through to the neighbour's in Kick Fish County, who had to run through the streets to fetch her.

"QING NI DENG YI XIAR."

Yes, he would wait, he told the neighbour.

As he waited, he saw the big metal gates she would rush through, with her snot-nosed brat in tow.

"*Ni hao.*" Bian Fu was on the line quickly.

"I got your e-mail. So they wouldn't give you a tourist visa, eh?"

"No, they refuse."

"Well, did they give a reason? Can you apply again?"

"They tell me I should not bother applying again. They said I have *immigration tendencies.* Those Canadians think they are so good. Not let me in. Of course I have immigration tendencies. What do they think I should have? My man is in Canada."

Jeff listened. He said, "Can you blame them?"

"What? You agree with them?"

"No, no, it's just that... Look, we give them an application saying you're coming to Canada and a single Canadian man writes a letter saying he'll pay your expenses. Purpose of the journey is to learn more English and see something of Canada. What do you think they're going to think? Shit, it never was a good idea in the first place. We didn't have a chance, this way."

"I know your meaning," she said.

"No, it's not —"

"You think I want to get out of China? That is your meaning. What is the matter with you? Don't suspect my love. It's not about immigration. Why do you think I can solve so many problems, get divorce from Li? I know your meaning."

"Please, listen."

"Not let me into country, I don't care. If you don't come back China, I will go to *Nanbian*, in Guangdong there are many beautiful Chinese women like me, and a rich man —"

"I don't want to hear it. I'm tired of hearing that. You want to go do that, fine. Just don't tell me about it."

There was a long silence.

"I want it too much," she said. "When I was young, my family was very poor. There was another girl in school with a blue dress. I want a blue dress like hers very much…"

Jeff listened to her story, one level down, thinking, and interrupted her when she started to say, "If you don't come back China…" again.

"Look, what are we going to do?"

"I don't know," she said.

"I have a suggestion. You think about getting your parents to write a letter to the Chinese government about our marriage, and I will try and find a job in China. This is not going to be easy. School has already started."

"When you come back?"

"Bian Fu, I don't know yet. I will phone you again next week. Bian Fu?"

"Yes?"

"Get that letter, please. We need it."

"I will do my best. But you don't believe I love you."

"Yes, I do."

"No, I think you do not. You do not understand me very clearly. Chinese woman depend on her man."

"Look, I'm doing my best too."

"When you come back?"

"Bian Fu, I love you. This is costing money. I have to go."

"Jeff," she said, "you try hard, but I am not the girl you want to marry."

"That's not true. Why are you saying that? You are the girl I want to marry."

"I want to hear that."

"You don't have to accuse me of something to get me to say that."

"You are angry. I say bye-bye now."

Later that day, when he was preparing the sauce for dumplings, he suddenly felt terrible. The image of the woman in the poem was all too clear. She is stooping to touch the ground outside her door. The husband's footsteps are still there in the moss, but faded because the moss is too thick to sweep; the wife is too tired and heartbroken to sweep it, and does not want to anyway because it is all she has:

> *Yi yi sheng lu tai*
> *Tai shen bu neng sao*

Other lines from the poem echoed: they were children once, and had grown up in the same village, without dislike or suspicion.

Without dislike or suspicion.

"You know, Jeff, you try hard, but I'm not the girl you want to marry, am I?"

"You are the girl I want to marry."

"Don't suspect my love," she said. "It's not about immigration. I'm serious, why do you think I have the ability to solve so many problems?"

We haven't got to the stage yet where they're our problems, he thought. We're still dealing with the baggage of your marriage and family.

He had not seen her for eight months. *Ba ge yue.* Eight months.

Ba yue hu die huang
Shuang fei xi yuan cao
Two by two the yellow butterflies pass
Over our western garden grass

He chopped garlic, nudging the slivers onto the blade and wiping them with his finger into the bowl of soy and vinegar. The smell filled his eyes with tears. He could not get all the slivers off the knife.

Jeff began his job hunt. He shook himself free of a great torpor and wrote an e-mail to the Chinese State Bureau of Foreign Experts, whose business card he dug out of his suitcase, along with many mementos of the past year. Tickets to the Beijing Concert Hall. Brochures outlining the features of Lu Xun's residence cum museum. A postcard of Gu Gong he had started to address, Dear Terry, but never sent. Dear Officials of the Bureau of Foreign Experts. He realized that the school term had already started. He had taught at Jian Hua last year, and availed himself of the marvellous opportunity that teaching in your remarkable country offers to all, etcetera. He pondered a sentence including the word "illustrious," and killed it. Too much. Wondered if his modest abilities as a writer and editor, honed through recent service with the BC provincial government, might serve some Chinese organization. Pleased to present the résumé of his modest qualifications. As he typed, he looked around his apartment: it gleamed. It was so uncharacteristic of him, this neatness he'd prepared for her coming, that he felt doubly alone. There was no airy happiness of refreshing his surroundings; rather, now he was readying it for his absence, an absence not yet certain, and so, flinging his e-mail off into the Web, he felt dislocated, not sure of his next move. He only knew that it wasn't likely to be cleaning the carpet again.

The reply came swiftly. A Miss Lin Wei Feng informed him that a magazine called *China Women's Monthly* was in need of an English polisher. The salary was comparable to what he had made at Jian Hua. Accommodation was provided — in the Friendship Hotel.

He groaned. The Friendship Hotel: he had passed it many times on Ba Shi Qiao Lu. It was a massive tomb, with the red tiled roof and upswept eaves common to all Chinese public buildings made to impress. It screamed simultaneously "late fifties Soviet official residence" and "five thousand years of history." It was several blocks square with many gates, each gate with its own impassive sentry. Bian Fu's visits, again, would be monitored. Another home he would have to sneak Bian Fu in and out of.

Don't be so negative, he told himself. It was a job, a chance. Maybe they would be having their honeymoon there, and soon. They would find a way.

He was interested, he replied. Did they need any more documentation?

As soon as he sent the e-mail he was visited by doubts about the salary. Jian Hua had not exactly been generous. Three thousand kuai a month! Jesus, a night out could cost two hundred. You're making more than ninety per cent of the Chinese, he reminded himself. Somehow this didn't help. English polisher? What infinite drudgery of propping his head up over a desk did that imply?

Annette dropped Melissa off that weekend, and when Melissa had run into her room to dump her things and say hello to her stuffies, Annette said to Jeff, "Well?"

"Well, what?"

"Is she coming?"

"I can't talk about it right now."

"Did you hear about her visa?"

"Annette, I need to think about this. I —"

"She's going to ask you, you know."

"I'll deal with it."

Melissa was out and looking from Mom to Dad.

"What do you want to do, Daddy? Can we go to the park?"

"I need to talk to your mother for a second, okay, hon?"

He walked into the hallway and waited for Annette to hug Melissa goodbye and she came out and crossed her arms.

"You're going back, aren't you?"

"I don't know yet."

"When are you going to know?"

"I don't know."

"You're not exactly being communicative, Jeff."

"No, I said I have to think about it. I'll let you know."

"Did she get a visa?"

"No, she didn't."

Annette sucked her lip. "Oh. I'm sorry, Jeff."

"Yeah."

"Was there a reason?"

"I can't talk about this right now."

"It would have been good if she had come."

"Yes, it would have been the perfect solution. But. It's not going to be."

Annette turned around and walked away.

He went in and began preparing dinner. Melissa got in behind him and, using the counter as a step, started to clamber on top of the fridge, where she liked to sit, head just barely touching the ceiling.

"What are you making, Daddy?"

"Chicken and potatoes."

"I can get up here and you can't. I like being small. I can get into places all small and scrunchy."

Jeff laughed.

"For Christmas this year I want a big stuffy and a radio of my own and I want a shirt with Pooh bear on it and I want a new bunch of markers and…"

"You should write a list," said Jeff. "Your birthday is coming up, too."

"For my birthday, I want a pool party, with all of my friends."

As he opened the oven door to slide the roasting pan in, Jeff thought, now is the time to say something. You've got to prepare her for the possibility.

But he said nothing. He asked her to set the table.

He got a response from the Bureau of Foreign Experts about the magazine job a couple of days later. The e-mail stated that the directors of the magazine were impressed by his credentials, and

wished that he perform an assignment to determine his ultimate
suitability for the position. The attachments were drafts of articles
written for the magazine; he was to polish their English. It was hoped
he could perform this task within a week.

He opened the attachments.

The first was an account of a Chinese government and NGO-
funded economic development project in a far-flung province. In
the article, he was introduced to a Wang Ning, who "*lived in poorness
deep and no future it seemed she was to be having, because of having five
children, and sickness all the time was with them, in a mud house, her
husband long ago in prison and with her relatives dead, mostly. Wang
Ning felt no hoping of her situation. She was relying on the other villagers
when their generosity afforded them the occasion of to give to her some
fuel-wood making her to light her stove, and sometimes food.*

"*The Xing Fu Hope Initiative for Economic Independence in Rural
China was introduced with the making of contributions by Ministry
for Interior Security, Ministry of Agriculture and all cooperations of
the International Poverty Relief Alliance, the Rural Benevolent Futures
Fund, all this happened to introduce to China the hope for a more gladder
prospect and was long before Wang Ning did hear about the opportunity
like other women had in hard-fortunate situation to take care of their
children, in the past.*"

He skimmed the rest. He made out that this fund had loaned
Wang Ning the money to purchase a grinder, with which she was
able to produce lamp oil from a certain seed, a process that involved
her working long "breaking of back" hours gathering the plants from
the neighbouring fields of peasants, which meant she had to swing
several subsidiary deals with the locals, so that, ultimately, she could
take a few containers of the oil to a market ten miles away from her
home and sell them. It hardly seemed like a complete rejuvenation
of her lifestyle; however, it did save her from "the situation bleak of
must prostitution as the case could be many women in rural China."
He thought he could break down and reconstruct Wang Ning's task,
given the prose at hand, but from a rewriting point of view he was
dismayed when Wang Ning and her sickly family disappeared mid-

article into a bewildering maze of statistics and pronouncements and poorly described other initiatives. He looked over the tortured prose, and checked himself. How well could he evoke Wang Ning in Chinese? "Wang Ning, poor, very poor, have many sick kids, sell a something get richer." He laughed at himself. All right, he would see what he could do. As Beijing jobs went, this might be halfway interesting.

He opened the other attachment.

Chinese Communist Party Central Committee Sub-Committee on Women's Emancipation Chairperson Makes Preparatory Policy Framework Statement on Beijing Declaration of Rights of Women Proclamation. He skimmed it. The article was a collection of pronouncements by a Hong Kai Zheng, a fierce figure in a padded jacket. He learned that the status of women in China, "*though are signs of showing improvement, are still in the condition of lowliest beside the men of China.*" He learned Mao had said that women hold up half the heavens. A sharp pain developed between his eyebrows when he read that "*all political change is to cause a reaction and especially the reactionary society's elements would be in the anticipation of improvements so that a vigilant attitude might be expected of those who are wanting a change in the matter of the women's freedom.*" The people desirous of this change were the masses, who, Jeff judged, were all those not ensconced in the palatial Women's Ministry building on Chang An Avenue and not married to high-ranking Communist Party officials. "*Women's progress is the following natural of revolutionary changes which by classes of society are in struggle to being the overthrowing of oppressive elements.*" "*The freeing of women from their obligations to existing in roles that are the feudal ones, this task is immensity before the Chinese society, and never before attempted by our ancestors has it been.*" There were five pages of this. By the time he finished reading it, Wang Ning's predicament, her seed-pressing and oil-collecting labours, seemed a literary masterpiece, Tolstoyan in its physical accuracy, clean and simple and unrhetorical, elegant as a mud-walled hut.

He set to it. By the light of his nicotine-coated monitor screen and the steady pulse of the cursor, he edited and polished the articles until they shone in standard English. He straightened out sentences; he cast paragraphs in a consistent, sunny tense; he rearranged the Wang Ning piece so that the dry groves of statistics were as fresh and green as the forests that Wang Ning skipped through on her way to market, her earnest face, her heavy baskets of seed always facing the reader. His own workdays at the government communication shop came and went as he edited the articles, and it wasn't lost on him that the announcements and complaints of local politicians and pundits were easily as abstract as anything the arbiter of progress, Hong Kai Zheng, had to say about the wheel of history and the flurries of reactionism. So too, the wanderings of the secretaries and female directors who surrounded him at work, from fax machine to cubicle, discrete office to coffee-station, seemed to him as dialectical as any army of Chinese women Hong Kai Zheng could conjure. Their clothes outstripped their salaries; their wedding rings flashed as they typed.

And he typed away, back at home, eyes shining with computer heat, as he slid participles to abut their subjects, took relative clauses that shivered and shook and threatened to spawn their own sentences and trimmed and tucked them neatly into Hong Kai Zheng's towering theories, which he toned down to the calm reason of a crusty oracle, as everyday as the acquisition of a beeper or a foreign boyfriend. He assumed that Bian Fu would read these articles and go, Bah! As he edited, he tried to ignore a blizzard of ironies. Emancipation of women in China. Fathers sealed away within the walls of the family home in hoary old Bing He, suavely offering thirty thousand kuai so that their daughters would marry the men they chose. Revolution couldn't be as simple as changing your mind, he thought, nearing the end of his revising. Not like here. The woman he had comforted and kissed in her confusion being told she must sleep with customers to benefit some shitty little company, and herself.

In a great fury he finished the work, and sent it off with a covering letter wherein he expressed his hope that the revised articles were worthy evidence of his ability to meet the evidently high standards of the magazine; as he did so, the figure of Kung appeared in his mind's eye. Kung was relaxing, his fingernails a little longer, his robes immaculate; he calmly lounged, piercing Jeff with his gaze. Jeff was apparently able to read Kung's mind. "What are you so upset about?" said Kung. "Did you know that I offered my own daughter in marriage to one of my disciples simply because he performed the ceremony of the white jade flawlessly five times?

"Well, what else was I going to do?" asked Kung. "You tell me."

He was up the next morning at four-thirty to phone Bian Fu.

"Jeff," she said, "how is it? Are there jobs you are applying for? When you return Beijing?"

"There is something that I'm working on," he said. "I should know pretty soon. Listen. I have something to tell you."

"*Ni shuo ba.*"

"I will not return to marry you unless we get a letter from your father stating he is aware his daughter is marrying a foreigner. Because that's what we need."

"Ah, he says he will write it, but he want us to be sure."

"He wants us to be sure." Jeff repeated the words incredulously.

"Yes, they are very angry at me leave marriage to Li. They don't want me make any more mistakes. Jeff, I miss you, love you. When you come back?"

"I don't know," he said. Then he started to talk quickly, angrily, across the Pacific. "Listen, I'm trying to get a job. I want to come. But I don't want any more of this bullshit. Your family has got to help us."

"I am doing my best. I can solve this problem, very well. Why are you angry, Jeff?"

"Dammit, I'm not angry at you. It's your parents. They aren't helping here at all. They prevent us from having any sort of life together. We can't live together. You won't introduce me to any of your friends. I don't even get to meet your father and have some chance to influence the situation. We get to sneak around Beijing again and hide our relationship. I get to leave my daughter and travel five thousand miles in order to wait for a man — a man who won't even try to communicate with me — to write a lousy one-page letter. He won't do it and you won't even demand it. After a year-and-a-half your parents are still making the decision, not us. Not acceptable. And they want us to be sure? They're *separated* for five years and they want *us* to be sure? Fucking hell —"

"You don't have to swear," she said, after the telephone line crackled.

"I'm frustrated," he said.

"You will abandon me."

"Why don't they just admit that they don't want a *lao wai* to marry their daughter?"

"I am doing my best!"

"I know."

"Look, they want us to be sure because of my marriage, it was a legal marriage and it ended, so they don't want me to make any more mistakes."

"You said that already. So they get to decide what a mistake is?"

If ever there were a sentence that encapsulated his naïvety, that was it.

"They are my parents. They love me very much."

"I know."

"Do you want to say bye-bye now?"

"No," he said. "I love you. I am trying. I will find out soon about this job."

"I wait for your telephone call."

"Okay, Bian-Bian. Good-bye," he said, and hung up. He got ready for work.

I love you and I will return to you.

At the Beijing airport, Bian Fu had hugged him, wheeled away from him, taken the wrong set of stairs, run back, and hugged him again, kissed him. "I love you and I will return to you," he had said. Yes, he had.

You always come back to me. Melissa had seen him at the Victoria airport and launched herself toward him, her eyes shining, left the ground running, and threw her little body against his and he whirled her around, ran his fingers through her hair, set her down and picked her up again, gave her a big smackeroo on the cheek. "You always come back to me," she said. "Yes, that's true," he said. "Always."

He lit a joint.

Jeff sat in front of his computer. It was late. He had spoken with Terry earlier:

"I got a job in Beijing."

"So when are you leaving?"

"I don't know yet."

"Soon, though, eh?" Terry sounded distracted.

"Tell you what, you free tomorrow? Meet you at Swan's for a beer," said Jeff.

Now, he stared at the e-mail on his screen. It was approaching midnight. The odd car swept past outside. The Bureau of Foreign Experts had informed him that the *China Women's Monthly* would employ him as an English polisher. That's me, he thought. English polisher. And my Chinese is very good. They wanted to know what flight he would be taking to Beijing: two weeks or three weeks from now. He clicked around inside the e-mail text with the mouse. Welcome you to China. You need to send your passport to the embassy in Vancouver to receive work permit, immediately. We need to know if you accept. Please give us your response immediately.

He no longer saw the screen. Instead, he was rubbing his nose, yes, his difficult nose against Bian Fu's cheek, searching her eyes, trying to get her to open her lips, to yield to him in a heated kiss. He felt her hands tugging his shirt down tight on his shoulders. Her hips were bumping against his. Her eyes were complicated, inner. How he wanted her back! Wanted the taste of her hair in his mouth, wanted to hear the long, suffering sigh she let loose when he entered her, her eyes filling and lifting to the ceiling, and then the hesitant, beautiful weight of her fingers working against his spine in the night. But he clung to her, hoping for something, in the glow of the computer screen. In her complicated eyes he was searching for something, and it would not come. No matter how he shut his own eyes and sent his mind out travelling, exploring the year ahead — for the contract with the magazine was for a year — he could see no certainty in her

eyes; instead he suffered the glinting maybes in them; he shifted on
his chair as he saw the long tunnel of her eyes, and what lay ahead.
The downcast looks when he pressed her for what he wanted to know.
The polite evasions. He saw himself standing on a street corner in
Kick Fish County, winter coming on, as she listened to him ask,
again, when her father would see them, and she shuffled her feet,
embarrassed, as always, by his directness, and lifted her eyes to him
and said, "Not much longer." He saw himself clutching documents
in front of silent officials, who offered him tea. He saw winter end
and the sandy winds from the Gobi lash her hair around as he told
her he did not know whether to go back to Canada or not. It's your
decision, she said. It's your decision. He saw her fear. He saw himself
yelling, shaking her by the shoulders on that dusty street corner, saw
her flinch and resist in her silence as a band of Chinese men passed,
observing them closely but saying nothing. He saw himself talking
himself hoarse on the phone to Bing He, and her father politely
asking for Bian Fu so she could translate. He heard Bian Fu saying
that her father was busy now, could he phone again some other time?
And worse imaginings: he saw them together in front of a toothless
neighbourhood committee work unit inquiring about an abortion,
Bian Fu so mortified she stared at the floor. He saw a slim Chinese
man take her hand and help her into the passenger seat of a shining
Miata. He would lose her, somehow. He knew this for a fact.

He dragged on the joint again.

He saw her sitting very still, saying nothing, as the voices of her
family bombarded her.

He felt a weight starting to shift within him, and looked around
the apartment at his things. There was a lot to do. He had to give
notice at work. Work visa. Landlord. He got up and walked in a slow
half-circle through his things, stunned by their number and weight.
The bookshelves, the computer desk, the couch, the futon, the beds,
the stereo, the food, the chairs, the dresser, the obstinate mass that
he had to lift and prepare for storage for an indeterminate period. He
walked around the room again, enumerating these. He sat down on
the couch.

Bian Fu waited, her lower lip puffed out, her arms crossed. He had to lift her out of her circumstances. He was exhausted; he doubted he could budge from his own.

He went to sit on Melissa's bed, amid the stuffed animals, their little eyes looking at him. Ralph, the feeling dog, was beside her pillow. He picked it up and held it in his lap.

I love you and I will return to you. I always return to you.

He saw his daughter, years away, taller, practised in the ways of balance beams and trampolines. He heard her voice, the timbre changing as she said, "Next year," and "Soon, I hope," and "I don't know." He saw her rangy, shooting through her years, suddenly practised at avoiding the question. She flinched, she said nothing, she silently endured the roughhousing of her friends' fathers. He clearly saw her licking envelopes to send a picture of her dog, a photocopied report card. He saw her open a drawer and touch a red *qi pao* he had sent, folded on top of other presents, admired ruefully once, never worn, the drawer difficult for her to close. He squeezed the stuffed dog and returned it to its pillow.

A stranger energy started to flow through him. He had to move. He grabbed his coat and before he knew it he was walking the quiet streets, his heart churning, towards Beacon Hill Park, the same route he and Samantha had walked, following the spoor of his own unfaithfulness. The dark trees swayed over him as he trudged up the hill. Orion was bright in the night sky. He stopped at the duck pond with its many willows trailing their leaves in the water. He breathed, and as he did, he smelled coal smoke. Beijing rose in him:

He was on his bike again, pedalling through the crowds, blasting out of Jian Hua's West Gate, pumping hard, dodging the minibuses and the queued Chinese with their eyes down and their mittens and scarves. He got hung up at the Kick Fish crossroads behind an old man pedalling slowly along hauling coal on his flatbed, then he cut in front of a taxi, and cruised through the market with its rabbits stiff on the tables and the Uighur vendors with their Russian hats and their Turkic language, and they yelled at him, hawked calendars and kids' clothes. He roared past the stalls and stalls of cabbage and nubbly cucumbers and the woman laughing toothlessly as she rocked in her padded Mao jacket beside a pyramid of cigarette packs, and the leather-jacketed farmers gossiping on their farmer cellphones and the lapdogs perky in the bicycle baskets, and the shouts and shouts of *Mai Le Ma, Yi Kuai Wu, Yi Kuai Wu Le!* The shapes swirled around him, and then, his breath catching, they dissipated.

He stood freezing beside the pond.

They had sat beside each other at the Chao Bai River a year and a half ago.

He slipped his hand in Bian Fu's. "Can I hold your hand?"

"Bah, you do not have to ask, I do not like it. If you do something I do not like, I will tell you."

"The river is lovely."

"Yes."

She looked shyly at him.

A fish jumped.

"Ho, it is a fish," he said in Chinese. "A beautiful fish."

"Yes, and it is a bird, a lovely bird."

"A bird and a beautiful fish."

"I am a woman and you are a man."

Suddenly, he saw Bian Fu standing with her bike across the pond, beside a tall stack of *baozi* steamers; the steam whipped through her hair.

"Here I am, how stupid, waiting for a man beside a stack of *baozi* steamers," she said, waving.

He laughed and called to her. "Let's go."

"Everyone has to face the truth," she said.

The pond lay still in the cold.

"Everyone has to face the truth," he said to himself. He was looking across the pond at the dark shapes of willows, in the middle of the night. A bird trilled once in the silence.

When he got back home, it was past three in the morning. He replied to the e-mail: He was sorry, he could not accept their offer of employment. He sent it. He made a pot of coffee and sipped it on the balcony, as the sky turned light. Then he called Bian Fu.

He told her his decision. There was a long delay in the satellite void before she responded.

"I do not know your meaning very clearly," she said. "What did you say?"

"I said I cannot come to Beijing. I cannot marry you. Our relationship is over."

"Why? Oh, I knew this. I knew you would not come. You would leave me, just like the other men leave me, always they leave me," she said.

"Or you leave them," he said, but regretted it. "I will explain why I can't come. I cannot leave my daughter. I cannot do that to her. And I don't have the money to come back and marry you and get you to Canada. It's too much."

"You say you would come back to me."

"I know. I'm sorry."

"You say, 'I want to marry you, Bian Fu.' You lie."

"No, I didn't. But I can't come. I cannot leave my —"

"Yes, I know, your daughter, you do not have to explain it to me like I am a little child. I am a grown woman. I understand very clearly."

The line crackled. Then she said: "I want to have a good relationship with you. If I have a life I enjoy and you have a life you enjoy, then we have something to share. I want to be myself, and I want to be part of you."

He said nothing. She started to cry, then she yelled, "I promised! I promised to always love you and take care of you, Jeff. I appreciate that about myself."

"I appreciate it too. But I will not do to my daughter what was done to me."

"Okay, I hate it. I hate it. I accept it. You say about your daughter, my eyes fill with tears and I admire you."

"I admire you too."

"How can you leave your woman?"

"How can you consistently put your family's interests before ours?"

He thought she didn't get that, but she was responding anyway. It occurred to him that they were not really talking to each other.

"Something happen to us when I was dreaming of the red carpet. Hesitation, suspicion, we start to fight, we lose the basis of our love," she said.

"We don't have a way to be together," he said. "Look, you think this is easy for me? I have many contradictory feelings. One day I want to get on the plane to Beijing, fuck it, fuck everything, I have to see you. The next day I never want to hear from you again."

"If you come Beijing will you call me?"

"Of course. Of course."

"Chinese woman need to depend on her man," she said.

"I'm sorry," he said. "I really am sorry." There was a long pause. "Bian Fu?"

"I listen."

"*Ban tu er fei,*" he said. "'I stop halfway.' *Ban tu er fei.*"

"Yes, I know *ban tu er fei.* Bah! Your Chinese is very good!" And she hung up.

"So, got things all lined up in Beijing?" said Terry.

Jeff paid the waitress for their drinks and took a long draught of his. "No," he said.

"Oh, shit," said Terry. "Oh, okay. Okay. Is that what you want?"

"I don't know. It's a decision."

"Are you sure you have to make a decision? How about the process? Last week you were going, 'Oh, it's hard.' Fuck, I know it's hard."

"Process," said Jeff. "I'm sick of the process. First I get sucked in and don't even know what's going on, and then I go all the way back to China and play games for four months until I don't know where I'm at and find out she's married. Married. Then I have to go back and do that all over again. Shit, I don't even know if we'd get married if I went back again. I'm not going to take the chance. Her and her parents — they have all the power. I'm just a *lao wai.*"

"Bullshit. Sure, that's how it all got set up. But now you're in a situation that you both contributed to. And who encouraged her? Who promised her that you'd return? Who said you wanted to marry her?"

"I did."

"And you're going to stop it. Okay. But just be clear about why you're doing that."

"I'm not." Jeff turned and looked out at Johnson Street, cars heading over the blue bridge, passing under the immense cement counterweights. "Clear. I... couldn't...I couldn't tell her."

"Couldn't tell her?" said Terry. "You haven't told her?"

Terry started to say something more, then stopped.

The waitress came and went; neither wanted anything.

"Excuse me," said Jeff. He walked around the bar, stood for a moment before a brass urn with its towering bouquet of snapdragons and lilies and gladioli, and then he came back and sat down again.

"Change your mind for a minute there?"

"She's in grade three. Her birthday is next month."

Terry reached out and gripped Jeff's arm. "Congratulations, my friend."

"Congratulations? Jesus, I fucked up."

"No. Take a drink. Just take a good long drink. Because I'm going to tell you something very true."

Jeff swallowed. "And what the hell is so true?" he said sullenly.

"Now you know what love is," said Terry.

A stream of daily e-mails between him and Bian Fu began to bleep across the distance.

"You never did understand me too well," wrote Bian Fu.

To which he wanted to reply, "An aspect of your behaviour is: You never really wanted me to understand you too well, and that is a great pity." But what he wrote was, "Perhaps you're right about that."

"Both of us try very hard not to get hurt, and we miss something, and what we miss is joy. That's our story and it is a very sad story," she wrote, with a dashing finality he found both irritating and endearing.

"You're definitely right about that. I didn't want to get hurt again," he wrote back.

"Chinese woman depend very much on her husband, who take care of her and support her, depend on her family, depend on her father. I try to be more independent, but I am still like this. Not much has changed," she replied.

"I can't keep a job more than a year, because they bore me. I try to be more responsible, but I am still like this. Not much has changed," he wrote. "I've been poor all my life. I don't fear poverty. I fear being owned. And we didn't have it all together to get married. Marriage has to have some sort of economic foundation."

"'Marriage has to have some kind of economic foundation'?" she wrote. "Is this the man I fell in love with? I thought you were romantic."

"I didn't mean to hurt you," he wrote.

"I make a big mistake lie to you about my marriage. You cannot trust me. That was a big mistake. I did my best. It is my fate."

"I made mistakes too," he wrote. "Many mistakes."

And the e-mails crossed the Pacific for a time, transmitting longing, their final and mutual possession.

Then they stopped.

He quit smoking dope, abruptly; his dreams became vivid. In one, he was walking down the main street in San Tiao, his arms laden with documents he had to get signed or sealed or stamped. There was a whole folder of them; he knew they were important, and he had visited many officials that day, but also knew, in that choking, conflicted way so common in dreams, when things thicken at transforming junctures, that something else was crucial; when he had finished with the documents, he would have to deal with it. It was hot and army trucks rolled by with the sullen soldiers dandling their legs from the tailgates. His steps lengthened and he wove among the shop owners milling on the sidewalk in their stained undershirts, taking breaks from the tedium of their businesses to spit sunflower seeds and take in the drama, such as it was, of the San Tiao street. Then he was in the College compound and stopped by a small, dusty garden, struck by something. Laughter. He could hear laughter, female, coming from somewhere. It took him a few minutes to figure out — the source was the College bathhouse, where the girls let their young laughter ring out, so happy were they to be clean. If the girls were in the changing rooms, then it was probably time for the men to have the bath. He stood for a moment in the hot sun, thinking of a time when he was certain he had said, or thought, "Surrounded by so much beauty, I desired." The strains of a radio playing a Wang Fei song mixed with the laughter. A couple of women passed lugging full thermoses. In the dream he said it out loud, "Surrounded by so much beauty, I desired," and, tucking his documents securely under his armpit, he marched straight towards the bathhouse. The girls were laughing all right, tittering, shrieking in their hidden games with towels and brushes. He entered the fungal gloom of the dressing room, where, on hooks on all sides hung identical, yellow sweatshirts and pants. Yet there was no or little sound coming from the baths. Splashing. He listened hard for the laughter — yes, still there, trapped in the awful summer fustiness of the wood building, barely audible above the cool rill of water through the pipes. He disrobed swiftly.

The bathing room was dim; he could not make out the lines separating the tiles. The air was steam. Slowly his eyes adjusted as he fumbled for the valve to open the shower-head. There were perhaps twenty young men on the other side, standing under the hissing showers, their motions a sleek undulance of yellow skin. They leaned in rapt attention upon each other; close together, mumbling, exchanging confidences at fractional volume. Their eyes canted and glinted in the steam. They were scrubbing each other with loofah mitts, biceps strained against spines and and hairless chests to chafe away dead skin. Some were on bended knee, working on legs. None of them making a sound. One by one, they recognized him, the eyes turning on him across the room. "*Ni hao,*" he said.

There was no reply, just the reinvigorated working of loofah against skin, and a few mutters.

He turned his head and saw at the end of the showers the tallest of them, attended by three men, process his presence, with eyes of a swollen blankness. The showers roared. Jeff ran his hands through his hair and shut his shower off and walked back into the changing room.

The yellow track suits exactly the same, every one. He got changed and left.

Then he was standing before a door. His apartment door in San Tiao. He could hear voices inside. He checked — no, he had not forgotten the important documents. Around his door were two brilliant red *chunlian,* the festive strips, one on each side, each with masterful calligraphy, reading *Jian wei zhi zhu* (from the very first inklings, one can tell how something is going to turn out) and *Wu ji bi fan* (when things reach their extremes, they begin to turn into their opposites). The voices persisted. Overcome by curiosity and anger — who is intruding in my apartment? — he opened the door and was met by a scene of sophomoric hospitality; his students from the class at San Tiao took up all the available chairs, along with the melon seller from down the road, everyone sucking on Popsicles and taking turns thwacking at a huge watermelon with a rusty cleaver, hacking out uneven wedges which they sucked to the rind and spat the seeds on his floor. Tian Kang was there. Jim and Tom were there. Han Xiu Ling was there. Robert, the Ugly Canadian from Jian Hua was there. Everyone was there.

(Save one.)

They were all glad to see him; they beckoned him in. Farther back, by the windows, he saw there was another (who, later, outside the dream, he will recognize has some resemblance to Bian Fu's father, from the clean throb of his forehead and the tiredness underneath his eyes) in a black robe, a little distant from the hilarity, saying nothing, refusing Popsicles and watermelon slices with a mere closing of his eyes and scant motion of his hand, and he saw that this was Master Kung. The voices, like swallows, looped and darted at Jeff. He sat.

"Sit, sit, sit, sit."

"We have something to tell you, Jeff."

"We in China have our rules, you know."

"In the South, we have a saying: Business first, then love."

"If you could understand what she is saying, then you would agree with it completely."

"It is easier to climb the mountain than to descend from it."

"You should get to know what her intention is."

"Oh, Jeff, very beautiful English student from Er Wai. She will learn English from you, I think."

"These Chinese women just want to improve their economic condition. Just wait until I get that big job in San Li Tun, I'll have two women hanging off me. And I'll say, I wonder why I never met them before?"

"Try not to put your feet up on the desk when you are teaching."

"Do you know the meaning of the Chinese word *rang?*"

"I do not think I will be a very good wife, tee hee. I do not think I will try so hard."

Robert, the Ugly Canadian, turned from the desk, where he had been going through Jeff's personal letters and papers, but there is never enough time in dreams to object, and Robert raised his hand, and said, "It's difficult for us to conceptualize the attraction.

"Suppose there were only three hundred Chinese girls who lived in Victoria. They come from a faraway land you haven't seen and in all likelihood never will see, though you have studied their language since you were in grade school. The Chinese girls can come and go wherever they want; many of them have been other places in the world teaching their language, travelling around, whatever. In a way, they epitomize freedom, and this message is reinforced by the many videotapes you've seen and the many books you've read. Although you are dimly aware that there is more to it than that, you nonetheless believe that the world they come from offers you much more than you can expect in Victoria. And the Chinese girls have money — they are constantly pulling it out of their pockets. They have credit cards, traveller's cheques. They are constantly complaining about how little money they make in Victoria. The Chinese girls don't understand you very well. They don't understand why you can't just change jobs if you feel like it, since they have done that all their lives. They don't understand that your family has to come first. But they do understand, sort of, that you and your compatriots have suffered greatly, and this is why they are content with whatever dribs and drabs of your language you parcel out, in return for being taken out to dinner, movies, nightclubs, etcetera. If you tell them one of your proverbs they become deliriously happy because they have been given something rich and strange. You resent them a little. Things are easy for the Chinese girls, and very difficult for you. A dream blossoms in you — if only one of these Chinese girls loved you and whisked you away from Victoria, where you have lived all your life with your eternally arguing relatives. What if they took you to China, that land of high incomes and modern convenience? But you must take no chances. If it is found out what you are doing with the Chinese girl, there will be severe consequences, for your society is fractious and viciously competitive. Your family could lose face. You could lose your job, get kicked out of school, ruin your chances of marrying a Victoria girl. You must trust nobody, least of all the Chinese girl. Despite your longing for the freedom they represent, and their surprisingly direct and permissive ways, you must make them commit to you before you commit to them. If you slip, the fall is a long one, and there are a hundred thousand ready to take your place, the place your family has struggled to maintain within the walls of Victoria…"

"It wasn't like that, it wasn't like that at all," Jeff shouted.

Master Kung cleared his throat and everyone became instantly silent. He adjusted his robe. He said in a certain, yet measured voice, "It is not that I do not love you, it is just that your house is so far away," then he turned his eyes toward Jeff and said, again pitching his voice so one could hear that it was Kung as personage speaking, "He did not really love her. Had he loved her, he would not have cared about the distance."

Then it was Kung's voice, direct, confronting him in the hot room with the ripe smell of watermelon. "What do you have to say for yourself?"

"I am a foreigner," he heard himself saying. "And you know what Lu Xun said: When they have power, they are ruthless. When they are struggling, then they trot out all the Daoist and Confucian philosophy, mostly to trick and cheat each other and because they can't deal with the reality of their own behaviour. When they are helpless, and realize that they will be crushed, they become fatalistic and accept what is going to happen to them."

Kung took this in but said nothing.

"Lu Xun said that about the Chinese, not foreigners," one of the students said quickly.

"I am Chinese. I am just not a very good-looking one," he said. And he said it again, convinced of his wit. And again he repeated it. But he could get no one to laugh. They stared at him. Master Kung turned and regarded the world outside the window.

And Jeff woke up.

Tie ma bing he ru meng lai. I dreamed of frozen rivers crossed by cavaliers. It was the last line of a poem by Lu You in his *Song-Tang* poetry book that Jeff read compulsively for several months; it was the landscape he returned to in his sorrow, his lost self, weighed down by armour, frozen, weary of crossing borders that infinitely receded. He forgot where he had wanted to go. The smell of his horse's neck comforted him a little. They were both getting thin. Occasionally he would look up from the plod, plod, plod and see the frozen branches woven around him, how delicate, how beautiful, catching little prisms of the sun in their ice-net; they made his eyes hurt. But he had to keep moving. Ahead, across the river, a slender figure with swinging black hair flitted through the bare trees.

The translation of the entire poem, *The Storm on the Fourth Day of the Eleventh Moon*:

> Forlorn in a cold bed, I'm grieved not for my plight,
> Still thinking of recovering our lost frontiers,
> Hearing the stormy wind and rain at dead of night,
> I dreamed of frozen rivers crossed by cavaliers.

He remembered Er Bao grubby-faced at the coffee table looking through her nursery comic-book of poetry. Her hands clapped as she recited.

Tie ma bing he ru meng lai.

The smell of ice dripping from the black branches.

North River woman. Bing He woman.

Their lost frontiers.

Eventually, he put the book away in his desk and did not take it out much at all.

Melissa pointed: "Look, Daddy. Look! Look at all the Chinese people going to eat *dim sum!*"

He did. Crossing Fisgard Street on that Saturday morning, neatly dressed and the small girls with ribbons in their hair, several family groups were idly chatting, looking forward no doubt to the shrimp and pork dumplings, the sticky rice wrapped in banana leaves. Melissa and he were within earshot — Jeff couldn't make out a word. *Guang Dong hua,* Cantonese, he thought, and he could hear Bian Fu's northern judgment — *Bah, niao hua,* bird-talk. He frowned. Melissa sensed her dad was having a difficult moment. She looked elsewhere, to give him space.

"Always remember," he said. "Always remember they're just as Canadian as you or I."

Melissa just looked confused, awaiting further explanation.

Stunned by the glib falsity of what he had said, and therefore by its truth, he pondered the statement's inverse possibilities, and felt dizzy. ("Er Bao, always remember, he's just as Chinese as you or I." Unlikely.) Melissa, he thought, how can your world be possible? Your father is a racist.

Or was it that, exactly?

Or is it that you recognized Bian Fu's difference from you; you could not *know* her, because you did not know yourself sufficiently.

They were almost among the families, and then, because he could see Melissa was bored with his innerness, because he was the only father she had, he grabbed her hands, and swung her up and caught her by the backs of her knees, inverting her, and carried her giggling through the laughter of the children and their parents.

The following summer Jeff was still working at his job, still had Melissa over every weekend, and Bian Fu was still on his mind, not every day, but sufficiently to snuff whatever lust flickered within him when he saw a good-looking woman. One hot day he wandered down to Dallas Road and descended the long stairway down the cliff; he sat on the beach and stared at the Olympic Mountains, clear blue and white, and thought, just beyond them is China, is Bian Fu. He just sat there.

He looked down the beach and there was a Chinese woman approaching, holding a black umbrella against the sun. She was beautiful. He watched her pass and walk daintily along the tideline far, far away. With a black umbrella.

Bian Fu used to take her newspaper and hold it over her head in the blazing Beijing streets.

If you stare at a poem long enough, he thought, you will eventually meet its characters.

An unknown Chinese woman approaching him, coming close, twirling her umbrella in a sort of antique mannerism and then infinitely receding along the shoreline.

Xiang yin bu dao yuan / Zhi zhi chang feng sha. I will come out to meet you and not call it far, as far as Long Wind Sands or where you are.

He closed his eyes.

He returned to Kick Fish County. The streets were empty. No policemen waved him on. The few souls he passed once he entered the wavy lanes cast their eyes down. There was a smell of orange peel.

When he leaned his bike against the *siheyuan* wall, there was plenty of space for it.

He was in her house; sunlight streamed downwards; the floor was brilliant. Her voice was coming from another room, like the room off the kitchen that housed the two students he was unaware of for months and months, but he sat on the couch and waited, he waited for her, but there was only her voice: emphatic, elusive, made of the wig makers and movie houses of Tiyuguan, her voice drifting out of the bedroom and reaching him:

> *When I was a little girl, there was a girl at school who wore a blue dress. My family was very poor. I wanted a blue dress just like hers. Years later I saw the exact same blue dress. It was nothing — it was very simple.*
>
> *When I saw it, I had a deep feeling of shame.*

THE END

Glossary

Ai ren — Lover. Also qing ren.

Baijan — Hindu devotional song.

Baixin — Cabbage, also called sui choy.

Bao bai — Transliteration of the English "baby."

Baozi — dumpling, meat bun.

Canting — Eatery.

Chang Cheng — The Great Wall.

Chengyu — A proverb of four characters, many of which allude to entire stories.

Chou — Rice porridge.

Dui — Yes.

Feichang hao — Excellent, very good.

Fuwuyuan — Service worker, can be applied to retail clerks, waiters, counterpersons, etcetera.

Gong Chan Dang — Communist Party.

Guanxi — Connection. Access to key people. Nothing much gets done in China without it.

Guazir — Watermelon seeds.

Hanzi — Chinese characters.

Hao bu hao — Okay? Is that good or not?

Hukou — Municipal ID. Chinese citizens used to have to register in one city, and could not work in another city without considerable bureaucratic process, often taking years. The system is loosening now, to accommodate the waves of workers from the country.

Jiazi — Hair-clasp, barrette.

Kang — Bed made of bricks, heated from below by coal, common in North China.

Kou — Mouth.

Kuai — Chinese unit of currency, also yuan, ren min bi. Kuai is like our "buck."

Lao pu, lao gong — Husband, wife. This is a traditional usage, often used ironically.

Lao Shi — Teacher.

Leng mian — Cold noodles.

Liang kuai — Cool.

Mei banfa — There is no other way.

Mei guanxi — It doesn't matter.

Mi fan — Rice.

Ming bai — Clear; I understand.

Nanbian — The South, which begins at the Yangtze River.

Ni shuo ba — Go ahead, talk.

Qipao — A long form-fitting dress with a high collar, often worn by brides. Literally, "bride-wrap."

Pengyou — Friend.

Ren Min Ri Bao — *The People's Daily.* (There is a Beijing joke about the *Ren Min Ri Bao* — "chu le rizi yi wai, dou shi pianji." — "Everything but the date is a lie.")

Ru guo — If.

Shan shui — "Mountains and waters," a style of landscape painting.

Shang kang — Hop up on the bed.

Shao kao rou — Barbecued meat.

Shei ya? — Who's there?

Shen me? — What?

Sheng qi le — To become angry.

Shi de — This phrase affirms what another has said.

Shi ma? — Really?

Shitang — Cafeteria.

Shou — Hand.

Shu cai — Vegetable.

Shui jiao — Sleep, sleep with.

Siheyuan — A particular style of Beijing house, with four compartments around a central courtyard.

Tian ah — My heavens!

TOEFL — Teaching of English as a Foreign Language.

Wei! — This is how the Chinese answer the phone.

Wo ai ta/ni — I love her/you.

Xian zai ba cu zai zhuo ya! — Bring the vinegar!

Xiangliar — Necklace.

Xiaojie, xiaojie! — Waitress, waitress!

Xie xie — Thank you.

Xin — Heart.

Xiuxi — Siesta.

Ya pin — Opium.

Yang rou — Lamb.

Yao cu, wo jiu yao cu! — I want vinegar, now!

Ye ye — Grandfather.

Yi kuai wu — A kuai and a half.

Yi, er, san — One, two, three.

Ying guo ren — Englishman.

Zai jian — Goodbye.

Zhong wen — Chinese language. Also called Hanyu, putonghua.

Zhongxin — Shopping centre.

ECO-AUDIT
*Printing this book using Rolland Enviro 100 Book
instead of virgin fibres paper saved the following resources:*

Trees	Solid Waste	Water	Air Emissions
6	161 kg	15,250 L	354 kg